TITLES BY STEPHEN HUNTER

GAME
OF
SNIPERS

A BOB LEE SWAGGER NOVEL

STEPHEN HUNTER

G. P. PUTNAM'S SONS | NEW YORK

PUTNAM
— EST. 1838 —

G. P. PUTNAM'S SONS
Publishers Since 1838
An imprint of Penguin Random House LLC
penguinrandomhouse.com

THE LIBRARY OF CONGRESS HAS CATALOGUED THE G. P. PUTNAM'S SONS
HARDCOVER EDITION AS FOLLOWS:

Names: Hunter, Stephen, author.
Title: Game of snipers : a Bob Lee Swagger novel / by Stephen Hunter.
Description: New York, New York : G. P. Putnam's Sons, an imprint of
Penguin Random House LLC, [2019]
Identifiers: LCCN 2018044740 | ISBN 9780399574573 (hardcover) |
ISBN 9780399574597 (ebook)
Subjects: | GSAFD: Suspense fiction.
Classification: LCC PS3558.U494 G36 2019 | DDC 813/.54—dc23
LC record available at https://lccn.loc.gov/2018044740

First G. P. Putnam's Sons hardcover edition / July 2019
First G. P. Putnam's Sons premium edition / June 2020
G. P. Putnam's Sons premium edition ISBN: 9780399574580

Printed in the United States of America
5 7 9 10 8 6 4

For Tracy Miller
and all the other Gold Star Moms
of the sandbox wars

I've noticed that I make people nervous.

> —Repp, Obersturmbannführer,
> 3. SS-Panzerdivision "Totenkopf,"
> known as "Der Meisterschütze"

PART 1

1

He saw Katie amid the prairie flowers. She sat, legs crossed, while the wind played with her hair, and it gleamed in the sun. She smiled brightly. She always smiled. Four years old was the age of smiles. She looked so happy, and around her the grass fluttered in the breeze, and it must have pleased her, for she turned to face it, tilting her little nose up.

"Katie!" he called. "Katie, sweetie . . . Katie!"

She turned to his voice, and her blue eyes lit with love.

"Daddy," she called. "Hi, Daddy!"

"Sweetie, I'm coming," Paul yelled, and lunged to run to her, to hold her tight, to smother her in his arms and protect her from all. It's what a father did.

But he could not make it.

He was handcuffed to a post. The sharpness of metal pulled hard against his wrists.

"Katie, I—"

"Daddy, I have to go."

"No, Katie, no. I'll be right there."

But his wrists would not yield, and though he yanked hard enough to draw blood from his flesh, the cuffs would not give.

"Bye, Daddy," said Katie, as she rose to run away. "I love you."

And then she was gone, and he was aware that he was awake. Dream finished, he was awake. But the odd thing was that the binding of his wrists was no dream, and he yanked hard, the steel biting. He could feel a solid post threaded through his bound arms, mooring him upright as solidly as Joan of Arc had been for the fire.

He blinked, it did not go away.

Other oddities revealed themselves. For one, a gentle wind pushed the smell of prairie grass against his nostrils, and, two, he felt the radiance of a sun above him, welcoming him—or damning him—to wakefulness.

He did not smell his own piss and vomit. He did not feel the crusty ripple of long-uncleaned skin. He hadn't shit his pants, or if he had, someone had cleaned up the mess for him.

He wasn't wearing that pair of ragged chinos, fifteen years old, filched from some garbage can, or that old pair of Adidas, two sizes too big. He was in turquoise surgical scrubs and white socks.

Paul blinked himself more fully awake, opened his eyes fully, waited for them to focus, and examined the world in which he now found himself.

It was not the world he had left, which was the alley

behind restaurant row, where he had unreliable memories of the effects of muscatel and methamphetamine, of his surrender to unconsciousness behind a dumpster a half block down from that Mexican restaurant in the alley where all the normals came to eat and drink and laugh every night and from whom he could occasionally cadge a buck or even a five-spot.

Where had it gone? What was happening?

Did I die? Am I in Heaven?

No, it was not Heaven, but it was definitely outside.

He saw grass, lots of it. The world was well lit. Details, vistas, landscapes dialed into focus. He saw vastness, mountains, pines. He saw a huge dome of sky, tendrils of wispy clouds spread across it, a sun that could have been hotter but not clearer, and green, green, everywhere, as he was confined to the floor of a valley that was bordered by forest, its pines rolling away to infinity mostly.

Confusion, not an unknown condition, took over his already murky mind, though for once, at least, the voices were quiet. He looked for human beings of any sort and soon saw them. A good fifty yards away, three men sat on deck chairs, coolly appraising him. One was holding a cell phone to his ear, talking to someone.

"Hey!" he called. "What is this? Who are you? Where am I?"

They did not respond to his calls, though the one on the phone glanced at him, then went back to his animated conversation.

More details: they seemed Mexican, from their hair

(long) and wardrobe (cowboy hats, jeans, boots). Sunglasses, a certain macho languor in body postures of amused relaxation. Was he in Mexico?

Oddest detail of all: standing apart from the crew was a man in black. That is, *all* in black, from the toes of his boots to the crown of his hat, including a black mask that covered his face, with slits for his dark eyes. Of them all, only this one was watching Paul.

Paul tried to assemble a series of steps by which he somehow ended up chained to a post in Mexico, cleaned up to some degree and placed before the world like a specimen. But rigor was long missing from the working of his mind, and nothing made any sense. His will crumpled against the effort. He wanted a drink, he ached for the blur and smear of the muscatel that drove his furies away, at least temporarily.

He went dizzy, leaned against the post to utilize its support. That small effort exhausted him. He breathed heavily, already in oxygen debt.

"Help me please," he shouted.

But now the postures of the Mexican steering committee had changed. The one on the phone seemed to be in charge, and he commanded the attention of the others. They joined the man in black in directing attention toward him, but not in empathy.

The moment seemed to elongate until it fell out of time. He heard an odd noise, not a blast or a burst, no sharpness to it, but it still carried sensations of destruction to it, as if something had struck in near silence against the earth itself. Immediately, the man on the phone began to speak.

Paul turned. About twenty-five yards out, a cloud of dust—debris from some sort of explosion, by the conical shape of it—hung gracelessly above the folds of scrub prairie, but was disorganizing in the breeze.

Again, he had no framework into which he could fit this puzzling event. It was just there, defying his attempts to classify and respond.

In the next second, another eruption occurred. The earth itself expressed the tremor of the released energy as a geyser suddenly spurted at the speed of light, easily ten feet of supersonic dust and dirt, roiling, climbing, disassembling in the breeze. It was much closer, and Paul felt the sting of pellet and grit.

He tried to place it, again seeking context, and rifled through the crazed index of his memories to find something and came to the conclusion that these were bullets striking the earth, delivering a violence of energy and purpose. He'd seen it in the movies a thousand times— at least, when he went to movies.

The ground beneath him shattered. He was smashed hard into the post by unseen energy, as the cuffs twisted and sliced his wrists. He tasted blood and copper in his saliva, and after a second's numb mercy, sharp pains began to clamor for attention, announcing the presence against his body of shards of debris, flung stones, supersonic grit.

He realized now: someone was shooting at him from a long way away.

The panic of the prey flooded his brain, and he tore away, only to have his motion halted by the cuffs.

"No," he shouted. "You can't do this. This isn't right," he screamed, but involuntarily began to sob.

They laughed. It was pretty funny.

"Katie," he screamed. "Forgive me! Forgive Daddy! Please."

He entered the light.

2

The ranch, Cascade, Idaho

What was there to complain about? The view from the rocker was superb, prairie meadows giving way in the distance to the mountains, snowcapped (as was he) and remote (as was he), been there forever (as had he). He owned everything he could see except for the mountains (ownership: God). The late-spring climate temperate, the sun not so strong, the breeze mild. Children successful. Wife content, as much as any wife could be. He just kept getting richer, not of his own volition but by the working of certain mechanisms. Health fine, even superb. The new hip (number three) felt great, his ticker still ticked. Horses— too many, all sinewy beasts with plenty of go in them. His guns? Some new ones, in fascinating calibers, maybe a new sniper round to test out, called 6.5 Creedmoor, which promised lots of amusement of the dry, technical sort he so enjoyed. Friends—more than he deserved, and in places he never thought he'd go, from NRA celebs to old snipers to a few journalists, to a lot of big-animal vets across seven states, plus dozens of former marine NCOs, as salty a crew as could be imagined. Pickup trucks? Could only drive one at a time, so what was the point in having any more?

I have everything, he thought.

His late self-education was progressing in his leisure. He was on to Crimea now, trying to imagine battles under gunpowder clouds so vast and brutal that no one could see their limits, the wounds nasty and greenish, headed into gangrene, toward, ultimately, amputation without anesthetic save whiskey. As a man whose life had been saved several times—and he had the scars to prove it—by modern emergency medicine, this fact alone sent a tremor of dread down his straight old spine. Everything was fine.

He knew it couldn't last.

It didn't.

It was the lowest category of rental car, in a shade of Day-Glo otherwise found no place on earth, pulling up the long road in from Idaho 82. It had to mean some sort of trouble, because friends never came without a call first, and not one of them would travel under such brightness. No mailbox shouted SWAGGER to the world at the otherwise unmarked gate, and the size and beauty of the house was not manifest from the highway: the road could have just as easily led to a broken-down trailer or a complex of heavily armed religious zealots or some other monstrosity that had taken root in Idaho's free soil.

He touched the .38 Super Commander holstered under the tail of his T-shirt, found it secure yet accessible in a second, though that was mere habit, as the arrival of a nuclear airburst fuchsia Tempo or Prism hardly presaged a gunfight. Actually, he would have preferred a gunfight.

The car pulled up, and he rose, and he was not astonished but mildly nonplussed by the driver, who got out and faced him. Woman. Fifties, maybe early sixties. Pantsuit, makeup, and the ubiquitous high-end sneakers that most American women wore most places these days. Her smile was tentative, not practiced and professional. Her face was slightly out of symmetry, as if parted and rejoined inadequately, but no scars showed. It was just an oddness of cast that suggested complexities. He couldn't help picking up a note of forlorn loss, however, when he added it all up. Something damaged about poor whoever-she-was.

"Ma'am," he called. "Just so you know: this is private property, and I'm not what you'd call a public fellow. If you're selling, I'm not buying. If you're interviewing, I'm not talking. And if you're campaigning, I don't vote. But if you're lost, I will happily give you directions, and a glass of water."

"I'm not lost, Mr. Swagger—Sergeant Swagger. It took me days to find out where you lived. I know you don't like interruptions, and there's no reason you should, but I would claim the right to a hearing because of the circumstances."

"Well—" he said, thinking, *Oh, Lord, what now?*

"My son. Lance Corporal Thomas McDowell, sniper, 3/8. Baghdad, 2003. Came back to me in a box."

* * *

They sat in silence on the porch for a bit. He didn't know what he could say, because of course there is nothing that can be said. He knew enough of grief to know that only time eats it down, and sometimes not even that, and death is the only ultimate release. So, it would be her show, and she seemed to need some time to gather.

Finally, she said, "It seems very pretty here."

"I like to sit a couple of hours each day. Just watch the weather and the grass change. Sometimes a batch of antelope wander by, sometimes a few mulies—a buck and his gals. Once a bull elk, magnificent rack, but they seem not much in evidence these days."

"You're being very kind to me."

"It's just my way."

"You think maybe I came for explanations. Context, history, the who, the why, the what, the physics of it. The ballistics. You would know such things."

"If it helps, I'll sound off."

"I've learned a thing or two since the notification team knocked on the door. Seven-point-sixty-two by fifty-four, 160 grain. Classic Dragunov. Velocity about sixteen hundred feet per second by the time it reached him. Steel-cored, probably didn't distort or rupture. Went clean through. It would have been instant, I'm told."

"Sounds about right."

"I should be grateful for that mercy, but don't look to me for grateful. Mom doesn't do grateful. Mom wants the man who pulled the trigger dead. That's what Mom wants."

He paused. That one was unexpected. Now, what the hell could he say?

"Mrs. McDowell, this ain't healthy. Not only because what you describe is murder, not war, not only because it could get you into a whole peck of trouble that would make where you are now seem like kindergarten, not only because no matter how it came out you'd end up spending all your money—and I mean all of it—on lawyers and various other forms of predators, not only because it's probably not even possible, and, finally, if you're trying to get me to go on some kind of revenge safari for you, I am too old, at seventy-two, and lack any wherewithal for door-busting, stair-climbing, and the stalking part of sniping and would only get myself killed or arrested."

She nodded.

"That is entirely sensible," she said. "The people who would talk about Bob the Nailer said he was a decent man and would not steer me wrong, and he would give me solid advice. And, for the record, nobody in the marine community or the shooting community or the intelligence community—and I have entered them all—has encouraged me. They think it's crazy."

"I would not use such a harsh word. Let's leave it at 'bad idea.'"

"But—" she said.

"There's always a 'but,' " he said.

"Yes, and here's mine. You can say it was war, that's all. He joined the Marine Corps of his own volition, he signed on to sniper school, he went to war willingly, he had a few kills of his own, and one night his number came up. Numbers come up, that's what war is about. But I'm not telling you anything you don't know. And the boy who pulled the trigger, the argument would run, he was just another boy like Tom, dancing to a politician's tune for policy goals that never made any sense, and, just like Tom, he'd rather have been at the mall or the movies, hanging out with girls, whatever. Is that it?"

"That would be the argument I'd make, yes. No peace in it, no justice either. The chances are also that that boy never made it out of Baghdad himself. There was a lot of killing there in 2003, if memory serves."

"There was."

"If I recall correctly, for a while they had a very effective sniper program, and our kids died at a significant rate. Some folks went over there, analyzed the data, made charts, and figured out where, when, and how these shots were being made, and designed new strategies. So our dying went way down, theirs went way up. I guess Tom went down before the experts figured it out."

"That's it exactly."

"Shouldn't you be mad at the Marine Corps for being so slow to get it figured out? Or at the president and the long line of men in gray suits who put your son where he was when he got taken? What about the newspapers that wrote editorials in support? That might be a way to channel your rage. Another way might be to see that those that died, in fact died for something, even if it was only to become part of a countersniper database, which ultimately saved a lot of mothers from feeling what Tom's mom feels. It meant something. It was a sacrifice not for nothing but for the betterment of all those who came after."

"I suppose I could feel that. But I don't. There's that 'but' again."

"All right. Tell me about this particular 'but.'"

"But it wasn't a part of the war. But it wasn't another kid who wanted to be at the mall. But it wasn't even an Iraqi. But he's not dead. But I know who he is and where he is."

It was a tale full of sound and fury. What it signified was as yet unknown. Only one thing was clear: it was told by a woman who was either insanely brave or insanely insane—maybe both.

She had been to Baghdad seven times. She had been raped four times and beaten three, once severely, which explained the somewhat odd shape of her face.

"The bones didn't heal properly," she said. "Big deal. Who cares?"

Three times she'd been bilked by fast operators. She'd used up the money she'd made selling her house on those. She'd borrowed money from her brother to pay for a six-month immersion course in Arabic.

"It's not like I can follow the nuances, because you know it's very fast, and so much depends on context or prior knowledge. But I can pretty much stay with it, I can negotiate, I can double-check, I can follow. Oh, and I became Moslem."

"You became Moslem?"

"I had to understand him. You can't do that from the outside, not really. So I gave myself another six months to convert, to really try and become Islamic, to understand it in history and culture and ideology and fervor of faith. I even experimented with the idea of blowing up some infidels just to see how it felt, but, crazy as I am, even I saw how wrong that would have been."

The story, so far. Tom's battalion intelligence officer had told her that the men opposing 3/8 in that sector of Baghdad were thought to be refugees from the 2nd Armored Assault Brigade of the 5th Baghdad Mechanized Division of the 1st Republican Guard Corps. Crack troops who melted back into society after the end of the war, mostly from the capital city themselves, so they knew it pretty well. They came together on a strictly ad hoc basis in the southeast sector of the city, where 3/8 had been placed, and began guerrilla operations against the infidel invaders. At first, it wasn't much: the odd IED, the bungled ambush, the sniper who missed, the constant betrayals, setbacks, mistakes, and sheer incompetence. But they learned fast.

So her first trip—and her second and even half of her third—was to find a veteran of that unit and of that campaign who would talk. Many false leads, much money stolen, many blind alleys in which, at least for the first time, the rape occurred.

Swagger had an image of this middle-class suburban American mom gone native in Baghdad, swaddled in the robes of the believers, knowing that at any moment she could be found out and be raped, beaten, or even murdered, at the same time being hunted by the alliance policemen who must have known she was there. She made mistakes, she got caught, she paid the price over and over, but somehow she kept on. Nothing scared her more than her son's death going unpaid for.

Finally, she met a man, an ex-captain in the 2nd, now crippled by a gunship chain gun, and needy of money to support wife and family, and, as well, angry at the leadership that had led him to this sorry, provisional life.

"Assiz"—his name—knew. Knew something. Maybe not enough, maybe not all, but something. He told her of the outsider.

"He was from elsewhere," Assiz told her, and didn't take money for it. "Brigade Command brought him in. He was said to be skilled with a rifle. We were canvassed for our best shots. I lost two excellent gunners from my IED team. They went off—where, I do not know. Someplace safe, where they could learn to shoot the rifle, not the AK but the other one, the sniper rifle."

She went on. When the men returned—there were just twenty-two of them—they were equipped with the Russian sniper rifle, the Dragunov. The sniper had a program, he scouted with them, he organized their escape routes, he was very professional. He had tricks they had not seen. A bomb would drive the marines back, under cover to all—save the sniper, who knew where they had to go, who had measured the distances, knew the adjustments, practiced the shots. The marines took refuge, unknowingly, in a kill box. The sniper fired quickly, taking as many as he could, but departed before organized return fire and maneuver elements came into play. The sniper killed and went to ground.

"He was an old hand," said Bob. "He knew a thing or two."

"Tommy was on perimeter overwatch. I'm told he had a premonition. He was on the roof of an apartment block, which 3/8 had taken as patrol headquarters. His job was to look for snipers through his scope. He moved positions every few minutes, a few feet one way or the other. If you stayed too long in one place, they might see you and zero you. But—"

"I know this is hard."

"But whoever the man with the Dragunov was, he was ahead of the curve. He knew where Tommy had to be. He set himself up where he had a narrow angle to target, knowing that, sooner or later, Tommy would have to occupy that position. The rifle scope was preadjusted to the range, and the sniper himself showed superb discipline. He didn't move a muscle in his hide, he just lay there, locked into the rifle, waiting, waiting, waiting until somebody took up the position in his zero, and when Tommy did, the shot was almost immediate. It was the headshot. Instantly fatal. Huge exit wound, though the hole in the face, just under the off eye, simply looked like a little black dime. Then nothing. There was a bounty on marine snipers, so whoever fired got a nice bonus that night. Maybe the Bossman took the shot, maybe he paid himself a bonus, maybe he kicked it into a fund for the party—I don't know. Again, it doesn't matter. He set it up, he made it happen, he entered their war and taught them things they were incapable of doing on their own. It was his training, his program, his planning, his initiative, that killed Tommy. It wasn't his country, right or wrong. It was this other thing: jihadi. He's the one that has to pay, and he's the one who authored that two-month surge in deaths where the casualty rate went from 2.4 per thousand to 9.6. Total kills for those two months was over two hundred and forty-five, with another fifty or so wounded."

"I'm surprised there were so few wounded. Usually, it skews the other direction, with a ten-to-one ratio of WIA to KIA. He must have trained them to shoot for center mass and wasn't interested in simple out-of-actions."

"According to my Captain Assiz, he had no use for that. The Qur'an says slay the infidel, not wound him, and he believed in it totally."

The story continued. The Corps brought in a countersniper intelligence team that applied special analytical skills to the problem and realized that the snipers always shot to pattern. The lack of improvisational skills again. Nothing left to chance. Do it by the program. They operated between 1600 and 1800, usually used cars for cover, the streets littered with wrecked and burnt-out vehicles, and fell back on a straight line to the nearest available building, where shelter had been prepared.

"Tommy was dead by then," said his mother. "It was too late. But on a certain day, the snipers went out early and placed themselves according to the doctrine. As soon as four o'clock came, every abandoned car on every company or battalion perimeter in Baghdad was taken out by TOW missiles, the wreckage sprayed with SAW fire, followed by grenades. Of the twenty-two, the Iraqi resistance lost seventeen that day. The snipers were never a problem after that."

"What happened to Bossman?"

"He vanished. He knew the tables had turned and that his program was now defunct. He'd done the best he could, but the game of snipers was over, and it was time to go on a nice vacation and begin to recover to fight another day in a war that's fourteen hundred years old."

"But his usefulness wasn't quite finished, if I'm not mistaken," said Bob. "After he was gone, the fighters put together a propaganda video. He became famous. Everyone feared him. The exploits of the twenty-two snipers were all attributed to one. It was said he killed hundreds of Americans. He was given a name, and the name was marketed. Great marketing, by the way. Madison Avenue quality all the way."

"You know the name, then."

"I heard it. He was called Juba the Sniper."

Darkness came. Julie arrived home from her office in town, from which she ran the Swagger empire of layup barns, and met Janet McDowell, and the two immediately bonded. Janet came easily out of her manhunter personality and warmed to Julie, who insisted she stay for dinner. Janet went with Julie into the kitchen, and the two worked quite happily together.

After dinner—a good time—Bob and Janet returned to the porch. It was time for the rest of the story.

"After he'd fled Baghdad, you lost him. How'd you pick him up again?"

She'd tried everything. More trips to the capital city after Bush's surge finally quieted things down, trips to Moscow to bribe her way into KGB files and see if the Russians had any contact or training with Juba, a trip to Chechnya to see if he was one of the notorious Chechen snipers, so ruthless and cruel to the Russians during that little war. Afghanistan revealed some possibles: an American colonel, highest-ranking officer to fall to a sniper off an exceedingly long shot—that seemed to suggest a much higher degree of skill than normal. The same on a senior CIA operative in Helmand Province. Using her son's death as an entrée, she met many marine snipers and intelligence officers, searching for hard leads. But everything was soft, a vague possibility, not proof.

"I almost gave up," she said. Left unsaid: if she had nothing to live for, what would be the point?

But then she thought: *What don't I know? I don't know the instrumentality. Perhaps that's the key.*

The rifles. She immersed herself in them, beginning with gun magazines, reading seven a month to familiarize herself. She read sniper memoirs, sniper fiction, saw sniper movies. She caught the upsurge in sniper as hero that pop culture suddenly embraced and followed the careers of Chris Kyle and other celebrity snipers. She learned ballistics, she studied rifles, she took shooting lessons . . .

"My son's father—we divorced when he was three— gave me two hundred thousand dollars. So I was able to keep going, though I am running out of relatives to pay for all this."

At a certain point, she decided to concentrate on the specific weapon. Juba and his team, according to every marine intelligence officer she talked to, had used the classic Dragunov, Russian-manufactured, and an issue weapon for close to fifty years. The marines knew it well. It had opposed them all over the world, and they'd been able to recover one in 1973 with CIA assistance.

"I've heard the story," said Bob.

"But the key wasn't the rifle. It was the ammunition."

"Good insight," said Bob.

"I never would have understood that. I thought you just put what I called a bullet into what I called a gun and pulled the trigger and that was that. But that wasn't even the half of it. Not even a tenth. So much to learn. I learned most of it."

The woman was determined. Nothing stopped her, not even the labyrinths of technical detail, shooting culture with its nuances, its contradictions, its loads of false information, its arbitrary names for things that made no sense and just had to be memorized.

"It turns out the most accurate 7.62×54R ammunition in the world was manufactured by the Bulgarian Arsenal AD in the '50s. It's called heavy ball, and it has a yellow tip. It ships in metal cans of three hundred rounds and has corrosive primers, so the sniper has to keep his barrel clean. I reasoned that Juba would always have heavy ball on hand."

"That's good," said Swagger, who had hoarded American .308 Match Target from Frankford Arsenal during his time in operations. You wanted the best. You had to shoot with gear and ammunition you trusted with your life, because you *were* trusting it with your life.

"So I reasoned that after he left Baghdad, he'd continue to have need for the ammunition, because in any further endeavors he'd need it. So I had to know: where do you get Bulgarian 7.62×54 heavy ball?"

"Next stop: Bulgaria?"

"Yes. It turned out that it was no longer being manufactured, and even when it had been, it wasn't turned out in mass quantities. Not in the tens of millions, but in the low millions. It was a slower process because the tolerances in the loading dies were tighter, the inspection of rounds more intensive."

In Sofia, she met a man who knew a man, and, twenty-five thousand dollars later, she was in the government archives, going through bills of lading for the heavy ball. It had been declared surplus in 1962 and spent the next twenty years in a warehouse. When the Russians moved into Afghanistan, their snipers quickly discovered how good it was, and the bulk of shipments went to the Russian army. It killed a lot of mujahideen there, and more in Chechnya. But by the new mandates of capitalism, the leftover ammunition—maybe ten million rounds—was exported to a variety of countries where the 7.62×54 was shot, mostly countries that had imported large quantities of the Mosin–Nagant, the Soviet/tsarist twentieth-century bolt-action battle rifle of the same caliber. It was a great Mosin round. So it ended up that the largest for-sale accumulation of Bulgarian heavy ball was an importer in Elizabethtown, South Africa, called SouthStar.

"You went there."

"Yes. Helpfully, it's another country where everything is for sale. After a few false starts, I gained entry to SouthStar's shipping and inventory records, for a single evening."

She reached into her briefcase and pulled out a computer printout.

It was a huge thing and it must have taken hours to master. But she'd gone over it before and certain shipments were annotated over the long years of SouthStar disbursement of the metal boxes, with their yellow dots painted on the sides to signify the superiority of the round.

It seemed that once every three months, five thousand rounds were shipped to certain spots in the world, mostly the Middle East. For a number of years, the destination was Egypt. For another couple, it was Iraq. Eventually, the printout put the recipient in southern Syria.

"The payment was always the same: money wired from the same Swiss bank. The last shipment shows he's still in southern Syria, far from the war."

"You think that's him?"

"I do. The trouble with ammunition is that it's so heavy by density. Which means he can't order a million rounds and be done with it. He's got to get a small, manageable amount every few months. If he's going to stay sharp, if he wants to stay at operational peak, he's got to have it coming in all the time. Clearly, it's the same customer, no matter the location or the customer name, because the method of payment is always the same. Don't you see what that gives us? Not an address, but a town. In this case, the last batch, only a month ago, went to a town in southern Syria called Iria. He has to be there. Somewhere in that area, convenient to whatever outlet receives out-of-country shipping, obviously with government approval."

"That's really not an address. It's not actionable."

"No, but a good man could infiltrate sometime when the next shipment is due. He could locate the point of arrival and mark the pickup. If it was impossible to follow to the source, he could ask around. Surely someone has noted a lone guy, quite prosperous, living in the far desert, doing a lot of shooting."

"I don't think so," said Bob. "If he's as smart as you say he is, he'll have snitches scattered throughout the town. If anyone shows up asking questions, that's the signal to find new digs. He'll move fast, and be chastened by his near miss and double up on his security. Maybe he'll stop receiving the heavy ball or find another source. He's probably worried because he's been getting it from SouthStar for so long. Have you gone to the Agency with this?"

"No. They've had me kicked out of so many countries it's funny. They think I'm the Madwoman of Baltimore. I'm nothing but trouble to them. They've even gotten me on the no-fly list, so I've had to become an expert at clandestine identity. That's why no emails, no phone calls, no announcements. I just show up and count on my pathos to get me an audience. I have no shame. So, no, I won't go to them. I want to handle it the same way I've handled everything else, which is on my own. I still have relatives, I can still pay a substantial amount. But it has to be fast, because he's skittish, he moves a lot. That's a pattern of his I've come to recognize."

"I see," said Bob, considering. "And you think I'm the fellow who could get in there, find him, and put him away?"

"Now that I've laid it out for you, I hope you'll alter your position. I can get you in on a very good phony passport. I'd get you a guide and translator, someone I trust. You won't even be in the country more than a few days. You find him in the Iria area, then you smoke him. One shot, one kill. Not only is it righteous, it's profitable. And you'll be doing the world a favor."

Of course it wouldn't go as planned, but, still, to end up with Juba in his sights and to see the shattered face sink into oblivion forever: that was quite an enticement. Everything about it felt right, no denying. But it was still wrong.

"No," he said, "I won't do that. Murder, not war. Revenge, not justice. Of no intelligence value, of no strategic value. May save some lives of some diplomats somewhere, but I don't care."

"There's nothing—"

"I didn't say I wouldn't help. You're some piece of

work, Mrs. McDowell. American suburban woman becomes her own CIA and outperforms the professionals. Outguts them too. Understands she'll get degraded and beaten and perhaps even killed, but goes ahead. You've got some sand in you. I respect sand. What do they call it? True grit."

"I'm not a hero. I just had to do something or the pain would have killed me. I only had Tommy."

"I'll tell you what I will do. None of it involves money on your part."

"That's a first," she said.

"I agree on staying away from the Agency. That was smart. It's full of idiots who think they're playing the long game. They've convinced themselves they're the masters of chaos. In this case, they wouldn't action this guy, they'd track him, see where he led them. If he led them to somebody bigger, maybe they'd sell that information, maybe they'd kidnap and debrief, but they'd do something so smart it would be stupid. And not to beat jihadi, but to outsmart the guy in the next cubicle, who'd be working on the same thing but from a different perspective. It's a mess. It's like an eighth-grade classroom with too many smart kids and a wobbly teacher."

She said nothing, but her silence suggested she'd reached a similar conclusion.

"Here's what I'm offering," he said. "I have a contact with a guy who's very high in the Israeli outfit, the Mossad. Never met him, but he ran an operation that kind of dovetailed with something I got involved in a few years back. So I heard he looked into me, and, as it turned out, I was his inadvertent benefactor. I know this because my daughter was a Fox correspondent in Tel Aviv, and he reached out to her and became a friend and a source. So I think, through her, I can put this before him. I'd guess this Juba operated against them too, and unlike our fellows, the Israelis take everything personal. So let me go to Tel Aviv and see if I can get them interested."

"I should pay your expenses."

"Guess what? I'm rich. Not sure how, but I'm just spending my dough on guns and an occasional trip to Cracker Barrel with my wife. It's an honor to invest in the takedown of Juba the Sniper. You pay me by sitting back and relaxing and not getting yourself beat up and raped no more."

3

Near Iria, southern Syria

I t was the same dream. He'd had it for years, he'd have it forever. Allah would not intercede. Allah had commanded it, and for a purpose: it kept him smart, scared, aware. And it reminded him of the hard reality of the world he had chosen to occupy and the price that he'd have to pay to dominate it.

In this dream, he crouched in the rubble. He imagined Americans in front of him. He imagined his Dragunov against his shoulder, braced solid against wall or fallen column or automobile fender, his eye to the reticle, his hand to the grip, the butt against the shoulder.

He had been thus many times. He imagined the scurry and twist of the Americans. The helmets were turtle-shaped, sand-colored, flanged to protect the back of the neck. They wore so much gear, it was a miracle they could even move. They looked like Crusaders, lacking only the flapping white tunics emblazoned with the Templar cross. In their armor, and with rucksacks and an abundance of weapons, they seemed to be a new crusade, and, in the way his mind worked, it wasn't hard to go from there to cities in flame, men burned at the stake, mosques desecrated, women raped, towns pillaged, despair everywhere in the land of Muhammad. All that had happened ten centuries ago meant nothing. Time was meaningless; there was no "then," as there was no "now."

The rifle was marvelous to his practiced touch. No tremble afflicted the chevron that dominated the center of the broad encirclement of his scope image. He put the point of the chevron where it had to be, gauging distance, adjusting the hold up a bit, down a bit, perhaps a bit to the right or left if heavy winds blew sand across the lens. Then the squeeze, almost automatic at this point, as the trigger resisted him slightly as he pressed it back, toward himself. No torque, no twist, the regularity of a robot's press, and the gun issued death in the form of Bulgarian heavy ball, which to Juba felt like a bit of smash to the shoulder and looked like a blur. Followed by the recovery of the system as it fell back to steadiness after its adventure in recoil.

Each one reacted differently when hit. You could never tell what was going to happen. Some went instantly still, some fought against the penetration of the bullet—that is, the penetration of death itself. Some manifested fury, some resignation, some even relief, as they went down into eternal sleep.

In this dream, the world was rich with targets, even if in the real world it was seldom so. Marines crouched everywhere, rigid with fear, trying to find cover, twisting their bodies into cracks and fissures in the rubble, trying to insert themselves into doorways or vehicles, anything to get away from the anger of the sniper. But the world was a kill box. His finger spoke for God. It nursed a bolt of heavy ball from the Dragunov without upset to the reticle image in which the infidel was pinned atop the chevron. He had lost track of how many times he'd sent infidels on their voyage to wherever Allah sent them.

But, every time, the dream turned. Each time, he encountered his own fate. As he sought targets, he came at last to settle on one sunk in shadow, not quite clear. He paused a fatal second, waiting for smoke to clear, and as the wind took it and spread it thin, he saw exactly what he knew he would see in life someday: a man, such as himself, hunched calmly behind the stock of a scoped rifle, its muzzle supported and, hence, stilled by the double vectors of a bipod. At that moment, the flash, a smear of disorganized radiance, lasting but a fraction of a second as the cartridge's unburned powder consumed itself. He knew he was doomed.

O Allah, hear me. I have served you with all my being and spirit and request humbly absolution for my sins and a welcome to Paradise.

He knew that's how he would die. Sooner or later, having been hunted his whole life, first by Israelis and then by Iranians and then by Kurds and then by Russians and then by Israelis again and finally by Americans, he would become the trophy to a man as skilled as himself.

He jerked awake—as always—in sweat, fighting panic. The desert night was calm. He rolled from the bed and went to the window to see the broad, empty plain outside. Far off, a light burned, a police station on the other side of the valley. Downstairs, his guards were quiet, though one of them was purportedly on duty. No point in checking, as nothing would happen today.

But his mind wouldn't settle down. Perhaps what lay before him had him unsettled—it still happened, even after so many years—and his biology was responding. No prayer could still it. He thought of a pipe of hashish, but that left him logy and imprecise in the morning.

Instead, he focused on his moment of glory. It was a gift from God. It was Allah sending him recompense for all that had been taken from him, for the humiliations and the disgrace and the echoes of a pain that never went away.

He thought of the bus.

4

S wagger found the address—less than a mile from
the beach, and less than a mile from his hotel—
which was a certain café with tables outdoors in
the sunlight. He sat at one, and the waiter came by, and
Swagger ordered an iced tea, though he didn't like iced
tea. He had been told to order iced tea. He sat for a while,
figuring that one team was observing him by means of
binoculars while another examined passersby for threats.
No bombs exploded, no machine guns sounded, no one
noticed, no one moved.

Finally, from inside the restaurant, a man came out
and joined him.

"Sergeant Swagger? I'm Gershon Gold."

"Sir," said Swagger. "Please sit down."

The man slid in. Like Swagger, he wore sunglasses.
Like Swagger, a short-sleeved shirt, open at the neck,
pale and gossamer, loosely woven for comfort. Swagger
wore a Razorbacks ball cap, while Gold wore a tropical
fedora with a black band. He had on dark pants, shined

loafers, and a Breitling watch with a green band. No color showed on his face, an ovoid specimen of milky whiteness built around a prim and unexpressive mouth. He looked like the rare man whose tombstone might read "I wish I spent more time at the office."

"Thanks for the chat," Swagger said. "I hope you find what I have for you useful."

"I've seen the FBI file on you," said Gold. "You have contributed much. Myself, I'm really just a clerk. For me, courage is not a job requirement. But I consider myself, nonetheless, of some utility."

"I was told by my daughter that you're the George Smiley of your organization. I guess that means 'a famous spy.'"

"Something like that. I lack a beautiful wife, however, and an encyclopedic memory. And unlike Smiley, I'm not a cynic, I'm still a humble pilgrim. By the way, I found your daughter extremely bright. I'm sure you're very proud."

"I am."

Gold nodded. "Please proceed."

"Is this place secure? Can I say a certain name that might be classified?"

"You are actually surrounded by young members of our counterterror staff. This is their favorite kind of assignment."

Swagger took a single breath before beginning. "Let me begin by asking, do you have familiarity with the name Juba? As in Juba the Sniper."

Gold sat back coolly, betraying no surprise. Yet the

microlanguage of his facial architecture—so subtle, few would have noticed—communicated a response. A stimulation. Then it was gone.

"A very interesting gentleman."

"Ain't he just?" said Swagger.

"I must warn you, much of what has been offered to us in re Juba over the years has turned out sourly. He is surrounded by misinformation. The man himself is quite clever in his security arrangements, as are his masters. This includes false trails, inaccurate leaks, bogus sightings, and the like. We have gone up many alleys to find them blind. He knows many things which we would like him to share with us—and I'm sure we could persuade him—but he seems more a myth than a man. A phantasm."

"You're telling me I could have been suckered, and this is just mischief, meant to eat up energy and leave everyone frustrated in the end."

"It might even be a distraction. You can never be sure. A whisper of Juba's presence orients us in a certain direction, and he operates in the opening left by our commitment to that lure. It has happened before."

"In other words, in this game I am an amateur and may be full of shit."

"With all due respect, at this stage anything is possible."

"Well, let me tell you the story and all about the remarkable woman who is its hero."

"Please."

Swagger narrated as succinctly as possible the odyssey of Janet McDowell, the one-woman CIA who'd gone from suburban matron to deep-cover penetration agent. The Mossad professional listened intently, occasionally sipping lemon water, but did not interrupt.

Finally, he said, "Is any of this backed up on paper? Do you have copies of the various documents in play, photographs of the individuals mentioned—proof, say, of her mistreatment on her journeys? Does this hold up to elemental scrutiny?"

"All of it, here in this briefcase. Moreover, I hired a private detective. Please, if you should meet her, don't tell her. I had the same questions. I also ran her paperwork by a friend of mine who's a retired FBI agent and extremely practiced in this business. In both cases, she passed the test brilliantly. Her zygoma was indeed fractured into four pieces in 2010, and she spent seven months in the hospital. Even then, the bones didn't quite heal properly. Her finances indicate funds coming in from relatives, an ex-husband, the sale of property. She doesn't have much left or much future to look forward to. She's two million in debt, with no end upcoming."

"So she is legitimate, though you wouldn't be offended if we double-checked?"

"Help yourself."

"But *her* legitimacy doesn't prove her *information* is legitimate. Perhaps this is another Juba game, conjured by some Iranian Ministry of Intelligence genius. I could name several. The brilliance of it would be discovering the woman on one of her trips, feeding her false information artfully disguised as the truth. Her belief—and she would have a need to believe, a need to achieve some justice for the poor lost boy—might be exactly the tool they'd put to use in order to achieve some sort of leverage over us."

"Sure. I guess," said Bob. "But it seems more likely that if they knew about her, they'd put a bullet in her head instead of going to all this trouble."

"And, other than being a nuisance, she is not under active CIA control or even in their awareness?"

"I don't know anybody there like I once did. But the mess that place is in now—again, it seems unlikely. Maybe this genius could play a game using her uniqueness, but right now everybody in the Agency seems really pissed off."

Gold nodded.

Finally, he said, "Why don't you let me run some checks. I'll call you in a day or two. Please enjoy our town. I will put everything on a Mossad account."

"That's very kind, but to keep myself untouched by financial interests, I prefer to pay my own way. I can afford it. Why should I just leave it to my kids?"

Gold's eyes crinkled briefly. "Ha. Why indeed?"

For two days, he enjoyed the sights and flavors of Tel Aviv, admiring the scenery, the women, the live-for-today ethos that seemed to animate the place. It had a gay living-on-the-bull's-eye quality to it, familiar from Saigon toward the end. They probably felt the same in Troy. He developed a liking for pomegranate juice and soda taken on the hotel veranda with the Med a blue pool in one direction and, in the other, scrub mountains sustaining what appeared to be thousands of apartments, all of this in splendid sunshine. Only occasionally did the percussion of what might have been an explosion jar his eardrums. Sometimes, but not always, sirens. He felt his face darkening in the rays from above, and his own step turning jaunty.

On the third night, his phone rang. It was not Gershon.

"You will be picked up tomorrow at nine," the voice informed him, then vanished.

And indeed at 9 a black Citroën pulled up, driven by a boy.

"Mr. Swagger?"

"Yep."

"If you please . . ."

The car wound through town and eventually made it to the suburbs, where, after a bit, it seemed to set a course toward a black cube of a building, looking all sci-fi in the light, gleamless, obdurate, implacable. He knew it was Mossad headquarters, a six-story glass block whose dark surface evoked the idea of being watched from the inside while remaining impenetrable from the outside.

Security was thorough, his documents vetted, his body scanned, even the labels on his clothes checked. The boy stayed with him the whole way, ultimately depositing him on the sixth floor in a shabby conference room, where he was awaited by what appeared to be a committee.

Gold didn't bother to introduce him to them or them to him. Names were irrelevant. The men were as somber as Gold, some bearded, some not. All had the game written on faces that might not have smiled in the past few years. Each of them had a folder in hand, and Gold seemed to be in charge.

"Sergeant Swagger, my colleagues and I will put certain questions before you. We do so in the interest of efficiency and probity. In some cases, you may think they are hostile. You might be right. I've asked my colleagues to divide themselves between advocacy and prosecution. No disrespect is meant, so please take nothing personally. Especially from Cohen."

"Who's Cohen?" asked Bob.

"I'm Cohen," said a small man with bright, combative eyes and a disorganized goatee.

"For some reason, our Director tolerates Cohen and his poor attempts at humor. Perhaps it's a lesson for us as to what not to become. Anyway: Cohen?"

"Are you fucking Mrs. McDowell?" asked Cohen.

Swagger knew trouble when he saw it.

"No," he said.

"Have you ever dreamed of her naked?"

"Are you kidding?"

"Does she have large or small breasts?"

"I have no idea."

"Would you consider her a sensual woman?"

"Do you find grief sensual?"

"How many men have you killed?"

"Ah. Too many. I didn't count. None that couldn't and wouldn't have killed me."

"Do you enjoy killing?"

"I enjoy the craft of shooting. It's what I was put here to do."

"Are you a gun nut?"

"I have respected them and they have served me. My family heritage is battle with the gun, for the sake of society, but also—and I have thought hard about this and can admit finally—it fulfills me. As I say, it's what I do, and if I am not doing it, something is missing from my life. But I don't have sex with them."

"Still, this whole thing could be a fantasy to get yourself in another gunfight, yes?"

"I often wonder about that. It's possible. But in all the things I've done since the Marine Corps, I was on the track of righting some wrong, usually recalling the sacrifice of someone like me who had been forgotten."

"Are you a psychopathic killer?"

"I am not psycho. I just have always found guns interesting and appreciate their capabilities, which, like my own, are at their highest peak when circumstances are at their most extreme. I have no need to kill. But I never dream about it."

Questions came and went. There seemed no pattern to them. It was like receiving fire from all points of the compass. As promised, Cohen was the most annoying.

"Do you consider sniping an act of murder or an act of war?"

"War. I have only taken out armed men. I take no pleasure in the kill, and I've made no money from it. I make my money taking care of ailing horses. I love horses. My wife is a good business manager, I have a reputation, and so we have prospered. I don't need money, I have all I will ever need."

"What moved you about Mrs. McDowell?"

"Her pain. Some people close to me have died in violent action. They were, all of them, too good to pass that way, but sometimes, by whimsy or evil, it happens. So I felt that."

"Do you think that could have clouded your judgment?"

"No. She was real. Her pain was real. Her courage is real. Her facts are true."

"Why are you here?"

"I was afraid if she didn't see progress, she'd commit suicide. I realized that we had reached a point—*she* had reached a point—where to proceed, we needed the support of state actors. Resources beyond our means, access to information beyond our scope. We just weren't big enough to do it no more. And every time she went over there, she risked her life. The next trip would have left her floating upside down in a river."

"It sounds more like you are hiring us, not us hiring you."

"I want Juba. For me, that's what this is about."

"If we decide to work with you," said Gold, "there is a precondition you must accept. That is, in our employ you will regard Juba as our property. Our goal is not to put a bullet in his head. That does limited good and would only satisfy in an Old Testament sense—"

"And nobody here believes in the Old Testament," said Cohen, and this time there was some laughter.

"Our goal," said Gold, "is to have a series of chats with him. We need to unravel his life. He harbors many mysteries and will settle many issues. Assuming our success at that enterprise, we will try him, then imprison him. He will live the remainder of his life in an Israeli prison. If you shoot him without cause, we will try you for murder. Though oceans of our blood have been spilled, we are not, as a culture, particularly bloodthirsty. We are justice thirsty. Do you understand?"

"I do."

"Can you live by those rules?"

"Yes."

"We are professionals, not avengers. We expect the same from you."

That seemed to do it. The session had lasted six hours, he realized. He was hungry. But the men at the table seemed to communicate by nod or even subtler stratagems, and after a pause for wordless communication, Gold went through the nature of the professional arrangements, involving contracts, payments, insurance, next-of-kin notification, and other bureaucratic necessities.

"Do you have any questions?"

"I am curious about one thing. What in the presentation convinced you this was worth following and not a scam or a dumb-ass initiative by amateurs?"

"On January fifteenth, 2014, an Israeli businessman, who was secretly our agent and very well known by many of the men in this room, was leaving Dubai. He was shot by a sniper on the tarmac as he waited to board the jet and killed. Very long, impressive shot. But mysterious too."

"Why?"

"He thought—and we thought—his cover was secure. He had been in Dubai for two weeks, attending to issues. On several occasions, he was accessible, we realized, to shorter, easier, more certain shots. We were baffled by the fact that it was not until his last day that he was taken from us, and the shot was much harder. But the bill of lading that Mrs. McDowell located in the SouthStar files provides the answer. Juba was out of ammunition. He had fired his quarterly allotment, and he would not move without the Bulgarian in his magazine. It arrived the thirteenth. He immediately was dispatched to Dubai. With his preferred ammunition finally in stock, he made the shot, though much harder than it could have been. The bullet was recovered, and indeed it was the heavy ball, although we attached no importance to that at the time. But now we see that it explains the timing."

"So again, the lady was right. She had a list of killings from around the world. Your people, ours, their own. Whoever. Juba is the one for the job."

"Juba is promiscuous," said Gold. "To our misfortune, he has had many encounters with us. And as you know, he's very good at what he does."

"You have IOUs to cash in as well."

"You don't know the half of it. Cohen, be unusually useful. Tell him about the bus."

5

Israel, the bus
June 14, 2015

You must do this hard thing for us, Juba," said the commander. "Bombs have lost their magic. Blow up two hundred and fifty people in the marketplace, and no one notices. It doesn't even make the news in the West. We need something with an edge to it, something that will make the bastards sit up and listen. And realize they cannot forget us for even a single second."

"I am in obedience, as always," Juba said.

The commander had told him of the politics of the situation, not that he knew or cared about politics. The Americans were attempting to negotiate with the Iranians, and if they got a mullah's name on a dotted line, it would be celebrated as a major event in the West. The idea would take hold that "progress" was being made, delusionary or not. But such arrangements made without the presence of the Islamic State at the table could not be allowed. It would suggest that such a way could lead to a "solution," when the only real solution was the eradication of the Zionist entity and its citizens. That was the solution that Allah demanded, that and nothing else.

An atrocity was needed that would shock the world and generate such heat that no accord could be signed and an important object lesson would be taken. The leaders had considered many alternatives, but all were difficult to arrange, needed heavy logistic support, and were subject to discovery and penetration.

Juba was one man, with extraordinary skills. With minimal assistance, he could move into position, strike his blow, and vanish. No networks risked, no valuable supplies eaten up, no large bodies of men required. Such was the magic of Juba the Sniper.

"The thought of the death of one by another, that is what scares them to their core. The bomb is impersonal. It has no charisma. It is anonymous and seems almost like the weather. It's like a tornado arriving. But the man with the rifle intimately acquaints himself with each victim. They are all narcissists, the idea of being not a victim of circumstance but of a conspiracy aimed directly at them—that is something that will linger in their minds."

"I understand," he said.

The trip in the hold of the ancient freighter was finished. So was the rumble through Gaza City traffic, the long trek hunched in the dampness of the tunnel, prone to discovery at any moment by Israeli security teams. But he had made it to the Promised Land.

In a nameless village in the Negev, not far from the

Erez Crossing, he climbed aboard a decrepit vehicle and paid his shekel passage. It was crowded, but he found his way to the rear and got a seat. Nobody looked twice at him. And why should they? He was of them.

He wore a loose tribal turban over his head and loose shirts and a scarf, all of it of the random sort picked up by laborers the Middle East over. His loose pants had seen so many other days and owners, his boots were scuffed from their own record of days and owners. He was the nameless one, the Arab, sustained by faith but otherwise oblivious to reality. He was the millions. If he had or had had a wife and family, it was all forgotten in the ceaseless turmoil and labor. This side of the wire, that side, this wire, that wire, made no difference. He was eternally on the move, and the only pleasures he could seek were religious or illicit. He had no place to go, he had nothing to belong to. To such, Allah would be everything, for in Allah and the next life was the only hope.

The bus coursed the Negev, stopping now and then in other nameless villages that had sprung up along the road. The desert here was vast, but not as cruel as much of its other territory, which was scorched land, inhospitable and dark, with stone rills running crazily this way and that. It could kill you fast if you didn't know what you were doing. Here, though, agriculture had taken hold. Still close enough to the sea, and the Jews had built their kibbutz, where they lived and sang and farmed and fucked, while, on the lesser land, Arabs farmed wheat or dates, mostly by the power of their own backs, and the sea temperature was mild enough so that that wheat and those dates usually were ready for harvest on schedule. The Jews patrolled in their machine-gun-equipped jeeps, young men drawn from the city, serving for only a few years. They knew nothing, their eyes saw nothing. It was a game of wasted time for them, until they had done their service and could be about better business.

But Juba knew it well. He had lived twenty years in such degradation, one of many children of a village chief in another country, virtually uneducated, beaten like a dog for any infraction, untouched by love from mother and father, for each had too much to do to spend precious seconds on that. There was never enough food. And the television reception—every house, no matter how poor, had a television—showed fuzzy images of some other world that was unreachable, unimaginable.

His life was defined by the wheat. From the age of eight on, he toiled in the fields. It wasn't any mechanical kind of farming but instead the ageless struggle of the Arab peasant, the harvest by hand, with flail and hoe, as the tough thistles on the stalks rubbed the fingers raw, and one had to bend to get to them, until the back knitted in pain, and the ground cut into the knees, while above the sun was merciless, and his father kept yelling, "Faster, faster, you lazy little insects. Do you want to die of hunger? This is survival!"

Only the True Faith was real, and only it offered some kind of escape. He could lose himself in the mandates of the Qur'an and the idea that somehow this life had structure and definition. So the only place he felt human was in the madrassa, where he applied himself hard, hoping to earn Allah's pleasure. It turned out he had a nimble mind, and at least one of the leaders said that among them all, he had the possibilities. He could escape from this world without tomorrows.

"You're smart," he was told. "There can be more for you. You can escape the great nothingness of your people."

"If God wills it, it will happen," he said, and believed.

One day after he turned eighteen, the letter arrived, informing him that he had been conscripted for two and a half years. He would be taken away and trained in some military skill. Maybe that would be his future, maybe it would open his eyes, maybe it will come between him and the life laid out for him, the life of labor and uselessness.

But the army was another delusion. A rural Arab conscript was the lowest form of military scum, and he was again laughed at and cursed and beaten and starved for his crudeness and ignorance. Sergeants mocked him, officers ignored him. He was invisible, his prayers without weight. God had forsaken him.

And then he discovered the rifle.

6

The black cube

He's Syrian," said Cohen. "A Sunni peasant named Alamir Alaqua, you can spell it any way you wish, with or without hyphens, it makes no difference to us. Born in 1970. Raised in the north, a hundred or so miles east of Aleppo, in Syria's narrow rim of arable land. His family are wheat people. His first eighteen years are unnoticed, and he never refers to them, it is said. One can imagine: working the fields, at prayer five times a day, beaten often, perhaps molested occasionally, part of a large family of minor distinction in a village named Tar'qu. To his father, and the rest of the world, he was but another beast of burden. That is all."

"If," said Gold, "you have some idealized vision of the international assassin as a man of erudition, you will be disappointed. This chap is a cold brute, utterly committed and sublimely talented."

Bob nodded. He'd seen enough bullshit about snipers on TV and in the movies to know that almost nobody ever truly got it: the closure of mind, the dedication to skill and art, the commitment to the faith. But Bob got it, and he would never take such a man lightly.

"It was in the army that he showed his extraordinary gift. He shot a sixty-year-old Persian Mauser so well that he was selected for sniper school. For the first time in his life, he felt special. He completed himself by putting the rifle in use to Allah's purpose.

"At the sniper school, taught by Saudi mercenaries, who themselves had been trained by American Green Berets, he was again picked out, developed, quickly promoted. And, again for the first time in his life, he had food in his belly. And respect from his elders. For the first time, he was a man.

"We assume he drew first blood in 1990. His targets, however, were not infidels but coreligionists. Under the first Assad's realpolitik, Syria had joined the coalition against the Iraqi occupation of Kuwait. No records exist, no tales of a legendary sniper among the Syrian forces of that war. Yet knowing his ambitions, it seems logical that he would have tested himself. I'm sure there are Iraqi widows owing to his efforts, the irony being that he served first against the men that he would later serve so ably for."

But his real experience, Cohen said, came as a specialist with the minister of defense's campaign to exterminate opposition to Assad and the Ba'athists in the '90s. That fellow, Mustafa Tlass, was a mediocre general, a mediocre politician, an excellent sycophant, and a first-rate secret policeman. He used snipers to isolate and eliminate non-Ba'athist pretenders to power to solidify Old Man Assad's rule. It was so much easier than raiding, interrogating, imprisoning, executing. One application of Bulgarian heavy ball from four hundred meters out and the problem was solved forever.

"In 2000," continued Cohen, "old Assad dies, to be succeeded by his surviving second son, the ophthalmologist without a chin or a scruple."

"What happened to his first son?" asked Bob.

"Ask us no questions and we'll tell you no lies," said Gold.

"Well, that's assuring," said Bob.

"Assad Two's first priority is to repair the enmity his father created by siding with the coalition and invading Kuwait in '90. Thus, in 2003, after the destruction of the Iraqi army and the occupation of Iraq by the Americans, he authorizes sending military advisors to the insurrection. At that point, he has the largest, most well-trained and -equipped army in the Middle East. Among the technicians and tacticians he sends is our Grim Reaper, Sergeant Alaqua.

"There seems to have been no initial plan to turn him into a legend," said Gold. "But he found the ruins of Baghdad an excellent place to practice his craft, he found these disgruntled ex-soldiers of the Iraqi Republican Guard highly motivated students. They were blooded, they were aggressive, they had no fear of death. They were the worst kind of patriots: they lived to kill or die, and it didn't much matter to them which. We could cite numbers and show you the marine reports, if you wish—"

"I've picked up enough from the fellows I know," Bob said.

He didn't like to think of it. The kids were fine as infantrymen when they had lots of high explosives a radio signal away, the American way of war. But the shattered wilderness of a city, all confusion and confinement, where the bad guys knew the streets so much better, the kids—at least the first rotation of them—were just so many sitting ducks.

Bob thought sourly that Tom McDowell had been one of those ducks.

"Against the sacrifice of Iwo Jima, Baghdad is nothing," said Gold. "But of course America—and the West and Israel—has lost the will to sustain casualties on a steady basis. When the numbers begin to rise, the parents begin to panic and the media begins to notice. It shows that the true realpolitik of the world is demographics."

"But we did turn it around?"

"The marine counterintelligence people did a brilliant job of analysis and counterplanning, and, yes indeed, it pretty much destroyed Sergeant Alaqua's sniper force in a single afternoon. He himself escaped death, barely, having killed much and learned much. But his name had been made in radical circles. He was eagerly recruited and offered not merely princely sums to keep himself available but, most of all, interesting targets. Upon returning home, he disengaged from the army and became radical Islam's go-to guy. We have him in Afghanistan, Africa, India, even the Philippines. He seems to have gone to work mainly for Tehran. But he helped the home folks too. In 2005, the prime minister of Beirut—occupied at the time by Syria—had run afoul of young Assad and old

Tlass. On February fourteenth of that year, he was blown up by car bomb in Beirut. The mystery was, how did the killers wire the bomb? The answer is, they didn't. Too tricky to use radio detonation in a heavily urban area, flooded already with transmissions. Rather, they planted twenty kilos of Semtex under the street, leaving a lump of highly volatile contact compound visible, possibly chlorine azide or silver nitrate. Perhaps it was camouflaged as dog shit. As the car passed over the bomb, from three hundred yards out, Juba, as he was now called, hit the compound with Bulgarian heavy ball, and the whole thing detonated. A great shot, a huge blast. Twenty-two others perished.

"Which brings us at long last," said Gold, "to the incident of the bus."

7

The old Arab's pony pulled his cart through the streets of Herzliya, a leafy suburb of well-appointed, well-landscaped houses, as well as luxury high-rises with ocean views, for the Israeli professional classes. Many lawyers, many engineers, many dentists, many doctors lived here, people far insulated from war and want and the anger of the Islamic entities. Twice the cart had been stopped by police patrols, and the old man offered to give them some of the fruit he had left over. They laughed, and one young policeman took a ripe banana. They checked his papers, checked his cart, warned him not to be out so late, and sent him on his way.

Somewhere between Yefet Street and Harmony Cove, the wagon drifted wide until it almost reached the sidewalk, and there a shadowy figure slipped off the vehicle's underbelly, rolled swiftly to a thicket of bushes, and slid deep into them. The wagon continued its meandering ways to a central road, which took it out of Herzliya, then it disappeared into the maze of streets in the city's Arab section.

The man who had slipped out lay flat in the brush for a good hour, not moving. Patience in these matters was everything. Possibly this site had been discovered. Perhaps it was an elaborate Israeli ruse, and perhaps capture and interrogation and ultimately surrender—no one held out forever—lay ahead. Having penetrated the Zionist homeland, he was risking everything, knowing himself to be a high-priority target.

But nothing happened. No commandos swept in for the arrest. Once or twice, late-returning citizens drove by, one in a BMW, the other in a Mercedes. He heard car doors slam, and a wife yell at a husband. But that was all.

When at last he felt secure, he slid back farther into the undergrowth. He knew the layout only from photos and diagrams. As usual, design diverged considerably from reality. The night was darker, the trees thicker, the turf spongier, the night smell of shrubbery and the sea more intense. His fingers probed, and for a second he experienced a whisper of panic. Suppose it wasn't here? Suppose he couldn't find it? Suppose he failed? Suppose—

But the supposition exercise became moot in the next second as his fingers came across, an inch or so under some low accumulation of loose dirt, the heavy canvas of a gun case. He pulled, the thing emerged, and he drew it to him.

Without needing to see, he unzipped the canvas bag and removed the object it concealed and protected. His fingers closed on the familiar configuration of the

Russian-designed Dragunov sniper rifle, a semi-automatic beast that shot the old tsarist 7.62×54R rounds, same as they had used in the Russo-Japanese War of a hundred-odd years ago. He knew it as well as one could know a thing. He had always loved the Dragon, from his first glimpse many years ago, such an improvement over the claptrap junkiness of the AK-47.

This Dragon, one of his best, was purely a parts gun, assembled from recovered battlefield castoffs. It had a Romanian receiver, a Polish stock, and a Russian barrel. An irony utterly lost on him was that it was universally called the Dragon, but its naming had nothing to do with that mythical beast. It was simply prosaic Russian policy to designate firearms by their designer's name, and the designer happened to be named Dragunov. This gun was highly tuned for accuracy, with minute filing of the trigger sear arrangements, the springs cut to a minimum for less vibration, the barrel cleansed to the atomic level, all of it lovingly reassembled, each screw torqued to the appropriate weight for maximum accuracy. It was perfect and it was untraceable and, therefore, expendable.

The scope, called a PSO-1, was Russian, of course, of the highest optical quality. It was affixed to the rifle by a clamp bolted to the side of the receiver, which held it, solidly and perfectly, over the piece, perfectly vectored to his dominant eye when he was in the prone position. He slid the rifle to his body, his right hand easing onto the familiar contours of the pistol grip, the buttstock tight, hard, without mercy, against the pocket of his shoulder, the support arm running directly under the rifle, jutting upward at the elbow so that the hand could grasp the wooden forestock, but not tightly, for a shooter's enthusiasm could compress the forestock so that it touched the free-floating barrel and thus bring imperfection to the system. He twisted, tested, squirmed, and wiggled, as any shooter will do, building the perfect position, so that the weapon was supported off bone, not muscle, and the legs splayed behind him, in full contact with the support of the planet itself. He lifted the rifle to his eyes from the ground a dozen times just to make sure he'd found his natural point of aim. He tested the electronics of the scope, switching them on to see the reticle etched in glowing red against the night, the chevron denoting point of impact, the crude range finder, an inverted arc in the right-hand quadrant, which denoted the height of a six-foot-tall man at eight ascending ranges, unnecessary to him because he'd already zeroed the chevron to two hundred and thirty-four meters, appropriate to task.

Now he attached the suppressor. Another battlefield pickup, possibly found still screwed to the muzzle of a marine M40 destroyed along with its owner in a roadside bombing and salvaged for use against its inventors. It was a well-machined tube that was something like a nautilus shell, encasing a series of chambers that ran its eight-inch length, each chamber leading to the next by a small orifice. The gases released by the shot emerged at supersonic speed from the muzzle but expanded into the surrounding tube, and raced, chamber to chamber, through the apparatus, so when they emerged at the end of the trip, they had lost most of their energy. The result could be measured in decibels by a sophisticated electronic device, but the number meant nothing. What mattered was that the blast of the rifle was reduced, not to the *pfft!* so beloved of the movies but a generic snap, like that of a door closing stoutly, not merely quiet but so diffused it was impossible to track. A small-arms genius somewhere in the Islamic State apparatus had machined a kind of linking device that united the rifle and the suppressor, which bore the name Gemtech.

That appliance threaded and screwed tight, he reached back to the gun case, found a zipper denoting a pouch, unzipped. And removed three ten-round magazines with the Bulgarian yellow-tipped heavy ball. He left nothing to chance. Each of the thirty rounds was selected from a larger cache of them, all weighed and measured to exact sameness, each tested for runout and found to have come out of the manufacturing process with perfect circularity. No group of mass-produced cartridges could be more accurate. He laid two magazines under his right hand so they'd be easy to access. The third he placed into the magazine well, rotated it into the gun until it clicked and was stable, then drew back the bolt and eased it forward, setting shell in chamber and firing pin at full cock. He was as ready as he could be.

He tried to relax, letting his body settle, letting his lungs oxygenate, letting his heart still. The moral aspects of that which he was about to do had been utterly replaced by the technical aspects. Before it was anything else, and after it was everything else, it was a pure shooting exercise, and he knew that Allah had put him on the planet to shoot infidels, he knew that his mission was blessed.

He prayed himself toward the nullity of complete relaxation and concentration, where he wanted his mind to be. *Praise be to Allah, the wise, the benevolent, the merciful. Praise be to He who watches over and favors His people so that they will always be under His protection no matter the ordeal. Praise be to the mission to which He has assigned me through his mullahs. Praise be to my training, my experience, my will, and my belief in Allah. Praise be to them all. And praise be to that which is about to happen, and may its purpose be achieved.*

In that steadiness of incantation, which evened his breathing and sharpened his vision, which calmed his hands and his nerves, he passed the time, not knowing if it were an hour, a day, or even a month.

When he opened his eyes and came back from the realm of prayer, it was light. A crisp day, still very early. Now and then, a sedan negotiated the street where he had concealed himself, usually a BMW or a Mercedes-Benz, but nobody was out for walks. The sky was clear and blue, though still blurred by the illumination of the rising sun. It had not yet cleared the small rise that had offered itself to him some two hundred and thirty-four meters down the road. From nowhere, it seemed, a woman and child had come from one of the great houses, she in bathrobe, he with a small briefcase, and stood at the curb. That meant it was time.

Juba drew the rifle to him, squirmed again to find the necessary position, set arms and chest in the correct opposing angles for the appropriate lockup of tension throughout the body, flicked the PSO-1 on, and put his dominant eye squarely to the rubber cup that cushioned the eyepiece. He was rewarded with the world swollen by a factor of four and the glow of the reticle against the crest of the hill.

He waited, not fighting the small tremble as the chevron responded to his own internal rhythms, the pulsing of his chest, the rogue twitches in his musculature, and watched as, slow, steady, dignified, the school bus rose over the crest, first its yellow roof, followed by its darkened windshield, behind which only the silhouette of the driver was visible, due to tunnel effect, against the opaque illumination from the rear escape door.

It was like any school bus from the world over, a lengthy van, a cab with a truck's snout, a flat windshield, the whole as aerodynamic as a brick. It was meant for slow, stolid transport of squirming treasure. It halted where it had to. The driver bent a bit to open the door, and he killed her.

The bullet spalled the windshield, and she slumped, an ejected Dragon shell popped free off the action of the breech, the acrid tang of decades-old Bulgarian powder rose ambrosia-like against his nostrils, and he rotated slightly to the mother, who just stood there, crucified by shock. She may have acted on instinct to throw herself around her child, but Juba was faster by a fraction and shot her in the head, which disappeared in a spurt of plasma, just a thumb smudge against the pristine perfection of the day. The infidel child, standing there, also dumbfounded, was next, dispatched by a side entry, in the chest, his little body spasming, knocked back by the impact of the high-velocity heavy ball.

Juba settled again on the windshield and saw some young hero had raced to the driver and was pulling at her. A shot, and he pulled no more. The children left inside, of course, panicked, filled the aisles in their desperation to escape, perfectly silhouetted by the illumination pouring through the rear door from the east, and he put the chevron to each squirming blur and brought it down. In time, the windshield was so occluded by bullet fractures that it became incapable of displaying detail. But movement was enough, and he shot until there was no movement, stopping at ten to switch magazines—ack, a cartridge had slid a quarter inch forward, and so he quickly pushed it back in line—ack again, his glove caught on the lip of the mag, so he quickly shook it off, forced the cartridge under the lip down with his thumb, snapped the box in with a dexterous aplomb, and came back to find a child had actually escaped and was heading toward tree cover. He was faster than she was.

Seventeen rounds later, it was over. No more movement. Nothing.

Praise be to Allah. Thanks be to Him for blessing my enterprise, for sanctifying my mission to completion, for rewarding my effort and virtue with success.

8

He looked at the crime scene pictures, or at least the ones taken outside the bus. Three bodies inert on pavement or curb. The bus windshield a smear of cracked glass, supernovas of fracture. Fragments glittered all over the bus's hood and the street.

He did not look at the shots from the interior of the bus. What was the point?

"And you want to interview this guy?" he said. "See, if it was me—and what do I know, I'm just an Arkansas hick—I'd cut off his face and feed it to the pigs."

"Alas," said Cohen, "we're a little Jewish country. No pigs."

"Dogs, then," said Swagger.

"Commendable enthusiasm," said Gold. "But Juba's secrets are more important than his life. Who can he identify? What is he working on? Who gives him orders, who supplies the logistics, the egress and exit? Who's in planning, who in execution, who is liaison? Which unknown state actors are influencing him? What has he heard of other operations? Perhaps most important, what is the source of their considerable funding?"

"Do you have a photo of him? What about DNA? Without those, he could be anybody that looks like anybody else named Mohamed."

"No picture," said Cohen. "No DNA. However, we have one good right-hand thumbprint. We believe it belongs to him, as it was taken from a shell casing found at the massacre. He would not allow anyone else to load his weapon. Prints don't usually show up on weapons or ammunition, but this shell had a slight sheen of oil on it, and so it registered. Perhaps an error committed under the pressure of expediency."

"By the way, did the plan work? Did he stop the treaty?"

"No, he didn't. Your Agency people were very fleet of foot that day, and even before all the first responders were on scene, your president was on the phone to our prime minister, begging him not to let this thing get out of hand. So instead of a massacre-of-the-innocents sensation, we prevailed on our press corps—more obliging than yours—to report it as a shooting in a suburb. No casualty figures were released, no speeches were given, no funerals were open to press and television. The dead were mourned in private. Rumors went wild, of course, but there are always rumors. And in the end, your State Department got its deal, and everyone pretended the world was a little safer. We realize that it goes that way, sometimes. I concur with Cohen, for the first time, on this one. We are just a little Jewish country. What can we do?"

"I vote for the dogs," said Swagger. "Anyhow, now what? Do you have enough? If so, how fast can you move? Who needs to give the go code? Is it just this room, or do you have to go to politicians who will decide on a dozen factors you have no control over?"

"No doubt other opinions will be sought."

"Meanwhile, a guy like this gets antsy. He knows how many people are interested in him. He knows no place is secure forever. Look at bin Laden. Thought he had it made in the shade until Santa and his reindeer dropped by on a midnight clear. I'm tight with some of those guys. Osama had so much SEAL lead in him, they didn't even have to weight him down when they chucked him overboard. Juba knows that. He will be ready to jump. His go bag is packed."

"We are aware," said Gold.

"And we just sit here?"

"We do."

"Are you waiting for electronic intel? Have you zeroed that area and are scanning for clues?"

"Yes, but it's less illuminating than you might think."

"So what is happening? Or do you consider it rude to ask?"

"Ask Cohen," said Gold.

"Mr. Cohen?"

Cohen said nothing.

"Cohen enjoys playing things out slowly. He gets more attention that way."

"Please, Mr. Cohen," said Bob. "I'm seventy-two. I may die before you get it out, if you don't hurry."

"Fair enough. The square mile containing the town of Iria in southern Syria has to be looked at not by us but by satellites. Ours is called TecSAR. It's very modern, I'm told. Its product will be flashed back to this building and examined by experts. They will debate like rabbis. They will come up with what looks promising to them. Drones will be dispatched to follow up on the promising areas. Lower-level, longer overhead, more precise cameras. They will return, their film will be developed, and that will be examined by the same experts to see what is what."

"When will all this happen?" said Bob.

"It happened yesterday," said Cohen.

It took a while for him to adjust his eyes. The room was dark, hushed, pristine, and without personality, full of cut-rate office furniture in the style of the '50s, and so air-conditioned it was like a meat locker. Cohen and Gold and a more somber man, who said nothing, sat around the table, waiting patiently as Bob examined the twenty-by-twenty-inch sheaves of photo paper placed before him, sometimes using the jeweler's loupe provided. He had trouble manipulating the awkwardly large sheets before him.

"You can't do this on a screen?" he asked. "And click on sections you want to look at closely? Like in the movies?"

"We haven't caught up with the movies, that's on next

year's budget. Then again, that has been the case with budgets for the last ten years. Always something happens."

"Okay," he said. "I'll try my best."

At first, it was just patches of light and dark, slashed by white streaks, occasionally with some kind of nubbin on the streak. There were, as well, dark smears of some kind of textured fabric, and occasionally a cluster of squares, some larger than others. It was abstract. A compass embossed on each photo established true north, and a rubric underneath issued data on time, altitude, position by longitude and latitude, as well as other information he didn't understand.

"The drones are quite helpful," said Gold. "They fly too high to be visible with the naked eye—even Juba's—but their camerawork is quite detailed. Time over target: six hours. Two drones on-site, ever since the TecSAR pictures looked interesting. This stuff is a few hours old. Perhaps our friend Sergeant Swagger might bring something to it our interpreters don't understand."

Bob went through the photos again, beginning to make sense of them. The streaks were road, the patches were field, the dark smears were hills covered by forest, the squares were farmhouses, the smaller squares compound outbuildings, the straight lines fences demarking patches of field. In time, he settled on two. He went over each carefully and finally discarded one of them.

"This one," he said to the men at the table, indicating the remaining photograph.

Cohen looked at it. "A-4511, seven miles northeast of

Iria, two miles off what passes as a main highway in southern Syria."

"Why that, Sergeant Swagger?"

"I'm looking for shooting ranges. This guy has to shoot, a lot, each day. He's very disciplined, very detail-driven. He has to have access to at least three hundred yards of open space, never less, maybe a lot more. The sun will be important too. He will, if possible, orient north-south or south-north. The other two wasted hours lost to the brightness of sunset and sunrise. And wind. It's so helpful if there's shelter. A stormy day, a windy ruckus—that can take a day from him, a day he can't afford. I see all that here."

"Please proceed."

"Another thing. The standard equipment of a range. He'll want a bench, or at least some kind of concrete pad, to go prone off the bipod. And at the far end, he'll want a berm—a roll of land, maybe just bulldozed dirt—against which to place his target. He'll want to see and analyze his misses, make adjustments. He has to see where the bullet hits relative to the target; that's why the target has to be surrounded by stuff that'll go *puff*. And then the target itself. I'm betting he's shooting at steel, which goes *clang* on each hit. He doesn't want to break concentration after a string and go to his spotting scope and track his hits with pad and pencil. Maybe they'd have a TV hookup or something computer-driven, but I'm guessing that's unlikely way out here. So I'm thinking steel. Looking at the south border of this whatever-it-is, I see a structure. Can't bring it up high enough for clear resolution, but it could be a jerry-built frame, exactly the sort you'd need to hang a chunk of steel plate . . . Can you get more resolution?"

"Perhaps later. Please proceed."

"At the other end, it's smooth, as if flattened out. Not paved, but someone had gone over it with a grader, scoured the grass away, rolled the dirt smooth. Just a little patch, but it orients nicely on the presumed target."

"Not much space there," said Gold.

"He doesn't need much. We think of shooting ranges as broad plains, but that's only for armies, cops, or hunters, for unit- or community-scale shooting exercises. This is one man. He needs a line, nothing on the lateral. So if you're looking for a field, you'll never find it. You have to look for a passageway or a lane. Because there are no regulations here, it will make no difference to him if he shoots over a road or even some houses. He's too good to whack some wandering peasant wheat farmer. On the other hand, accidents do happen, but it's not something he's concerned about. Again, get me some more resolution and I'll tell you if I see indentations from prone shooting or indications of a portable shooting bench being wheeled in. Can't tell from this altitude. If you want to be certain, send the drones in lower or with bigger cameras."

"Anything else? Temperature, humidity, rotation of earth, sunspots?"

"Not really. This ain't benchrest, where you try for a group of five in the same hole. He's shooting at men, has to hit them in the thoracic cavity, heart, lungs, spine, spleen, so his kill zone is about eighteen inches by eigh-teen. That's all the combat accuracy he needs."

"Night shooting? Will he use night vision?"

"Not at longer ranges. That stuff can clarify to maybe two hundred yards maximum. Fine for sniper work in a city, but not the kind of reach-out hit he wants for this. And that worries me. A lot."

"Why is that?"

"He's teaching himself to hit from way out. Beyond security service worry zones. Really, beyond infantry ranges. He's not training for battle but for assassination. It seems in this last operation, the one in Dubai, that he was out farther than he'd ever been. He's teaching him-self how to hit the long ones off the cold barrel. I have to tell you, that's way outstanding stuff. The long shots in Afghanistan came at the end of a sequence, where the shooter was either able to walk his rounds in unnoticed or had already zeroed in on that spot the day before. Juba can't afford to walk rounds in against high-value targets, he'd give up his position and get return fire in a second. Choppers, SWAT, the whole security apparatus, silencer or no. So he's got to train himself to the cold barrel. That's another advantage of the dirt backdrop."

The comment was met by the sound of men breathing.

Finally, Cohen: "Again, you go with this one? No sec-ond thoughts, no doubts, no little suspicions?"

Bob put his finger on A-4511.

"Here's your huckleberry. It's got all the necessary components I just described. As I said, you can see at the southern end where someone has chewed up a furrow with a backhoe or something to chart the bullet strikes against the raw dirt. Do you have distance? I'd guess close to a thousand yards."

"About right," said Cohen. "Ten twenty-seven, to be exact."

"If you know so fast, that means you've had your photo hotshots on it, and this is the one they went for too. They've given you all the numbers."

"Sergeant Swagger is no fool," said Cohen. "He misses no nuance. Continue, then."

"A thousand yards. Very long shot, by combat standards, but not so much anymore for sniping. The great shots in Afghanistan are much farther, well over a thousand, even over a mile. A couple of things to look for: if he's teaching himself to go this far, he'll need a better rifle. The ballistics on the Dragon 7.62 round drop way off, and, yep, you might get some hits from over a thousand, but you'll get a lot more misses. He's right at the distance limits on the Dragon. So he'll upgrade the hardware."

The somber old man whispered something to Cohen, who nodded, then turned to Swagger.

"Our Director is a man of few words," he said, "and I am a man of many. So he turns to me to blabber for him. He said: 'Add it up.' What he means is, given all that you have learned from the photos, what is your read on the situation? Can you project a scenario in which all this information comes into play?"

"Sure. He's a long way from being retired. If it were my call, I'd say he's in this location with this setup for a specific purpose. He's preparing for a job. It's a big one too, because look at the assets they've invested in it. They scoured the country and found exactly the place where he'd be safe, they went to great trouble to keep it secret, and we tumbled on it only because of Mrs. McDowell—"

"God bless Mrs. McDowell," said Cohen.

"Look," said Swagger, "maybe I'm out of place here, it's your country, but what I'm getting seems sort of undeniable. He is getting ready for *something*. He's either going operational or on to another step in his training before he goes operational. That means at any second he could disappear. It's your business, not mine. But if I was you, I'd chopper in the tough boys and hit this motherfucker tomorrow. Payback for lots of bad shit, yes—but, more important, you make sure there's no more bad shit down the road. I'd go tomorrow."

"Why tomorrow, Sergeant Swagger?" said Cohen. Do you think us miracle workers? We couldn't possibly hit him tomorrow."

"So when can you go?" said Swagger.

The Director spoke for the first time.

"What about," he said, "in two hours?"

9

He hated his father. He hated his mother. He hated the madrassa. He hated the beatings, the punishment, the molestation, the degradation, the hopeless, endless despair of it. He hated everything he thought of as "before." Except for the wheat.

He was in the wheat. He was of the wheat.

He had watched the sun go down over the western hills. He was a few hundred meters from the house. Prayers were over, the day's efforts over, and now he sat among the stalks. The darkness was deep and lovely, a vault of towering stars and silence. A mild breeze rustled the wheat, and it whispered to him. He turned, grabbed a handful of stalks, and brought them close to his eyes.

He observed the genius of the heads, their complexity so staggering that only Allah could have designed them. Intricate, tiny structures, each identical to the others, arranged in rows, waiting to ripen into something life-sustaining. The wheat would become grain, the grain would become bread, the bread would feed the Moslem nation and make it strong.

The wheat had created him. It demanded that his back be strong for the bending, that his legs be limber for the weeding, that his arms and hands be remorseless for the cutting, that his coordination be superb for the flailing. Later, the huge machines reached the commune to take so much of the misery out of the stooped labor. But in his time, it was all muscle: the weeding, the cutting, the flailing. You found a rhythm; you guided the beating stick exactly. It was his gift, and he had it from the start. He flailed more wheat faster, more accurately, than anyone in the province. Afterward, to amuse his brothers and the villagers, he would do tricks, which also came naturally. Put three eggs on a table and, with three cracks of the flail, smash each one perfectly. Toss an egg into the air, toss a second, toss a third, and before any of them reached the ground, whizz the beating stick to intercept them, catching each egg in the center and turning it into a spray of yellow yolk, bringing cheers and laughter. He got so he could do it one-handed, left-handed, and behind his back. He had gifts. He remembered those harvest festivals with joy. He was probably happier then than at any time in his life.

But, of course, the dark times came. Which war was it? He couldn't remember, there had been so many, and what did it matter? The fear of starvation everywhere, the sounds of hungry babies screaming as their mothers tried to calm them to sleep. Though the killing and dying were far off, the government took everything to support the soldiers, and the imams demanded obedience in their holy quest for survival, then hegemony. Easy to demand, hard to sustain.

To make things worse, a drought had scoured the earth, the clouds going heavy and dark but not bursting, the irrigation was primitive, there was only so much water, and what was left after conscription had to be rationed strictly. Many wondered how Allah could forsake His obedient children so fiercely—but the sniper did not. Instead, he nursed his misery, felt it harden into hatred, and found in it the determination to continue. I will survive, if Allah allows it. I will fight, if Allah permits it. I will die a martyr to Allah. But be pleased, Allah, do not consign me to the meaningless death of a starved peasant in a forgotten backwater of what was once a great empire. That would be waste, and what good—this was apostasy, he knew, but could not deny it—would my death do? Allah must have more in mind for me. He must enable me. Like the wheat, He must let me grow and ripen and do my part. If not, why did He give me the gift of the flail?

Now, so many years later, so many battles fought for Allah, he tried to forget, for memories of the past were of no use at all.

What mattered was tomorrow. The task. You survived the past, you fought as a soldier of Islam, and will do so yet again. You became what you became and were permitted to do your part.

Allahu Akbar, he thought. God is great.

Then he heard the helicopters.

10

The reasons to deny him were many and excellent. They were explained to him with great patience in the Land Rover as it sped through the Tel Aviv night to the air station.

"You're too old. Your reflexes are too slow. Your vision is impaired. You have a steel hip that could pop or break at any moment. You could not pass the exacting physical demands of Unit 13. You do not speak or understand Hebrew, so you would not understand commands. Do you think, under the circumstances, we should provide you with a translator? Hardly possible, and even if it was, there is the issue of time. Then there are weapons. You are not up to speed on ours. To know how to operate them efficiently, you would have to be drilled with them thousands of times under intense pressure and by mandate of our doctrines. This our Unit 13 people have done, you have not. Also procedures. With raiding, all members of the team must know the target intimately, must be in agreement on tactics and intentions, and if they must improvise, they improvise from that plan, and as soon as possible return to it. You don't know the plan.

Then there are the men. All of them will worry about you, not about the mission. They will be agitated to have a stranger in their midst. It's an unfair burden to place on them. And there are diplomatic concerns. You are an American citizen. You have no authorization from your government to participate in our combat operations. I don't know the legal repercussions, but if an American dies on an Israeli combat mission, there could be harsh political consequences. There are many in America who despise Israel and would use the tragedy as leverage to pry us further apart. Conspiracy theories would spring up like germs. Occlusion would be general where clarity is demanded. And consider journalism. Your newspaper rats would probe your death, expose your past life and your secrets, bedevil your survivors, blow security on Unit 13, breach its security, shine a light on its missions when what is most needed is darkness. I cannot under any circumstance imagine this man"—Gold indicated the Director, sitting obdurately next to him, smoking a cigarette, barely listening—"would authorize such a thing."

"Okay," said Swagger. "Just hear me out. If it matters, my eyesight *has* degraded: from twenty/ten to twenty/twenty. I spend three hours a day on horseback. Ever see any fat cowboys? No, because the horse works your muscles like an exercise machine, keeps you limber and strong. As for the guns, that's pretty much all I do. I can shoot with or against anyone in the world and either win or tie, and if I tie, I'm dead, but so is he. Raiding? I did an extended tour in Vietnam with CIA Studies and Observation Group—'commandos'—and that's all we did was plan raids, raid, look for new raids. I come from raid-ers. My father raided five Japanese islands. My grandfa-ther raided the Huns for eighteen months in the first big war. Ask the Germans about him, they still remember. He also had a spell raiding motorized bank gangs for the FBI in the '30s. Note the lack of a motorized bank gang problem now? Too bad you don't have either of them, I agree, but you're stuck with me. As for diplomacy—really, I've signed a contract, and to the world I'll just be another hard-ass contractor trying to get his kicks. Happens every day all over the world."

The Director looked at him impassively. Not a guy to go "Gee, wow!" easily.

"But all of that is irrelevant," Swagger continued. "I can stay here with you Mossad rabbis under the presumption that everything is going to happen exactly as it's planned. Has there ever been a mission like that? Even at Entebbe, the best special op in the history of the world, your commander got plugged. So if things go bad—say, there's more resistance; say, militia units from nearby get on-site faster than we expect—you need someone to eye-ball that place. Maybe you get Juba, maybe not. And if you don't, you nevertheless have to learn what he's plan-ning. You need a sniper, a gun guy, to read Juba's setup. If I see his equipment, his targets, his ammo, his scopes, I can do that, and we can draw conclusions. And from conclusions, we can move on to intercepts or prepara-tions, whatever. And if we do that, we can save lives. So the priorities here have to be these: nail the big guy first, or, failing that, get hard intel on upcoming activity. Anything less than that is failure and not worth the effort. I'm not the afterthought; I'm the thought. I'm the whole goddamned dog and pony show. Do you understand?" he added for the Director.

"I suspect he does," said Gershon. "He went to Harvard."

The Director looked at Swagger.

Finally, he said, "It's Lieutenant Commander Motter's mission. We'll let him make the call."

"You'll be fine," said Cohen, smiling at Swagger. "Motter went to Harvard too."

That this fellow Motter was a lieutenant commander, not a major, meant that Unit 13 was, like the SEALs, a navy thing. You couldn't tell from the man himself, all geared up in mushroom-cap helmet, his Kevlar strapped with frags and flares and fighting knives and various kits and packs that might come in handy, a Glock Kydexed to his chest, his face smeared black to match the night. He looked like any special ops jock, from SEAL to Delta to Pointe du Hoc Ranger to Spartan at the Hot Gates— same war, different day—to the horse raiders under Sergeant Major Odysseus outside Troy that fateful evening. He smoked a cigarette, listened impassively, as the Director spoke to him. His eyes were dead, his emotional engagement somewhere between calm preparedness and existential meaninglessness.

"Sergeant Swagger," he said. "I read the accounts of Sniper Team Romeo-Two-Bravo against the North Vietnamese Second Battalion, Third Shock Army, in the highlands outside Nha Trans in 1974. That was a hell of a fight. But you were twenty-six then. Now you're seventy-two."

"The only thing I can't do now that I did then is win at hopscotch. A weapon will equalize me out just fine."

"To be frank, I'd much rather go drinking with you, hear your stories and learn your lessons, than lead you into combat. But let me ask the fellows. We're tight in battle, but I like democracy in the unit."

The young man turned, wandered off to where a dozen or so other guys were arrayed on the tarmac, all identical helmeted dogs of war. They gathered and talked, quietly and briefly, and finally Motter waved Bob over.

"Welcome to the team, brother."

Men crowded, slapped him on the back. One guy kissed him. Names came at him, and he kept nodding as if able to remember them while answering "Bob, Bob." Like the SEALs, 13 was clearly a first-name-only kind of outfit.

"Too late for gear," said Motter. "We're airborne in three." He turned. "You, sentry, over here please."

Swagger hadn't even noticed air force security guards at the perimeter of the loading area. The fellow loped over.

"Last-minute addition. Don't have time to check an M4 out of the armory. Sergeant"—he looked closely at the name tag on the sentry's Kevlar vest—"Sergeant Mappa, he needs your vest, your Uzi, and your ammo."

Such was the charisma of Motter that no resistance was offered. The sentry seemed pleased to play with the cool kids. Smiling, he stripped off his Kevlar and handed it over to Bob, who tossed his sport coat on the tarmac, pulled the vest tight over his polo shirt—helpfully, black—and clicked the links closed, feeling it tighten and solidify. Where the helmet came from, he never knew, but it more or less fit; strapped, it was reasonably secure. Someone handed him a piece of charcoal, and he rubbed it over his pale features, feeling the grit. Soon he was of the night. Finally, he took up the ancient submachine gun, and even though he'd never touched one, it felt so familiar, like he'd known it all his life, so iconic was it. Short, with an open bolt, its weight centralized in the grip, which housed the twenty-five-round 9mm magazine in an elbow joint, with another twenty-five-rounder hitched on, all under the density of a telescoping bolt, it felt solid and useful in his hands as he looped the sling around his neck. He seized the nearly perpendicular grip, conspicuously pronging his finger upward, far from the trigger, noting that the grip safety had been clearly taped flat, so there'd be no problem if he had to shoot fast and didn't come up square on the grip.

The sergeant pointed to a horizontal slide lever, labeled in Hebrew, over the trigger guard of the blocky little thing. He said, "First position, safety on. Second, single shot. Forward, *bap-bap-bap!*"

Bob nodded. He knew their doctrine was chamber empty, and the guns didn't go hot until they were safely on the ground, advancing toward the objective. Then, and only then, would the boys pull the bolt to get ready for the man dance. As policy, the Israel Defense Force didn't want anyone jumping out of a chopper with a hot gun.

The three choppers began to whine. Slowly at first, gathering momentum, quickly speeding to a blurred fury, their rotors sucked at the air, and the boys self-divided into squads to file aboard, six to a ship, Swagger being the seventh on the Command ship.

"You're on me," said Motter, pulling him along.

"Got it," he said. He turned to the three Mossad wise men—stolid, two smoking, one not—but they simply witnessed the ritual in silence.

"Let's go to war, brother," said Motter.

Three dark birds hurtling over the dark landscape. Running hot, running low to avoid radar. The raiders were silent, knowing that when they hit the landing zone, it could turn tragic in a split second, and would definitely turn complex in two. That was the nature of the raid, and if you couldn't handle it, you were in the wrong business. So each man smoked, prayed, dreamed of sex, wondered if the Tel Aviv Guardians would beat the Jerusalem Bobcats, then wished they'd told their dad how much they loved him or hated him, and told Sally Sue either to wait or to move on with her life. Each guy had his little thing.

Up front, wedged into the hatch next to the inert but watchful Motter, Bob was pleased to note that the Israeli pilots wore FLIR goggles, so, to their eyes, the darkness ahead was illuminated. A good way to avoid telephone poles and other nasty possibilities. Didn't have them in 'Nam, and too many good men went down in pointless wastage. The birds vectored north by northwest on a heading the pilots knew by memory, just as they knew the landforms and city features that marked the route until they passed from Israel into southern Syria, where it all went dark. The machine vibrated familiarly—it was, after all, a Sikorsky Black Hawk, a kind of Vietnam-era Huey on protein shakes—and Swagger knew, from a thousand flights in three tours, the *whup-whup-whup* of the rotor, the buzz of the engines, the octane scent of the fuel. But inside—bigger than the Huey but still the cabin of a combat chopper—it was dark except for the glow of somebody oxygenating the burning stub of his butt.

Time elongated, but, at the same time, it contracted. Maybe it just couldn't figure out what to do and decided to go away.

Red light blinked.

Motter—Gadi, by first name—spoke with the pilots into his throat mic in Hebrew, pulled his legs in, un-strapped himself. In the darkness of the craft, Bob sensed the boys doing the same: butts out, minds blank, throats cleared, goggles down, bolts checked, straps tested, tightness of Kevlar and mushroom observed, knives and grenades and flares at the ready, Glocks and aid kits prepped, relationship to God figured out. Bob duplicated their motions and found himself crouched in the door-way of an assault chopper about to land someplace inter-esting. He had no fear.

The plan was easy enough, so simple as to almost be no plan at all. The birds down a hundred yards out at three points of the compass, the thirteen guys out, cocked, hot and fast, headed straight in. Classic L. Two elements hit frontally, from slightly different angles; a third sets up horizontal at the house's rear, to take down any escapees. If they run, they have to be shot; if their hands go up, they're gestured to their knees and flex-cuffed, and the op moves on. All three elements converge in one minute, each under a shield of fire from the other two. Gadi's team would hit the door first, and Gadi would enter, followed by others, for house clearance. Swagger was not invited. His job was to wait at the door until all the rooms were cleared and then move in with a second team while a third team formed a perimeter facing the road to Iria, seven klicks away, its militia being the only Syrian force in the area. Job done, Juba either captured or dumped, the guys would take their prisoners back to the choppers and home to Tel Aviv for beer and cheeseburgers by dawn's early light.

Simple, but what had not been counted on was that whatever bad guy was on sentry was not asleep and certainly not overwhelmed by the arrival of 13. It was as if he knew it could happen at any moment. So before the birds touched down, fire lashed from the house, traced stitches of dust across the zone, threw the odd tracer blur through the air, and whanged off the fuselage. Instead of a quick walk to the target, it was advance by fire and movement at the quickstep.

Swagger stayed close to Gadi, who pushed ahead. In

keeping with doctrine, he kept his chamber virginal so that he wouldn't stumble and kill three Israelis by clenching the trigger by instinct. Meanwhile, fire rose from three points on the upper floor of the house, but the shooters had no targets and could only enfilade the area. Their flashes documented them, however, and steadily any 13 guy who had a shot took it.

War is hell, it is true, but to Swagger, his soul be damned or exalted, it was also cool. The exhilaration of rounds overhead and nearby, peeling through the air and leaving a vacuum where they passed. Heat, light, noise, grit, dirt, adrenaline, energy long forgotten blossoming like an instantaneous orchid. Swagger raced into the melee, looking for someone to shoot. Hoochie Mama, ain't the beer cold!

Gadi went down. Swagger was on him.

"Fuck," the Israeli said. "Leg."

Swagger looked, saw, as usual, that God favors the bold, and that the wound was a through-and-through in the left calf. Not much blood, no spurt or gush. Just an ugly pucker in and an ugly pucker out.

"You'll be okay."

"Tell them to keep moving. They can't get hung up here."

"What do I say . . . what's the phrase?"

"Well, it's—"

Two other men came and hovered, the three talking in Hebrew. One, a sergeant, stood and waved the boys forward. With no Gadi to be his sponsor, Swagger felt himself freed from obligation, and he moved fast as any of them on the house, heard a cry, which he knew had to be "Grenade out," went flat as three large concussions ripped up dirt and debris and filled the air with dangerous stuff, but he was up. The fire volume rose, and everywhere in the brush fast smacks of dust displayed the random pecks of bullets as the defenders fired blindly at men they couldn't see. He made it to the door and realized—Hello! Ding-dong! Eureka!—it's time to go hot. He slid back the Uzi bolt, felt it lock, and he shoved the handle, at that point disengaged, forward. His thumb made certain the lever was pushed to full auto, and, last of all, he yanked on the folding stock, getting it to telescope out, and though it was no ergonomic masterpiece, it gave him something to lock between arm and rib cage. That done, he did an appraisal of the house. He was alone. He reached for a grenade, realized he had no grenades. He made ready to enter under his own full-auto cover, but then, out of the night, two more commandos showed. One had a frag in hand, nodded at Swagger, who nodded in reply and pulled back. The man tossed it. In an instant, it transformed into pure energy—lots of it.

He waited a second for pieces of stuff to cease whirling about what used to be a room, was the first to enter the boiling atmosphere, and when a figure emerged from another doorway across the space, he put six Uzi nines into him fast, melting him to the ground at light's speed, feeling the jerk of mechanism, peripheral vision noting the spew of spent cases and smear of flash at the muzzle.

Behind him, he heard men climbing steps to deal with upper-floor resistance, but his job was to push through to any sort of shop.

He rushed ahead, found nobody else to shoot, came to a door, kicked it open to behold a shooter's headquarters: targets on wall, components on shelves, heavy reloading bench, arbor press. A smashed laptop lay atop the bench, its screen a look-alike for Bonnie and Clyde's windshield. A man crouched at the bench, struggling with a lighter while holding an opened eight-pound plastic jug whose label proclaimed Hodgdon H1000, a smokeless powder applicable to reloading cartridges. It was highly volatile.

Bob thrust the Uzi muzzle at him, finger on trigger, but did not pull down.

"*No!*" he screamed. "*No!*"

Another commando was at his shoulder, rifle zeroed, also screaming, but more helpfully in Arabic.

The lighter lit. The fighter laughed, showing white teeth.

"*Allahu Ak—!*" he screamed and dropped it into the jug. If he expected a blast, he did not get it, for smokeless burns incredibly fast but does not explode. What he got, rather, was an instantaneous transformation of the universe, of which the central feature became the Devil's blowtorch, which His Satanic Majesty had just ignited. All the mythic furies of lethal flame proclaimed the presence of that which melts everything in a fraction of a sliver of a fragment of an instant. The man himself was wardrobed in flame. The fire simply cloaked him alive,

GAME OF SNIPERS   87

engulfing him to the atomic level, as all eight pounds of H1000 went. He was not a man on fire but a man of fire. Yet still, in the heart of the heart of the burning, he had some rational impulse left and spun backwards, where, in a corner, a collection of similar powder jugs had been stashed.

The result was ten more satanic blowtorches so bright, it hurt to see. The world became flame. The commando grabbed Bob to pull him out, for clearly the room would be completely lost to fire in seconds, the house in a few more, but Bob pulled away, screaming in English, "I have to check it out."

Few men run into fire; he was one. Though he could feel his skin blistering, he shoved himself forward three or four feet, then five or six, yanked his goggles off for better vision, and saw what he could see of the components above the bench before they were consumed by flame. He saw the green boxes of Sierra bullets, the yellow of Berger, the yellow-and-black of Swift, and others. He wasn't close enough to grab one but had the impression, not clearly confirmed, that the calibration on all the boxes was .338.

Two or three subsequent cans of powder went, and their Devil's breath spewed plumes in on him. He saw his sleeve was on fire, twisted, tried to find his way out in the flames, which were now general, and suddenly remembered the laptop. He twisted back against the wave of heat, and though each particle of skin was being clawed with hurt, he managed to reach out, snag the laptop with one grasp, and pull away. He stumbled a step or two, unfortunately gasped and took in some superheated atmosphere and lost another second to a racking cough. At that point, on one knee and in recovery from his hacking spasm, his eyes caught on a large gun case, steel, expensive, a wealthy sportsman's piece of equipment, leaning against the far wall, buckling as the heat crunched it. Two of three initials engraved on the case in exquisite calligraphy six inches tall were briefly visible, and again he thought he registered them as *A* and *W*. Then they were gone.

Fire propelled him to the door, and though it seemed to take hours, he reached it and spilled out. The room before him was empty, though beginning to ignite here and there too. He passed the entryway and felt the coolness of uncontaminated oxygen. Two men grabbed him and pulled him back to where the commandos had gathered and the fire's heat was not lethal.

"We thought we'd lost you, brother!" yelled Gadi.

"Damned near," said Bob, sprawling in an ecstasy of oxygen debt, sucking desperately for some air to inflate his life force. Someone took the laptop, someone else peeled the Uzi off his shoulder, and the Kevlar vest was sprung next. Cool water from a canteen gurgled in his throat, and he gulped it down. He was done for the night. Maybe for the year.

"Medic!" yelled Gadi. "Get some salve on this arm."

He was quickly tended to. Gadi gave the signal, and the party fell back to the landing zone and popped red flares, even as the three birds broke orbit and swooped down. Swagger still had fire flaring in his mind, his left arm and left shoulder hurt badly, his night vision shot—perhaps forever—by his encounter with the big flame, and his mind wasn't ticking properly. He turned back, saw the house now all gone to flame. Nothing left.

The next thing he knew, men were pulling him aboard a chopper and flattening him out on the deck. A quick radio count was made and confirmed that all who'd landed were back aboard, and the birds roared airborne, 13 homeward-bound.

11

Southern Syria, in the wheat

Juba watched. Three Black Hawks, expertly flown, as one expected of the Israelis. They did nothing poorly, they never quit or surrendered, their timing was exquisite. He hated these guys, but, damn them to the deepest chamber of Hell, they were good.

The helicopters landed, their cargo of commandos disembarked, and the birds were airborne again in seconds and climbed and vanished to a holding pattern above the fight. The operators moved fast; the question was, how fast would his people react? He knew that battles turned in the split second between action and reaction. His fellows were the best, ex–Republican Guard Special Forces, and they didn't let him down.

The volume of fire rose quickly, and the night was speared by the blasts of grenades. From three hundred yards out, he could see the automatics opening up. His guards had not wasted time wondering what was happening but got straight to the guns. The Israelis would win, with surprise and firepower on their side, but how much data would they collect in the aftermath of the raid? The guards knew their duty: to serve Allah by holding off the assault long enough for someone to detonate the smokeless powder and leave no trace behind.

It was close. A detonation came from within far too early, meaning that the commandos had gotten close enough to use grenades to room-clear and advance. Indeed, with his superb vision, he saw the figures of commandos scurry low through the doors, and now the gunfire came from within the dwelling as its assaulters closed in and flooded it.

Adid, he thought. *Adid, you swore to me you'd succeed. I trusted you.* But maybe Adid had taken a bullet in the head on the first exchange, and all his zeal and drive and hatred of infidels hadn't been enough to drive him to the final act.

Adid, I pray to Allah that I have not sacrificed you for nothing. Be a martyr in the battle, you who have given so much over the years, you who—

The powder went. Adid! Adid the Martyr had somehow, under the very eyes of the Israeli commandos, gotten it done. It was a bolt of incandescence, Allah's lightning, that blew out the shopwindow, and it was followed a second later by another bolt—larger, faster, hungrier—that seemed to rip through the house, and everywhere it struck, it ignited, and in another few seconds the whole dwelling was in flames.

Now, he thought, *I must run.* Suppose they hunt me

with heat-seeking lenses and machine guns from the air. It would be so like them, for the Jew loved his gizmos, much more than a blade for stabbing or a scarf for strangling. It was evidence of their depravity.

He turned and raced through the wheat.

12

The black cube
A few days later

He thought the wheelchair a bit much. But the doctors insisted, and you do not argue with Israeli doctors in an Israeli military hospital. Nurse Susan rolled him out of the ambulance and through security, where, even still, he was scanned by electronic wand. These boys didn't take chances.

He'd come to cleaned and bathed, but he was in pain. His burned arm felt like it was suspended in oil, which was simply antibiotic cream meant to lessen the chance of infection. The burns were second-degree and would heal, no skin grafts needed. He felt well enough on the second day to talk to his wife and assure her it was no worse than some kind of Fourth of July accident or maybe from staying too long at the beach—that sort of thing. Her unexpressive voice told him she didn't buy it, but there was no way to fix that.

And now this. Dressed in surgical scrubs, shaved, smoothed, hair cut, he found himself being rolled into the same conference room as before, once again to a rabbinical audience of men who had done much and who spoke little. As before, it seemed Gershon Gold was in charge. The Director would sit, imperturbably unimpressed, in his central seat, and the comedy material would be supplied by the man called Cohen, who announced, "Freshly returned from his recon in Hell, the possibly insane Gunnery Sergeant Swagger, USMC. How did you find the weather down there, Sergeant Swagger?"

"It ain't the humidity," said Bob. "It's the heat."

"Excellent," said Cohen. "If he can banter at a time like this, he's ready for the rabbinate."

"All right," said Gold, "no need to go over tactical details, as Lieutenant Commander Motter and the others have been debriefed extensively, and all accounts are in accord. Time now to hear Sergeant Swagger's read on the situation and his action recommendations. I suppose there's really only one question, in the end. Our soldiers— I include you, sir—killed eleven men that night. We were able to get right thumbprints off of ten of them. No Juba. So, have you reason to believe he was the eleventh man— that is, the chap who melted himself before your eyes? He was obviously impossible to fingerprint."

This hadn't occurred to Swagger, and, in a second, he realized why.

"No possibility. Because whoever he was, he died the happiest man on earth. You could read it on his face. When the lighter flicked on, he knew he'd won. He'd done his job. I'd guess that job was destroying the evidence, and he knew also that Juba had not been taken.

He was happy to face his god. You don't see that much in the West. Then he was gone in flame. As to the implications, I don't know. But I can read the signs for indicators, if you want."

"That is exactly what we want, Sergeant Swagger."

"Sure," he said. "I didn't get a clear look, and it was a little hot to be taking notes—the pen would have melted. Still, I think I got something. I was in a place I'd been before. I was in the shop of a dedicated shooter, and he was in the midst of, or possibly had finished, a serious project."

"And that is?"

"He was trying to find a load."

"The meaning evades us," said Gold. "Can you be more specific? We are not NRA members."

"Sure," said Bob. "Most folks think shooting is divided into two components. You have a bullet, number one, which you put in a gun, number two. Pull the trigger, and a hole appears somewhere, wanted or not."

"I take it there's more."

"A bit," said Swagger.

"Is this going to be long and boring?" asked Cohen.

"I'll certainly try to make it so, sir," said Bob. "Turns out each gun—not each *type* of gun, but each individual gun off the assembly line—has peculiarities of construction: screw torque, variation in machine tool setting, metallic composition of barrel, precision of fit of moving parts, and on and on. This is where it can get really long and boring, Mr. Cohen, so I am cutting you some slack here."

"You are a humanitarian," said Cohen.

"All these little things affect accuracy. In most applications, it don't matter. In most applications, you're just trying to hit the target in the fat part—man, beast, or paper. In three applications, it does. Those would be hunting, benchrest shooting, and sniping. So people who do those things pay special attention to details."

"Fascinating," said Cohen, as his face said the opposite.

"What they have learned—and remember that the gun and its ballistics is one of the most studied, engineered areas in human behavior—is that these elements can make an immense difference in accuracy. In the rifle itself, it can be the barrel, the rifling in the barrel, the trigger pull, the fit of the stock to the action—all of these can make a difference in determining whether the rifle is just accurate enough, accurate, or superaccurate. Questions?"

The rabbis appeared to be paying attention but had no questions.

"But that's even more true of the ammunition. Thus, what's called *reloading*. It gives the shooter control over many more factors. He takes a spent shell, pops the spent primer, cleans the case. He reshapes it under pressure, primes it, puts a new and different kind and amount of powder into it, and loads a new and different type of bullet—same caliber, different shape, design, weight, material, whatever—and assembles it in a press. He documents all this carefully. It's about recording each step in the process. Then he shoots it, usually in groups of five. He wants all five to go in one hole, or close enough to it.

He very carefully documents the results of the shooting—that is, group size, response to wind, velocity, muzzle energy—and he compares it to factory ammo or, more likely, his other attempts. Maybe it's better, maybe it's not. The point of this trial-and-error process is that he is searching for a combination—it's almost a musical thing, hunting for a chord—that gets the absolute most out of the rifle's potential. Usually one load—a certain brand or make of shell, a certain ritual of preparation, a certain bullet weight, a certain bullet design, a certain powder, a certain amount of powder, a certain length of cartridge, a certain high degree of concentricity, and maybe half a dozen other empirical things—will produce the best load. That is the cartridge that meets its goal for accuracy, velocity, perhaps lack of muzzle flash, in combat considerations. Anyway, that would be his ideal, and it would be his round of choice. It would be significantly better than factory ammunition, across the board, for any usage."

"And there is an industry that supports such behavior?" asked Gold.

"Yep. Chemical companies make dozens of different powders—different burning rates, different-shaped crystals, different fillers—while gun accessory companies make measuring devices, powder scales, reloading dies, primers, primer loaders, and bullet companies make different weights, shapes, interior structures, tips, composition materials. He's just trying to find that right chord and build his harmony around it."

"Superb," said Cohen. "The Mozart of the sniper world. But do you also have a point?"

"Given that he had pounds and pounds of different kinds of smokeless powder, boxes and boxes of bullets, boxes signifying Wilson reloading dies, an arbor press for squishing all the stuff together, it seems to me he was doing a methodical search for a certain round for a certain task that would be far more efficient than anything he could obtain on the market."

"He's setting up for an extra-hard shot where maximum accuracy is mandatory?" said Gold.

"It gets worse," said Swagger. "You haven't asked about caliber. I am all but certain—remember, I was in Hell, and the Devil himself was trying to turn me into a marshmallow—that the bullets were of a diameter of three hundred and thirty-eight thousandths of an inch. This would mean the load in question was a caliber called the .338 Lapua Magnum. It's currently the go-to sniper round in Afghanistan for long-distance situations—which are most situations in Afghanistan. In 2009, a British sniper named Craig Harrison used the .338 Lapua to hit the longest documented shot in history. He popped a Taliban machine gunner at over twenty-three hundred yards. That's a mile and a half. That's the point of the .338 Lapua: it lets you strike from a different time zone. So I would conclude that Juba is putting together a .338 Lapua Magnum load to put someone down from a long, long way out. He's methodical, skillful, dedicated. He's going about it the right way. However jazzed up his jihadi half is, his shooter half is professional, cool, cunning, taking no chances, no shortcuts. They've spent a lot of money and a lot of effort getting him exactly what

GAME OF SNIPERS 99

he wants. There don't seem to be no limit on the purse strings. My guess is, he's got either a stolen or a recovered Accuracy International Magnum—the best sniper rifle in the world—and all the gadgets to support it. All that stuff had to be somehow gotten and smuggled into Syria. So you're looking at a major effort by someone's intelligence agency. Only one conclusion: he's going after a high-value target."

"This news is extremely bad," said Gold.

"One small advantage we may have: the distance of the range he was practicing on was only 1,023 yards, if I recall. There's not really any advantage to the .338 Lapua over any one of a dozen other long-range cartridges at 1,023. The point of the Lapua is the long, *long* shot. No point in going to all the trouble they've gone to if it wasn't a long one they were planning. So my thought is, he ain't done. He'll have to find somewhere to test his stuff out to Harrison's range, another thousand yards or so. He'll need to have made that shot a hundred times in practice before the real thing. So maybe that gives us a little time. He's got to find someplace to shoot where the distance, the climate, the wind patterns, the weather all match up with his target zone. But it's taken him a bit of time—we don't know where in his program he is—to get to 1,023. If he's planning to take someone further, he's got to move on to that next stage and become friends with it. Seems like in Syria there wouldn't be too much trouble finding fifteen hundred or two thousand yards to go shooting."

"No, but it's the climate," said Gold. "Syria is desert,

as is Israel. Much less humidity, much more wind, odd temperature patterns. Maybe shooting at that range elsewhere in Syria wouldn't teach him what he needs to know because he's not operating in Syria. He has to travel to wherever that is, or to its duplicate."

"It's a damned shame we don't know where he's gone," said Swagger.

"But of course we know," said Cohen. "We're Mossad. That's what we do."

13

On the run

He would be all right. The preparations were in place, the contacts set, the logistics arranged, the codes known, the schedule activated. It would all happen as planned, nothing could stop it.

False leads, clues within clues, switchbacks, deviations, deceptions, booby traps, the full genius for Ottoman deception and betrayal woven into one grand plan certain to do horrendous damage. Cities would topple, fire would engulf infidels, the mighty would fall, death would be general. It couldn't fail.

But it depended on a cold bore shot only one of the best in the world could make from a distance until a few years ago thought unreachable. Maybe Harrison of Afghanistan could make it, maybe not.

But even that was not enough, for Harrison was safely within his own lines and had no difficulty slithering through enemy territory. He could have had a nice cup of tea before he shot and then gone back to bed behind the barbed wire and sandbags. Juba, on the other hand, would be the most hunted man in the world afterward, and it was mandatory that he escape, leaving only hints that pointed to another man.

But . . . what did the Jews know?

How had they found him?

Had they intercepted a message?

Was there a leak?

Was he in jeopardy?

All of that was premised on the idea of Israeli intelligence having tentacles as yet unseen. It would represent a penetration so subtle and devious, it would be among the world's best. Yet if that were the case, would they have hit him with three helicopters full of commandos, in and out in seven or so minutes? The best thing to do would have been an American smart munition takeout of the whole site. Even if subtlety was desired, a larger engagement force—at least a company of 13's best, maybe more; a gunship recon by fire; boots on the ground in the dozens; night vision everywhere; drones scouring the area—a real show. But, no, this was limited, fast, lethal.

The other possibility: it was a raid motivated by simple vengeance. After the school bus, he was the first name on their kill list. Anywhere in the world they located him, they would strike quickly. It had nothing to do with intelligence; it was raw vengeance. And they would never stop hunting him, would never let him escape. At any moment, an Israeli commando could knock in the door and finish him.

He favored that second possibility. It was the simplest, as the operation itself was so secret, only a few in the world knew of its far-reaching possibilities, much less its target, much less its location.

That meant he had great advantages still. He could be headed anywhere. Without a destination, they were helpless. A worldwide alert for a shadowy figure called Juba the Sniper would do them no good at all and would be ignored in the West, where security services were too busy wiretapping mosques to find the odd angry imam trying to cajole losers into shooting up homosexual bars.

Meanwhile, having made his first contact, he had picked up a package of superb credentials and identification that would get him across any border in the world. He knew his cover story forwards and backwards. He would become three totally different people on his journey, each unconnected to the other two. The whole thing, with so much money behind it, was first-class.

He was in a cheap hotel in Istanbul, smoking cigarettes, awaiting a flight to his next destination. Tonight's whore had been good, a lively Turkish girl with dark eyes and pretty hands who gave generously of her skills. Later, there would be no time, and security would be too intense, for such a risk. So for now, it was the flesh, the tobacco, the prayers, and the slow but steady passage to the destination.

He tried now to understand what the Israelis could have learned from the farmhouse. The blaze of light—searing and brilliant—told him that Adid had lit the powder and that everything in the shop was obliterated. But assume nothing. What if a Jew got in there and at least got a look?

So, did they see? And if they saw, did they understand? It might have meant nothing to a Zionist commando— the boxes of American bullets, the jars of powders, the reloading manuals, the targets. Still, assume nothing. He saw it. He reported it. The rabbis studied his reports and interpreted them correctly. But there was nothing in the house that carried an indicator of the mission. None of the guards knew the scope of the mission. They would know only that there was a mission. But, then, there was always a mission, so what did that tell them?

He had but one worry: had Adid destroyed the laptop along with himself? He remembered it was on the desk in his quarters. He had told Adid over and over of its importance. Certainly, even in the gravity of the situation, the arrival of raiders, Adid would have remembered the core of his mission and taken the laptop with him as he fell back into the shop and its powder cache. No piece of electronic equipment could stand up to that sort of conflagration. It would have been liquidized under the affront of the flames.

I am safe, he decided.

If they didn't have the laptop, they knew nothing.

14

The black cube

What laptop?" said Swagger.

"He's being coy," said Cohen. "It'll play so well when Spielberg films it."

"What laptop?" said Swagger.

"Sergeant Swagger," said the Director, speaking to him directly for the first time, "you graciously visited Hell on our behalf and did not come out empty-handed. If we had the time, I'd give you a medal. But as you're about to learn, we don't have the time."

The Director lifted his briefcase from the floor, opened it, and took out a plastic bag holding a curled and blackened laptop computer. Someone had put a burst through its screen, turning it into a spiral nebula of fractures surrounding large holes that showed clean through. The keyboard had modulated into a wave, and most of its keys were shapeless nubs.

"Do you remember?" asked Cohen. "Gas and flame, your arm on fire, your Uzi too hot to hold. Somehow you reached out and snagged it, and, in another second, another jug of powder went, and then all of them. Somehow—God favors the insane perhaps?—you grabbed ahold, staggered out, and collapsed."

"Wish I'd done that," said Bob. "It seems pretty cool. Also, by the way, I tripped over a gun case with the initials *A.W.* on it, the third letter gone to fire."

"It's all coming back?"

"The only thing that comes back is that fire is hot, and you don't want to die that way."

"An excellent lesson," said Cohen.

"Cohen might know a bit about this one subject," said Gold. "He was shot down four times."

Cohen held up his left hand. It was plastic.

"Okay," said Bob. "I'm impressed."

"He shot down fifteen of theirs. Net gain for our side: eleven aircraft."

"Triple ace," said Swagger. "Again, I'm impressed."

"Odd that he turned out so annoying," said Gold.

Bob nodded. "Anyway, that thing looks pretty well shot to hell to me."

"Forensic computer science is quite advanced," said Gold, "and we have people who are practiced at it."

"You got something?"

"There was an undamaged sector header on the otherwise quite useless hard drive. The process is called file carving. Our people were able to extract bits of information from the header, including IP addresses recorded on the data sector. The data sector was gone, the data, therefore, was gone, but not the Internet Protocol addresses. They came from a server in Manila, in the Philippines. We've just penetrated it remotely, located the origin of the IPs, and learned that many were created in Dearborn, Michigan."

A silence settled into the room.

Finally, it was the Director who spoke.

"That is why, Sergeant Swagger, in one hour you and Mr. Gold are taking off for Washington. Your FBI shares our concern. The evidence is irrefutable. Juba the Sniper is headed to America. He is going to shoot a high-value target from a long way away. And probably quite soon."

PART 2

15

Working group MARJORIE DAW

Dearborn's a bitch," said the special agent in charge of the Detroit Field Office, Ronald Houston. "Everybody knows everybody. Everybody talks to everybody. Everybody listens to everybody. The radicals are buried in the general population but operate with the general population's tacit support—and, in emergencies, active support. And Arabs—not to stereotype—being volatile, bristly, highly verbal, crafted by a millennium in the marketplace, haggling about everything, haggling for the sheer love of haggling, get lawyered up, are smart about politics, understand leverage and patronage and election support, so the local judiciary has been penetrated and subverted. It's really hard to get a subpoena for a wiretap, and if you do get it, the folks who are the subject will hear of it before you. To get a warrant is even harder, and to serve it by force—that is, to raid—is almost a legal impossibility. No midnight door-busting in Dearborn. So you can't tap, you can't raid. I suppose you could surveil, but the community is wired so tight that any vans or teams in apartments or street-level retail are blown before they're even inserted. On top of that, if you do make some kind of initiative, it better be executed perfectly, because, if not, you will be sued, your litigants will be all over the tube, claiming harassment and bias and anti-Islamic prejudice, the academics at Ann Arbor will join the hallelujah chorus, the protestors, with their genocide signs, will be out in the hundreds, and suddenly you're teaching at a junior college in Tennessee for the rest of your life. That leaves snitches. Please note, I do not say 'our' snitches, because although we have a lot of them, we're never quite sure who they're working for. They are expert at playing both ends against the middle, can switch allegiances in midsentence and switch back again before the punctuation at the end. Can they be trusted? Yes, no, and maybe. Penetration? Forget it. You'll never get a double into the cells. They know each other too well, and have for a thousand years. Doesn't matter if we're talking Lebanese, Syrian, Iraqi, Jordanian, Palestinian, Egyptian, or whatever, them-against-us will always trump them-against-them. Shiite or Sunni—whatever—makes no difference. That's the realpolitik of the situation, gentlemen. You're up against a system that is thirteen hundred years old and has stood against opponents for twelve hundred of those years. They know the ropes. They invented the ropes."

"Thanks, Ron," said Nick Memphis. "At least we know where we are. Mr. Gold, with your experience in that part of the world—I can't help thinking the situation sounds a lot like Tel Aviv's problems in Gaza City—I wonder if you have any suggestions or observations."

The briefing was not being held in the FBI Detroit Field Office. It probably hadn't been penetrated, but both Gold and the SAIC, the special agent in charge, agreed that you couldn't be too sure. So it took place in an Ann Arbor library conference room, forty miles northwest of Dearborn. The SAIC came in one car—his own—after hours, his assistant in another. The entire MARJORIE DAW working group, a co-FBI/Mossad task force consisting of Nick Memphis, Gershon Gold, and consultant Bob Lee Swagger, who shared the room with the federals, assembled itself.

It had been a crazy couple of days, way too full of meetings for anyone's pleasure, but you couldn't put stuff together like this without suits sitting around tables in fluorescent-lit rooms, making decisions. The most important had already been made, however, and that was to grade MARJORIE DAW priority one, and Nick, dragged out of retirement because he knew and was trusted by Swagger, reported directly to Ward Taylor, the Assistant Director of the Counterterrorism Division, with copies to the Director himself. What was the budget? Priority one essentially meant there was no budget. At the same time, it was to be separated and shielded from Taylor's same Counterterrorism Division, at least for the immediate time being, on the idea that the fewer people that knew about it, the more likely it was to stay secure. It's not that Counterterrorism had been penetrated; it's that it was big, too big to control and monitor, and things always squiggled out of it, and if anyone was watching, those squiggles could be assembled into information.

"It sounds a lot like Gaza City," said Gold in response to Nick's question. "I agree on penetration agents. No luck with that in Gaza City either, and too many have died trying. I could suggest observation by drone, with a small team examining the photographic evidence, but, again, drones are cumbersome to administer in any number without ample notice being given, and surely word would quickly reach the ears of exactly those whom we wish it not to. Thus, I'm afraid we're left with our eyeballs, and again I concur with Special Agent Houston. The more eyeballs, the better. But also, the more eyeballs, the worse. More eyeballs means more chances of a leak. So I would restrict our observer corps to those in this room. I would obtain a variety of utility vehicles—mail trucks, UPS vans, television repair vans, telephone company units—and I would invest the hours it takes to move about the city in irregular intervals, from target to target, looking for anomalies."

"How would you prioritize the targets?" asked Nick.

"Surely Special Agent Houston has an idea of which mosques are home to radicalized imams and which are not. I would take that list and invert it. I think it far more likely, given the expense and effort they—whoever 'they' are—have taken with this operation, that they would prevail on a mosque known for its docility to harbor Juba."

"Are we so sure he's going to be in a mosque?" asked Swagger. "Thinking like a sniper, I'd go for the best hide, but certainly not one that's already on a list."

"Very good point, which gets at a congenital operational weakness among the brotherhood. As leaders of a theocracy, the mullahs and imams will always want control. We have found that although operational assembly points might not actually be within the mosque itself, they will always be near it. The leaders want close-by fellows as their assault troops, men they know from families they know. We have found, furthermore, that they tend to administer all ops from within the mosque—meaning that if food or other kinds of support are necessary, it will come from the mosque. Though, I might add, there aren't so many pizza delivery shops in Gaza City as in Dearborn."

"If we had time, we could open a pizza shop," said Nick. "That'd get us into places we might not otherwise get into. But we don't have time."

"Counterterror can get you three or four clean agents," said Ron Houston, "to help with the outside surveillance. When I say 'clean,' I mean they are new to my office and haven't yet interfaced with any Dearborn customers. They can take up the slack. I'm seeing a patrol pattern, driving by each of five mosques once an hour, changing vehicles frequently. I see walkers-by too, again nonchalant, no observational tells, just ambling, spelling the vehicular orbiting. Standard anti-mob procedure. Never stopping, but eyeballing on the move. We're pretty good at it by now, all the energy and time we've put into working the dope trade. I can arrange to borrow at least a U.S. Mail van and a UPS truck. Detroit Metro has a surveillance van dressed up as a plumber's truck. I know people there, and I could get it discreetly and unofficially."

"It has always helped," said Gold, "if we have very specific behaviors for the observers to focus on. I would like to see each of us, and each of the new recruits, given a list. If they know what they're looking for, they may see it. If they're, generally, just staring, the chance is less likely."

"Such as?" asked Houston.

"Groups of unknown men entering and exiting. Certain entrances blocked off. Hyperactivity among security personnel. Upgrades in countersurveillance. Men in groups leaving with packages or groceries."

"Another thing," said Swagger. "Remember, Juba ain't no cosmopolitan world traveler. So one of the things he'll do here is go out with a group of guys to get acclimated to America. They'll take him places, brief him on public transportation, taxis, Uber, anything practical that'll prepare him for movement in America as he manipulates his way closer to his target."

"That's good," said Nick.

"Swagger has gifts for this game," said Gold.

"Hey!" Swagger said, looking at Houston. "You said getting an agent in was impossible? I know an agent who could get in."

All eyes came to him.

"This person knows the routines. This person has passed among them before. This person has the clothes. This person knows the prayers, the ranks in the mosque, the literature, the culture. This person has done undercover. This person is brave, speaks the language, and is highly motivated. This person has a very low profile."

"Sergeant Swagger," said Gold, "I don't think we could ask—"

"No, she'd do it in a second. They took her son."

16

Dearborn, Michigan, and thereabouts

His name was Jared Akim. He was twenty-four. He was from Grosse Pointe, and his father was a periodontist.

"Are you blooded?" asked Juba.

"No. I'm not a fighter. Look how thin my arms are."

"It's not the arms, it's the spirit."

"Brother, I have the spirit. No arms, plenty of spirit."

"I would like a man who is blooded," said Juba to the imam.

But he got Jared instead.

"Brother," said Jared, "if I were blooded, I would be on somebody's list. The FBI would be watching me. I would have no freedom of movement. I would lead them straight to you. Unblooded, they have never noticed me. Even with two years in university in Cairo, they did not pay me any attention. I am a virgin in this business, and I am told of your importance, so I infer that you need a virgin as your assistant. I speak English as well as I speak

Arabic. I'm cute, so people like me. But I am ready to fight, willing to die, and I will get the job done."

Juba appraised him. Skinny, tousle-headed, lithe, quick, beautiful, earnest, a smiler and a charmer, a boy full of words. Juba didn't care for men full of words, as they were often too clever and saw through everything and believed in nothing, but he had no real choice in the matter.

"If I sense weakness, I will dispense with you quickly. You understand that?"

"I do."

"Then proceed."

Jared learned quickly. He never forgot. Once spoken to him, it became a part of his mind-set. Currency was first, and after absorbing the values of American coins and bills, it moved swiftly to the culture of the exchange.

"You must be facile with the money. Americans notice very little, but if one is clumsy at the paying, they will notice that."

No haggling. If that's what it says, that's what it costs.

No looking disappointed at a price.

No counting coins or bills out one at a time as if they were being torn from your flesh.

"They have so much money, they don't care about it at all. Only another Arab or a Jew makes something of pennies. Most Americans don't bother to pick up pennies or nickels anymore. Money is shit. Pay it no heed. That's what they expect. That's what lulls them to nothingness."

Transportation: elemental, necessary, difficult.

"Cab is best. Pay in cash, no records. Your driver will

be a Russian, another Arab, some sort of black fellow or other. He will pay you no attention. He will read you for threat before he picks you up, and seeing none—make certain you look forlorn and defeated, your body sags with melancholy, your cheeks are hollow—he will pick you up, take you, and forget you."

Public transportation is slow but generally anonymous. Best to understand the payment system up front, however, so as not to struggle awkwardly trying to fit the right number of nickels and quarters into the hopper. This new thing—private cabs contacted by iPhone, Uber, Lyft—is useful, in that it picks you up where you are and it leaves you where you want to be. But as it's all done via credit card and the Internet, records are kept. If unobserved and working with a card that has been validated, it's okay, but the card should never be used operationally.

On to peoples. Jared was not kind in his evocation of various ethnic groups. To him, stereotypes were market research, the accumulated wisdom of millions of transactions between tribe members, and he brought a certain bourgeois zest to profiling those he considered inferior, which was pretty much everyone who hadn't attended prep school. In political correctness, he was well schooled, but he did not care to burden Juba with its precepts. He knew it could get him killed.

Then on to the police, any race.

"Give them no attitude. They are not clever men or they'd be making some more money elsewhere. They are usually big; they like to hurt people and are always looking for an excuse to do so. But their obsession is with their local area, and they rarely see a bigger picture. They pay more attention to paper than to people, so keep your documents up to date and learn your story forwards and backwards."

"My name is Awari el-Baqua, as the papers say. I am in the country on a six-month visa, legally admitted. I have some education, but I am here as a laborer to work construction for my uncle, who is a builder. I hope to raise enough money to continue my education back in Syria. I have three brothers. Do you want the names?"

"No policeman will ask you that. A federal agent might. But if the papers are good, you should be all right."

"The papers are good." They had been produced by the best forgers in Chechnya.

"Also, smile a lot. They like smiling."

"I can do that."

"They say you're obsessed with rifles. Bury that part of your personality. Never mention a weapon, never look at one, never ask about one. Many people are frightened of them and consider them evidence of malice. Don't read magazines about them or go to where they are sold and talk to people who own them. A brown man with an interest in guns is a problem."

"I understand."

They went over it, over and over, on their walks. At first, they walked on Warren Street and the streets just off it, which felt like his own culture to Juba. But, each day, the young man took him in a new direction, and he visited the large city of Detroit, he visited malls where the Americans consumed out of any possible proportion to whatever needs they could have, he went to a famous university town and felt its absence of fear, in stark contrast to the city itself. They took every form of transportation. They visited museums, restaurants, hospitals, office buildings, schools, pizza parlors. They dressed casually, in jeans and running shoes and T-shirts and the kind of sweatshirt with a hood that zipped up the front. They wore sunglasses. They admired monuments and went to the lakefront. They went to the stadium and watched the crowds file in, though Jared could not get Juba to actually attend.

"I won't try to convert you to the religion of baseball. But it will be a sad day when Allah wipes it from the earth. This, alone, I do not like about jihad."

"You are a blasphemer," said Juba. "It is only because you are so negligible that Allah does not punish you. But you have been very good to me, so I forgive you. I will pray for you tonight, and perhaps Allah will extend your time."

Jared's phone rang.

"Uh-oh," he said. "Only the mosque has my number, and only for emergencies."

He took it out, put it to his ear, and listened. Then he returned it to his pocket.

"They caught a spy," he said. "A woman. Probably FBI. We'd better get back there."

17

Dearborn

N o heroics, Janet. You understand that?" said Nick Memphis.

"I do."

She sat in a rented suite of offices in a low-intensity industrial zone just outside of Dearborn, where the MARJORIE DAW working group had rented a building in a warehouse complex by the railroad tracks. All were present, also some technicians and some SWAT officers on loan from the State Police. But they were casually dressed, simply there for the briefing. They wouldn't go hot until she was in play.

"Mrs. McDowell, can you go over it one more time?" asked Agent Chandler. Chandler, whose cuteness had evolved into serious beauty in the time since she'd worked with Swagger, even if she tried to pretend such a thing could never happen, had been flown in to relate to Mrs. McDowell when all agreed—finally—that Mrs. McDowell was the best option. But it hadn't been an easy sell for Swagger.

"She's untrained. You can't put a civilian in this kind of situation without formal training, and if she slips up, the whole thing goes down," argued Nick. "On top of that, this is the most highly graded top secret operation we have going. She is not cleared for it and can't be vetted in time. On top of even that, if the CIA finds out we're using someone on their nutcase list, they'll become highly interested, by which I mean irritated, and all sorts of political ramifications could come onto the board that we cannot control."

Swagger said, "I don't know nothing about the politics. There shouldn't be any in this situation, but if there are, let's pretend there aren't. It seems to me she can be brought in on the statement that an action against Juba the Sniper is under way, no further details available to her. She will accept that. She wants to be a part of this."

"You're not just sentimentalizing things? You're moved by her, you feel sorry for her—so do I, and who wouldn't?—but you want to improve her mental health by bringing her in on this and feeling like part of the solution when it is explicitly her amateur status that risks it?"

"Maybe I am. But trying to take my feelings out of it, we're not sending her in to get the plans for the X11 bomber or to blow up a bridge. She knows mosques, she's been visiting them for fourteen years. Her job is to determine, as casually as possible, if anything seems out of the ordinary. There are too many mosques, and we do not have enough time to run deeper hunts of each of them. She can save days, maybe weeks, and if we can nail this bird here, think what it'll mean."

Gold was agnostic. "I've seen cases where passionate amateurs have performed brilliantly. I've seen them where they've turned triumph into catastrophe. As she's an American citizen, I will not take a position."

"These people are not amateurs," said Nick. "They are ruthless and violent and do not believe that killing an infidel is a sin. We could get this poor woman's throat cut."

"We can cover her the whole way," said Swagger. "Do we need a warrant if an undercover's life is in jeopardy?"

"Houston?" asked Nick.

The Detroit SAIC answered. "We can get an emergency verbal warrant. It's rare, but it can happen. But suppose we need it, and the one judge likely to provide it has gone to the movies?"

"It's too damned dangerous," Nick said. "And getting a civilian killed could be a bigger scandal than letting Juba proceed. And if we go without it, nothing we acquire will be usable in court."

"No, but Israel can extradite because of the bus. His number is fixed if we nab him."

On and on it went, according to the immutable law that the human factor is more responsible for administrative inaction than any failure of policy, plan, or hardware. Finally, the need for speed became the decisive factor. If Juba was here, it wouldn't be for long.

Nick said, "We have to cover her. Let's figure out how."

So Agent Chandler had to make sure Janet was locked in on security.

Janet said, "I check into the Dearborn Holiday Inn tomorrow afternoon under the name Susan Abdullah.

My story: I married Saleem Abdullah, an Iraqi psychia-
trist, thirty years ago. We lived in Baltimore, Maryland,
where he had a private practice. I converted to Islam
shortly before the marriage. I learned my pidgin Arabic
from him. He was radicalized after nine/eleven. He went
to Baghdad in 2012 as a volunteer aid worker for the
International Red Cross and Red Crescent Movement
and was killed in an American air strike. I have come to
Dearborn to worship at the big mosque at the American
Muslim Center because I'll never be able to get to Mecca.
The big mosque is as close as I can get. I will embrace
Dearborn because it is as close to my husband's native
Iraq as I can get. That will be my first mosque. Then I
am to enter five mosques, as listed, and attempt to ascer-
tain if anything is subtly amiss. But I am to be strictly
observational—no eye contact, no questions, no opening
closet doors or going down hallways or trying to get into
the basement. Just what I pick up in an informal way.
Sewn into the hem of my hijab is a small bead containing
a GPS transmitter. If my life should be in danger, I am
to crush it through the material. When it stops transmit-
ting, that will be the signal that something is amiss, and
the SWAT team, orbiting outside, will hit the mosque
under the doctrine of police endangerment."

"Good, good," said Chandler.

"Thank you so much for this opportunity," Mrs. Mc-
Dowell said. "I know you can't tell me what this is about,
but I presume it's something important, and I am so
pleased to play a part in it."

* * *

Of course, she violated every admonition within minutes. She looked aggressively into the mosques. After ablutions and prayer from the carefully delineated women's section, she rose and wandered. She tried closets and stairways. She peeked into men's rooms. She went into offices, recreation centers, basketball courts, weight rooms—all the appurtenances of the modern American house of worship, as much community center as prayer platform. Her hijab made her bold in this world, as it always did. She looked for burly security types, and, with the first four mosques, found none. She asked other women worshippers about changes in mosque operating procedures, or evidence of heavy traffic or other business at night, when all was supposed to be quiet. She wondered if the calls to prayer were on time. She wondered about strange deliveries. In all places, the women were eager to gossip, and she had no problem. The fact that no one paid her any attention she took as the ultimate indication that nothing was amiss or held in secret in each building. Twice she spoke to an imam and found both to be charming, educated men, eager to make conversation with an American convert and sympathetic to the tragic death in Baghdad of Saleem Abdullah, M.D., at American hands.

She came to the last mosque on the list, another domed building with administrative wings off of it. It was far from majestic, but, at the same time, far from shabby. It was no storefront, with an angry young imam in blue jeans and teenagers hanging about, talking of jihad. It looked sedate, unlit, almost slumbering. But even though the last evening prayer was done and darkness was falling on Dearborn, she entered the dim space and quickly noted three women performing ablutions. She joined them and started to chat them up, and it seemed to be going quite well, when one said to her, "Sister, you have many questions."

"As a visitor," she said, "I like to learn of new places. This city is almost a shrine in itself. To walk the streets, to buy from the shops, to hear the calls to prayer, it's like the trip to the homeland I'll never make."

"Many of the men here are suspicious. My suggestion is, enjoy the closeness of Allah but not the closeness of men. It seems Imam el-Tariq has surrounded himself with some tough ones. I tell you this only for your own good. I should not even be seen talking to you. But God be with you, sister."

With that, Janet was abandoned.

She waited a bit, put her socks back on, and turned to the domed prayer chamber. A few prostrated solitaries were there, but none paid her any attention. It was as if the place were deserted.

She went to an outer circle of the chamber and went to the mat herself before Allah, His name be praised, and she praised it aggressively. No watcher, if there were any, could doubt her ardency. She prayed hard, believing if her goals were not the goals of her coreligionists, they were still the goals that the true Allah would find virtuous. When she had been there for some minutes, she felt safe, under His protection.

She rose and made as if she was headed for the door but diverted to the women's restroom instead, went in, washed, calmed herself, again absorbed the silence of the place, listening for signs of habitation but heard none. She exited the room, but instead of turning left, to the door, to escape, she turned right and came to a corridor. It was empty.

She turned down it and made her way tentatively as if lost. She peeked in each door, finding an office of some sort, nothing of any ramification. Finally, she came to a stairwell.

Don't do this, Janet, she told herself. *Don't.*

But she did it anyway.

Courageous or not, she learned nothing on the second floor. It was just another office corridor, with doors along each side, from where the imam ran his enterprise, made plans to visit the sick and the lame, gave comfort, supervised goods for the bake sale, coached his basketball team, and raised money, much as any other clergyman did in any other house of worship in America. She turned, started back down the hall, when a flash of movement jerked her out of serenity, and, in a second, she realized that she was confronting a man with a strange package in his hand.

It was a pizza.

"Mogdushani?" he asked.

"I don't know," she said. "Nobody up here now. Maybe downstairs."

"Thanks, lady," he said.

He was young and black, and he turned and bounded down the steps. Someone working late wanted a pizza, the universal snack. Yet . . . it did seem odd. Why would someone in a mosque order a pizza, especially long after the hours of administration? Who but her would be here so late?

She followed her nose. Tomato, cheese. Terrorists? Juba the Sniper? To the main floor, then a quick look in the stairwell, darting down it just to make sure, then a quick turn, another corridor—nothing—another turn and—

"May I help you, sister?"

The man was Arabic, dressed casually.

"I just got confused," she said. "I'm just trying to find the way out."

"This way. I'll show you."

"Praise be His name."

"Praise be."

He led her back to the upstairs, where they ran into the pizza man.

"Hey, thanks," he said again, and departed.

"You were here before?" asked her escort, pausing a second.

"Ah, I blundered about, in my confusion. I ran into that young man. I didn't really help him, I only told him to go downstairs."

"But what were you doing upstairs?"

"As I say, I was confused."

He thought about this intently for a bit, decided it was problematical, and said, "I think you should see the imam."

"Oh, I hate to bother him. I'm just a visitor. I'll leave now, and that'll be that."

Again, concern clouded his face, and he said, "I do not wish to offend, but something here is amiss. I must ask you to accompany me. I just want to make sure he's comfortable with this."

"Why, there is nothing to be comfortable with. I tell you, I merely lost my way and—"

"Please, madam," he said, and took her elbow, "humor me, or I will make the imam mad at me."

Not force, exactly, was applied against her, but strength, communicating his need to fulfill his instructions versus her feeble explanations, and he took her this way and that and into an office of no particular significance, no RPGs or sniper rifles lying about, just desks, one messy, one not so much, and asked her to sit. He vanished. Was the door locked? Was she a prisoner? But to investigate would be suspicious, the actions of a spy, so she simply sat, waiting, feeling her heartbeat increase.

He returned.

"This way, please," he said.

"Of course," she said, and followed him into the well-appointed office of Imam Imir el-Tariq, who was sitting behind his desk, in his robes but with his hair uncovered. A handsome, bearded man in his forties, as befit his rank, with the face of the earnest and the committed, but with brown eyes that were not the sort to be found in zealots.

"Madam, please," he said, gesturing to a chair. "We're not comfortable with strangers wandering about. We have no secrets, of course, but, alas, we do have enemies, and many nonbelievers hold us responsible for things over which we have no control."

"I assure you, Imam, I have no agenda save the faith."

"May I ask for credentials of some sort?"

She handed her purse over.

"Here, examine the whole thing. I have no secrets either, and I hope I have not given offense."

He looked at her driver's license.

"Mrs. Abdullah. Yet you are not Arabic."

"My husband was. And, under his auspices, I joined the faith."

She told her story.

"I am sorry for your husband, sister. Many have died unjustly. The pox of our times."

"If I enter the houses of worship, great or small, it helps me find peace," she said. "I am content here, and the emptiness in my heart is not so severe."

"Allah, His name be praised, is merciful."

"His name be praised, He is always merciful."

"I hope you will not mind if I give your license to an assistant to run a check."

This was the best news. Her legend had been constructed by professionals of the highest quality, and she was assured that it was invulnerable to scrutiny.

"Of course. I should have offered it to you earlier to save time, Imam."

He touched a button, the assistant entered, took the license, and departed.

Simple chitchat followed.

First time in Dearborn?

What did you think of the Great Mosque?

I hope you will wisely stay out of the bigger city. It can be dangerous.

It went on for a bit, seemingly untethered in time, and she kept up with the insignificant patter easily, fully confident that, as promised, her license would check out, the backstory would stand up to vetting, and she'd be on her way in a bit.

The assistant returned and whispered to the imam.

The iman nodded and turned back to her. She heard three more men enter.

"I am confused," said the imam. "Indeed, your husband's name is carried on the Maryland Board of Psychologists, as is the date of his death. All seemed perfect. But then—"

"Is there a problem?"

"I have a very good assistant on the computer. We try to stay up to date. In any event, he was able to get into the Social Security database, and though we found over forty Susan Abdullahs, we were unable to find one living in the Baltimore area. Are you new to the city?"

"No, no. Actually, I think my Social Security number might be listed under my maiden name. I never worked again after I married my husband. I tried to be a good Islamic wife, you see."

"Impressive. You will not mind if we run that name?"

"Isn't the Social Security database off-limits? Aren't you hacking something illegally? I'd hate to get you in trouble. My thought is, perhaps you could call the police. Surely their techniques surpass yours, and they could verify me. I am a little hesitant about my Social Security number. That, actually, was something my husband was adamant about. It's not to be trifled with."

"I can't help but notice that while you're not seeming to evade, you are, in fact, evading."

"I want to cooperate, but you don't have any right to hold me against my will. You can call the police, and if you are not satisfied with their explanation, you can bring charges against me for trespassing. It would be a waste of everybody's time, but I do understand your anxiety about the mosque's security and will happily wait until the police arrive. Perhaps we can continue our conversation about Dear—"

"You see, you could be a scout for some kind of guerrilla attack. Someone wants to bomb the mosque, but they want to know where to place the bomb. This is information you now have, and it appears to be information you've gone to some trouble to obtain."

A cold breeze of fear swept through Janet. She had been in these situations before and each time the results had been disastrous: forceful hostility, beatings, rapes, hatred at its most naked.

"Sir, please, I beg you. I am no bomber, no fanatic, I am just an American woman who has seen the way to the faith and is still in grief over her husband's death. The worst you can say of me is, I sometimes act irrationally. I know that. It gets me in trouble all the time. Perhaps my need to go to mosques for the therapeutic value makes no sense, but I can't really seem to help it."

The imam considered for a bit.

"I am in an unfortunate position, Mrs. Abdullah. Alas, I owe more to the mosque and its followers than I do to you. You understand, no? Now, let's start over at the beginning. Please give me facts—facts that can be checked. This may take some time, but I would like you to stay until I am satisfied that you are of no danger to us. Or, perhaps admit that you are an FBI agent seeking to penetrate our security based on some intelligence you may have. Then we could easily disprove that intelligence—many false things are said of Moslems in the United States, many false conclusions are drawn— and you could go on your way. Would that not be the simplest?"

"But it would not be true. There is no FBI, there is no intelligence, I am merely—"

"Enough," said the imam. "I want this to be pleasant, but you're provoking me to behavior that I find abhorrent. I ask again, please do not make such a provocation."

Janet thought of something to put between herself and them, something that would baffle, slow, confuse them. Nothing occurred. She felt her fear rise, and the urge to beg for mercy came over her hard. She couldn't go through another beating. The last one had almost killed her. But when she opened her mouth, she said something that surprised even her.

"Please," said Mrs. McDowell. "Torture me."

Swagger stared at the blip. It had not moved in an hour.

"Okay," he said, "maybe we have a complication."

"Maybe she's helping put up decorations for a dance," said Nick.

They stared at the screen of the monitor that was receiving the signal from McDowell's GPS.

"Where's the team?" said Swagger.

"They're in orbit around the building," said Chandler. "They can pop the raid in a minute if I send them the go."

"Hold on," said Nick. "Folks, we have nothing here to go on."

"A, she's been in that building for over two hours," said Swagger. "B, she's in a room in the administrative section, not in the prayer center, so she's obviously either imprisoned or undergoing interrogation."

"Maybe she's watching a ball game with some of the kids in hopes of overhearing something."

"I just don't like it."

"We are on very thin ice here," said Nick. "This is not the vacuum of combat where the only criterion is taking the objective. It is Main Street America 2018, and the rules are different. We cannot raid an innocent mosque with guys in Kevlar and carrying HKs. These folks are savvy, they're on the phone in seconds, lawyers are there in a few more seconds, and, in minutes, TV is there and the *Free Press*, and we have a major administrative fuckup. MARJORIE DAW is disgraced and closed down."

"None of that has anything to do with a woman's life in danger."

"What do you think, Houston?" he asked the Detroit guy.

"In this town, it's always better to take it easy. You do not know the can of shit you are opening if you do something wrong. It will land all over everybody in this room and never go away."

"I would add," said Nick to Bob, "that maybe your read is that she's in danger because you're overcommitted to her, and maybe you've seen so much combat that everything is always combat. I'd hate to have to testify to a condition of 'danger' on such flimsy evidence at my board hearing."

"Fair enough, and always a possibility."

"Chandler?"

"Not fair to put her on the spot," said Nick. "She's junior and under Bureau discipline. Chandler, you don't have to answer."

"Yes, sir, but I will. Mr. Swagger, I'm FBI all the way. If the agent in charge—that is, Agent Memphis—makes a decision, I will obey it. Period, end of message."

"Okay, she's a good marine," said Swagger. "We knew that."

"Mr. Gold," said Nick, "you've got more experience than any of us. Please jump in here, tell us what you think."

"It would be different in Israel, where the courts and the media favor the government in its anti-terrorist efforts. So I cannot advise, because your context and nuances are so unique."

"You have to say something," said Nick. "Sorry, but you are here to advise, and it's no help at all if you don't."

"Then I would say cock the hammer, point the gun, but don't pull the trigger."

"Okay," said Nick. "Houston, you call that U.S. Attorney for a verbal warrant, so that if it does come to a raid, the State boys can hit the door in a second."

"I'm going to move them across the street," said Chandler. "That'll shave even more time off their reaction interval."

"Good move," said Swagger, hearing in his mind the slide and click of MP5 bolts setting up for action.

Sister Abdullah, don't be ridiculous."

"I am not. I want you to be comfortable with me, and the fastest way I can do that is endure a great deal of pain. I am not afraid of pain. My faith will enable me to forget it quickly. And if I am beaten to a point where you believe I could no longer lie and would say anything to avoid further pain and I do not deviate in my story, I will have proved by ordeal its authenticity."

"This is ridiculous."

"I give you permission. I see it from your point of view. I will not file charges. I will go back to my room and heal and then go back to Baltimore, proud that I have served my faith."

"You may give me permission, but the state of Michigan does not. I could end up in prison for ten years."

"The state will never find out."

"A guarantee you cannot possibly make."

"Perhaps you should think this through a little more clearly. FBI agents are young women, athletic. I have varicose veins, and I haven't seen the inside of a gym since high school. Would the FBI employ an old thing like me?"

"Young and beautiful FBI agents exist only in the movies. Who's to say one couldn't look like you?"

"So what do you recommend, the towels with water? I will undergo that. Many of the faith have."

"I can only recommend what I've initiated, which is a detailed interrogation session, and these men will vet each answer on the Internet. It will be a long night. There will be great psychological pressure on you, if you are a spy, to avoid a mistake. We will see if you can stand up to it. When your story collapses, we will deal with what remains."

She didn't know if she could do this. The slow grind of it all, the utter concentration it would take to keep her details in trim, the mental effort against the deep fatigue— it would be too much.

Crack the button, she thought. *Get the cops in here. Shake this place down, see what's cooking. Smack el Tariq and his pals around. Get them to talk. Get Juba that way. Find him, get him, kill him. You killed my Tom, and I turned into a different woman and I tracked you down and I killed you dead.*

But—if she pushed the button, and they found nothing, the word would get out that the FBI was hunting a certain terrorist in Dearborn, and, if he were here, he'd know and vanish. Instead of hurting him, she'd have helped him.

"Mrs. Abdullah, you blacked out there."

"I took a little nap," she said.

The door opened. A man came in and set something on the desk. It was a file. He leaned and whispered to the imam, who listened intently, nodding.

"All right," said the imam. "Perhaps this may move things along."

He pulled out a picture.

A knife cut into her heart. How had they gotten it?

It was taken on November 12, 2002. Boys' Latin had just beaten Gilman in football, and Tom, a tight end, had made a spectacular catch, late, to keep the drive going, to keep the ball away from Gilman's offense. There was Tom, his helmet under his arm, his arm around her, on the happiest day of his life. His radiance was like the blaze of the setting sun at the end of a stormy day, promising much for tomorrow.

How had they gotten it?

"A handsome boy, Mrs. McDowell," said the imam. "It's a shame what happened to him. But perhaps we will now proceed with the truth."

She cracked the GPS bead in her hijab.

18

We'd better get back there," said Jared.

"Give me your phone," said Juba.

He took the thing from the young man, set it on the pavement, and crushed it with the heel of his shoe. He removed the SIM card and put it in his pocket for later disposal in river or fire.

"Wh-what are you doing? How can I call my mom?"

"We will not go back there. Ever. It no longer exists for us. That phase is ended and must not be revisited. It is compromised, everything in it is tainted and potentially of lethal danger. We must think clearly and move quickly. How much money do you have?"

"I don't know," said the boy.

They stood on a street corner somewhere in the revitalized Tomorrowland of downtown, so sleek that it was devoid of human beings. A few retail outlets remained open—a Subway, a McDonald's, an old auto-themed pub, a late-night Sprint—hopeful of snagging a few late customers. The glow of each establishment spilled out onto the dark sidewalks, while mute monoliths that by day were full of suburbanites loomed blankly overhead.

Jared pulled out his wallet, checked the cash, and saw that he had about thirty-five dollars in bills.

"But I have this," he said, pulling out a red Bank of America card. "I have a thousand in my checking account. We can get eight hundred dollars out tonight, from an ATM machine, the other two hundred tomorrow."

"Get the eight hundred now. Then the card is to be destroyed. It may have GPS. Our goal is to leave Detroit as quickly as possible."

"To go where?"

"Away. We will need money and an automobile."

"I can't just walk out of my life. I have to call my folks, I have people I have to say good-bye to. I suppose I could borrow some money, but we've got to get a car, and that will take some time. I have contacts, and—"

"You're an idiot child. Assume that in a short while they will know everything about you. Your picture will be flashed to every policeman in the state. They will net you by noon tomorrow. You will talk, giving them an explicit description of me and an account of our conversations. You will cooperate with an artist, and a drawing will emerge. I will be the most famous man in America by five-thirty tomorrow afternoon."

"I don't—"

"Assume and operate on the principle of the worst of all possibilities. No other course is safe but immediate escape and evasion. Now, where can we get a car and ten thousand dollars?"

"I . . . don't know."

"Well, I know. In this city, in certain areas, there are many drug transactions. We will rob one of them. Do you understand? They will not go to the police. Eventually the police will hear, but by that time we will be long gone."

Jared could not keep the look of fright off his face, or the series of dry gulps coming out of his throat or the clumsiness overcoming his limbs.

"Those guys are really tough. They will not take any shit lying down. It's well known in the community that you do not fuck with them. Fuck with anybody, but do not fuck with dope guys."

"Little American boy, you say you are a jihadist. This is jihad. It is about action, commitment, discomfort. It is about will. Your faith should give you that. You cannot talk and posture and affect any longer. You must become my right hand—and, thus, Allah's right hand. You have been chosen. Now you must contribute."

Oh, fuck, thought Jared.

The car was not a problem. Juba selected a '13 Taurus out of a parking lot, jimmied the lock with his knife, ripped the plastic shielding off the keyhole, did some fast wire twisting, and the thing came to life.

The car led to the ATM, which led to eight hundred dollars in crisp twenties. Next stop: Drugland.

"You're sure this eight hundred dollars isn't enough? We can get a long way—"

"Suppose we need to bribe? Suppose we need a new vehicle? We will need new clothes, we will need money for motels. The one thing necessary for surviving on the run is cash. I know, I have been on the run many times. Do not think of your old life and how things used to be. You have given your life to Allah. He will do with it as He chooses."

Great, thought Jared, who was finding transfiguration from the theoretical to the actual more troublesome than he ever imagined.

His mood was not improved by the ghastly terrain south of Seven Mile Road. Abandoned crumbling houses, lawns overgrown, the stiff grass blowing in the wind off the lake. Now and then, the fluorescent, dead-bone illumination of a late-night mart or liquor store turning anyone caught in it into a zombie. Abandoned cars, broken toys, gardens that looked jungly and foreboding. About a tenth of the houses were occupied.

You didn't want to be out here if you weren't really good at the game. This was the big league. Predators or guppies, nothing in between. You could tell the whores from the dealers easily: the dealers looked better. They were everywhere, like specters, standing in the wind, oblivious to its chill. A hoodie over a T-shirt, baggy jeans, big white sneakers off some astronaut's moonwalk, ball caps worn backwards.

"These guys?" he asked Juba. "They look uncooperative to me."

They discussed strategy, Jared smiled and licked his

dry lips, and, in time, they found their mark. Jared rolled out.

"Yo, little A-rab boy," said the dealer. "What yo' wanna be here fo'? You wanna score? If not, git yo' ass outta here or some brothahs gonna turn yo' shit to hurt."

"Ah, actually," said Jared, fighting a rise of phlegm in his throat, "I wanted to hook up with some stuff. Hard, you call it, right? Got some pals, we want to try it. That's what I'm here for."

The dealer sized him up. "Think yo' know some shit cuz yo' calls it hard, just like a bro wif two nines and a mouf-ful of gold and a shiny diamond? What yo' know? Yo' don't know shit."

Jared shrugged. "But the money is green. That should count for something."

"Gots to try the ride? Yeah, man, dis shit give yo' the ride. Yo' show me the green—or is dis some bullshit fraternity test, see how long yo' last on Seven Mile?"

"No, no, I have the money," he said, pulling out his roll. The dealer looked at the thickness of the wad.

"Yo' heavy, man."

"Eight hundred, man. I want to buy that much."

"Yo' don't know nuffin'! Yo' think I got that much? I do nickel and dime bags, man. And it's late, I done most of my business. Got two nickels and a dime left. My man be comin' by soon. I got to put in a request, and he go load up. Then yo' git yo' eight dimes and go off to yo' white-boy A-rab par-tay with all dem Beckys."

"Shit," said Jared. "How long do I have to stand here?"

"Yo' come south of Seven Mile, that's what happens, man. Okay, go 'way. Go back to that car wif yo' friend. My man be by in a bit."

"Do I give you money now?"

"Give me two hundred, down payment. That's so's I know yo' come back, and also yo' don't go to no other dealers. I'm Ginger. Yo' come back to Ginger, yo' don't go no other dealer or yo' lose your two hundred dollars, get it?"

"Yeah."

"Go 'way, come back in forty minutes, 'kay? He come, I tells him, we go load up, yo' pay up. Yo' gits yo' bags and yo' gets yo' scared little Peter Pan ass outta here."

They drove around the block and parked. Juba slipped out. He slid through the overgrown yard of one house, across an alley mainly used by rats, and through another yard, until he had a good vantage on the dealer.

Nothing happened for a time—no traffic, no pedestrians, no whores, no cops—but then a black SUV pulled up, and the dealer man went around to him. Juba watched as they exchanged words through the window and, finally, some cash and a plastic bag with new, but short, replenishment.

Juba turned, raced back the way he came, and jumped into the car. He pulled down the street, screamed around the corner, hit the street where the drama had played out, and turned. A couple of blocks ahead, they could make out the taillights of what could only be the SUV.

They rolled through back streets, closing the distance. Juba was counting on poor security from the runner. He wouldn't be alert. Under normal circumstances, Juba would have followed at an eight-block increment, pulled off, waited for the next run, then eight more blocks, finally arriving near morning. But time was short. The only thing he did was turn his lights off, keeping eye contact with the taillights ahead. They turned, he turned, and when he got to Seven Mile, he had to guess which way the supplier had turned because he hadn't made it to the street in time to see. He guessed left, put his lights back on, and pressed pedal to floor. Ah, yes, there it was, a black Jeep Cherokee, well-polished, glittering in the more vivid light of Seven Mile. He fell into place six car lengths behind, careful to keep a regular interval, low profile, nothing aggressive or hostile.

At least one person was impressed.

"Wow," said Jared, "you're on this guy's tail like glue."

"Concentrate. Eyes on the car. When it turns, I'll go straight ahead. It's your job to see if it turns left or right the next street over or continues."

Jared nodded, swallowing.

The game played itself out for another three-quarters of a mile. Then, helpfully, the driver ahead signaled, slowed, and took a right.

Jared saw, from the vantage point of his own car, the SUV slow down in the middle of the intersection, saw the taillight signal, saw the vehicle swing around.

"He went left," he said.

Juba accelerated through his block, took the right on

two wheels, and pulled up at the corner, waiting for the SUV to pass him and for the chase to begin again. But it didn't come, and he got out, ran to the corner, and saw the SUV parked in the road half a block down. A sudden shear of light signified the opening of the stash house door as the driver was admitted.

"Okay, that's it," he said as he got back. "Now we check it out."

Slowly, they drove by the house. It was dilapidated, like all the others, but three lights burned in various windows. Otherwise, it was quiet.

They pulled around the corner, parked, and, catty-cornered, observed, sheltering in the lee of an abandoned place across the street.

In time, the dealer came out. He had a large paper bag with him.

"Okay, he's loaded up, headed back with your eight dime bags," said Juba. "We'll give it a few minutes and then we'll hit them."

"Hit them? With what?" said the boy.

19

**Interrogation room A, task force MARJORIE DAW
headquarters**

The interrogation of the Imam Imir el-Tariq didn't
take place until nearly 5 a.m., after various administrative tasks had been completed. The
imam's lawyer had to arrive and meet with his client, the
relevant federal attorney had to be roused from bed and
brought on scene, the FBI evidence retrieval had to work
the room found in the basement in which a single man
had lived for a week, Mrs. McDowell had to be medically
attended to, cleared, debriefed, and her testimony inte-
grated into the strategy Nick would take, the evidence
collated and mastered—all of these activities backed by
paperwork and cyberwork.

Finally, Nick, SAIC Houston of the Detroit Field Office, and the sleepy federal prosecutor, who was instructed to keep his mouth shut since he knew nothing,
sat across from the imam and his lawyer, a well-known
firebrand named Kasim. Swagger, Gold, and Chandler
observed via closed-circuit TV.

Nick began by speaking into the recording device, identifying each participant and his allegiances, the date, the circumstances. Then he began in earnest.

"Imam el-Tariq, as your lawyer has undoubtedly told you, the government will indict you on the following counts: detaining a federal agent against her will, use of force against a federal agent, conspiracy to assault a federal agent, and, if necessary, kidnapping a federal agent or conspiracy to kidnap a federal agent. This could amount to a federal prison sentence of more than fifteen years. And please note that we do not anticipate filing state charges, so that the cases will not be tried in the somewhat dubious Dearborn judicial system. Hard time is a distinct possibility."

Kasim was fast on the reply.

"Special Agent Memphis, the government's case is extremely weak. Your own officers will testify that no doors were locked between Mrs. McDowell and themselves. There were no firearms, nor weapons of any sort, found within, according to your own evidence team. No marks of bondage were discovered or documented. No bruises, no abrasions, no physical evidence of any kind of abuse has been documented, nor can it be. At no time did the woman merely say, 'I wish to go home.' Had she, compliance would have been immediate."

"She tells a different story, and the situation as discovered by the SWAT team—four men grilling a single woman under harsh lighting—is itself prima facie evidence of most of the charges. Moreover, the courts have long held that psychological intimidation—the suggestion, the intimation, the subtle inference of force—*is* force. Bruises are not necessary, only witness testimony of intimidation as to direction."

"Our position is unassailable: the woman discovered to be representing herself under false identification was asked to discuss her presence on private property after hours. She agreed to do so. That discussion was ongoing when the officers—well, we can't say *burst* in, since no bursting was necessary through the unlocked doors—but they *strolled* in. That is all that happened."

"If Mrs. McDowell represented a threat to you, you had recourse to the law: merely phone the police. She would have been taken into custody, examined, and her case processed as the law found. You had no right to take her captive, to threaten her—verbally or nonverbally—with violence, and to detain her. This is true whether she's an FBI contract employee or not. It further seems that your true methodology here was deprivation, as you meant to wear her down by denying her sleep. That is torture, by any definition. It is actionable, if we deem it appropriate."

Kasim replied that Mrs. McDowell was hardly irreproachable herself. "It turns out she had appointed herself a one-woman crusade and has bedeviled your security forces with paranoid conspiracy stories of Islamic evil for years. We are sympathetic, given the tragic loss of her son, but only to a point. The fact is, her irrationality has been long documented, I am learning, and more evidence will be forthcoming. That makes her an unreliable witness. On top of that, I can promise you adverse publicity, demonstrations and other sorts of highly unflattering and bothersome attention, if you proceed with this issue. I hope you do. I think the good people of the United States would be interested to learn their tax dollars were being spent on wild-goose chases of purely anti-Islamic hate under the aegis of a crazy woman. I'm sure allegations of an out-of-control Bureau would not be welcome, given the situation you find yourself in."

"Publicity cuts two ways, Mr. Kasim. I'm told there are many wealthy, conservative donors who support this mosque. Those donations could dry up if it became public the imam was involved in possible terrorist activities, to say nothing of kidnapping, intimidation, and torture. Moreover, the three other men in the room are not members of the dance committee but members of mosques known in the area to be far more radical in orientation. Two of them have prison records. Does the imam want that to become public knowledge? Whatever good he hopes to do his cause he cannot do if his position is lost and his reputation is tarnished."

"Since we both have much to lose," said Kasim, "perhaps it is incumbent upon the government to consider a less dramatic course of action than a terrorist trial against a Dearborn imam, certain to stir controversy and attract national attention no matter the outcome. There is no reason this has to go any further, and if the TV cameras go away before the noon news tomorrow, few will remember in a couple of days. All will be restored."

"Restoration might be possible, but only if the imam cooperates with us. Judging by the quality of the other men, he is the only one of sufficient intellect to explain what was going on and to identify the mysterious visitor sleeping in the building. We have to understand who he was and why he was here."

"Let me confer with my client, please," said Kasim. He and the imam rolled away on their chairs to a far corner and, there, chatted for a bit.

When they were done and had returned to the table, Kasim said, "He might be willing to acknowledge certain unusual occurrences within the mosque over the past week. No names can be given, nor any telephone numbers, and no computers will be turned over, but we will work to inform you of what little we know, and you will see how misplaced your apprehension is."

But at that moment, Chandler entered. She walked over to Nick, whispered in his ear, and deposited a folder in front of him. He nodded, opened the folder, and read the first document.

Restoration is possible," Nick was saying on the screen, and Bob, in the television room, turned to Chandler and said, "See, this is where I'd attach the electrodes to his ears."

She didn't laugh. She just shook her head sadly and leaned past Bob toward the third member of the audience and said, "Mr. Gold, can you control him?"

"I believe the record shows nobody can control Mr. Swagger," said Gold.

"Chandler, it was a . . . Oh, you were joking too, now

I get it. No, I didn't really mean to electrify him, and, no, you didn't mean for Mr. Gold to stuff a sock in my mouth."

"I get your point," she said. "It's boring. Laborious exchange of legalisms. So let's speed it up. It's time for my cameo."

She smiled and rose.

"Pay attention, boys, you're gonna like this!"

Nick set the folder down.

"Hmm," he said. "Seems like the stakes have changed."

But to draw out the theater of the thing, he nodded to the prosecutor and Houston, and they rolled backwards and muttered among themselves, while the defense attorney and the imam watched without a lot of enthusiasm. Then the threesome returned to the table.

"This just in. Our evidence team managed to collect some latent prints from the faucet of the lavatory immediately adjacent to the basement bedroom, and two more from the leather straps inside the suitcase, which was otherwise packed with newly bought underwear and shirts of Canadian manufacture, as if someone were trying to hide his origin. But fingerprints don't lie. We ran the prints against not only our own but the Interpol database, and one print, the right thumb, came up with a hit. That print belongs to a former sergeant in the Syrian army named Alamir Alaqua. It turns out Sergeant Alaqua has quite a record, much of it in Israel, where the same fingerprint was found at the site of an atrocity involving the shooting deaths of seventeen children. Sergeant Alaqua is known by his work name, Juba the Sniper."

"We had no idea—" started Kasim, but Nick cut him off.

"Juba is on Interpol's list of ten most wanted international fugitives. Specializes in long-range shooting. Blamed for killings in most of the known world, except, of course, in America. So right away the charge against the imam jumps up to aiding and abetting. That's a big one."

He let it sink in.

"Furthermore, if we are unsuccessful in stopping Juba from whatever his mission in America is, we could nail the imam on accessory before the act. That's a real big one. Suddenly we're looking at twenty-five years."

"If Allah so wills," said the imam, "then let it be so."

"Yes, easy to say now. You tell him, Mr. Kasim, what twenty-five without parole can do to a man. You've seen it."

The two men said nothing.

"And yet still another possibility is that the Israelis will file charges against you for aiding in the escape of a terrorist wanted by them. Possibly they'll file to extradite, and, with nothing to lose, I think we'd almost certainly comply without demurral. Off you'd go to Tel Aviv. I don't think you would enjoy a visit with some very angry Israelis. I suspect they would go after any information you have a lot less civilly than we do. No friendly late-night chats in rooms with your lawyer present."

Again, the two men were quiet.

* * *

The Israeli threat was enough to get el-Tariq's mouth running," said Nick to Mrs. McDowell in her hospital room the next day. "Now, I can't tell you what the issue here is, as it's classified, and you are not cleared. Sorry. But let me say again: we think you did a great job."

"So—it was worth it?" she asked. "I didn't pop the button too early?"

"These clowns could have turned ugly. If you waited, you might not have gotten a chance. You're here, you did your duty."

"I'm so happy to be of use."

"Here's what you got us: we confirmed that Juba is in America and that he's sheltered at this mosque. That's the first step of a long process. We didn't get him, no, but that's just the way the cards fell. He was out 'learning' and was smart enough to get away when he was alerted the imam had busted you. If the cards had been different, he would have been down there in that little basement room and it would have been game over."

"I'm so sorry."

"Can't be helped. Tell her, Mr. Gold."

"Mrs. McDowell, the importunes of providence in these affairs are always puzzling. Enough to suggest that God's favorite weapon is His sense of randomness, which keeps any of us from getting too smug."

"But," said Nick, "we also learned a lot. El-Tariq has connex with a previously unknown terrorist cell, which we'll track and bring down. We learned that through these guys, el-Tariq had access to Dark Web intelligence penetrations, including the Social Security database and some kind of facial recognition technology. They got your face from your driver's license, ran it, and came across the photo in *The Baltimore Sun* of Tommy and you, which ran with his obit. That's big-time facial ID software, so it proved again there's a lot of money and ambition behind this. But now we've got our computer people working on any leads that dope may run to."

"And the kid," said Swagger. "We got the kid."

"Yes," said Nick. "Potentially, the game winner. We've got a picture and other ID of the boy who's running with Juba. We've got all his credit information, which has been flagged for instant law enforcement notification if accessed. And his picture has been sent to four thousand police agencies, so we think it's only a matter of time."

"What do you think, Mr. Swagger?"

"I'm surprised that Juba has hooked up with this kid. It's not like him. I mean, look at him. He could be any kid at the mall."

They had the file on Jared before them. He was Grosse Pointe all the way, his father being one of the most successful periodontists in the suburbs of the Motor City. Jared graduated from Deerfield Academy in Massachusetts, did two years at Princeton, followed by two years at the University of Cairo in Egypt, the site of his radicalization. Since then, he'd accomplished little of merit, just hanging around the fringes of the rad scene in Dearborn, threatening to go join the ISIS armed fighters in northern Syria, but not wanting to be too far from an ATM that delivers monthly support from his father. He liked being on the edge of the gulf between legal and illegal, as if he had the guts to cross it, but there was no evidence that he had—yet. One could easily see why the imam picked him as Juba's tutor in the ways of America, for it would enable young Jared to indulge in his fantasy life, but safely. Except now he was on the run, stuck.

"Juba's normally more self-reliant," said Nick. "But remember, he's a stranger in a strange land and probably paranoid and unarmed. He thinks, *One mistake and I'm gone*. He needs an enabler. Meanwhile, we've got legal intercepts on Jared's parents' and his friends' phones, as well as emails. He'll be the one that cracks. He'll miss Ma and Pa. He'll get lonely. He'll sneak away, put in a phone call, and once we've got a heading on that, it's over."

"Don't hurt him," Janet said. "He's young, he's stupid, and people have always lied to him."

No one had to ask how she knew.

20

First rule of the raid: recon," said Juba.

"Do you mind if I wait in the car?" said Jared.

"You follow on me and keep your mouth shut."

The older man led the younger across the street, well down from the stash house. They waited in the alley, and when they heard nothing, they edged forward, surrounded on either side by the hulks of abandoned houses. The wind rushed, the stars were clearly visible, and their breath turned to vapor. Jared was already huffing.

They reached the property line, noting three gleaming vehicles parked in the alley: another SUV and two slick Mercedes S's. All looked brand-new, freshly waxed, and preposterous here in the back alley of a rotting city. All three made the point that nobody fucked with these guys.

Juba crept through a fallen fence, edged through overgrown bushes, and shunted low across the yard, coming to rest in the lee of the house. Jared followed, a good deal less adeptly.

It was a prewar bungalow, brick, maybe prefab from Sears, Roebuck. Really, just a single story, with a few windows, probably a couple of small bedrooms off a hall, a living room, a dining room. There was a bit of an upstairs, under the eaves of the mansard roof. It looked like every other house in what had been an autoworkers' neighborhood in the salad days before the Japanese attack—on Detroit, not Pearl Harbor. The house was old and sad and broken. It wanted to die.

"On your belly," said Juba.

He crawled to the window, went still under its amber glow, waited for Jared to join him. Then he squirmed out and very slowly stood, surveyed, and ducked down.

"Three men, laughing. Lots of money. Lots of weapons—shotguns, mostly, and pistols. The windows are barred. A TV."

"Must be the rec room," said Jared.

"What?"

"Nothing."

"If it's only three, we're fine. Come."

They repeated the drill at the next window, then slid around back. At each window, Juba took his recon, and in none did he find more men. Upstairs might be another matter, but he didn't think so. He also stopped at the rear door. Leaving Jared behind, he squirmed around to the front, slid under the windows, showing nothing, and examined the door.

When he returned, he drew Jared back to the bushes and into the alley.

"Only the three. Maybe upstairs some women, but they'll be no problem."

"Maybe you underestimate women in the drug trade."

"Okay, we kill them too."

"No, I didn't mean that. Let's not kill any women. Actually, I'd prefer if—"

"We follow Allah, little boy. We do what must be done."

"I can't kill a woman," said Jared.

Juba looked at him squarely. "Are you jihadi?"

"I guess," said Jared.

"Okay."

He abandoned the boy and went into the bushes. After some effort, grunting and tugging, he emerged with a straight ten inches of branch, from which he was busily trimming smaller limbs and twigs. He turned to a patch of unruptured asphalt in the alley and set to sharpening one end by aggressively turning and grinding it at an angle and, in a bit of time, had manufactured a pointed tip that looked like the business end of a bayonet.

He turned to the boy.

"We go to front and—"

"Whoa! Wouldn't it be better to go back? Nobody to see. Suppose a cop happens to drive by?"

"The back door swings outward on hinges. You can't get through it. The front swings inward. Also, it's a new hollow-core door and it doesn't look very strong. Locks come out of the wood easily. Understand?"

"Yeah," said Jared without enthusiasm.

"Remember, you don't touch, you don't spit, you

don't rub. You don't shed hair. Take off your sweatshirt and wrap your head to prevent hair from shedding. Also, cover your face, since if anybody sees it, they must die. If there are women there and they see your face, they must die. Or, maybe easier, I'll kill you, let them live."

"Ha ha," said Jared. "Now you're the funny one."

"It's time. Be a man."

They crept to the lee of the house again, low-crawled down the side, turned the corner toward the front, and reached the front door.

"Go on," said Juba. "Do it! Now!"

Jared swallowed and stood. More gracefully, more fluently, more practiced, Juba stood next to him, back against the door.

Jared pounded hard on its surface, feeling the rebound of the wood with each blow.

Nothing. He pounded again.

Sounds of scuttling inside.

Then the *thump-thump* of someone racing down the hall.

"Who the fuck is that?" came the call from the door.

"Ginger sent me. Man, he's hurt bad. They jumped him, beat his ass, and took his shit. I think he's going to die."

"Who the fuck are you?"

"Ginger told me to come here. He may be dead by now."

A view hole in the door opened, as whoever was in there had to check out the messenger before deciding what to do. Juba pivoted and without pause or hesitation, but with full strength, commitment, and great accuracy, jammed the sharpened stick through the hole.

Jared heard an unprecedented sound. It had both the qualities of crunch and slurp to it, something cracking, something squirting, and the stick disappeared as whoever now received it surrendered to gravity. Juba, fast as a snake, reared back and drove the sole of his right foot at high velocity into the door, just above the lock, and the wood splintered as if it were balsa. The impact sprang the door, ripping splinters and chunks with it, as bolts and chains clanked with their sudden release, and Juba was in, followed by Jared, who got just a brief look at the guard. He lay against the wall, about six inches of raw stick protruding vertically from his left eye socket, a torrent of blood washing down his slack face and running onto his black satin shirt. Jared had never before seen the devastation to flesh that violence brings, and it froze him solid for a second.

Juba had no time for coaching. He snatched up the man's weapon, a short-barreled semi-automatic shotgun, pivoted, throwing its bolt even as he lifted it to his shoulder, and stormed down the hall. Another figure, in the full animation of urgency, appeared, Glock in hand. But he was way behind the action curve, and Juba put what had to be six gallons of buckshot into his center chest, shredding it, and him, lifting him off his feet, where he bounced against the doorframe and went to the floor like a shock of wheat.

The ear-stabbing blast of the gun, and the acrid smell

of burnt powder, snapped Jared free of his trance, but also set his ears to ringing like all the alarms in the world. Following Juba, he raced down the hallway, while struggling to get his hoodie wrapped around his skull, and he ended up looking more like a bedraggled mummy than Juba, whose wrapping was tight and efficient.

Juba reached the doorway out of which the man had come. Instead of bursting through it, he went prone and snaked around it low. Whoever was in there expected no such move; for his misinterpretation, he got his own six gallons of buckshot in the knee. He went down, tried to rise on his one good leg, and Juba sent buckshot in an angry cloud into his genitals. Juba rose, strode in, and Jared heard the headshot.

But he became aware of scurrying upstairs. He had paused halfway down the hall at the foot of the stairway.

"*Stop!*" he screamed in English. "If you come down, we'll kill you. Stay upstairs and hide until we're gone."

But suddenly a large woman materialized at the head of the stairs, her face bulging out with fury, and she came leaping down the stairs at Jared. She was immense and full of adrenaline. He swallowed as she launched from five steps up and filled the sky like a crashing dirigible, huge enough to squash him. But some instinct caused his legs to spring, and he jumped to the right. She thundered past and landed with what sounded like meat smashing into wood at three hundred miles an hour. He knew if she got her hands on him, it was all over, so his cowardice poked him into action, and he kicked her, hard, in the face. And then he kicked her again.

She went prone, but was still breathing and struggling to move, rolling over like a large farm animal caught in the muck, and, the next thing he knew, he was using her face as a trampoline—up, down, up, down. And then Juba pulled him back.

"Good," Juba said, "you are warrior now. *Allahu Akbar!* God is great! Now, come on, we have to get the fuck out of here."

Jared looked at the carnage he had unleashed. The woman's face was pulped, and squalid splatters of blood reflected greasily in the yellow hallway lighting. Her wounds had swollen so quickly that she looked as if tumors had overtaken and eaten her features. Her immensity made her stillness even more apparent.

Hideous detail, never to be unseen: a dental bridge, with two gold teeth and one white one, all twisted and bent, sitting in the puddle of blood that was oozing across the floor.

21

A few hours of sleep, a shower, then back in to file reports, read the wires, scan the incoming reports, Nick on the phone with D.C., everyone busy.

They finally got together at 4.

"Hope you all appreciate the lie I told Mrs. McDowell yesterday. In fact, not picking up Juba at the mosque, alerting him and letting him fly the coop, was a total catastrophe. They are not happy in D.C. Don't know how much longer I'm going to be around."

"If you go, I go," said Swagger.

"Appreciated, but not helpful," said Nick. "Anyhow, in this room, we all understand that, but once it's been acknowledged, we have to forget it and move on. So if anybody has any bitches—complaints, recriminations, bitterness—now's the time to let fly, because after today it's a closed file."

Gold said, "It does no good to compare to Israeli methods. I feel, however, that psychologically your people—I don't mean anyone in here, but more generally—have not made the kind of commitment that is necessary to deal with this sort of existential threat. I hope I am wrong."

"You probably are not," said Nick. "Passive-aggression haunts our every move, even in the Bureau's Counterterrorism Division. We haven't committed as yet to the path of total destruction. Many still believe some sort of rapprochement is necessary."

"Do you yourself, Agent Memphis?"

"Tough question, soft answer. I hope so. Deep down, however, nobody wants to go full theater. It's not in our character. Look at our wars and how equivocal we've been, at least since 1945, and the two months immediately after nine/eleven."

"Then your task will be harder."

"I understand that. I will help in any way I can, as I have an intense investment in seeing Juba eliminated."

"Anything else?" Nick said.

There were no murmurs.

"And we did gain," said Nick. "A, we confirmed that he's here. B, he's supported by an expensive maintenance system of unknown provenance and sophisticated capabilities. C, he's unsure of his ability to maneuver here in America. And, D, he's with this Jared Akim, whom we can track. Now, Chandler, update us."

"Got over a dozen responses from the wired picture of the Akim kid, but, in all cases, they're outside the cone of possibility. He couldn't have gotten there that fast by car. So I low-prioritize them. There are many reports of stolen cars, but nothing unusual in them, no way of knowing if one of them was taken by Juba and Akim. We have upgraded priorities on the license numbers of those taken after Imam el-Tariq put in his call to Akim and warned him of the spy. El-Tariq said that was about six p.m., and on his phone there indeed was a call to a number at six-oh-seven p.m. confirmed as Jared Akim's."

"And I'm guessing there's no further intercept data on that phone. Surely Juba would be smart enough to destroy it."

"That's correct."

"And there's no intercept intelligence from the phones or emails to Akim's parents or any of the seven friends we've identified?"

"Nothing, chief."

"Mr. Gold, do you think he'll split up from the kid? He's used to operating alone."

"He's used to shooting alone. He's used to escaping alone. But in all his operations, even going back to his housecleaning for Assam's henchmen, he was serviced, transported, and sustained by an in-place network. He is used to having a chaperone. He is a star, in other words, and is used to people doing things for him. He's the artist, he has to be free to create."

"He sounds more like a director than a sniper," said Nick, but "Director" had a different meaning to the staff than to movie-crazed Nick, so nobody laughed.

"I believe he already has a new network in place and will work quickly to find it," continued Gold. "This situation would be among the eventualities he planned for.

As I see this, I think he has to go from network to network to keep advancing. Might I suggest you assign someone to find organizations capable of sustaining him over the next month or two, getting him what he needs, transporting him, assisting him in his movements and his logistical needs? I could guess, furthermore, that it will be a criminal organization, but it won't be radically Islamic in tone or tendency."

"Yeah, good," said Nick. "And that's also more indication of the money behind this op. If he's got a criminal organization helping him, that kind of work doesn't come cheap."

Gold nodded.

"I'll forward a memo to our gang intelligence people to be on the lookout for any kind of pattern of unusual activity."

"I agree."

"Meanwhile, we wait. But we have to anticipate. Mr. Swagger, what're your thoughts?"

"Well, gun stuff, for one," said Swagger. "I believe he's prepping up a .338 Lapua Magnum shot. Those rifles are damned expensive, and they're prized by people with passionate urges to shoot from a long way out. It's a small community. Someone—me, I guess—ought to canvass it and see if anything has happened and left tracks in that community.

"I also—not sure of the legality here—but it's a community serviced by just a few retail outfits, some mail order only, some brick-and-mortar, and the gear is very specific, very well made, very expensive, mostly from specialized machine shops. He—or somebody—would have to make some purchases to get him set up. Can we monitor or question those limited outlets, again looking for unusual patterns? Also, there's a series of competitions where fellows shoot over a mile. I don't think he'll be competing, but those boys might have picked something up—rumors, odd patterns of purchase, questions coming in from an odd source, stuff like that. It could all lead us to Juba through a different route."

"That's good. Don't you think that's good, Mr. Gold?"

"I do, yes."

"Other than that," Swagger continued, "I remember that Mrs. McDowell said he was not a great one for improvising. So I think it's fair to assume that now that he's on the run, he'll try to get back to his plan as quickly as possible. He only knows we know about him, but he has no idea the extent to which we've penetrated. He will get back on schedule."

"Okay, lay out the schedule. As you see it."

"I believe he has to find an area with at least a mile of clear space to get zeroed in. He has to work with his reloading program until he's satisfied he's found a load that will get him on target from the appropriate distance with the appropriate killing velocity still left in the bullet. He's got to shoot and score five hundred times so he's comfortable. I also think at a certain point he'll move on to living targets. He'll want to see what the bullet does. He might find an accurate load and bullet, but not be pleased with its penetration and expansion powers, and know, from that, that if he don't hit heart or lung, the boy he's shooting at will probably survive. So he's got to have a bullet that deforms or mushrooms or bursts into splinters and cuts everything to ribbons. No point coming all this way, spending all this money, time, and energy, only to knock whoever-it-is down for a two-day stay in the hospital. He's got to know he's got a one-shot kill package. So he'll shoot at something alive from this distance, and somehow we might be able to connect by finding such a site."

"Satellite recon, as with Mr. Gold's operation in Israel, would seem in order," said Nick. "Unfortunately, the United States is a lot bigger than southern Syria, so we can't just send the drones and satellites out. Can you put together for me a profile of what he'd need? Then we can task a recon satellite to look for it. Or maybe we have computer programs that can do such a thing."

"Yep."

"I'm going to hook you up with a Cyber Division hotshot we have named Jeff Neill. Lots of big-case experience. Maybe if you tell him what you need, he'll be able to put something together that could facilitate finding it fast."

"Now we're perking," said Swagger.

"Chandler?"

"Well, we're not all drones and boy-genius hackers. Manhunt principles: flood the world with photos of quarry, run commo intercepts on likely allies, find a track, then raid. That's how they've done it since Rome, and it's worked before."

"Sure, I agree, bu—"

Her phone rang.

"Detroit Metro, Homicide," she said, looking at the dial.

"Take it," said Nick.

The crime scene was indeed a crime scene: standard urban tragedy, case number 1,708,887. Bodies, blood in lakes and tributaries, the shooter's progress written in the trail of shotgun shells he left as he took out all living things that crossed his path. Style points for the guy with the stick in his eye—the cops had never seen that and thought it was pretty funny—and the poor woman, so pulped her face looked like it had been taken over by malignancy. That, under the mashed and merged features, she still breathed lowered the score a bit, but a special bonus had to be awarded for the twisted false teeth in the blood.

"You've seen this shit before?" Nick asked the boss detective. "What are you getting?"

"Out-of-towners. No Detroit crew would hit this house. It's a Black Pagans franchise, and the Pagans are the biggest, toughest gang in the city. They've got about eighty percent of the hard trade. 'Hard' being Motownese for heroin. So if you hit them, they will go medieval on your ass and wipe out all the living generations of your family. If your parents are dead, they'll dig them up and kill them all over again. Whoever did this didn't give a shit about the Pagans."

"What do you make of the shooting?" Bob asked the detective.

"It got the job done."

"No, I mean as skill."

"High-quality. The Pagans and their competitors, all four of them still alive, aren't known for their finesse. That's why so many innocent bystanders go down when they're settling scores. But this shooter put all his blasts into kill zones. The first shot was about forty feet, dead center to the chest, and it had to be made fast. He came around the door low on Reggie, put one into his knee, to bring him under the table, then the other into his balls. A fourth shot, close-range, finished him. Muzzle distance: zero feet. Ejected shells were all twelve-gauge double-aught Remington. We also found an empty box of shells in Reggie's room, so presumably one of the bad guys filled his pockets."

"Anything on the gun?"

"Probably stolen. That's where the Pagans strap up, mostly. By the spray pattern, I'd say a shorty, sixteen inches. As I say, well-shot. He hit what he was shooting at dead solid perfect. The guy knew what he was doing."

"How much do you think they clipped?"

"Plenty. Fifteen, twenty, twenty-five thousand, small bills. On a weekend, much bigger, so if the point was to hit a stash house, they would have waited till Saturday night. Hitting one on a weeknight doesn't make any sense robbery-wise."

"They needed the dough to get out of town," said Nick. "Strictly travel money. What about the woman?"

"Different guy. Unarmed. Theola was a formidable woman; she'd been shot three times, and we believe she had at least four kills on her, two bare-handed, but nobody would think of snitching her out. Anyhow, this was amateur hour. He kicks her in the head after she fell down, jumps on her face like it's a pogo stick. You can see his tracks in the blood. Size: about ten and a half. I've seen plenty of those tread marks, they're Vans, a shoe suburban kids think is cool. It's not a ghetto icon. The other guy was in size eleven cross-trainers, probably New Balance or Nike. So it's an odd combo of a pro and someone suburban with zero experience."

"But they knew where to hit. How'd they know where the stash was?"

"Followed the runner's car, I'd guess. He'd been out servicing the street pushers."

"So I think we'd like to talk to the street pushers. They might have something."

"Sure, so would I, but I can't do that right away. After something like this, they'll all go to ground, because they don't know how it's going to come down from here. They don't want to be standing on their corner when the retaliation starts turning the air blue."

"Got it."

"And one more thing. See that fat guy with his balls splattered on the wall? His name was Reggie 'Candy' Peppers. A legend in this town. Anyhow, he had a 2017 Mercedes S, jet-black, shiny as sin. His pride and joy. We found two cars out back registered to the two other vics, but Candy's was missing. I'm thinking your boys not only ripped off money and guns and ammo but the car as well. We can put out a statewide on the license plate and a descript of the bad guys. Maybe tighten it up with street pusher info to be collected later."

"Do that, please, Lieutenant. But as you say, the main guy is a pro, and he'll be good at evasion. He may have dumped it for another car by this time. It's been, what, twelve hours since all this occurred?"

"Get right on it, sir."

"So they needed dough and a car to travel," said Nick to Bob. "Best way to get each fast is to hit a place like this. That we're on it so fast is a break for us, thanks to a cop's sharp eyes. Still, they're out and on the road."

"Fuck," said Bob.

"Yeah, and for someone who hates to improvise, he's doing it pretty goddamned well."

Next day, nothing, no reports of an abandoned Mercedes S, Michigan 4C55 409, jet-black. A few replies to Jared's photo, but all useless. Another Assistant Director showed up to sit with Nick in his office. No comment on the subject of the chat. Bad news from latent prints: nothing for Juba. A few that presumably belonged to Jared Akim, but since he'd never been fingerprinted, that couldn't be confirmed. Bob on the phone to the long-range retail shops of America, to the president of the Mile Benchrest Club in Pennsylvania, to MidwayUSA and Brownells, which owned Sinclair International. Nothing tangible. The .338 Lapua Magnum was mainstream enough that no unusual activity on behalf of its sustenance could be identified. A few hours for nap breaks, but nothing else.

The day after was going the same way, until Nick hung up his phone with a crack.

"Okay, let's jump," he said. "Get that State Police chopper over here, Chandler. Email intercept from Jared Akim to a pal, asking him to tell the folks he was all right, would be home soon—this was the coolest thing."

"Did they get a locality on it?" Swagger asked.

"Yeah, the GPS record puts it at a Kmart in Germantown, Ohio. About one hundred and fifty miles south of here, right on the state line."

"Let's go to Ohio," said Bob.

22

On the road

The Mercedes-Benz was a sweet ride. But at a small-town strip mall two hours out of Detroit, by way of Ann Arbor on 127, Juba slipped out of it, popped the lock and the ignition of a dark blue Chevy Impala, sitting in the neon wash of a coffee shop, and drove away. Another hour, and he spotted a low creek, shrouded in bushes, and directed Jared, who'd been following him in the Benz, to pull off. It took some arranging, but once they'd removed the shotgun—a Remington 1100 Auto-Tactical—and the canvas sack containing $23,650 in small bills from the Mercedes, Juba sent it through the bushes and into the water. It sank low, until only the roof was showing. Nobody would notice it, at least not routinely.

They drove on in the Impala, and finally Jared said, "Man, I am almost dead."

"All right. Small motel, you go in and rent a room, pay with cash. Make sure you know this license number so you don't struggle."

This proved within Jared's range of abilities, and soon he was zzzzed out.

He woke at 4 in the afternoon, suddenly disconsolate. What would his parents say? God, he'd been such a disappointment to them. They'd given him everything, he'd given them nothing. Now his mother was battered by tears and pain, his formidable father was being bedeviled by FBI agents, black cars were parked all around the block.

But maybe his friends thought he was cool.

Someone knocked.

"Yeah."

"Come on, time to go."

"Let me grab a shower."

"Hurry."

He cleaned himself but climbed into stinking clothes.

"You drive," said Juba, his eyes everywhere.

"I think we're okay," said Jared. "I signed with a false name."

"Oh, what a clever boy," said Juba. "He knows all the tricks."

They drove on, staying off the interstates, which were patrolled by more vigilant Highway Patrolmen, confident that they could outsmart small-town cops. Soon enough, they came to a Kmart, mooring some other stores in a downscale strip mall. Juba pulled in.

"Okay," he said. "You go in. Buy some underwear. Me too. Also buy me a heavy file—a carpenter's file, no fingernail stuff. And a light jacket, any kind, size fifty-two. But, most important, you buy a disposable phone. You know how they work?"

"Yeah, you buy a card with minutes on it, she activates it at the register, and we're all set."

"Yes. Don't buy anything unusual, like toothpaste and a toothbrush, along with underpants. We'll buy that some other place."

"Shall I wear my sunglasses?"

"No. It's dark out. You don't want to be noticed. Tell yourself: I am nobody."

"I *am* nobody."

He got out and entered the bright zone of the store. It was sparsely populated, every clerk a composition in disinterest, and he got his stuff together in a short time, stopped for some Milky Ways and some protein bars, and got through the line quickly.

But it was too much. The melancholia broke over him quickly. Sitting on a stool at the hot dog counter in the front of the store, he quickly activated his phone and dialed the number of a pal back in Grosse Pointe.

"Hello?"

"Jimmy, it's Jar—"

"Holy Christ, man, what are you up to? The FBI has been here, and everything."

"I can't explain now. It'll be okay. Look—real quick, just send my mom an email to Shareen at AOL-dot-com. Say you heard from me, I'm fine, I'll be in touch in a bit. That's all."

"Where are you?"

"You wouldn't believe it if I told you."

"Okay, I'll send the message."

"Great. And thanks, man. When I get out of this, we'll have a good laugh."

"You got it."

He rose, put the phone in a trash can. He went back to the store proper, got another one off the shelf, and bought it, feeling very Secret Agent Man. He'd be able to present an unopened plastic-sealed phone to Juba, who'd never know he'd made a call. What were the odds that the feds were intercepting his parents' emails?

Are we going anywhere? Or are we just going *away*?"

Juba looked at his watch, pulled over to the edge of the highway.

"Okay, little boy," he said. "I need to make contact. Phone?"

Juba took it, ripped it from its plastic packaging, which he threw out the window, scraped clear the code of the calling card, tapped it into the phone. He had fifteen minutes.

He dialed a number.

"Yes, I am fine. I need a new pickup. Tell them I am on U.S. Route 127, just past the border of Michigan. I will stay on 127. How much time will it take to intercept?"

He paused. A car passed, then a van.

"Okay. Yes, we are in a dark blue Impala. License: Michigan L11 245. Thank you."

He turned to Jared.

"Okay, a town called Greenville, about three hours ahead. We will go to a shopping mall on the south side of town—Walmart, not Sears. We are looking for a van, a Chevy, tan, license 276 RC678. Can you remember that?"

"No."

"276 RC678. Pay attention."

"What state?"

"Ohio."

"How did they know we'd be in Ohio?"

"They know everything. Now, get rid of that phone. Sink it in water."

Jared did as he was told. The phone went into a stream he found about fifty yards in. It occurred to him that this would be a great time for Juba to dump him. Or, he could dump Juba. He could take off now, disappear for a day or so in the Ohio farm wilderness. Then he could turn himself in. The best criminal lawyer in Michigan, whom his dad would hire, would get him a deal. He'd snitch out Juba, and they'd drop whatever thought they had about putting him away for mashing Mrs. Potato Head.

But he knew he couldn't do that. He'd crossed the line. No matter how much he missed the easy pleasures of his old, meaningless life, he could never go back to it. He was jihadi now.

And, of course, Juba had not left.

About an hour further on, Juba, confident they were not under observation, ordered Jared to pull over. He reached into the Kmart bag, pulled out the plastic-wrapped file, and climbed into the backseat.

"Continue to drive. Eyes open, under the speed limit, nothing stupid."

"Got it."

Jared drove on, as one of the drearier sections of rural Ohio, its northwest corner, rolled by monotonously, but it wasn't long until he heard some—well, what? Grinding? Sawing? Some kind of mechanistic sound. The rearview revealed nothing, but he managed a quick look-see on a smooth section of road and saw Juba, hunched over in concentration, his arm like a piston as it plunged ahead, was withdrawn, and plunged ahead again. In a few seconds, Jared realize what he was doing: shortening the shotgun stock.

Juba looked up.

"I cut it down. Easier to hide, and I can cover it with a jacket."

Jared gulped. He did it again when the filing stopped, and he heard the weird *thunk-thunk* of Juba inserting more shells into the extended magazine of the shotgun.

23

Greenville, Ohio (I)

At the Ohio Highway Patrol station on U.S. 75 outside Dayton, Nick stood at a much-abused lectern and addressed the troops.

"You need to be very careful. We think this guy popped three drug dealers in Detroit. He will shoot. Big, tough Arab guy, we don't know what name he's operating under, but over there, where he got his start, he was called Juba. He may be with a kid, early twenties, slight, American citizen of Arabic heritage, sort of his interpreter and facilitator. But he may have dumped the kid, as he knows we're all in on the two of them."

The guys on the folding chairs were police-appropriate: crew-cut, gym-big, crisp as Honor Guard Company in their immaculate uniforms, seeming to share a single expression of wary attentiveness. They had faces built for Ray-Ban Aviators and flat-brims, and they all carried plastic Glock .40s on their patent leather Sam Browne belts. They were duty guys, and what more could you ask for?

"Sir," someone said, "a triple first-degree is big-time.

But we know you got here by emergency chopper from Detroit. You're FBI, but not out of the Detroit Office, and that fellow with you is a 'consultant,' meaning a guy who knows a lot about a certain thing. So I'd like just to ask, politely, what's going on?"

"As some of you may have surmised, there is a national security connection, but I am not at liberty to divulge it. The Detroit thing is a helpful pretext to get me troops without having to explain things. Let me just say this guy is thought to be very dangerous in ways not connected with Detroit, and that it is in the highest national interest— and urgency—to take him off the page right now."

He watched them watching him. Like most State cop shops, it was a shabby installation off the highway, in- nocuous except for the OHP shield on a sign outside and the two dozen black-and-whites outside.

"Why here, why now?"

He backgrounded them, finishing on, "We're working on the theory they stole the Impala in Hudson—blue, plates Alpha-Four-Five-Five-Charlie—and dumped the Benz outside of Hudson. So they're headed south on 127. Since they'd been going forty-eight straight, I think they bunked somewhere and got on the road again maybe late last night. Still heading south. Don't know if it's random or they're aiming toward a certain destination."

"But you see it as this part of Ohio?"

"Yeah, and so far they've shown a tendency to stay off the interstates, because they know that's where you guys are and they fear you guys. They know you pay attention.

So my bet is, they're still on 127 headed toward Greenville. So our target would be a dark blue '13 Impala."

Nick had more.

"Really, guys, do not go all heroic on me and try for a one-man intercept. This guy has tons of combat experience in the sandbox and he is a world-class shot. He's got a twelve-gauge semi-auto and a box of double-aughts, stolen from the drug stash. With that gun, he's too good to go man on man against. He will not miss. He will not go down to .40, unless it clips the central nervous system. Are you that good while taking incoming double-aught? I didn't think so.

"So, note road and direction and pass on by. Don't even pursue at a distance. You've done your job. Last thing we want is a rolling-felony-stop massacre as in Dade County. We can't catch him, we've got to ambush him. We've got to be there in force or we're looking at a shooting event like you wouldn't believe. Like you wouldn't survive. If we get the ID, we'll go to helicopter then, airborne, try and monitor them while we throw together some kind of roadblock, way overgunned for the occasion. I've got SWAT people coming in from Lansing and Columbus and Dayton; they'll do the rough stuff, if it comes to that. They like rough stuff."

Nick turned to Swagger.

"Can you think of anything?" Nick asked Swagger, standing just off to the side of the lectern. He turned back to the men before Bob could answer and said, "My associate here has been in more gunfights than probably anyone this side of Frank Hamer, and, as you can see, he's more or less alive."

There was some laughter.

Bob just said, "As Nick has said, I have been in many shooting events and had to put some folks down. This guy scares the hell out of me. I'm supposed to be brave, but I would run like hell until I had twenty guns backing me up. So bear that in mind if you get bitten by the hero bug. Your widow gets a folded flag, your kids get nothing, and you get dead."

The accoutrements of the wait: cold, stale coffee made slick by degrading Styrofoam, intense cigarette hunger even for those who shook the monkey years ago, finger-drumming jazz variations, playing games on the iPhone with half an ear toward the cop-talk frags that come over the loudspeaker.

"Hector, this is Lima Five, just swept up through and past Greenville on 127, no contact."

"Continue your route, Lima Five."

"Hector, Lima Nineteen, am on binocs at Walmart parking lot, looked at a lot of cars, but no '13 dark blue Impala."

Nick said to the supervisor, "You know what, another tell might be a bad spray-paint job. And yet another is a different license plate. He might have changed."

"Also, one of the guys might have gone flat in the backseat, or been dumped, so there won't be two profiles," said Chandler.

"Good on that, Chandler."

The supervisor put that out, said, "They'll find him."

"If he's there."

Swagger stretched, yawned. Another headquarters day: a room decorated with radio shit and maps, with chalkboards all over the place, the radio people being mostly dowdy civilians, because why tie up a trained State cop sitting at a mic? Pictures of the governor, the president, the vice president, and various officials of meaningless rank. Fluorescent light pouring down, turning everything pale ghost gray even if outside it was a sunny midwestern day and prosperity's engines were turning smoothly, except where they weren't. Seemed odd to be hunting a shotgun-armed jihadi in Yourtown, U.S.A., and Swagger worried that if Juba saw what was ongoing, he might divert to the nearest mall and start blasting citizens until someone brought him down. He'd go out the obsessed, mercy-free jihadi way. Whatever you could say about these guys, they were hard men, in it to the end, willing to back it up with guts and fast to offer their own lives in the transaction.

Crackly noise.

"Hector, Lima Seven, have a possible Impala, no matching tag, maybe a '13, tan, but the tan looked ragged to me."

"Identify location, Seven."

"Greenville. I'm north on Oakton, he's south, just past Miller, inside speed limit. I haven't turned on him."

"Nearest unit—ah, let's see—can you get to Oakton and Biddle, park, hide behind your vehicle, get an eyeball on this guy as he passes, but stay low."

"This is Lima Nine, Hector, wilco that."

It was silent except for the gravy train of static, amplified so much that it became especially irritating to those who hadn't made peace with it.

"Go to chopper?" asked Bob.

"Not yet. Maybe it's a no-go."

Then, "Hector, Lima Nine, tan Impala just passed, black woman, three kids in backseat."

"Got it. Good try, Lima Seven. Everybody stand down and—"

"Hector, Hector, Lima Nineteen, now at Walmart Plaza. There he is, parked near the store entrance. Sorry, can't see if car is occupied, but it's still dark blue and it's got the Michael Charlie plates."

Nick said to the supervisor, "Get your people on the south side, out of sight. Get 'em to assemble—I don't know—close by, no sirens, no squealing brakes. We'll take a look-see from up top and issue procedures at that time."

"Got it."

Nick turned to Swagger.

"Let's go," he said.

From above, the small city of Greenville was mostly elm canopy, pierced here and there by church spires. At the edges, a few industrial tanks stood out like white mushrooms. Nick had instructed the chopper pilot to orbit from a mile out, never coming directly over the Walmart and its wing of the mall. Nick and Bob worked their binoculars carefully.

"Okay, I got it," Bob said. "Dark blue sedan, south entrance, in the row up from the main entrance on the east side, no action, no motion."

Nick found it and focused, and there was the car, a long way away. Given the vibrations of the chopper, it was hard to hold it clearly for more than a few seconds.

"Yeah, I see. Looks empty to me."

"Sure, they're probably in the mall, getting a burger. But they could also be hiding on the floor, waiting for something, ready to roll when the time comes."

Nick went to SEND mode.

"Hector, this is Fed One, you getting me?"

"Yes, I am," came the voice, now clearly an older man's, probably the State Police commanding officer, over from Columbus a few minutes ago.

"Sitrep, please," said Nick. "What assets on the ground?"

"I've got my own SWAT in an armored vehicle, I've got twenty black-and-whites, we're about a block away holding in the parking lot of First Methodist. All my people are armored up, cocked and locked. I've got an auxiliary SWAT unit from your office in Columbus, but they don't have any armored assault car. I've got Greenville P.D. ready to take over traffic and isolate the mall from civilian ingress quick-time. And we've got the vehicle identified and are ready to launch."

"Real good. Colonel, what's your thought?"

"You don't know if they're in the car or the mall, is that right?"

"Yes, that's it."

"Okay, my call would be to move five black-and-whites in through the five entrances on two streets to the mall. I have my SWAT people in an armored vehicle, ready to hit the site and deploy. I will move Columbus and Dayton SWAT around the back of the mall as primary assaulters in phase two. On my go, the armored SWAT vehicle and the five squad cars hit the pedal and race to the car, establishing a perimeter and firebase if they're there."

"And the guys in the squad cars, all in body armor?"

"As per instructions."

"Good. One call to surrender, then you can shoot," said Nick.

"Got that. But if they're not there, those officers fan to the east-side mall entrances and, once deployed, the SWAT mall assaulters hit from the two northernmost entrances and begin to sweep through. Your up-armored FBI team hits from the southern entrance, their job is the Walmart itself. Meanwhile, I'm blocking all mall exits with troopers, who, when signaled, will move in to coordinate with the mall teams. Encountering fire, all will rally to that point. How does that sound?"

Nick turned to Bob, putting his hand over the throat mic.

"You're supposed to be a consultant. So consult."

"It's good," Bob said. "Two targets, the car, then the mall sweep. He's got his priorities right, it's straight-ahead, no fancy timing or tricky feints and bluffs. Plus, these guys will feel better taking instructions from him rather than some out-of-state FBI guy. And these are supposed to be the best guys in the state, so I believe in 'em."

Nick took his hand away from the mic.

"Real good," he said to the colonel. "As soon as you hit the vehicle, my pilot will land and drop me off, and I'll come to you."

"My Command Center will be with SWAT at the car. I will move in with them if the car is empty. Y'all have raid jackets?"

"We're in 'em. Ball caps too. Please don't shoot us."

"Haven't shot an FBI agent in years," said the colonel.

"Okay, give your guys a few more minutes to get settled, then we go. You call it, Hector, you're on the ground."

"Roger that, Fed One."

They could see the squad cars converging on what had to be the target car.

"Take us in," said Nick to the pilot. With the zooming rotors' angles shifting, the helicopter banked left like a fighter jet and began the long swoop in, leaving stomachs far behind.

Swagger thought of his last helicopter adventure, which ended with second-degree burns on arm, shoulder, neck, and face.

"Reminds me I hate helicopters," he said to nobody but himself.

24

Greenville (II)

Juba wanted to destroy America but for one thing: the French fries.

"I like these," he said.

"You've been all over the world, you've never had French fries?"

"I was not on tour. I was on jihad."

"Yeah, busy, busy—I get it."

They sat in a booth at a McDonald's halfway down the mall's hallway. To the right, the broad opening to the shiny paradise of Walmart beckoned. The hall itself was darker, a corridor of dying retail, with a cheesy plastic garden in the middle. A lot of mom-'n'-pop new-media stuff, DVDs and games and phones from obscure networks, a couple of other fast-food troughs, a shoe chain, an Old Navy, the whole place dying. The brick-and-mortar was losing to the 'Net, as Jared knew, but he thought this was not a topic that would fascinate Juba.

"No," said Juba. "I've seen these places, you know? They're everywhere."

"I remember when they were just another snake cult," said Jared.

"What?"

"Nothing. Bad joke."

"Jihadis do not joke."

"But they eat French fries?"

"I make the rules."

"That is true," said Jared.

Next to Juba on the seat was a hoodie wrapped tight to obscure fourteen inches or so of semi-automatic shotgun stoked to the gills on 12-gauge double-aughts. But the man carried it with such insouciant naturalism, it would never have occurred to anyone that such a package could conceal such a weapon. Juba was completely calm, at peace. He had prayed in the car, something Jared could not get himself to do even now, explaining to himself his attraction to the cause was more identity politics than faith.

They had made the drive down 127 to Greenville without trouble, skipped the Sears mall, found the Walmart mall with equal ease, and realized there was no time frame set up. Jared found a space, close to one entrance.

"Want me to get another phone?" he said. "Maybe they're here already. Do you know where they were coming from?"

"Detroit, same as us. It's where they were to pick me up. But then things went wrong."

"Who are these guys, may I ask?"

"No. Suppose I get away and you get caught. You will give up all your secrets. So, the less you know, the better."

"Okay, just asking . . . Do we wait in the car? That's kind of suspicious."

"I agree. Go inside, one at a time, meet at . . . Where will we meet?"

"Hungry?"

"Yes."

"I see by the sign, the golden arches, there's a McDonald's inside. Meet me there? Easy to find."

"Fine."

They left the car, each going a different way, eyes hunting the presence of the tan van, neither seeing it. The mall swallowed each and, in time, reunited them at the McDonald's.

After the meal, Jared said, "So, now get new throwaway?"

"Yes, little boy."

Juba sat, drinking coffee, appearing uninterested, as Jared went to run his errand. He was a good boy, it turned out, and his cheer and wit, something long missing from Juba's life, paid off as a small pleasure. He trusted Jared enough at this point that he felt no anxiety as the boy disappeared—and no relief when he reappeared twenty minutes later.

"You get it?"

"Yes."

"Powered up?"

"Yes. You want to make a call?"

"Not now. We go to the car, wait there. They drive by and we hop in. Who would notice?"

"Nobody."

So they ambled out, headed down the mall amid strangers who paid them no attention at all, came to the entrance that yielded the car and headed out.

It was all fine—and then it wasn't.

"Whoa! Whoa! Whoa!" said Jared, pulling the larger man back just inside the doors.

Juba wheeled on Jared, caught off guard by the physical contact.

"See out there," Jared said quickly, "a mile out? That helicopter?"

He pointed. Above the trees, a speck moved horizontally through the air, its faintest of buzzes only barely reaching their ears.

"Yes . . ."

"I saw it fly by when we headed in a half hour ago. It's still there. Farther out, but still. Could they have us?"

"Are you sure?" said Juba.

"Yes."

"Go out, look about," said Juba.

The boy sauntered out, pretending nonchalance, headed back.

"Okay," he said. "I see the white roofs of police cars at major intersections. As if they're . . . waiting for a signal."

"How will they come?"

"God, I don't know. Go to the car first, then sweep the mall."

From far off, five squad cars punched out in a squeal and roar as they raced into the lot and blazed toward the sector where the Impala was parked, led by what looked like an Abrams tank but was some kind of black SWAT thing, moving too fast for its treads but clearly a war machine. All over the perimeter, gumballs lit up as officers moved to restrict access at intersections. The helicopter roared inbound.

"Okay," said Juba, slipping his hand into the package he carried. "Little boy, you run away. When this is over, you surrender. You are no longer jihadi, you are kidnap victim."

Jared was struck by this sudden mercy. The man had human graces after all and didn't require of Jared his pointless death. But he knew it wouldn't work.

"Not with my size tens on Oprah's face. Come on, we can still make it out."

He pulled the larger man to him, back to the main corridor, where they veered toward the Walmart at the end of the mall, while Jared said, "Call your friends, tell them we'll be at the south end, down where the shopping carts are. The mall is hot, it's about to be cop city."

"No. I stay and fight. I take as many infidels—"

Jared saw his man walking down the corridor, methodically blowing up housewives and baby buggies and old guys with walkers until the State cops hosed him down with full auto. He'd have two hundred bullets in him.

"You don't have to die today. *Call them!*"

As they moved, Juba dialed the number and spoke rapidly to the responder.

They reached the maw of the big store and plunged into Walmart, skidded past people loading up for the next seven months, past the Chinese menswear and the

Filipino furniture and the Japanese electronics and the Brazilian shoes, turned hard, past many shoppers, skipped sideways and through the lines at the cash registers in front, hit the exit.

But instead of bulling his way directly out, Juba sidled up to a woman pushing a large shopping cart and said, in English, "I help," and smiling, showed a crown of white teeth. It was there that Jared noticed something for the first time: Juba was a strikingly handsome man, square of face, strong of jaw, and regular of feature, and, with the baseball cap off, his shock of thick dark hair turned him almost debonaire.

The woman—she hadn't been looked at by a man in decades, Jared guessed—lit up and instantly yielded to his charm. The two of them walked out into chaos, Jared a little behind but clearly a part of the same triad.

Sirens. Rushing, careening squad cars. Jared glanced northward, observed the Impala, surrounded by ninjas in black armor with subguns who'd just poured from a giant black armored truck, while squad cars with flashers and shotgun cops set up at every entrance.

They turned right, unconfronted, because as a self-contained, inward-directed family unit, they were off the cops' radar. They went to the curb, the feds too forward-oriented to look peripherally, too busy setting up exactly as ordered, too hungry for a genuine terrorist to notice them.

It would be seconds before more cops flooded the area, and now the olive chopper took over the auditory universe as its rotors beat the air on the descent. Risking a peek back, Jared saw it land two hundred feet from the Impala, and two more men hurtled out of it.

They stood there, naked to all eyes yet rendered invisible by the beaming woman, who was having the time of her life.

A van materialized before them.

"My dear, I must leave," crooned Juba, and gave her a kiss on the cheek. She sighed, having had a wonderful date, if a bit of a truncated one.

Men pulled them in and flattened them out.

"Lie in here," someone said, opening a hatch in the floor like the lid of a coffin, and they rolled in, seeing the light disappear as the hatch was closed behind them.

But Jared had gotten a glimpse of the save team.

They were Mexicans.

25

Greenville (III)

The sweep was done, and they had nothing.

"Fuck," said Nick.

"This guy's the best," said Bob.

"I know my people were on plan," said the colonel who supervised Ohio's Highway Patrol and stood with them near the garden at the center of the mall under plastic palm fronds and next to gurgling toxic water in a filthy open sewer among the palms' fake terra-cotta pots. "Nobody got out after we commenced our operation. There was just a few seconds there where the cars hadn't quite gotten to all the exits."

"Colonel, your people did fine, I'm sure," said Nick. "And a nod to Greenville, they helped too. I'm just thinking I should have sent the cover cars in first, without siren and flashing lights. When they were in position, we hit the Impala with SWAT."

"There was hardly time to consider everything," the colonel said. "The doors were covered within two minutes, maybe one. I don't know how anybody could have made it out."

"Anybody couldn't have. But this guy, he could have," said Nick.

The search continued, but now at a slower pace. Closets opened by heavily armed police, civilians cleared and let go, aisles and bins explored and probed, storerooms and break rooms penetrated. It might, it could, maybe it would, yield something—but neither Nick nor Bob held out much hope.

Meanwhile, FBI techs dusted the car for prints and in a fast first pass had come up with two of Juba's right thumb, and lots of others, which meant that one trophy of the operation—a consolation prize, to be sure—would be a whole set of prints. They also noted a pile of plastic grit in the well of the backseat and half the butt of a shotgun.

"He's cut it down for practicality," said Bob. "He can hide it better, pull it out fast."

Nick nodded, then he had to go back to the phone for the tenth time. This round, he was on it with D.C. for a long time, explaining, taking responsibility, offering his resignation twice, both times turned down, because the people there only were interested in one thing: what does Swagger think?

"They think you're a god. Don't worry, I won't tell them the truth. Anyway, talk to them." He handed the phone over.

"Swagger."

"You're on speakerphone with the Director and four

Assistant Directors and the head of the Counterterrorism Division," said the voice.

"What can I do?" said Swagger.

"Your read, please, Mr. Swagger."

"We almost got him. We know he was there. In my humble, Director, Memphis put together a brilliant plan on the fly and—"

"Swagger, no, leave that for later. Tell us where you think we are and what you think is next."

"I would just add that we have consistently underestimated this guy." *Oops, maybe that was selling out Nick. Can't do that.* "I mean, *I* have continually underestimated this guy. Everything we throw at him is nothing new. He's done it before. He doesn't panic, he doesn't quit, he improvises. He's a pro's pro."

"Your next move would be . . . ?"

"Well, I wouldn't set up roadblocks. He'll never give in to that. On top of that, we don't know who helped him split, and in what vehicle. He may be with another cell—four guys with light machine guns and RPGs, and if some country cops out in the haystacks bounce them, it could go to guns in a bad way, with a lot of people— cops and civilians—going down. The one thing we know is, he's got a cut-down Remington 1100 on him, and that's a big, bad toy. You don't want him going Remington on you, which is what he'll do if you corner him. You have to ambush him. You have to be there first, and let him walk into it, and take him hard, with overwhelming force. Still dangerous, but maybe one degree less so. So I'd go back to the brainiac stuff."

"Our analysts?"

"I think some hard thinking by your top people should come up with some possibilities that would narrow the search areas. Given what we think he's going to do, he's got to have certain things. We have to anticipate him. Along those lines, Nick wants to set me up with a computer genius. I think that's a good idea. I have a series of attributes he will need to have at his disposal to move on to the next step, maybe you could use that as some kind of index or filter, or something."

"All right, taken into consideration. Put Memphis back on."

So Nick talked to them for a few more minutes, and then a Greenville detective came up, whispered to a sergeant, who whispered to the colonel, who indicated something to Nick.

Nick ended the call.

"We've got them on surveillance footage from McDonald's. You guys want to take a look?"

It was him, no doubt. Not in the center of the frame, not in the cone of focus, but definitely a man of intimidation and danger. He sat in a booth just off the cash register and delivery counter and, by a twist of fate, facing toward the camera, while his companion, sitting across from him, was just the back of the head.

He wolfed down two burgers and a soft drink, seemed to savor the French fries, and looked to be engaging in conversation with the boy. Meanwhile, in a box in the corner of the frame, integers raced by that indicated number of frames and time of day.

"Looks like McDonald's has a fan," said Nick.

"Nobody don't like them fries," said Bob. "Freeze it, please."

They were in the mall security office, amid a bank of video screens, all of them recording and feeding from various key spots around the installation. The McDonald's had three cameras, because ruckuses were most likely to start in spots where teenagers gathered. Thus, all things considered, it was a pretty good show.

"We'll need to ASAP this to D.C. Our labs can enhance. Maybe we'll get a clearer picture, something we can put out. That would cut way down on his maneuverability and operational freedom."

Bob looked at the blurred image.

"Can you bring it up?"

"No, sir," said the mall security boss. "It's mainly meant for figuring out what kid hit what other kid."

"Got it," said Bob.

He stared at the image, but the more he bored into it, the more incoherent it became, until it was just a fuzzy mess of pixels, losing all form and content. What he saw was what he expected, but nothing actionable. His head was big; it went with his big frame and big hands, which were seen dwarfing the individual French fries as he ate them. He was clearly in command, but, in actual point of fact, he didn't look particularly fierce: a big guy, but no different from a million other men in other malls. Not bad-looking. Baseball cap—black, no insignia—a hoodie, jeans, the shoes not visible. Clean-shaven, not that fake tough look movie stars and podiatrists affected these days. Everybody wanted to look tough, while this guy, and all true tough guys, just wanted to blend in.

At one point, he sent the boy on an errand, got himself a cup of coffee, returned to the table, and just sat. He didn't appear to be unusually wary or agitated. It was clear he trusted the kid, who, after all, could have sold him out as a way of walking away from flattening Theola Peppers's face. But the kid was back, and the sack revealed—another freeze, thank you—that he'd bought a phone.

"Disposable," said Nick. "One call, then into the river. If we track the phone, the GPS signal just takes us to the river. Standard operating procedure."

The two rose to leave. Upright, Juba was large for his ethnic grouping, with that linebacker's body and the sparkle, the large and powerful muscles evident with each step, even though he was slightly pigeon-toed. He and the boy ambled out of Mickey D's, back into the world, all proteined-up for fresh outrage.

"Is that it?" Nick asked.

"One more segment we think is them. Another camera, looking down the hall toward the west parking lot exit, number 2B."

"Please," said Nick.

This one, at least, explained something. The two were shuffling nonchalantly to the doors, Juba with fourteen inches of sawed-off shotgun wrapped in what appeared to be a hoodie. They opened the doors, stepped out, the doors closed behind them, and—

A second later, they were back, their postures changed radically. Now their faces were clenched, in fear or anger, clearly alarmed, bursting with a palpable need to move or flee or pull guns on something.

"Freeze it," said Nick. "He saw us. The kid, I mean. Mr. Supervisor, as far as I can make out, that entrance looks directly east?"

"Yes, sir," said the security chief.

"That's exactly where we were laying off, goddammit. So the kid sees the chopper, and the plan is shot. Little fucker. Look at the time."

According to the data window, it was 16:13:34 p.m., thirty-seven seconds before the moment the SWAT truck and its five wingmen began to rush the Impala.

"Okay," said Nick.

The images started moving again. Juba was speaking urgently to the boy and seemed to reach into his package as if to unlimber the Remington and get ready to go to war. But the kid grabbed him and began to pull him. They advanced toward the camera—another freeze, unfortunately, didn't provide a better facial of either—and disappeared, clearly to exit, one way or the other, off camera.

"So the kid talked him out of going jihad on Greenville, Ohio," said Bob. "Saved a lot of folks from getting whacked."

"I'll be sure to mention it to his parole officer . . . Mr. Supervisor, that's it? You don't have any exteriors of these guys pulling away in the seconds before the squad cars arrived?"

"Nothing my people could see," said the supervisor.

Nick gestured to Chandler, who'd made it down by car and joined the party a few minutes earlier.

"Jean, I want people to go to every retail outlet on every street surrounding the mall and check the security cameras. Maybe somewhere there's coverage on who picked them up and in what kind of vehicle. Meanwhile, arrange for our tech people to get the stuff Supervisor Gray's cameras covered back to D.C. for analysis."

"Yes, sir."

Nick's phone rang. It was D.C.

"Fuck, not again," he said. "How many times can I resign?"

He slid it on, ID'd himself, said, "Yes," and listened, nodding. It was a detailed conversation, perhaps three minutes long. "Yeah," he finally said, "good. Late but good. But it points the way."

He hung up and turned to Bob and Chandler.

"It was Cyber Division. The kid emailed his buddy. Fifteen fifty-nine. Off a disposable. Juba sends him to buy a disposable, he does, but he sneaks in a quick update to Johnny Jones, to give his mom a heads-up. They just accessed the GPS to give us the location, which, unfortunately, is where we're standing right now."

"The jihadi who missed his mom," Swagger said.

"Yeah, but it's the pattern. Whenever Juba needs to make contact with whoever, he sends Jared out to buy a disposable. One call, then into the river. But Jared sneaks in an email or a call to his pal, to reach his mom, and we're on that. See, if we can nail the area, get our reaction team in place, ready to chopper to the site, we can nail him. That's how we've got to do it."

"So we've got to anticipate where he'll be," said Bob. "We get the area tight enough, everything falls into place."

"He'll do it again. He misses Mom. He'll always miss Mom. So you'll work with the computers to come up with a filter to pinpoint the area, we'll scour the wires for reports, and also look at it from the weapons acquisition point of view, all of which will point us to an area. The kid is the key to the whole thing."

26

The dream again. Now, after so long.

In this version, he is trapped. He is unarmed. He cannot move his arms. The American sniper smiles, fiddles, takes his time, locks himself into the weapon skillfully, slowly. He peeks up from the scope just for the pleasure of seeing it all laid out before him.

The flash.

Juba awoke. Where was he? It was dark, someone was near to him, he felt the closeness, the movement in and out of the other's lungs, their limbs tangled, the sourness, the vibration, the motion, they couldn't move, they were oppressed under some kind of lid. The coffin's?

"You are awake?" asked the boy.

"I am. We are still in the truck?"

"It's been so long, I hardly remember. I'm numb. I'm also very hungry."

"I'll tell them to stop for more French frieds," said Juba.

"French *fries*," the boy corrected.

At that point, at last, the lid above them raised.

Three men peered down at them, the silhouettes of their cowboy hats showing against the highway illumination.

"All right, my friends," said one in Arabic, "it's time to come out."

Slowly, hands helped Juba unwrap himself from the boy, supported him as he searched for power in his legs and arms, hoisted him clear so that he could almost stand, though his legs were soft and weak, and one momentarily gave out.

"Where are we?" he said.

The vehicle sped through the night. Outside, an occasional light slid by, nothing prominent, merely a sign of human habitation. He looked forward, saw nothing but the cone of headlights illuminating a road with a pair of lines down the middle of it. The lines flashed by like tracers. The beat of the engine came through to him, concealed under every surface he touched.

"We're going west," said the Arabic voice. It seemed one of the Mexicans was along as translator, for he had Arabic skills, and even in the dark, squinting, confused, Juba could tell that his face had significantly different features. He was some kind of transplanted Syrian, judging from the accent.

Next, they pulled the boy out.

"About time," said the kid. "I am so thirsty. Got anything to drink?"

"Who is this?" said the Syrian. "We were told only one."

"He is with me," said Juba. "He is fine."

Jared jumped in with, "I'm his go-between. I'm the guy who introduced him to America. I happened to be with him when the shit hit the fan, that's why I'm here."

"He is jihadi," said Juba, in English.

It was the best thing anyone had ever said about Jared.

They stopped, and a man ran into an outlet for food. Burger King, not McDonald's. Better hamburger, French frieds not so good.

They drove again, through the night.

The Syrian caught them up.

"We got you guys out just in time. How'd they know? Is there a leak?"

"This is what they do," said Juba. "It is their job. No leak, just them reading the signs."

"Maybe so," said the Syrian. "Anyway, we were stuck at a roadblock for a while, they were doing a search of vehicles headed out of Greenville onto the interstate. We thought we might have to use this."

He patted something on the floor covered with a tarpaulin, pulled the canvas back, exposing a Russian PK on a bipod, its long belt of 7.62 RPD gathered in a heap under the receiver.

"Bad news, but then a few car lengths before we got there, they tore it up and pulled out. I don't know why."

"The hand of Allah?" said the boy.

"Possibly they didn't want a gun battle on the highway," said Juba.

"Ever since, we've been driving without incident. The

radio says something about murders in Detroit, three dealers."

"It was necessary," said Juba.

"It's of no importance. All the same, I wouldn't return to Detroit any time soon."

"Who are you guys?" asked Jared.

"Cartel," Juba said. "They have the capacity to support my enterprise. They have been paid a great deal for their interest."

"You will meet Señor Menendez shortly," said the Syrian. "He is a great and powerful man. A visionary. With his might behind you, you cannot fail. We will also abandon this rattletrap van and continue our journey in comfort."

"Where are we going?" asked Jared.

"Little boy," said Juba, "you do not ask men like these such questions. They are professionals. You show them respect by allowing them to do their jobs."

"Anyway," said the Syrian, "you should know that all items you requested have been acquired and are where they need to be. Your rifle came in from Mexico with a recent large shipment and awaits for your hands to assemble it. You will not be bothered at the shooting range we have for you. All things will happen as they have been planned."

Juba sat back. He settled into the seat. He seemed, for the first time, without tension. The van rolled through the dark.

Dawn cracked the eastern horizon behind them. Gray light spilled from the sky. They shared the road with semi-trailers, a few SUVS, all of which flew by them in the left lane. Lights came and went, and the only sound was of men breathing. Jared was full of questions, but he asked none. Cartel? That bothered him. They were ruthless, had no ideology except greed, and became allies only via payment. But Juba clearly trusted them, and without them, he'd be sitting in a Greenville cell, waiting for his father's lawyer to arrive, wondering if he had the guts to take the fall for the woman or sell out Juba for less jail time. He hoped he never had to discover the answer.

They slowed, the blinker was activated, and the van left the highway, taking an exit, somewhere in the vastness of rural America. He wanted to ask, "Are we there?" but thought it a bad idea.

The van pulled into a farm, drove around the back of the house to the barnyard, where a large black SUV awaited. The van came to a halt.

The Syrian said, "Sir, that package still in the compartment, that is a weapon, no?"

"It is," said Juba.

"You must leave it there. You must not be armed in the presence of Señor Menendez."

"I understand. I have no other weapons."

"And you?" he asked Jared.

"No, of course not."

"All right, out. Enjoy the fresh air."

They climbed from the van, and indeed the fresh air seemed like a reward. Jared inhaled, almost becoming dizzy from the pleasure of it. He was still ticking, despite it all.

A man got out of the SUV and opened the back door. Another man got out, thin, handsome, Hispanic, of grandee heritage, in a well-tailored blue suit and black loafers. His Rolex was gold as were his tie clip and his cuff links. His teeth were white and perfect, his hair thick and well cut, his manner smoothly aristocratic.

"Sir," he said, "I welcome you. I am Menendez."

The Syrian translated from the English to the Arabic.

"It is an honor, señor," replied Juba.

"As you have been told, all is in waiting. From here on, things will go smoothly. Your visit is much anticipated."

"Excellent," said Juba.

"And this young man?"

"He is my assistant. Young but eager. Has proven himself in action twice during the past few days. Jihadi to the core."

"I am Menendez," said the grandee. "Welcome, and congratulations on your accomplishments. If you have impressed the great Juba, you have impressed me."

"Thank you," said Jared.

"You are a very brave young man," said Menendez. "And you are safe now."

He clapped him on the shoulder to point him on the path to deliverance, but the hand had a gun in it, and he shot the boy in the back of the head.

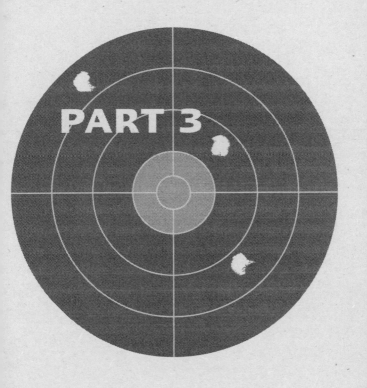

PART 3

27

Zombieland

It got big fast after Greenville and Detroit. It wasn't just the three murders; it was the concordance of the Juba prints with Israeli intelligence files, a wide circulation of his curriculum vitae at high echelons, as well as Juba's own awareness that he was being hunted. The zombie posse, as Swagger had christened them, decided to move into a larger operation.

Task force MARJORIE DAW ceased to exist. It was seconded to the Counterterrorism Division, which put unlimited manpower and computer time at the disposal of those hunting Juba. But the unit wasn't broken up. Instead, Nick and his assistant Chandler and consultants Swagger and Gold were moved to a suite of rooms on the Counterterrorism Division floor in the Hoover Building, and Nick had direct access to Ward Taylor, the Assistant Director in charge of CTD. They were to be the intelligence staff, the out-of-the-box thinkers, who provided guidance and zeal to the larger, more plodding operation. Taylor and Nick were friends. Taylor had worked under Nick in Dallas and done very well, while at the same time not being one of those guys who could never be wrong and had to get ahead or die. He was okay.

Swagger's first matter of business under the new setup was to meet with the computer genius Jeff Neill, another Nick ally from way back, and see what could be teased from the mysterious machines on the floor down one flight.

"Not much," Neill explained to him and Gold, whom Bob had dragooned for his elegant speech and manners. "Mr. Gold's people had a village name, therefore a specific area in southern Iraq. Their possibility index was quite limited, a few square miles. They didn't even have a program. They just took pix of everything."

"Our program was Mr. Swagger," said Gold. "He performed exceptionally well, up to the point of carrying an Uzi on a commando raid against the target."

"I wish we could get ours to do that," said Neill with a laugh. "But ours just sits there, hums and filters and occasionally freezes up."

"So," said Swagger, "if we run the attributes against imagery from the U.S. national weather satellites, we'll come up with too many."

"By a factor of several million, I'd guess. You need a more precise limiting function. The smaller, the better. Region: too big. State: too big. County: probably too big. Sector of county: now you're talking. We can task a bird to snoop it out, we can design a program to hunt for the things your eyes looked for and saw, all that shooter stuff, and we could probably find it. But until you get me that, I can't do much for you."

"Okay, I'll put that one on hold for a bit. Now, another question."

Bob explained about the sustenance of a long-range shooting program, via reloading tools, powder acquisition, premium bullets in .338 caliber, perhaps virgin shell casings, a chronograph, wind direction vanes, a Kestrel Pocket Weather Meter, perhaps a computer and app for solving the necessary algorithms for sight adjustment, as well as the optics and mounts and cleaning tools themselves, and other things too numerous and Mickey Mouse to mention. "Not available at your local Sportsman's Warehouse," he said. "A couple of retail outlets, one in Colorado, one in Pennsylvania, both of which also do considerable mail order, plus a bigger outfit, called Sinclair International, all of which service that community. It'll grow; we're lucky it's still pretty small. The big lick in competition shooting is something called Precision Rifle Competitions, popping up wherever there's room, the west mostly, but the big suppliers haven't really gotten on that bandwagon yet.

"If we can we get into their mail-order systems and determine if anyone has made a big purchase of this stuff recently. If we come up with something odd, we could check his name against the lists of competitors at various competitions and see if he's legitimate. If he checks out, okay. If not, if it's a sophisticated order from an unusual person—say, a city address, an address next to a mosque, something like that—then that would be worth looking into."

"You didn't come up with a question."

"Sorry, too tangled up in my own thoughts. The question—two of 'em, actually: Can we get into those records from here and is it legal? And if it's not legal, can we get away with doing it anyhow?"

"It's legal," said Neill. "We can put it before the FISA court for a ruling. FISA is the Foreign Intelligence Surveillance Act, passed in '78 but punched up after nine-eleven to give us some latitude in our pursuits. Juba is clearly a representative of a foreign intelligence agency, no matter who he's working for now. The Israeli documents prove that. So you'd work with Legal—Chandler'll set it up for you—and you'll draw up a request. It has to be tight, limited in scope, not a fishing license."

"I can live with that."

"It'll be limited in time, so you'd better have your team ready to hop in and ride hard. Once it's gone, it's gone. The act is designed to help you hunt for one thing and one thing alone, not as a general scouting expedition."

"I've got that."

"It's so much easier the Mossad way," sighed Mr. Gold. "We just do it and sleep well at night."

"You have an advantage," said Neill. "You're at war. We're playing a party game called Don't Make Anybody Mad."

The paperwork was expedited, the FISA ruling achieved, and at that point the Director of the Cyber Division ruled that Gershon Gold, of Mossad, was not cleared to assist in the search, being a representative of a foreign intelligence service, even though a friendly one.

Bob immediately resigned.

"Don't be ridiculous," Nick said.

"Who's being ridiculous? He's the best cyberguy in the world. A legend. That's why he's here. And now you're telling me he can't take an elevator down a story and sit at a monitor just like the one he has in Tel Aviv."

"That's what I'm telling you. It's federal law, and, in their way, the Cyber Division is right. If anything goes wrong and it is later revealed that we illegally let an Israeli national highly educated in cyberwar into our nerve center, that could be used against us by the usual sources. Different agendas here: you are trying to catch Juba, the Cyber Division is trying to ensure the Bureau's integrity and invulnerability to partisan or press attacks."

"Maybe Gold is the only guy in the world who can break this thing. Would you want them partisan jerks to know that he was sitting upstairs drinking bad coffee while we were fucking up downstairs, thirty feet, as the crow flies, from his instrument of war?"

"Cyber Division is playing the odds. It's the smart move, bureaucratically. Our smart move has to be to figure out how to get around it. Nothing personal against either man, it's just another obstacle we have to get over."

"Can we bring Ward Taylor in on this one?"

"Sure, but he'll tell you the same thing. He has to. He has no choice."

It was Gold who ended the contretemps.

"Sergeant Swagger, this battle is fought each day in every intelligence or law enforcement entity in the world. I have seen it at play in Mossad as well. We even have a nickname for it. We call it the Gray Foolishness. It can't be defeated, it can only be outsmarted. I would counsel you to waste no energy on this, and we will work out a way to get around it. The important thing, for both of us, is not what makes sense in this building but to catch or kill Juba before he brings yet more chaos and death to the world."

"That's what a grown-up sounds like," said Nick.

"So it's on me," said Swagger, "and I don't even know where to start."

So Gold gave Bob and Chandler a rough tutorial in the investigation they would have to run by themselves.

"You also must be skilled in pattern recognition, knowing that the little bit you learn here may seem meaningless, but it must not be discarded, as it might fit into some larger scheme and its importance become paramount."

"In other words," said Swagger, "I have to become a lot smarter than I am, and really fast."

That afternoon, Swagger passed into a top secret computer center, and then into a special room, where he and Chandler—she did the keyboard stuff, being younger and faster—went hunting in cyberspace.

Their targets were the mail-order customer lists of EuroOptic Limited in Montoursville, Pennsylvania, Mile High Shooting Accessories in Erie, Colorado, and Sin-

clair International in Montezuma, Iowa, all purveyors of
high-quality and high-cost equipment for the sport of
long-range shooting, the first two the only FFL dealers
of Accuracy International rifles in the United States.

"There are other marks," said Chandler. "Surgeon Rifles, JP Rifles, Cadex, Sako, MHSA. Savage is in the game,
so too is Ruger, at a much lower price point. How do you
know he didn't do one of those?"

"Well, I don't," said Swagger. "But my thinking is, AI
was the first and the most famous. It's also hard combat
tested, the others not so much. It was, most importantly,
the weapon system used by the British Corporal of Horse
Craig Harrison in his mile-and-a-half shot in Afghanistan in 2009. Juba would know that, he would have
heard of that, and, in the way his mind works, he wants
to duplicate that. Thus, he's going to put together a kit
identical, or nearly identical, to Harrison's '09 hit. That's
part of the intellectual appeal."

"What did Gold say?"

"He thinks it fits the personality—that is, the bastard's methodical way of thinking and doing. He ain't no
experimenter. He will very slowly and precisely follow
exactly what happened before, to get the same result,
with the when/where at his choosing."

"How about Mrs. McDowell? She's the world Juba
expert."

"You know, I didn't think to ask her," said Swagger.
"She was so worried that she hadn't done well in her
little undercover thing that I couldn't get it into the conversation. Want me to call her?"

"No, let's save her for when we're in a *real* jam."

"Makes sense."

"Gold is enough, I guess," said Chandler. "But one of the things we might look at is a history of sales, or specials, or something, from these outlets. The reason I say that is, maybe Juba didn't himself place the order but had some minion of whoever is working with him do it. And his agenda might be different. Maybe one of these places had a real good buy on Steiner Optics, and the guy decided to save five hundred bucks by going Steiner instead of Schmidt and Bender."

"Good point, Chandler. Damn, you're smart. Ever make a mistake?"

"Only once. I married a guy who thought I actually cared about sex."

"We fall for that one every damned time, don't we?"

"It was nothing a divorce couldn't solve."

A few minutes later, out of nothing but his cogitations, it happened: a palpable thought.

"Oh, and this," said Bob. "The rifle Juba's using, I'm betting, was stolen from somebody here in the U.S. It was probably a high-ranking competitive shooter. Now, that guy would also want the Harrison rig duplicated for exactly the same reason. Yeah, the other stuff might work, but Juba'd *know* the AI rig works. And so would the theoretical original guy. He's probably got some sniper buzz going on using the right stuff too, though he'd never admit it. So we have to look for a listing of stolen guns."

"Got it," she said.

The first stop, then, was the National Firearm Registry, a listing of all stolen guns. Wouldn't it be nice if someone had made off with the weapon of choice and that could lead right to the heart of the matter? But no such luck. A Barrett .50 caliber was the closest thing, but a quick call to the jurisdiction revealed that it had been recovered.

That possibility exhausted, they moved on to the sales records of the three companies.

First pass of all three sales records over the past five months—an arbitrary period, to be sure, but they'd go back further only as a desperation measure—yielded nothing of much interest. Filtering, courtesy of one of Neill's programs, for "Accuracy International .338 Lapua Magnum," they indeed encountered a cult based upon the worship of that rifle and that caliber. But all the purchases seemed to be more along the line of adding geegaws to the system—like dedicated cleaning kits, AI optical mounts, transit cases, wrench sets, a mirage band to stretch down the barrel and thus kill any reflection from its metallic surface, headspace gauges, bolt-cap-removal tools—all the little bitty Tinkertoys that so many in the culture told themselves they absolutely *had* to have.

"They're like little girls collecting Pretty Ponies," Chandler said.

None of the purchases was particularly big-ticket, none of them was absolutely mandatory to the shot, except for the scope, but Bob assumed that most of the shooters already had scopes, and, furthermore, granted the assumption that somehow Juba's rifle was initially stolen in America, it would have been scoped as well. None suggested someone trying to get into the AI .338 Lapua Magnum in a big way all at once. It was all about adding a little of this, a little of that.

"Any feeling or buzz?" asked Swagger.

"You're the rustic genius. I'm just the little grind who went to State U and got straight A's. I'm as creative as a block of wood."

"Let's filter for 'L.E. Wilson dies, .338 Lapua Magnum.'"

"What the hell is that?"

"If you want to reload for superaccuracy, it all turns on the accuracy of machining in the dies. Everyone in the game knows that Wilsons are the best. These guys will get every angle perfect to a hundredth of an inch. They're that good. Plus, Wilsons, not being screwed into a big, sloppy press, can be loaded at the rifle range on an arbor press—that's a hand-portable device—which makes it easier. It's not for high volume, but it's the one most of the benchrest guys use. It's very accurate, no wobble or slop in the construction, the parts fit like a Mercedes engine. More, I saw one in Juba's shop—bright yellow box, very compact—in the second before the guy lit it, and himself, off."

She typed it in, pushed Return, and in a few seconds the computer scanned, filtered, sorted, and presented nine purchases in the past five months of Wilson die sets—neck size and bullet seater—in the .338 Lapua Magnum size, plus specific neck-sizer bushings for the first die, three at .366, two at .367, and one more at

.368. From this they got nine names, which they ran against several data fields already in place, being the membership in the North American Long Range Shooting Association, which was the governing body of most of the matches, as well as entry in long-range shooting schools all across the west, part of the training craze in all the esoteric gun skills of Special Forces operators that currently gripped the shooting world. Of the nine customers, eight were in one or the other, the ninth being a wealthy South Carolina gun collector who was on the Board of Trustees of the NRA.

"Too bad it ain't him," said Bob, a little sourly. "The newspapers would go crazy."

"He's not the type?"

"I met him once. Rich guy, big in the NRA. He owns a batch of auto dealerships, and Subaru millionaires don't turn into jihadi terrorists."

"Good point," she said.

Eighteen hours in, and they had nothing.

"How much time left?"

"Six hours."

"We're not getting anywhere."

"Maybe we've proved there's nowhere to get. Maybe we've excluded a possible avenue of investigation. That's worth something."

"I suppose," he said, yawning, checking his watch. "Let's take a break."

"Sure."

They exited security and went back to their own floor. As it was night and rather late, the Counterterrorism Division was pretty much empty except for the operations sector, which always burned lights day or night. But they passed it, went to the lounge, meaning only to sit on sofas and mosey off into a private anywhere that had no Accuracy International mail orders in it.

"Mr. Gold!" said Bob, seeing the portly Israeli at the table, going through paperwork.

"Yes, hello."

"You're still here?"

"I thought I might be of some assistance."

"I wish you could be."

"You have had no luck?"

Chandler narrated their adventures, rearranging it efficiently so it seemed less random.

"Seems to be very thorough," said Gold.

"I thought we might have something on the neck-sizer bushings. But, no. All of them checked out. And that would be the one thing anyone running a .338 Lapua Mag program would definitely need to have."

"Yes, I see," said Gold.

"Any suggestions?" said Chandler. "We've got some time left before the FISA mandate runs out."

"Nothing of a practical measure. However, there remains a possibility."

"Yes?"

"Your subconscious has figured it out. It is trying to get you to pay attention. But your brain is clotted with meaningless things."

"Sounds like you're suggesting a drink. Only problem is, if I have one, I end up three weeks later in Calgary during the rodeo season, married to a calf roper with four kids."

It was a familiar line of his. Usually, somebody laughed. Not this time.

Chandler leaned back against the cushion of her seat and closed her eyes, as if to relax.

"All I see is my sisters' husbands trying to cop feels over a long, long holiday weekend."

"Any of 'em jihadi snipers?" Swagger asked.

"No, just doctors, lawyers, and one would-be poet who sells real estate. He's the worst. The poets always are."

So she got the laugh.

"All right," she finally said. "I am getting something on numbers. Three of them: 8-7-1."

"Are you of numeric imagination?" asked Gold.

"I'm of no imagination. I'm just good at math."

"What that means is that in the presence of numbers you are relaxed. Thus, there is less to oppose the flow between conscious and subconscious."

"Maybe. But I just see 8, 7, and 1, from somewhere, sometime—recently, I think. Don't know why, can't connect it with anything. Where would there be an 8-7-1? Swagger, do you recall that in our hunt?"

"Lots of numbers. Phone number, zip codes, catalogue numbers, calibers, trigger-pull weights."

She pulled out her iPhone, went to Safari, ran the number 8-7-1.

"It's not an area code," she said.

"Try a zip code. The first three numbers of a zip code."

She did.

"Okay, it's Albuquerque, New Mexico—87102 through 87123—twenty of 'em."

They let that lie for a second. Then Gold said, "Contiguous zones. So that would mean that no matter if the town or suburb were different, the physical sites could be quite close to each other."

"Yes, and what are the odds of so many different .338 guys living so close to one another? Probably, in the west, lower than elsewhere, but still pretty remote."

"Okay," she said. "Let's go back into Cyber Division and see what our 8-7-1 gets us."

28

The wheat

By midmorning, they reached the wheat.

It rolled for miles and miles to the horizon, golden, turning almost liquid by the wind rippling its surface, broken here and there by a farmhouse, a silo, maybe a stand of trees. Now and then, a huge red or green machine—thresher, combine, packer—moved like a heavy tank across the surface of the earth. The sky was blue and vast, the clouds hazy, the weather crisp and precise. He'd never seen wheat like this and was glad he now had.

These people may be infidels, he thought, *but they are excellent wheat farmers, maybe even better than the Russians.*

He said nothing. What would these Mexicans know about wheat? The answer was, nothing. It was an alliance of convenience—financial, for the one, and practical necessity.

Across from him sat the grandee Menendez, who

spent all his time jabbering in Spanish on the phone, perhaps dispatching orders to the far ends of his empire. Juba didn't know the details—no need to—but he knew the sort of man Menendez had to be and had no illusions about him. The matter of the boy, Jared, had made illusions impossible.

He didn't care for that. There had been no need. The boy had proven himself. He didn't deserve sudden death in a farmyard in someplace he'd never been in his life. But, at the same time, Juba was under mission discipline. He worked not for his intelligence masters or for the mysterious source of all the funding but for Allah. Allah required his self-control. And that is what he gave Allah, not Menendez.

Now Juba's life and mission were in the hands of this Menendez, for how many millions of dollars, one didn't know, and there was nothing to be done at this point except to go passive, offer no resistance, merely the softness of the sniper in him. He would observe, calculate, and record, and that would be enough—for now.

Beside Menendez was the one called Jorge, the translator, his face an odd mix of the Arab and the Mexican. What godforsaken, blasphemed union had produced such an offspring? He had the mealy look of a grub worm, obsequious and frantically obedient. He was disposable, a fact known to everyone except himself. He probably thought he was quite important, not realizing that the mere luck of his dual upbringing made him valuable to Menendez, but Menendez would squash him if the need arose. His face wore a perpetual expression of guarded optimism. He thought he was in with the big boys. Juba despised him on principle.

Meanwhile, he of course had no idea where he was—Kansas, from the little he knew, seemed about right—because he couldn't read the frequent highway signs, nobody spoke to him except for offers of food or drink, and he himself refused to betray his curiosity. In any case, it all changed when at a certain point they diverged from the highway into a small city, coursed through its outskirts, and arrived at a minor airfield.

"Now, my friend," said Menendez through Jorge, "it's time to move more quickly. I didn't feel it safe to divert to air immediately in the area of your escape, as airports would have been put under close observation. Where we are now, nobody notices anything."

Juba nodded.

They passed through gates, around empty parking lots, and arrived at a hangar. Nearby, a number of parked planes sat angled in the sun, all with their tails low to the ground, with props thrust skyward, all with glinting, bright steel, acrylic canopies of one configuration or another, riding plump tires and looking speedy though sitting still. But they continued on, and, instead, the driver took them to the end of the runway, where, already fueled up and its engines roaring, a sleek white twin-engined jet awaited.

As the car approached, the jet's cabin door opened and a stairway unfolded.

Menendez spoke by phone to whoever his necessary assistants were, then put his arm on Juba's shoulder and indicated the way toward the stairway. They walked to the plane, and, in seconds, both men were inside, in a plush tan-leather interior, attended by an unctuous steward, who offered alcoholic beverages—Menendez took a brown liquid over ice in a squat, wide glass; Juba refused politely, secretly annoyed that nobody realized the faith forbade liquor—and ushered them to seats.

They strapped in.

29

As it turned out, spread over the three retail outlets—EuroOptic, Mile High Shooting Accessories, and Sinclair International—there had been nine transactions that dispatched product to an 871×× zip code. Of the nine, three had received two shipments, so it amounted to six different addresses spread over the four Albuquerque area codes, but to a single name.

"Sounds generic," said Chandler. "Brian Waters. Mean anything?"

"Not sure," said Bob. "Maybe a whisper of a buzz. Keep going."

Taken together, the nine separate orders amounted pretty much to an advanced kit for the care and feeding of an Accuracy International .338 Lapua Magnum, but more or less camouflaged as a series of small orders of no significance.

"Here's an interesting one," Swagger said. "He orders

the Wilson bullet seater and neck sizer in one package, but he orders the .367 neck-sizer bushing in another. Yet for the system to work, you need both, meaning he's putting together the reloading kit but in increments that nobody would ever notice, save for Chandler's 8-7-1 pickup."

"So the implication is that 'Brian Waters' is putting together the reloading kit but wanted nobody to know it, particularly snoopers coming at it from cyberspace—namely, us."

"Not only that but this 8-7-1 has ponied up for a ballistic engine, that is, a handheld computer prekeyed with possibilities and algorithms for figuring out corrections for wind and distance. You pop in .338 Lapua Mag, Sierra 250-grain HPBT MatchKing bullet, 89 grains of Hodgdon H1000 powder. Wind south-southwest at one-half value, barometric pressure at 30.12, humidity at fifty-four percent, range: 1,922 meters. Push a button, and it gives you a solution based on your zero, which you've preentered. It'll say something like 'windage left: 12.7 mil dots, elevation: 14.44 mil dots.' You crank your knobs—elevation and windage—to that location and squeeze. Nineteen hundred and twenty-two meters away, something falls dead."

"I think we've connected."

"More here. To one address, a Whidden Bullet Pointing Die System. It's a new, hot lick by which you can 'sharpen' the bullet point, which assists greatly in long-distance shooting. And, if I'm not mistaken, this other thing is an electric annealing machine, by which you heat-treat prefired brass and make it more consistent."

"This guy must read all the gun magazines," said Chandler.

"No, this stuff ain't been in the magazines yet. He's that far ahead. And that fits in neatly with Juba's patient, plodding, one-step-at-a-time methodology, very thorough, not rushing, not making any mistakes. Both Mrs. McDowell and Mr. Gold make that point. All *t*'s crossed, *i*'s dotted. Not that he did the ordering, but he provided the operating plan and the security requirements to whoever was working with him on this."

"So here's my thought," said Chandler. "Let's run the addresses for each of the six locations and see what we turn up."

"Good move," said Swagger.

It didn't take long to pull the data free.

"No homes," said Swagger. "They're all FedEx Office or UPS outlets, all places that take packages for people."

"Yes, and though usually those places rent you a post office box," she said, "in this case Brian Waters requested or paid extra not to list a P.O. box but just the street address of the little shop. I suppose that was part of the camouflage operation."

"Yeah, and, moreover, most mail-order places won't ship to post office boxes, only to residential addresses. But it's not a rigorous system. The guy at the sending end isn't going to check. If it's just an address, he doesn't have the time or the interest to make sure the street address is a house, not some retail thing."

"Well, let's run the credit card number that paid for all this stuff."

Another quick discovery: Brian Waters again.

One man with six addresses, each FedEx Office unknown to the other five, had ordered all the goods.

Swagger went to his list of competitors.

"He placed highly in the thousand-yard championships at the NRA range in New Mexico. He's a shooter. They had to use him as the fulcrum of their operation, alive or dead, probably dead."

He thought of this fellow. Shooting geek, maybe a little private money, lived for nothing more than putting five .338 bullet holes inside a couple of inches at a mile. To what purpose? If you weren't a sniper, it had no purpose, it was just damned hard to do, and he had decided he'd become one of the few men in the world who could do it on demand, off a cold barrel. That's all his life was: he lived in a world of numbers and weights, and certain refined body movements, and one night someone snuck in and put a silenced bullet through his brain. They took his rifle and reloading stuff and shipped it secretly to Syria, where a cold-minded fellow named Juba became him, mastered his rifle, learned his tricks, all with some dark purpose in mind that would leave a lot of other people dead. Swagger shivered.

Mrs. McDowell wants you for her son. The Israelis want you for the bus. The Marine Corps wants you for Baghdad. But I want you for the shooting geek, who never did no harm and got sucked up and spit out for something he couldn't understand.

"Now he's here, he's got the rifle, he's used the credit

card to reorder the stuff he had in Syria but was too bulky to smuggle in. So they've been replacing it."

"Whoa!" she said. "Isn't that leap a little far?"

"No," Swagger said. "His name was Brian A. Waters. In the burning shop in Syria, I saw his gun case in the second before the flames took it. I saw the two initials, *A* and *W*, the *B* was already roasted. They need a pigeon. He's the pigeon. Somehow, some way, this is going to turn on him. I mean, what good is an assassination conspiracy without a Lee Harvey Oswald?"

30

The ranch

The jolt of landing awakened him. No dreams of American snipers this time. Instead, he saw the blank look of existential nothingness on Jared's face as he went down, bullet in head. This was fiction. As Jared had been turned, Juba had not seen the expression, and the flash of the pistol's cartridge from the muzzle did not illuminate it. Still, awaking, he could not shake the grief and the hurt, which surprised him. Mission discipline, he ordered of himself: push it all out, make it go away.

He shook his head and came fully awake as the plane came to a halt.

"Enjoy the nap?"

"Yes."

"It's not far now."

The steward opened the door, sliding it sideways on its rollers, then pushed a button to lower the stairs. As the door cracked, bright light flooded in. Juba blinked, but felt the rush of natural air, warmth with perhaps a tang of grass to it, a suggestion of wildflowers. He stepped out to cooler temperatures and a sense of being engulfed by mountains. They were everywhere, green and lofty, some cragged with solemn old faces, others, higher up, still capped with snow. It was a small airport somewhere, presumably for rich people, as the other planes on the ground all seemed to be jets, with swept wings and sporty paint jobs featuring impressions of blur, speed, lightning, and other symbols of modern, comfortable transportation for the elites.

A Land Rover waited, with its driver inside. Next to it sat a Mercedes S, with four men deployed, well-dressed, but of the thick variety that reminded him of the American contractors in Baghdad, standing about, hands loose. Bodyguards, they'd have weaponry secured in the vehicle, quick to come out or packed against their bulked-up bodies. All wore sunglasses, all had snail earplugs, all watched warily, not the arrival but the horizon, for threats.

"Now, my friend," said Menendez, "it's just this last little bit, and you will have everything you require, most of all absolute security and privacy, as required."

"I am very impressed with your preparations," said Juba.

"We are bigger than many Fortune 500 companies," said Menendez. "I am proud to say our growth, though stymied at times, has been remarkable in the past several years. There is money for everyone. I know money means little to you, and politics everything, but it is only with money that political ends may be achieved."

"True. But that's not my concern. I leave it to others.

Allah has seen to give me a gift for a certain kind of war and I will use it in the infidel heartland to strike a vital blow."

"And that is why I am so eager to assist. The money, it's nothing. It's the ends, really, that make all this so interesting."

They climbed into the Land Rover, and the S fell in behind. The convoy set off along roads through a valley, beneath the peaks on either side, and again, in more time than he expected, drove and drove and finally reached a gate of no particular interest.

"From the road: nothing," said Menendez.

The car passed through and rolled down a one-lane blacktop, climbed a small hill. There it encountered a second perimeter, this one of barbed wire, with a sentry post at its locked gate. Two men with M4s, also sunglassed and earplugged, operated the gate to let the two cars pass. They surmounted the crest and started downward.

Juba had no sense of architecture and had no way of knowing the elegant log mansion in the valley before him was famous and dated back to Teddy Roosevelt's time, though of course it had been much upgraded. In fact, TR had stayed there on one of his many western hunting trips. To Juba, it was just an immense log house, and his idea of a palace involved marble columns, cupolas, and gold fixtures. This building reminded him of cowboy movies he had seen as a boy, all juts and angles, with gables and balconies in roughly cobbled wood.

Jorge the translator was kept busy, as this Menendez, after so much silence, had much to say.

"If the editors of *Architectural Digest* understood who owned the famous Hanson Ranch, they'd be stunned. Especially if they comprehended that it was their own children's enthusiasm for our product that paid for it."

The grandee was a man of boastfulness. He could not help himself.

"I own several houses—Mexico City, Acapulco, Cap d'Antibes, the U.S. Virgins, even Malaysia—but this is my favorite. It is very private. A small army guards it. Come, you'll see."

Juba had no interest in a tour, but he had been raised in the tradition of hospitality and pretended to appreciate the rooms through which he was led. He saw lots of tribal patterns on the walls and floors, brown-leather furniture of the heavy sort, paintings of bears and mountain lions and prairies and cowboys, sculptures of animals— what was "an original Remington"?—and a glistening gun cabinet, presumably full of the famous American Winchesters.

"This will interest you," said Menendez.

He opened the gun case and pulled a weapon out— but it was no Winchester.

"I keep it to remind me of how I got here," Menendez said. "Of course, it reflects the gauche tastes of the Mexican peasantry, but what it lacks in class it makes up for in earnestness."

Jorge had trouble with "gauche," but Juba didn't care. Menendez handed him the gun.

It was an AK-74, but plated in gold. It was also encrusted with diamonds and rubies in a somewhat primitive array along the receiver, as if dribbled into place by a child. It glittered with surreal brilliance, the two themes—lethality and decadent bad taste—making even less sense than the mistranslated word.

"It was presented to me by my former competitors, now vassals, when my absorption of their organizations became complete. It is an object of veneration, respect, and, I suppose, fear. The gems, by the way, are real, and the gold is indeed twenty-four karat. Estimated value: about three million dollars. A fighter like you would think, what a waste of rifle! A connoisseur like me would think, what a waste of three million in diamonds! But to the men who gave it to me, it had real meaning, and, thus, I keep it, enjoying it both literally and ironically."

This made no sense whatsoever to Juba, but much of what the slick and sophisticated Menendez said made no sense. He did get that it was in some sense special.

"Magnificent," he said. "But, then, I would expect no less from a man of such accomplishment."

"Yes, yes, appreciated. But I know you yearn to see the shop we have built and equipped for your work and the ranges to which you will have access. But first"—he gestured emphatically—"this fellow will be seen lurking about. He is my body man, my most trusted bodyguard, my assistant, a very large part of what I do and how I do it."

A lithe but powerfully built man appeared at a door, advanced to Menendez, and bowed. Like the others, his duty uniform was a well-fitted black suit; like the others, a radio wire ran to his ears; like the others, he crackled with messages of skill and intensity; but, unlike the others, he was wearing a tightly fitted black hood, its tightness more akin to a sock than a hood. Only his eyes showed.

"As a part of his commitment to his craft, Señor La Culebra prefers to keep his face mysterious. He values his anonymity. He will always see you before you see him. He has the gift of cunning, stealth, and grace. He would have made an extraordinary sniper, but his hunger is to kill at more intimate levels, with the blade, at which he excels. His skill level is perhaps the world's most dangerous. Policemen, detectives, journalists, competitors— they have all been awakened by the hiss of their own throat being cut. His very presence at my shoulder is an extraordinary asset when I am in meeting with my peers. Of course, when I meet with, say, my fellow suburban Los Angeles Subaru dealers and Carl's Jr. franchise holders, I leave him in the car, behind tinted glass. He is not for the bourgeois."

"My respects to such a talented man," said Juba, nodding in greeting.

The hooded man nodded back, his eyes intense behind the slits of the hood.

That ceremony completed, Menendez led Juba first to a bedroom—nice, but Juba had no interest in bedrooms—and laid out eating arrangements, as well as laundry and maid service, and then out a back entrance, through a garden, across a stable yard, where Mexican boys could be seen exercising and otherwise caring for some beautiful horses, and finally to a small, corrugated prefab cottage, clearly temporary.

"Sir," said Menendez. "To your liking, I hope. If not, corrections will be made."

Juba took the key and entered.

It appeared perfect. Every item he ordered was displayed on a heavy worktable against the wall. He went quickly to the heart of it, the yellow packaging from L.E. Wilson, and saw several containers of neck bushings that ran from .366 to .368, as well as the crucial boxes containing neck sizer and bullet seater. Another box contained a Whidden bullet-pointing die, to sharpen the tips of the missiles themselves, and they were close by, boxes of Match bullets from Sierra, Nosler, Hornady, and other makers, all .338 Match grade. Next to the bench was packaging from Oehler, signifying a high-grade chronograph, to measure velocity. And an iPhone 8, lying on the bench. Seemingly innocuous, it had been programmed by its original owner with data onto a ballistic app, the Hawkins Ballistics FirstShot software, which offered instant solutions to the equations that ruled the universe of long-range. Canisters of smokeless powder, bright as pennants leading the Saracen army, stood on higher shelves, and a brand-new arbor press, as well as boxes of Federal 215M large-rifle Magnum primers, chamfer tools for both neck and primer hole, seven reloading manuals—all had been placed around the central icon in what was almost a crèche of infidel devotion.

And its icon was a rifle.

31

The zombies were hungry. Pink-faced, blue-suited, white-shirted, red-tied—they sat around the conference room table, champing their jaws, screaming for flesh, starved for protein to be washed down by blood.

They were the creatures Bob had always hated. So far away from it, so sure, so absolute, so magnificent, so clean of fingernail: who could not hate them? If you lived behind wires and sandbags, and shit in a hole and got shot at a lot, it was mandatory to hate zombies—not these particular ones but zombies as a class. Yet where would the world be without its zombies?

"All right, Nick," said the head zombie, "who, what is, and why should we care about a Brian A. Waters of Albuquerque, New Mexico, who has no record and no footprint, and, by all accounts, is a pleasant, accomplished, well-respected fellow?"

"Mr. Gold, would you speak to that?" Nick said, then checked for zombies who had trouble keeping up. "Swagger found Brian Waters, but Mr. Gold identified him as only a theoretical possibility, so Swagger worked off that, isn't that right, Bob?"

"Completely," said Bob.

Gold was not a zombie. Somehow being an Israeli meant you could never be a zombie. Swagger wasn't sure by what principle this was, but it was a principle nevertheless, perhaps having to do with all the shit they'd been through, their tenuous grasp of survival, and perhaps most of all the subtle intensity that underlay the Israeli faces, as opposed to the theatricality of these American intelligence and enforcement executives.

"Gentlemen," said Gold, "it has to do, eschatologically, with the different meanings of terror in the Middle East and here in the West. In the Middle East, terror is force. It is about killing lots of people as efficiently as possible. In the West, terror is metaphor. This is a feature of asymmetrical warfare at its purest. It is not the act itself, tragic though it may be, but the resonance of that act in the public imagination. The West cannot be destroyed through numbers; it must be destroyed through its imagination. Its capacity to fight will not be eliminated, but its will to fight can be, and that is the object.

"Thus, this operation against the United States, extravagantly budgeted, extravagantly planned, extravagantly slow in gestation, is not merely about killing a certain high-value target. It is about subverting via its brutal didacticism. It means to be 'a Big Event,' in the way the assassination of John F. Kennedy was a Big Event. It means to resonate for decades, to haunt and cripple and dispirit. In order to do that, its execution is not enough. It must have arrived caparisoned in legend, and it must reveal a perpetrator of legendary proportions."

"A patsy, is that what you mean?" asked zombie 4.

"Exactly," said Gold.

"How does Mossad see it accomplishing this goal?"

"It's not merely that the sniper kills. It's that the blame is put upon a certain figure, and that figure must have status and meaning of disturbing weight."

"And that would be Brian A. Waters."

"Exactly. He cannot be a piece of unimpressive trash like Lee Harvey Oswald or James Earl Ray. His meaning must be immediately accessible. The press must uncover— or think that it is uncovering—a paper trail of meaning. What that meaning will be, we don't know yet."

"Sounds like they want to do Dallas again."

"But better. This time, controlled, managed, brilliantly syncopated. These people are very clever, and in Juba the Sniper they have found the ideal instrument of their will. And in the unfortunate Mr. Waters, they have found the ideal vessel."

"Agent Chandler?" said Nick.

"He is, or was, forty-two years old," said the perfect one, "born in Corpus Christi, Texas, with a superior technical education at Texas Western University and a master's in petroleum geology from Rice University. Four years working for Phillips in the Geology Department, fast promotion, excellent reputation. In 2004, he resigned, though he was next in line to take over the division, and opened his own survey-and-development company. Fabulously successful, and in six years he sold it for seventeen million dollars. Never married, no kids obviously, a man of extreme intelligence, self-discipline, and drive. Well, I should say, he *did* marry. He married a rifle.

"His obsession is long-range precision shooting, and he bought land enough in New Mexico for a mile-long range, as well as a collection of rifles capable of accuracy at that distance. He's spent the last eight years on an odyssey to put five holes in a bull's-eye a mile away. It's been done by about fifty men, Mr. Waters hopes to be the fifty-first.

"He has no vices, no politics, no angers, no hatreds, has never said a bad thing about anybody on earth that we can find. But he is an isolate. Being entirely alone with his obsession, he is perfect prey for men who would use him. And we feel he has been used."

"Do you believe he is dead?"

"Yes, sir. Well, dead in reality. That death is not known. To his few friends and neighbors, he's simply disappeared, but he disappears a lot. He travels all over the world to shooting matches, he hunts in Africa and Asia and New Zealand, he goes to conferences. His friends are elite shooters, the world over, who share his obsession and speak his language."

"What is his current official status?"

"He—or somebody with access to his email—has announced to his friends that he's going on a hunting trip in Southeast Asia and will be incommunicado for several months. We have checked with every known outfitter, and he is not on any trip docket. He has applied for no visas or hunting permits in any Southeast Asian country. His house is closed and locked, a lawn service attends to the yard once a week, prepaid via the Internet. He has vanished, but without any alarm being raised. That is why our hope for his survival is so low. It would be so much easier for them to kill him, help themselves to his life, and use him as an avatar to their purpose under a false flag. So he is being kept alive—well, not physically, but by reputation and counterfeit footprint."

"Is there any evidence or is this just a working assumption?"

"Well, sir, no physical trace—that is, face-to-face, eyewitness accounts—have been documented with him in several months. Physically, he seems to have vanished from the earth."

Nick continued, "We believe that a part of this operation is to implicate him as the perpetrator of whatever crime it is that Juba the Sniper means to accomplish. A 'legend,' as those of you with intelligence experience will recognize, will be or is being created, and a paper trail will be uncovered, skillfully counterfeited by the best covert people in the world, to suggest that he did this, he did that, he believed this, he believed that. All of that information will play in a certain way to create a certain meaning—certain ramifications. That is why we must stop this thing."

"Since we seem to know he's being used, it seems like we can quickly counter any—"

"May I?" said Gold. "Nothing is *known* these days.

All fact is conditional. Modern media allows any interested party to influence millions of people. Who brays the loudest or frames the most skillfully or feeds prejudices the most earnestly is the most believed. False news—particularly if it is backed with credible journalistic sources, as uncovered by reporters who believe they're doing God's work. We will be telling another version of a story, and who's to say ours is better than theirs?"

"Where are you now?"

Nick ran through it: the guise of looking for Juba as a triple murderer and the boy as a felony assault perp in Detroit, which enabled circulation to all law enforcement agencies, as well as maximum social network and media exposure. The penetration of long-range shooting culture to obtain any hints of unusual activity that might have indicated preparation for the shot Juba was to take. The monitoring of criminal enterprises—cartels, more traditional mobs, gangs, crews, paramilitary organizations—for indicators of unusual activity in support of such an operation. The use of satellite technology to discover shooting-range layouts on private property that might also support Juba's enterprise. The hunt for traces of "Brian Waters," for provocative statements and clues meant to establish his legend but which might lead to their creators. Finally, the alerting of all field office SWAT teams for high readiness so that apprehension or interdiction could commence immediately upon acquisition of a breakthrough in the hunt.

"Counterterrorism is in on this?"

"Yes," said zombie number 9, who happened to be

Ward Taylor, division chief and Nick's pal and ally. "Assistant Director Memphis has been extremely solicitous of our participation. No turf wars from Nick, I'm happy to report."

"Good, I like that," said zombie number 1. "Now, Memphis, CIA liaison?"

"No, sir."

"They won't be happy."

"I suppose you could say, 'Too many crooks spoil the broth'"—a little laughter at Nick's pun—"but there's more: CIA involvement doesn't complicate matters by two but rather to an exponential degree. Their agenda can be so murky that even they don't know what it is, and it can vary, week by week, or even office by office or cubicle by cubicle. It's not that I don't trust them—it's that I don't trust them. When the time comes, we'll be happy to go to them."

"What about Secret Service? If the target should turn out to be Executive Branch—"

"That's when we'd come to them. At this point, to alert them to the possibility is simply to set up leaks."

Zombie number 1 nodded. "Your next move?"

"I want to put a clandestine forensics team on the ground in Albuquerque. I don't want our mobile lab units and three hundred technicians showing up at the closed-down Waters house. I need to get a good workup on what is missing from his house, I want to know if there are any forensic discoveries that could lead us another step—prints of any sort, DNA, who knows whatever clues. But I don't want them to know we've picked up on this. If they do, they'll take steps to cover further footprints, they'll enter a higher state of vigilance, and they may alter their plans. We want them confident that they've evaded for now, which will give us time to track them down, then we'll jump."

"Mr. Swagger, you've been hunted. You're also a rifleman of great skill and experience. Where is Juba now? Mentally, psychologically?"

"He's happy as he's ever been. He's made his getaway, he's got his rifle, he's working with it, which for a man like Juba is not a duty but an obsession. A pleasure. He's a sniper with a target, and a sense of importance and contribution, according to the tenets of his faith. He's one happy boy."

"Your job is to make him unhappy," said a zombie.

"Swagger's a sniper," said Nick. "Unhappiness is his business."

32

The shop, the ranch

The rifle is not beautiful. Its designers yielded on aesthetics from the very start. They knew and loved the look of rifles—the sweep of dark wood, the glow of deeply blued metal, the grace, the symmetry. It was in their blood, but they knew, as well, that they had to ignore that siren call. Theirs was a single-minded objective, not dedicated to the kill so much as to the shot. There was no kill without the shot and thus the shot was everything.

The rifle acquired the configuration of a prosthetic limb with a hole in it, and two giant tubes organically absorbed into it. The hole afforded the shooter's trigger hand purchase on the grip, just under the bolt. Its placement was not arbitrary, its angle was not arbitrary, its size was not arbitrary, nothing was arbitrary. Everything was designed, tested, adjusted, and retested, before it became part of the specifications. The stock behind the thumbhole was itself a spectacular construct: it was a monstrosity of bulbous swellings and pads, all in play at the convenience of screws. They could be adjusted almost infinitely, so as to fit length of neck, arm, and hand, the thickness of shoulder, breadth of chest, strength of muscle, firmness of grip. All human variables were accounted for, and the shooter before he took his first shot needed to find the ideal harmony of parts, so that the whole fit to and against his body and took advantage of his unique skeletal alignment and musculature. All these adjustable parts were issued in high-strength plastic, giving the thing in question the dull gleam of, perhaps, reptile skin, something without warmth or life. It was not meant to be loved, but respected. It was not meant to please the shooter's heart, but the intelligence officer's, the general's, the president's, the mullah's. It was policy as firearm.

All angles machined into it were true. All springs of the finest metals. All steel of that superb blend of strength and flexibility. The trigger was almost as soft as a woman's most private part, and it took a refined finger that had already pulled a trigger a hundred thousand times to nurse the finest action from it. People don't realize how much of the gun is about the machinework and what miracles a man who has spent his life shaving pieces of metal to an exact measurement can do. The receiver is epoxied and bolted into the stock, so that the hold is again true, so that no oddities of alignment will haunt a shooter years on down the line. You could use it as a hammer and build a house with it, though to its owners such a thing would seem a desecration. The barrel—barrel making is an art in and of itself—drew even more attention than the other parts, because the barrel, that long steel tube embracing the supersonic missile driven down its bore toward the target, couldn't be merely excellent, it had to be perfect. Perfect is never cheap, neither in effort nor cost. The men who made the barrels had practiced their crafts for years in such British houses as Purdey or Holland & Holland or Westley Richards. They knew the interior dynamics of steel and how it responds when grooves are engraved along the tube's polished interior. They hunted with spectroscopes for inner flaws that might play hob with vibrational patterns, because they knew the vibrations must be true as a violin's strings to deliver the kind of accuracy that they demanded. None of this happened easily, but only after so much experimentation, so much trial and error, all of it piled atop the years of experience.

Then came the scope. It was German, as are all the best optics, a thirty-four-millimeter tube of aluminum, steel, plastic, and polished glass, studded with dials that control adjustments for magnification, focus, windage, elevation, even a laser whose pinprick of red light focused on the target's center, making it stand out to the shooter's eye in the dark world of the lens. Its magnification runs from a power of 5 to 25. And the internals on such an instrument are dazzling, as is the machinework that makes everything not merely function but function smoothly as if sheathed in petroleum lubricant so that the sliding between focal distances or in and out of magnification is accomplished without notice by the adjuster. All scopes do this reasonably well, but the S & Bs do it better.

But, of course, the scope does not make all things copasetic. For if the scope magnifies the target, it also magnifies you. That means every tremor, tremble, or twitch, every breath, sniffle, gulp, burp, or fart, is instantly transmuted into action. Accuracy demands mastery of these animal impulses, which a few can achieve but most cannot. And the farther the range, the stiller the body attempting to engineer the connection must be. It is no small thing, and a Juba or a Bob Lee Swagger or any of the great rifle killers have subsumed stillness to a transcendental level. It is a skill that even with talent takes years to master, a discipline that clamps steel expectations on something so prehensile and spontaneous as a human body. Take the trigger finger and the little twitch that fires the weapon: so easy, yet so hard. You can do it a million times and fuck it up on one million and one. Why? Because for the greats, it is a part of their identity, yet beyond knowing, becoming that way only by those endless repetitions, in concert with breath, muscle, and sheer willpower.

He now opened a package and removed a cartridge. Remington—green-and-gold box—.338 Lapua Magnum. He would of course not use factory ammunition in his shot, for so much more could be gotten out of a hand-loading program, half of which he was already through. Still, the round itself was instructive, even inspirational. It seemed like a small missile, heavier by far than one expected, more than three inches long and almost half an inch wide. It was dense, far heavier than it looked, and indeed it looked heavy. It also looked absolute, without any softness about it. It was a serious thing—in its way, more serious than anything.

He held it in his hand, feeling its cool weight against his palm. He turned it to look at the perfect concentricity of the rim, the primer in the perfect center of the head, which was a perfect center again. He traced the smoothness of the brass, with its slight taper, as it rose to the shoulder, where the cartridge reduced itself and formed a neck to sustain a bullet. The bullet itself was all seriousness—copper sheathing over some kind of lead alloy, again concentric to an extreme degree. These bullets were from Sierra, a world-class expert, and since the ammunition was premium, no expense had been spared in achieving their perfection. He looked at the shanks of the thing, admiring the perfect grace of its curve in accordance with the laws of streamlining, the smoothness of the skin, for a nick or a gouge might throw it from true to meplat, as the technical call the tip, and saw again concentricity as a small hole that precludes the tip from becoming a point, absorbing the rushing atmosphere as it flies, and work, with the spin facilitated by the grooves in the rifle's barrel, stabilizing it during its time in flight before it arrives exactly at its destination, for better, for worse, for whatever purpose filled the head of the shooter.

The statistics of the event are impressive. Muzzle velocity is near twenty-five hundred feet per second for a 250-grain bullet, the kind Juba would shoot, and at the muzzle it delivers 4,813 pounds of energy. It was with such an instrument that the British infidel Craig Harrison had killed in Afghanistan at a distance of 1.54 measured miles.

Now what remained? He'd continue his development, having found three loads of three different powders, three different seating depths, and two different primers that were superior to all the others. Now he could shoot at eleven hundred yards, twelve hundred, thirteen hundred, moving a hundred at a time, easing his way so that what seemed gigantic at the start seemed tiny by the end. He knew how far he had to shoot. He knew where the sun would be, what the temperature should be, what the humidity should be, what the velocity of the breeze should be. All these facts had to be factored in until he could do it on the first shot, cold bore, over and over again. Because on the day when the time finally came, after all the months of preparation, he would have only one chance to speak for God.

33

Zombieland

S wagger went on the raid, just as he had gone on the raid in southern Syria with the Israeli commandos. But unlike that episode, this one was strictly routine.

The house and property of Brian A. Waters were deserted. The Bureau team entered from overland, a mile away, after midnight, using night vision. No problems. A law enforcement–affiliated locksmith cracked the door easily, pointing out to Swagger that it had been cracked before, as evidenced by the toolmarks on the lock. That meshed perfectly with the assumed scenario.

Two gifted dogs quickly searched for explosives and drugs and found none. Once inside, the investigators used their infrared to discover that Brian Waters was systematic, neat, organized, thorough. His books, CDs, and DVDs, for example, lay on shelves in perfect, parade-like dress, alphabetized. There were books on American history, books on marksmanship, riflery, the history of the rifle, company histories, anything about the gun.

There was no porn, nothing at all of a salubrious nature. This was a man dedicated to and caring for one thing: rifle accuracy. To that end, he had no family, though pictures of his nephews—towheaded boys frolicking in a backyard—were arranged perfectly on a shelf in the living room. They lent a certain human dimension—a little anyway—to a room otherwise without character and style. He seemed to have no tastes or eccentricities. It could have been a rental, for all the home furnishings revealed. Only his framed NRA Life Membership and certificate proving he'd gone Distingushed Expert–Rifle suggested an ego. These hung in perfect symmetry over his bed.

The killers—ISIS, the Iranian Ministry of Intelligence, ex–CIA contractors gone rogue, *cartelistas*?—had probably put a .22 bullet, suppressed, into his brain as he slept. No signs of a struggle, no signs of anything being neatened up after a struggle. The agents took his pillowcases for analysis, hoping to uncover microscopic traces of blood from the shot.

The shop could have been a museum. Again, the neatness was spooky, and it indicated why Brian Waters had never brought a woman into his life: no human being could live up to his standards of precision. Swagger noted that his many yellow boxes containing L.E. Wilson neck sizers and bullet seaters were arranged in ascending order by calibration, beginning with the humble .222 Remington, America's first dedicated varmint cartridge, and working up to the gigantic .458 Lott elephant bouncer. But again, his neatness had tripped up his murderers and fooled them into leaving behind traces of their presence;

when they'd plucked out the .338 Lapua Magnum boxes, they'd been smart enough not to leave a gap by pushing the remaining boxes together to hide the missing ones. However, they'd done so sloppily, so that the row was slightly out of whack, the boxes not perfectly dressed on one another. Waters, Swagger already knew, would never have done such a thing.

The locksmith cracked the gun safe without much trouble, and Swagger examined the firearms that had captured Waters's imagination. He seemed to have a nice collection of vintage 1911 target pistols, as upgraded by the armorers attached to each service's marksmanship units: from army, marines, navy, and coast guard. He had other .45s from masters of the bull's-eye craft like Jim Stroh, Armand Swenson, Bob Pachmayr, and Jim Clark, on up to modern masters of the craft of building a handgun that could put five into an inch at fifty yards, offhand.

The long guns were equally to the point. He liked sniper rifles, and had one each of the chosen weapons of Our Boys since War 1: a Springfield, a Winchester Model 70 with Unertl, an M1D, a Remington M40 from 'Nam that Swagger knew well, and an M14 with Leupold 10× scope, which the army folks had chosen. Not quite so comprehensively, he had variations of other countries' War 2 choices: an Enfield .303 No. 4(T), as sniperfied by the geniuses at Holland & Holland for the Brits; a Mauser 98 with a Hensoldt scope on a claw mount and with SS runes on its receiver, making it not Wehrmacht but genuinely Nazi. He even had a Barrett .50, looking like an M16 after years of pumping iron, which had proven so useful in Afghanistan, and when it delivered, it landed with such force that the guy on the other end usually pinwheeled through the air, he had so much energy loosed against his poor bones. But, of course, no Accuracy International, in .338 Lapua Magnum. And, of course, there was a slot empty near the front of the gun safe's rack, where presumably that rifle, his current number one and his match gun and the font of his recent dedication, his intensity, his high-IQ brain, and his quiet passion, had lain.

But all in all, the event had to be categorized as confirmation, not progress. It strongly suggested incursion, murder, careful looting, without leaving a trace. It was a quality intelligence operation. Whoever had done it this time had done it before, or something similar, and they'd left little to track, nothing to go on, no next step.

Annoying?

Yes, because he'd thought it would take them somewhere instead of nowhere, and it left them with nothing new to do except to monitor reports on the whereabouts of the missing criminal and his little buddy Jared Akim, presumably under the aegis of some masterful criminal organization. But nothing specific emerged, and none of the divisions responsible for monitoring such organizations reported anything untoward, any hints of maximum preparation—vibrations of extra effort or deep planning—occurring within their precincts. It was very frustrating, until it wasn't.

Jeff Neill, the Cyber Division guru, came to call. He was in the paper-distribution network and saw everything Swagger, Memphis, and the others did, only a bit later.

"Okay," he said, "I want to run something by you."

"Let's hear it," said Swagger.

The younger man laid two photos on the desk. They were taken using infrared illumination at the Waters house the night of the search. Bob looked and saw only what should have been there, which was the interior of a closet stacked neatly with packaging.

"This guy was ultra-organized," said Neill. "He didn't just save stuff, he catalogued it and stored it alphabetically so that he could access it in seconds. He'd be the rare individual who always sends in the warranty card on the first day."

"That's him."

"So this is stuff he bought this year—he's probably got the other years saved in a storage unit somewhere. Or, rather, the packaging from it."

"Okay . . ."

"Look closely."

Bob looked. He saw a few gun shipment boxes; as for convenience, Waters had a Federal Firearms License, an FFL, and a license for Curios & Relics, both of which enabled him to receive firearms at home by common carrier. There was no evidence he operated at the retail level with his purchases, as he was strictly a shooter and a collector. He just had to enter them in a book for the occasional ATF examiners, who must have treated him like a pal, as he offered no threat and kept transparent, perfect records. Bob saw packaging that was probably left over from his last big-ticket get, the Accuracy International. He saw supporting implements, plus other mundane things, such as a box for a new Cuisinart, a new speaker for his nifty hi-fi system, book packages from Amazon—quite a bit of stuff from Amazon, in fact, as Amazon was the perfect abettor for such a lifestyle.

"Am I supposed to notice something?" Bob said.

Neill put his finger on a slim piece of packaging lodged neatly between two larger pieces, almost indistinguishable. But part of the overlapping cover art was visible on the edge, and Neill had identified it.

"If I'm not mistaken, that's the world-famous apple with a bite taken out of it. The corporate pictogram for the world's largest computer outfit."

Bob squinted. Yep, there it was: a bitten apple, a little leaf up top.

"That's the package the iPhone comes in. I would know because I've just picked up my X and spent an hour or so programming it."

Swagger carried an iPhone 3, or something Cro-Magnon like that, and wouldn't have noted such a thing in a million years.

"Okay," he said, "I'm with you. But where is this going?"

"Well, it fits, doesn't it? A tech and engineering guy like this, he'd have the latest variation of iPhone, just as, upstairs, he's got the latest variation of desktop system—he's always upgrading everything. He's probably got an X on order, it just hasn't come in yet."

"So?"

"We got into his desktop system and found nothing much of interest, other than that after a certain date, when he told his few friends he was going hunting, it hadn't been accessed."

"Okay."

"So he's got the 8. Now *they've* got the 8. They'd have to take it, because he'd no doubt downloaded his ballistic app into it, I'm guessing FirstShot. Anyone smart enough to use the rifle at highest capacity would know that that's the best. Anyone taking the rifle would take the iPhone and use it to set up his really long shots. Juba would have to have it."

Bob nodded. Seemed right so far.

"Here's the issue. The later iPhones—the 8 and the X—are really a bitch to crack if you don't have the code. Those fuckers at Apple are smart, you can bet on it. One of the things they're selling is security. When one comes up in a case—say, recovered in a drug raid—we can't even crack it. It has to go off to one of three or four high-tech computer labs, where the engineers can diddle with it for weeks before they can finally get in. And I'm guessing next that Waters was the kind of guy who shut down every night before he went to bed. So if they plugged him and they need to get in, how do they do it?"

"You don't think they'd take him?"

"No, because if he's alive, all sorts of complexities are added to what is already too complex. Security, support, interrogation, the fact that they would assume someone like this tough-ass, high-IQ Texas oil engineer wasn't going to give up his secrets easily, which generates another major headache and more drama for them. No, they'd probably cap him and trust they could crack it by their own devices."

"Could they?"

"As I said, there's a handful of labs that could do the work. But they're not going to a lab."

"Of course not."

"So they'd go into crime world. And, as it turns out, there are about three guys in that world capable of cracking a late-gen iPhone. They don't hang out in small towns like Toad Lick, Mississippi. One's in Boston; one's in Seattle, obviously; and one's in Dallas. We know all of 'em, have for years. Sometimes they help us so that we will leave them alone. Putting them in the slammer is of no use at all. Plus, we get tips from them on stuff they hear."

"You're guessing it was the Dallas guy."

"I'm guessing he was paid a pretty penny for his work. So we bust him, work him over hard. We leverage him. He can tell us who paid him, what he did, what was on there, whatever. Again, I'd do it real low-profile, bust him on another charge, never move him out of Dallas, maybe just pick him up privately and take him to a parking garage, someplace anonymous, no drama, nothing to cause any ripples in the water. Maybe he leads us to whoever's funding this thing, and we can track them to the source."

"It's two things," said Bob. "It's our best lead and it's our only lead. Let's go to Nick."

34

The range

Much was known now. He'd finally settled on 91.5 grains of Hodgdon H1000, once-fired Hornady brass, Federal 215M big-rifle Magnum primers, overall length 3.73 inches, a Wheddle bullet die-sharpened Sierra 250-grain MatchKing hollow-point boattail bullet, as loaded by an L.E. Wilson bullet seater, with a .367 neck bushing. Fired, it delivered a muzzle velocity 2,755, plus or minus, and of course each individual round he made was tested in a Hornady concentricity gauge for circular perfection. The result was a brilliant chord of power and accuracy, the MatchKing bullets being the most accurate in his ambitious testing program. He also rolled them—the bullets themselves—before seating them, for consistency, on the Hornady gauge, making certain that they were perfect.

They produced a thousand pounds of energy at twenty-one hundred yards, enough to splatter any living target, human or animal, save perhaps the great thick-skinned and heavy-boned beasts of Africa. They could pulverize the thoracic cavity of a man at that range. It would be a wound there'd be no walking away from.

Now he sat at the bench, constructed by Menendez's clever carpenters seven feet off the ground in a solid beech tree. Before him, though edged by pines that led to mountains—lofty, green, snow-covered or not—was more than a mile of heavy grass. It was yellowish, full enough to wave in the breeze. Three hundred yards out, water—too big to be a pond, too small to be a lake— gleamed in the sun. It spread for a couple of hundred yards, a kind of swampy stew under the tufts of grass, before yielding to more solid land. Finally, 1,847 yards away and sixty-seven feet lower, at the edge of the meadow, was his target. The range was perfect, the height difference too, exactly to his specifications and verified many times over by range finder.

He peeked through his spotting scope, a Swarovski 60×. In the circle of that magnification, he saw what he had to see. The image at 60× was one hundred and thirty feet wide, more than enough to make out the scene. A post had been driven deep into the earth. It had a medieval look to it, something the great Saladin would have erected as a site for execution by fire of cowards and traitors. Moored to the post, though hanging limply unconscious from it, was a man.

He stirred, shook, then twitched hard, as if gripped in the talons of a nightmare. Juba had no interest in what those nightmares might be. What he saw was only a target, something to be hit solidly with one 1,847-yard shot. He knew that the Mexicans sat a few feet to the left, their Land Rover not far from the scene of the action, which promised to amuse them greatly. They had brought a cooler of Diet Cokes and Tecates, and some lawn furniture.

The phone on the bench buzzed. Juba picked it up.

"My friend," said Jorge, in Arabic, "we think he will awaken soon. You won't have to wait long, although these drugs are tricky."

"It's fine," said Juba. "I have no rush. Besides, I have some calculations yet to make."

"Excellent. We have bets going on how many shots it will take you to hit him. I bet two."

"Probably too few," said Juba. "The program never works perfectly the first time. We must learn its refinements."

"Ah, well, it's only for a bottle of tequila."

Juba put the phone down, pulled on surgical rubber gloves, and picked up the iPhone 8. Always with the gloves so that not only would his fingerprints be protected, so would any oily excretions, any flakes of dead skin, any strands of hair that might adhere, all of which would reveal that the DNA was not that of Brian Waters. Of course, on the great day itself, the thing would be carefully scrubbed with acetone and seeded with some souvenirs of the late Mr. Waters—saliva, mucus, oil from his fingers, hair—which were the key part of the deception.

He held it, pressed the HOME button. It blinked awake and asked him for the code behind which lay all its treasures. Expensively, this had been found. He keyed it in and immediately emails came up, not many of late, but a few, saying such things as "Can't wait to hear your stories, buddy" and "SE Asia! Now, *that*'s for the man who's done everything!" and "Have fun, pal, but I wouldn't go anywhere that didn't have Magic Fingers in the motel rooms."

Juba only went to the icon page and knew exactly where to look. His finger hit the one that said FirstShot, the icon a tiny bull's-eye.

FirstShot came up, the menu offering him a selection of previously installed load choices, each one of which Waters had run through the program in his search for a winning handload for the matches. The newer were Juba's experimental loads, the last the load he had selected, simply marked as #12. He clicked on it.

The number 12 load page came up, everything entered. It displayed his previous selections: bullet brand, bullet weight, bullet length, velocity, twist rate of barrel, height of scope above barrel, all the aspects of the bullet that could determine, support, or reduce its accuracy. Additionally, the point of zero was registered, for it would be the baseline off of which all further computations would be calculated. He had selected fifteen hundred yards for zero, verified that synchronization among rifle, scope, and load at that range in his last session.

He poked it again, and a blank menu called CONDITIONS arrived, and this is where the weather aspects under which the shot would be taken were factored in. But it wasn't necessary to laboriously measure by Kestrel Pocket Weather Meter and enter them, one at a time.

The genius of the FirstShot program is that pressing the GET CONDITIONS button at the bottom of the screen, the machine downloaded them from the U.S. Weather Service. Thus, in a second he learned, watching these numbers deploy in their slots, that it was 74 degrees Fahrenheit, with a southwest wind of 4 to 8 miles per hour, the humidity was 51 percent, the sky was generally sunny (18 percent, or intermittent, cloud cover), the altitude 2,842 feet above sea level. All these figures would be factored into the algorithm the little genius inside the box was about to solve in nanotime.

He pressed CALCULATE. Magically, a table rose before him on the screen. The machine decreed the amount in minutes of angle by which the scope had to be moved off its fifteen-hundred-yard zero to put the crosshairs on the target in these conditions. It was indexed by distance. He surfed the lengthy listing via the left-hand distance column until he got to the nearly exact value. It was 1,845 yards. Moving his eye right to left, he came to the elevation column. It read 13 MOA. Since each of his clicks was worth a half of an arcminute, he multiplied by two to come up with the number 26. He carefully turned the elevation knob atop the scope up 26 clicks. In the next column, the windage was listed; it gave him 4 arcminutes left. Factoring 4 times 2 equals 8, he cranked the windage knob eight snicks left on Herrs Schmidt and Bender's magical tube.

That would do it. Now he found another turret on the tube and illuminated the red dot at the center of the—

His phone rang.

"Yes?"

"Juba, he's up. Confused. Just discovered the cuffs. Seems to think he can pull his way free."

"I'll spare him his effort shortly. You must watch and report to me on the impact of the shot if I miss so that I can make the corrections."

"I will."

"I am going to fire now."

The most sophisticated ballistic software program in the world is of no use if the shooter lacks technique. Juba did not. It's a thing acquired over long years of practice or, instantaneously, by genius. He had both.

The rifle, solid on its Atlas bipod, came to his shoulder. Important: all shoulder must touch flat and consistent against the crescent of the butt. Without thought, Juba did this. He eased his thumb through the thumbhole, came around with his hand to place his remaining four fingers and as much palm as possible on the grip itself, as well as applying rearward pressure, tightening it to shoulder. The adjustable comb was set to support his cheek weld precisely, given the length of his neck, and, laying his cheek upon it, positioned his eye instantly to the center of the scope. He anchored his left, supporting hand over the grip, pressuring it downward toward the table. He had made himself as solid as the inevitable caliphate of the future.

The world of twenty-five magnifications, centered by a red glowing dot, yielded amazing resolution, though still tiny. It was indeed a tiny world, everything small and perfect. Clear and stable, nevertheless it offered up a man exploring his new reality. Dressed in surgical scrubs, he pulled this way and that against a post. It did not budge. Juba watched as he yelled to off-scope witnesses and grew agitated when they clearly did not respond with anything except indifference. He had unruly hair and a prophet's beard. He was agitated—and who would not be, going to sleep among garbage cans and in dog shit and awaking in Paradise chained to a stake, offered up for burning.

Behold man: he tugged, he screamed, he addressed God. He was enraged one second, in tears the next, perhaps resigned at the end.

Juba's heart slowed, and between the beats his fingertip played God by moving the trigger straight back two millimeters. The rifle barked and leapt, a heavy and powerful beast, pushing mightily in its fraction of a second of energy release as its primer fired its powder, which obediently alchemized into an expanding pulse of energy and sent its missile down the launch tube. Its report was muted by the Thunder Beast suppressor screwed to the barrel, tricking its escaping gases to take the long way into the atmosphere and spreading the considerably diminished sound signature over a broad, untraceable area. The rifle rose an inch or two off the legs of its bipod, settled down, and, through this action cycle, Juba's finger remained stoically against the trigger, pinning it. Little air came into or out of his lungs, his heart was still, his muscles tight, his cheek steady upon the stock.

When the tiny world settled again, and the time in flight had expired, he made out a wisp of dust and the man, having turned at the sharp disturbance in the soil, trying to imagine what had caused such an occurrence.

His phone rang.

"A miss. I would say by a good twenty-five yards. The line to him seemed right."

"Yes," said Juba.

He was annoyed. This was the first test at distance, and why had the device not worked as it was supposed to?

He broke his position on the rifle, put his fingers to the elevation knob, calculated quickly that he was at least a full arcminute off, and therefore clicked in the appropriate improvement. One arcminute: two clicks.

He worked the bolt, gently ejecting the spent cartridge case, shoved the bolt forward and locked it down, thereby reloading and cocking. He assumed the same careful position, and when it was time, and he had settled into stilled perfection, his finger rewarded him with a shot.

The same ceremony of recoil and recovery through time in flight. He waited for everything to settle and the phone to ring. He saw dust at the target, roiling and buzzing, eventually clearing to reveal the man, untouched.

"Just a nick off. Hit near his feet. Maybe a whisper to the left."

"Yes, yes," said Juba, confident that he had it now.

He made adjustments: one click of elevation up, one click of windage to the left.

Into position, rifle steady, on scope.

And there he was, tiny, human, frail, doomed and knowing it, pulling hard against the stake, his face raised to God for mercy or maybe forgiveness. For this man, the time was now, the place was here, and the next world, whichever it may be, beckoned.

The rifle fired, rose and fell.

Time in flight: 5.1 seconds.

Juba was back on by then and saw the point of impact. Somewhere in the lower chest, the body's midline, right at the boundary between chest and entrails. The bullet emptied its total remaining power into him, a thousand pounds' worth, and the shock drove him backwards into the post, hair flying, body in spasm, a trace of dust vibrating off his clothes from the hit. He was dead before he went limp against his chains.

"Thank you, brother," said Juba. "You have helped me. May God be merciful on your soul."

It was the only prayer the fellow got.

35

His name was Lawrence M. Wakowski. His nickname, in certain sectors of his life, was Whack Job. In other sectors of his life, it was Mr. Wakowski. To the FBI, the nomenclature was determined by who held the leverage. Sometimes they called him Whack Job and enjoyed making him squirm and whine, other times it was Mr. Wakowski and he was treated with deference, respect, and other trappings of fealty.

"Thanks for coming, Mr. Wakowski," said Jeff Neill.

"Agent Neill, we meet again. And Agent Streibling, Dallas Field Office, Cyber Division rep, an old friend indeed."

Streibling, the local agent who'd set this meet-up, nodded but, knowing his place in the pecking order, said nothing.

"These other two fellows, I don't know," said Mr. Wakowski. "Kosher, though, I assume?"

"Totally kosher. Names not necessary," said Neill. "One is high-ranking, experienced, in from Washington.

The other is his associate, expert in certain arcane areas, known to be an extraordinary detective. He uncovered the string that led us to you and this meeting."

"Gentlemen . . ." said Mr. Wakowski, nodding his head.

"The accommodations—suitable?" asked Neill.

"Sure. Out of the way, unavailable to chance encounters. Way off my beaten track, and yours."

It was a cheesy suite motel near the airport, off the interstate. Left-hand neighbor: strip bar; right-hand neighbor: Best Tacos in Texas, which was true except for the other places in Texas that sold tacos.

"I checked," said Mr. Wakowski. "I wasn't followed."

"Actually, you were," said Neill. "By us. We're very good at it. The point, however, was to make sure you weren't followed by anybody else. You weren't."

"I feel secure in the bosom of the Federal Bureau of Investigation."

"A good start. Now I'll turn the meeting over to my superior officer."

"I'm Nick," said Nick.

"Nick," said Wakowski, "I'm Mr. Wakowski. How may I help you—that is, except by going to prison or getting myself killed?"

"Perhaps four months ago, certain parties almost certainly approached you with a job. They had a newly acquired iPhone 8. It had to be cracked. It takes even the best labs weeks to crack them. You are reputed to be one of three men in country who can do it in days. Am I right so far?"

"I could lie," said Mr. Wakowski. "In fact, the best course for me would be to lie."

"Not a good idea. We would have to stop calling you Mr. Wakowski then. We would have to call you Whack Job, and there's an issue outstanding about someone who built software to evade the cybersecurity at the First National of Midlands job a few weeks ago. We know who did it, a fellow named Roy Heinz, because Roy himself told us. It was decided that Whack Job would be left alone, as he might prove more useful to us in the future. That judgment can be rescinded. And if Whack Job goes to Huntsville, being soft and weak and white, what do you suppose happens to him?"

"I'm so disappointed in Roy," said Mr. Wakowski. "He was recommended to me as a stand-up guy."

"Everybody talks, in the end. Which is why we're here."

"May I ask—"

"No," said Neill. "But be advised that Nick and his friend wouldn't be here if this weren't of highest priority, of national security declination. Let's be polite, as we're all wearing ties, which signify politeness. But we do need your help, and we do expect your help."

Mr. Wakowski took a deep breath. He was mid-forties, with a face lacking singularity or charisma but notable in its ovality. He could have played the title role in the new *Egg and I* remake. Black frames, thick lenses, receding sandy hair, charcoal suit, black shoes, a face rather like butterscotch pudding. You wouldn't pick him out in a crowd of one. Except at Huntsville.

"Very dangerous people," he said. "That is why I hesitate. Betray them, see my kids tossed into acid vats. My wife handled by twenty-five grinning caballeros with eagles tattooed on their necks. All this before they stake me out naked for the vultures, with great big gobs of greasy, grimy cow guts smeared on my genitals."

"Those guys," said Nick.

"Yep, those guys." He shivered. "Why, oh why, did the Good Lord give me so much talent?" he said. "Without it, I wouldn't end up with the vultures going sushi on my dick."

"But you'd be living in a tract home, and both wife and kids would hate you for being a failure," Streibling said.

"True enough," said Mr. Wakowski.

He swallowed.

"You will protect my future and my children's future?"

"For now. It could change."

"Okay. Yes, it was an 8. Hard to beat, those motherfuckers at Apple go to sleep every night grinning about how hard it is. But Whack Job knows the way. Wasn't easy to figure, and it helps to have an IQ of 450, but he can, with much intensive labor, get it done in four days. I'll spare you the details. If you ain't a 450, they'd be meaningless anyhow. So they come to me, the money is, shall we say, quite convincing, as is their reputation. In my world, better to be friends with them than enemies. Enemies get the vulture thing."

"So you got in."

"Yes. The guy who set it up had to be some kind of supershooter or something. Most of the data space was eaten up by some program called FirstShot. I gather it helps you put little pieces of metal in certain places from a long ways out. It figures all the little bitty factors and influences, but it's basically a spreadsheet. It solves the problem at muzzle distance and extrapolates out to infinity from there."

"Okay, that's our guy," said Nick.

"Anyhow, that was important to them. They did need access to it, they made that clear. Excuse me for my lack of curiosity, but I didn't ask the fellow what this was necessary for. I figured I'd read it in the papers."

"And you will, right before the vultures come for a visit, if you don't get on with your story."

"So I unlocked it for them and got them access to the ballistics data. But they had another requirement: they wanted it hardwired for fast access to the Dark Web."

"For boys and girls who don't read *Computer Monthly*, explain 'Dark Web,'" said Neill.

"What you see when you click on, that's about two percent of the web. There's a whole other region. Its access is guarded, and it is superprotected by three Russians and a Chinaman who are even smarter than me. Only four of 'em, I guarantee you. Getting on it is part of the trick. Navigating it is the other trick. Using it is the final trick. All twisty, complex, under multiple two-factor codes and sliding algorithms. Grad students and psychos only. But it's where you can find a hit man, snuff porn, actual explosive manufacturing supplies and RPG missiles in bulk at a good rate, that sort of thing. It's the superego of the 'Net. As I say, hard to get on."

"And you made it easy to get on?"

"I set up a site for them, but the key ingredient was that it had to be findable, traceable. I had to build factors into it so someone like Agent Neill or one of the Israeli wonderkids could deconstruct it and trace it back to its origin, which would be the i 8 that I had in my hand, presumably linkable to someone else. It sounded like a key to an elaborate plot."

"You did all this?"

"I did all that."

"What was the website called?"

"I don't know. I showed them how to set it up, but they didn't want me to see what it was. So I just know it's there, and all that will be revealed when the time comes."

"Can we find it, Neill?" asked Nick.

"Without a name or a web address, not likely. There's more—they probably haven't posted it yet. It's all set up to go, but they don't want anyone discovering it prematurely. So it's ready, and they dump when it's appropriate to their plans—that is, when they want us to find it."

"Not helpful," said Nick.

"Yeah, but you still learn stuff," said Mr. Wakowski. "I'll play Agatha Christie here, if you don't mind. Their plan is to use the ballistics program to snipe somebody. The shot will be taken from Pluto. They will leave the iPhone so it will be found. Agent Neill will hire a lab to crack it, and they will see something that leads to the website, deconstruct it, and track it back to whoever the

Mexican vulture keeper stole the iPhone from. Ergo: he's blamed, no one even knows they were in play. Maybe he's dead. That's what I'd do if I were (a) running this thing and (b) totally insane."

"I think we figured that out on our own already," Nick said. "But since you're a genius, let me ask a more general question. Does this seem like the sort of thinking you'd affiliate with the kind of criminal organization we're talking about?"

"Excellent question," said Mr. Wakowski. "The answer is no. Our boys—the happy tots who reached out to me—are more forceful and direct by far."

"What is this thing typical of?"

"It's got high-IQ intelligence agency written all over it. CIA, Mossad, MI5, Chinese Ministry of State Security, Russian MV—real big boys in the game. Someone used to playing deflection shots, in love with the false-flag paradigm, fully aware of media tendencies and how it's all going to play out on a stage when the cable morons get on it and distill it to mouth-breather level. In my experience, they love to do that sort of thing."

"Middle East?"

"A stretch. But I see smarter guys."

"Okay," said Nick, "I guess we'll have to keep calling him Mr. Wakowski. Oh, wait, am I forgetting anything? Gee, I wonder what it could be?"

Wakowski hesitated, then said, "I was hoping you'd forget."

"Too bad for you, pal, I just remembered it. All that is nothing without a name to put with it. Cartel, yeah.

Bad people, yeah. Sworn enemies of all that's good and holy, for sure. But I need a name, and it better be a right one or . . . vulture chow."

"You didn't hear this from me. You don't even know me. I don't exist. But the name is Menendez."

36

The range

He thought it might be the climate. So target number two paid with his life for that experiment. Clearly, the weather data from the service was too generic. It would have been downloaded from the nearest regional U.S. weather station, and that could be miles away. Good enough for TV, good enough for government work, but not good enough for man killing at a mile's distance.

So instead of doing it that way, as FirstShot allowed, he laboriously filled in the blanks of data from his own Kestrel there at the range. Tedious, but tedium was a material snipers trafficked in. Wind speed, direction, altitude, temperature, humidity, and other subtleties of weather reality that only meteorologists knew, stuff so arcane, no TV guy even bothered with it.

He took his shot.

Better, but not good enough. The first one hit about fifteen yards shy. And although he dispatched target number two on the second shot, on The Day he would not be allowed a ranging shot. It didn't work that way in the real world. He had to know he was on with the first press of the trigger.

There was really only one thing to do: check the precision of the scope clicks and do the math. So the next day, instead of shooting at a mile, he shot at a hundred yards, at benchrest targets.

The exercise: five targets vertically arrayed a hundred yards out, stapled to blank cardboard and mounted in a frame. But the hundred yards itself was not simply lased for distance, it was hand-measured—again, not from the muzzle of the rifle but from the elevation knob of the Schmidt & Bender—for the most accurate possible hundred yards. He started at the bottom, fired a three-shot group. He moved the elevation knob up one click and fired three more at the second target. Then the third, the fourth, and the fifth, in the same one-click increments. Of course, for every click, the three-shot cluster moved up a bit. But how much? Was it the one minute-of-angle Schmidt & Bender's brilliant minds said or was it more? Or less? Working the target sheet with calipers, he determined that each click produced a rise in strike of not 0.552 inch, as per specs, but 0.489. It was so tiny an increment, it would have meant almost nothing out to three hundred yards, but with each leap in distance, it grew larger and larger. Thus, he was able to reconfigure FirstShot algorithms so that the click measure was 0.489.

Target number three: first shot, via FirstShot, was an ankle hit. The man—large, black, and dissolute—slid down, screaming, his lower leg shattered. Not good enough. Juba corrected a click, fired again, and eternally stilled him.

Target number four: close—closest yet—but low stomach. Probably not survivable, but given the speed of arrival of emergency personnel and the sophistication of trauma medicine, survival could not be ruled out. He had to hit the chest, destroy the heart and both lungs, sever all arteries and veins converging at the nexus of the heart. That hit, with a thousand pounds of energy and a sharpened missile more than a third of an inch wide, was the only guarantee.

Target number five.

Target number six.

Target number seven: a tough one, a fighter, he wouldn't stop moving, he yanked, pulled, twisted the cuffs that restrained him and was still squirming heroically at the arrival of the bullet.

But all succumbed to the first shot of the finally correct program.

He was done with prayers. His food had been delivered and eaten. He had worked out, sweated hard, spent forty minutes on Systema Spetsnaz, sparring with a bag, and finally showered. Now he settled down for a good reread of Jack O'Connor's *The Complete Book of Shooting*, a favorite text. He could read what might be called shooter's English, having taught himself first rudiments, then technical terms. At first, it was very slow, but with dedication, energy, and time, he'd mastered enough to read texts that dealt with his subject, and his mind could stay with the math, which most could not. He was absorbed in "Revolution Theory II: The Wind Factor" when the knock came.

He opened the door to find Señor Menendez, accompanied by Jorge, the translator, and by the fellow with the black sock over his head.

"Yes."

"My friend, we must talk."

"Certainly."

He admitted them. He sat on the bed. Menendez took the chair, the socked one stood behind him, at his right shoulder, quickly assuming perfect stillness. More twitchily, Jorge positioned himself to the left of Menendez, but somewhat forward, where he could hear both men clearly.

"I have heard that the shooting is going very well," said Menendez, absent recently at the range.

"I have addressed the system to the scope and the ballistics of the ammunition so that the precision I require is attainable. Other factors, of course, must come into play. These sorts of things are always delicate, and what happens if The Day arrives and it's rainy or blustery? What happens if there's a change in schedule, some sort of confusion or event near the target area? These are all factors I cannot control, yet I worry about them still. But not for much longer."

"Yes, yes, then your time with us is limited?"

"Yes. There comes now the shipment of the rifle to certain people, who will place it where it must be, and my own progress toward that destination, which must be carefully handled. The effort is exhausting. If I were not so true a believer, I would have long ago faltered. But I am no fool. I know Señor Menendez is not here to chat about my fortunes and my mood."

"No."

"How may I assist?"

He could see Jorge swallow, a sure indicator that something thorny was coming up. He felt the eyes of the man in the sock on him intently. Did they fear his reaction may cause Juba to attack? This was not promising.

"Yes, well, I'm afraid there have to be some changes made to your schedule."

"The schedule is set," said Juba. "I will adhere to it."

"If only it could be so, my friend, but it cannot."

Juba said nothing, wondering where this was going. Had the Jews found out and offered Menendez more money for Juba's head than his sponsors had paid for their assistance?

"You are aware that I control a considerable empire. I have built it from nothing, I have learned on my own and from my peers all the hard lessons, my discipline for security is intense, my arrangements have been brilliant, my mastery of many elements that people frequently take for granted has been exemplary. And so I have power."

"I have assumed as much."

"In all this time, I have never been seriously threatened. Neither by competitors nor by law enforcement."

"But now?"

"It's the turning of luck. You can plan for everything

except bad luck. And now by a stroke of misfortune, it seems I am in jeopardy. I, me, myself. And if it comes to pass that I am arrested and put in jail, even for a few years, things become tenuous. It cannot be then ever again as it is now. The system I have built will erode without me, its caretakers—good men all—will make wrong decisions, competitors will see weakness, potential defectors will be emboldened, law enforcement efforts will double and redouble. You can see why I am concerned."

"I can," said Juba. "But you must know that my mission is a mandate from God Himself. I cannot be deflected from it due to your concerns."

"Alas, it seems I need a man of your skills. Badly."

"What about this fellow right here, in the mask? He is said to be a technical of the highest degree."

The man in the sock made no acknowledgment.

"He cannot do what you must do. And that is, kill a man, from afar."

37

The Doll's House, Route 16, Grapevine, Texas

Whack Job was gone. The agents had no urge to sit in the squalid motel room, not when there was a squalid titty bar next door. So they ambled over to The Doll's House, found it three-fourths deserted, and a blonde cogitating onstage in lights that showed off every blue vein and stretch mark, her inflated breasts a-tumble, her hips equally active, but her face a mask of lacquered ennui. She'd had better days.

The men sat at a back table, ordered Lone Stars and Buds, with Bob doing his Diet Coke routine, asked the waitress to ask the boss to turn down the disco tunes a bit, as it wasn't the '70s anymore, plus they had serious talk ahead. They all looked so cop—short hair, beefy, badly fitting sport coats—that this wish was swiftly granted.

"Okay," said Nick. "Streibling, you're up. Tell us about Menendez so we don't look stupid tomorrow when we go through the files."

"Menendez. Big, smart, tough, tricky. More sophisticated. Not just feeding men to vultures and cutting women's heads off. Oh, they'll do that if they feel it advances their interests, but it's not SOP."

"Who's Menendez?"

"Raúl Menendez. About fifty. One of the few, maybe the only, cartel hotshot with American citizenship, joint with Mexican. He was born in Cambridge, Massachusetts, where his dad was getting his Ph.D. in economics. Dad went on to become the head of the Econ Department at the University of Mexico, until he died a few years ago, maybe out of grief over his son's chosen path."

"So Raúl has brains from his dad's side."

"His mom's too. Well, maybe that's where the refinement comes from. American citizen, grad student in art history, when she met and married Raúl's dad. She's dead too, maybe of the same grief."

"They should be proud he chose such a growth career," said Nick.

"Supersmart Raúl used tony family connections to apprentice under some of the bad dudes, then went independent ten years ago, having paid his dues, having learned the business from the ground up, having made peace with the older cartel generations so he himself didn't end up staked out for the vultures. He seems to have been guided by a vision for what a cartel could be, not just a Nazi Murder Battalion that, incidentally, sold drugs to the bean people but an international entity, penetrating society at many different levels. They use money to buy allies in other realms of society."

"Smooth?"

"Snoot Spanish and American all the way. No mestizo blood in him. That is why, alone among them, he's also cultivated the outer world. He seems to be headquartered in L.A., where he owns some auto dealerships, shopping centers, fast-food joints, has been mentioned as a possible investor in various sporting franchises, dabbles in movies, sits on several charity boards, has a wife and three kids."

"Meanwhile—"

"He's got SoCal, NorCal, and the Pacific Coast. New Mexico, especially Albuquerque, which he owns. He moved into Texas a few years back and took out a bunch of people who objected. We found them in unhappy circumstances. Meanwhile, Raúl is flooding the barrio with the latest in designer shit, he's big into meth and fentanyl, as well as pushing the old favorite, Mexican Mud. A late big move has a touch of genius to it: he owns an opioid pharmaceutical plant in Guadalajara and produces extremely good counterfeit merchandise, right down to the packaging. He sells cut-rate to a lot of hospitals, infirmaries, and pharmacists, and even if you go to Walgreens in Cambridge, you may be buying his stuff. He makes big dough off that. Anything that makes you go buzz seems to originate from him. DEA would do anything to bring him down, and if it happened, a lot of our beefs, particularly for the ditch floaters and alley bleeders found all over the southland when he first got here, might get cleared up. But he's too tricky for that."

"Can we hit him?" asked Bob.

"See, that's just it. You can't. He's so lawyered up,

you'd never get a warrant from the locals without him knowing about it. The local cops would find excuses to do nothing, even the emergency room docs might go on strike."

"At the federal level, we could get action."

"You'd think. But DEA has tried that route, and it's never panned out. He knows if someone is poking around, and next thing you know, smart guys from Harvard and the town's biggest white-shoe law firm are visiting the federal judges, doing a real soft-soap approach, but making it clear that no matter what D.C. says, the locals don't want any ruckus here. Because they know that when the mandarins go back to Peking, the blood will flow, and it won't be—pardon the harsh truth—out of the veins of any mandarin."

"Okay, he's tough and smart."

"As for the warrant, here's another wrinkle: it only works if you can find him. He has no headquarters. His headquarters is his brain, which he takes with him everywhere he goes. And he goes a lot. He likes big, fancy houses, and he owns a batch of 'em—penthouses, places in Europe and the Far East. Under his name, under his wife's name, under various corporate and dodge-company names. DEA doesn't even know half of them. Sees family in L.A. about once every two months. So we don't know where he is, even if we could get the warrant without loud sirens going off. So nobody's ever made the big commitment of assets necessary to raid. It just hasn't seemed worth it."

"Any penetration?" Nick asked.

Streibling shook his head. "Very tough security, lots of checks and cross-checks built into the system. He travels with a crew of twelve ex–Mexican Special Forces guys, SEAL-quality gunfighters, and a spooky guy who always wears a sock on his head."

"What's that about?" asked Bob.

"Nobody knows."

Nick summarized his conclusions.

"I can see that he would be perfect for Juba and Juba's people. Solid, secure, able to provide Juba with logistics and privacy. Able to get him around the country. Everywhere he goes, he'll have operators with him. They're the guys who picked him up in Ohio and got him where he is now."

"And ambitious," said Neill. "Saw a chance to link up with some sort of extranational or transnational entity and took it. Not just for the money, but for the experience of going international. He's a globalist."

"What about cyber?" asked Nick.

"Well," said Neill, "we can at least go full-press war on him, now that we've got a target. Somewhere, sooner or later, there's a crack."

"That's what they say about us," said Nick, with a humor-free laugh.

"Yeah, but we can keep trying, and, sooner or later—"

"Later ain't no good," said Swagger. "He's on schedule right now, and we're not sure how much time is left. These Mexican operators get him into position, he pulls off the shot, and they get him out of there. All the forensics points to poor Brian A. Waters, loner and gun nut.

Depending on who he hits—and, I bet, we can all guess—some kind of major shit hits some kind of major fan, and suddenly, somehow, it's a different world."

"Ah, Christ," said Nick. "This one is tough. I don't see how we can proact. We can monitor, get ourselves included in the loop of every agency that encounters Menendez, we can apply our analytical skills and our imaginations to various scenarios and pick the most likely one and go against them. But we'll always be behind the curve, action-wise, never in front of it."

"Well," said Streibling, "something could be happening."

All eyes went to him.

"Enlighten us, Agent Streibling. I must say, you seem well informed."

"I am. I'm about sixth-generation Lone Star law enforcement with Texas Rangers, Dallas Metro Shotgun Squad, Border Patrol—all that good DNA in my veins."

"Go ahead, spill some beans."

"As I say, cop people. Cops, cops, cops. They talk to cops who talk to cops. Agents, supervisors, techs—whatever—everybody talks, and some of us listen. And who do I listen to, especially with two martinis in him on a Saturday night? My wife's sister is married to a guy very high up in DEA here in Dallas."

"More beans, please," said Nick.

"This is so hot, it hasn't even hit the gossip circuit yet. You've got to know that Menendez drives DEA nuts. They want him so bad, it makes them crazy. They don't care about anything but Menendez. Major effort, so much work and man-hours and lab time, and, so far, nothing. Until—"

He paused for the theater of it. Then he gestured to the waitress that he'd like another brew. Nothing like milking the big moment. Meanwhile, a new girl came onstage. Asian, somewhere between twenty-two and seventy-two, left arm tattooed with dragons fighting tigers and empresses telling off warlords. *La fille jaune* had eyes like headlights edged with coal tar, a good, slim bod, the upstairs rack with the required silicone filled to the brim. Her hips seemed rocket-fueled; the music was really bad. Bob tore his eyes away and returned to the moment, in which Streibling was finishing his first swallow.

"Menendez, as I say, is supersmart and supercareful. But I hear, from my brother-in-law, that he's made one slipup. He's committed a major crime of violence, one that could put him away for a long time."

"How do they know that?"

"They have a witness who will testify to it and whose testimony will stand up to any cross, no matter how tough. That's because Menendez shot him in the head. Somehow he survived. His name is Jared Akim."

38

The ranch

"Y ou see, my friend," said Menendez, "this isn't a request, it is what must be. You are the tool of my deliverance, and my god, or yours, has put you in my hands at exactly the right moment, while at the same time it in no way jeopardizes the bigger operation for which you were sent. It is a sideshow, a little extra fuss, perhaps best regarded as a training exercise. I want your friendship, I value your skill, I admire your courage, but I must have your cooperation."

Juba considered, while Jorge caught up with the translation. Really, what choice did he have? With these monsters, one never knew what could happen. They had no morality, no commitment, no belief in anything as perfect as the caliphate, no belief in God.

"And if I don't?"

"It would be so regrettable."

"You realize that if you go back on your deal, the people who believe in me will declare war upon you."

"What a waste that would be. Many would die, and

for what? We should be brothers. We have common enemies, and slaying them is so much more important than petty squabbles."

Juba sighed. He had no choice, not here, not now, not so close. But it was a breach of etiquette he would not forget.

"With that superrifle of yours," said Menendez, "it seems to be no problem at all. You can kill a gnat at a mile. Here, you would kill a gnat at a quarter mile."

"I cannot use that rifle. I must use a different rifle, and I must have maximum security, minimum time in the vulnerable shooting site, and a clear and efficient escape."

"Is there something wrong with the rifle?"

"There is nothing wrong with the rifle. But I have spent months working with it—the scope and the ballistics software and the ammunition—to achieve a state of perfection. I cannot now take it on another operation, where I have to change all the settings, where it's liable to be banged about, treated roughly, perhaps dropped. Then I'd have to readjust, retest, and sometimes you can never quite find what you once had. Second, if I use that rifle—a .338 Lapua Magnum—the Americans will understand exactly why I am here. They may or may not know already. I'm not sure what the Israelis learned from their raid and what they shared with the Americans. For all the Americans know, I'm merely suspected of the nebulous crime of terrorism, which could be anything from blowing up a shopping center to poisoning the water supply to filing a suit against a Hollywood movie."

"I see. I can work with that. I am quite reasonable. Let us know what is required. It shall be done."

"I prefer to plan my own operation. I will see things that your people could never understand. To use my gift, you must let it express itself. Without my own plan, my confidence will be considerably lessened. This is not an easy task. I will need to acquire, zero, and test a new rifle. I will need to study the site, consider time of day, distance, weather—all those factors. Like so many, you think this can easily be done."

"Rifle?"

"The caliber will be called 6.5 Creedmoor. Made by Remington. Heavy barrel, perhaps the police model, easily acquired. The Model 700: they used them against us to great effect in Baghdad. They used them in Kuwait. They used them in Vietnam. It's a wonderful rifle, and shooting it will be a pleasure. You must also acquire a Leupold scope, at least 10×. I need ten boxes of ammunition, Match-grade, preferably Hornady, as the caliber is their creation, so they would understand it best. Preferably, this weapon is bought used, the scope mounted and zeroed by the previous owner. If it must be purchased new, have the store mount the scope and zero it. That saves considerable time, and time is something we need. And I need a few days here to work with it. I need also plans of the site, location of the target, distances, mean weather conditions, time of day of shot."

"My people are all Special Forces. They have experience. They will scout and assemble a preliminary plan. Yours will be the last say."

"All right," said Juba. "That seems all right."

"It shall be done," said Menendez.

"Oh"—Juba nodded toward one of the men—"and keep that one away from me. He makes me nervous."

"You mean La Culebra?"

"No, he's all right. I mean Jorge, the talker. He makes me jittery."

As he changed from Arabic to Spanish, Jorge acquired an ashen look. He swallowed, smiled awkwardly, licked his lips.

"I understand," said Menendez, and nodded to La Culebra.

La Culebra cut Jorge's throat in one second, and Jorge died in seven.

39

For the record, this is Special Agent Jean Chandler, FBI, about to commence interrogation of Jared Akim, suspect in re triple homicide in Detroit, Michigan, affidavits on file, other charges also listed in affidavit. Also present is Agent Gershon Gold, of the Israeli intelligence agency, Mossad, a contract advisor on terrorist matters by formal arrangement, documents also on file. Mr. Akim is without legal representation as per his signed agreement with the Drug Enforcement Agency, on file, reference C445-002. The session is being witnessed and videotaped."

They were in a safe house DEA ran on the well-protected grounds of McConnell, four miles outside downtown Wichita. Now and then, F-18s howled into the air, and the place vibrated like a tuning fork. Bob and Nick and Neill watched the proceedings from behind a rather obvious one-way mirror into the squalid interrogation room. Outside, various DEA officials muttered and stewed, having lost sole custody of their prize, having lost the administrative war with the FBI, and having once again had their noses rubbed in their low status in the federal law enforcement pyramid.

The boy sat in orange scrubs, his head still bandaged. But he did not look groggy. Quite the contrary, his eyes glittered with wit and intelligence, and he seemed relaxed, even happy. He got that they were playing head games with him by putting a beautiful young woman in front of him—in real life, she'd never date him!—and a portly, scholarly Jew. They were supposedly the bête noirs of his fevered jihadi imagination, but he merely thought it was kind of funny. He liked pretty girls, and, actually—don't tell anybody—he liked Jews. So the idea that a Jew and a babe would shake him was patently absurd! What, they thought he was an idiot?

"Mr. Akim, how do you feel today?" Chandler asked.

"I'm fine."

"The head?"

"It hurts, even ten ibuprofens in, but if it hurts, that means I'm still breathing, which is good news."

"You're out of concussion protocols?"

"Yeah, but I still hear the sound of bad music."

They spent a few minutes running through the mundane facts of Jared's existence: age, place of birth, education, disposition, parents, family, intellectual journey into radicalism, anger at white girls, so on and so forth.

"For the record, please describe your current circumstances."

"Okay, you don't want the Marcel Proust version, you want the action-movie version?"

Chandler tilted her head, caught off guard by his wit. "That's exactly what we want."

"I got involved in some dope stuff. Stupid, but I needed money. One thing turned to another, and I'd partnered up with this heavy dude named Ali La Pointe. I had no idea how heavy. I thought we were going to this drug house to see The Man and buy a large chunk of product, which we were going to move in Grosse Pointe, where I have lots of connex. It was a very win-win deal."

"It didn't work out that way?"

"This guy Ali goes nuts when one of the dope guys pulls a shotgun on him. We were unarmed! But he'd made a kind of spear thing and got him in the eye. God, I was not ready for that. *Squosh*—like, that was the sound. He grabs the shotgun and goes all SEAL on the other guys. *Boom-boom-boom*, and he's put them down. Some crazy woman comes downstairs, and I don't remember the next part. Anyway, by the time I sort of get straight, we're in a Benz S, heading out of town, with a pile of dough and a shotgun in a stolen car."

"So you claim to be the victim of Ali La Pointe as much as the others?"

"Ma'am, if you'd seen what a guy looks like with six inches of stick in his eye, you'd have been an obedient pup too. Really, no way I was going to do anything he didn't want me to do. I knew what he was capable of."

"For the record, all the forensics indicate it was you who beat the woman."

"I thought she was dead. She must have had a skull thick as the polar ice cap to survive that pounding. Yeah, well, as part of the deal, that's sort of going to be dialed way, way down to second-degree assault, time served. So I'd rather not talk about it. I don't think I have to, legally. Anyhow, this Ali La Pointe and I make a run for it. Again, he's calling the shots, I'm the punk. Somehow he has a number for somebody big in the trade, and we arrange a pickup. We just make it out of a couple of bad situations by a hair, and we're heading west. I had no idea we were even in Kansas.

"So, early in the morning, we pull into this abandoned farm. Another vehicle is waiting for us. The head guy is some silver-haired fox out of the Ricardo Montalbán school. He was all charm and smoothness, and he smelled like rich Corinthian leather. He welcomes us, he's the boss, and as he leads us to his SUV—it was the size of a PT boat—he puts his arm around me like I'm his son or something, but he has a gun in it and shoots me in the head."

"Why aren't you dead?"

"Good question. Perhaps I am the chosen of Allah."

"Perhaps you are a chronically immature delinquent from Grosse Pointe, high IQ, but still in so far over his head, he can't see the surface," said Chandler.

"Hmm, I wonder which one? Anyway, as they explain to me, it was dark, and maybe I lowered my head to see where I was stepping, and maybe he held the pistol slightly upward. It's all about the angles. At ninety degrees, the bullet excavates the Lincoln Tunnel through my brain. At thirty degrees, it blows out a chunk of scalp and hair, bleeds like hell, and whacks me into total unconsciousness. I wake up—surprise, surprise—in a hospital guarded by the State Troopers who found me in the bushes. It's three days later. They've got me on the Detroit thing. Since it's drugs, another state, they turn me over to DEA. DEA interrogates me, and when we come to the silver-fox guy, their eyes turn to saucers. They don't care about Ali La Pointe, he's a low-level guy, and the system will eat him alive sooner or later. They want this Menendez, even if they can't figure out what the hell he was doing riding shotgun in the pickup of a low-level dealer. But that's not my department. A little of this, a little of that, my dad hires me a hotshot Kansas City lawyer, and a deal is struck. I ID Menendez and testify against him, they forget everything they have on me, and after he's in, I go Witness Protection. I become Jerry Smith of Bone Fossil, Idaho, or something. But I'm alive, I've put the fox away, I'm a hero, I have a life, and I get to see my folks once in a while."

"You're a very lucky young man," said the Jewish fellow.

"I owe it all to clean living and a fast outfield," Jared said.

"If I may, one thing. This other man, Ali La Pointe. Interesting."

"He's out of the picture," said Jared. "I mean officially, as per my agreement."

"Yes. However, it is interesting that Ali La Pointe is the name of the charismatic and illiterate terrorist hero of Gillo Pontecorvo's *Battle of Algiers*."

Was that a twitch engulfing the young man's Adam's apple? A swallow, a flick of dry tongue over dry lips?

"Now, that could mean three things," said the man. "It could mean this chap was really named Ali La Pointe, after the movie role. Possible, perhaps. Or it could mean that an intellectually promiscuous, rather smart-ass young man decided to put one over on the dumb American police and use a name that every highbred radical Arab teenager in the world would recognize but no DEA functionary would. Or—and I believe this one, actually—as an inexperienced junior terrorist undergoing his first interrogation, he chose the first name that came to his mind, which was from his subconscious memory of that movie—it's superb, by the way—and named the mystery figure in the narrative, Ali La Pointe. Later, he possibly regretted it but was stuck with it. This last possibility, I must say, seems more like you."

"Who is this guy?" Jared asked Chandler.

"He is assisting us," she said.

"Okay, who's *us*?"

"Us is the Federal Bureau of Investigation. You would know that if you'd been paying close attention."

"Yeah, but my DEA deal still holds. I don't know what you guys are here for, I really don't. This is straight drug shit, I'm going to help them get Menendez; otherwise, I go into the general population at Kinross and last about six seconds before they kill me."

"Actually, your deal is now off the table," said Chandler. "It was conditional on your willingness to tell the truth. In all things. You rather artfully constructed a narrative that gave DEA what it wanted and yet you hid your real mission, which was to help Juba the Sniper. So your deal is undone, and off you go to Detroit and then Kinross. If you want, I can help you pick out panty hose for your new life as a bitch."

40

The ranch

The new rifle was fine, the new translator a great improvement. He too was elderly, calm, seemingly amused by this situation, so clearly he did not know what had happened to the man he had replaced. His name was Alberto, and he was one of those awkward figures caught between opposing cultures, the Mexican part of him not happy with the Arab part, or maybe it was the other way around. He was skinny and thin of hair, but he had about him a teacher's air. He also had watchful eyes, a trait Juba admired.

As for the rifle, it was indeed Remington's 700, the police model, with an oversize bolt knob and a shorter barrel for easy maneuvering, in some kind of spongy camouflaged stock from Hogue, the whole thing in a sort of coyote gray or dun desert camouflage, not so much for practicality but so that American shooters could get a sniper buzz off of it. The scope, a Leupold 4–12×, was also new and had been mounted in the gun store, wherever that was, by an armorer using Leupold rings and mounting hardware. The kit included a new Leupold range finder with proprietary ballistics software.

The armorer was a sound craftsman, and Juba found everything tight, the scope properly indexed to dead zero, and was pleased. Additionally, it was prethreaded for a suppressor with the standard dimensions of eight by twenty-four, and from somewhere in Menendez's store of armaments, among the gold-plated AKs and the ruby-crusted Glocks, a Gemtech suppressor had been found that fit those dimensions, and it screwed right on. The range finder was preprogrammed and indexed to common commercial loads, and Juba's 140-grain Hornady Match was one of them.

He zeroed in with several shots at a hundred yards and discovered that it delivered sub-one-inch groups at that distance, through the suppressor. The next day, he moved the target to two hundred yards, and then to three hundred, zeroing carefully each step of the way. This new cartridge, the 6.5 Creedmoor, was living up to its hype. It kicked less than a .308 and yet was more accurate. The cartridges fit perfectly into the magazine well, being essentially a .308 round necked down to accept a .264 bullet. It would have made a great sniper round, he thought. Working with the Leupold ballistics software program proved without issue. He dialed in the weather and the velocity—as tested, not listed by the manufacturer—and came exactly to the right windage and elevation clicks at three hundred yards. As a midrange shooting system, the outfit was up to his standards.

On the fourth day, Menendez brought him explicit diagrams.

"This is no good. I must see it myself."

"You will. I bring you this for familiarity only. You will see how professional my people are. They know many things."

The sniper said nothing, eyes betraying nothing, body betraying nothing. He simply addressed the document.

He saw a street grid, one block marked 4th Street, on which stood an immense building, as described by a rectangle, some kind of official structure, judging from its size. A diagonal line had been drawn across the map, passing over two blocks, tracing the trajectory of a shot. Its source was a circular structure, part of some kind of connected complex. Sounding out the letters, he could tell that the name of that street was Market.

"You have no issues using an infidel religious site for your work?" asked Menendez.

"It is nothing to me. If it offers the position, I will use it."

"You will be in the dome of a Catholic church called the Cathedral of the Immaculate Conception. It's perfect for our purposes. One of its six windows faces the target zone exactly, clean, unobstructed shooting. It's easy to access, at that time of day likely to be largely empty, and its priests will yield quickly and without drama to our functionaries. A glazier will accompany you to the selected window—it's an ancient building, everything is at least a hundred years old—and he will remove the glass from your shooting position."

"I will have to examine it myself and make certain that all is as you say it is."

"Why would I lie?"

"You would not lie. But you might see what you want to see, not what is there. I also will need a tripod on which to place the rifle. You can acquire one at any camera or large sporting goods store."

"Of course. Your target will be the stairway into the Fourth Street entrance of the federal courthouse. At two-thirty that afternoon, a carload of U.S. Marshals will deliver this witness to the courthouse. In the brief seconds that he is ascending the steps, he will be accessible to you."

"Your intelligence is very good."

"And expensive. Now, if—"

"There is more. I want a demolition, radio-controlled, placed nearby. Its point isn't to destroy but to stun. When it detonates, the party will halt, look around—all of them—for the threat. It's basic animal behavior. It must be detonated as they reach the top step. He will be frozen for perhaps a second, and I will take him. Time in flight from that range is less than a second, and he will still be at least that before everybody realizes what is happening and pushes him forward. It'll be too late by then."

"I appreciate your confidence."

"I do not miss. Now, tell me how we shall escape." He parsed the diagram closely.

"No elevator down," he said. "It will take some time. Upon detonation, a car should pull up outside. Probably best to leave the rifle, as its awkwardness makes it difficult to maneuver."

"Fine. It was bought under untraceable arrangements."

"We leave, transfer cars quickly, and—"

"To the airport. Where my jet awaits."

"All the men with me, they will be armed. Just in case."

"Heavily. Well-trained, ready to fight and die, if necessary, to make your escape good."

"It shouldn't come to that."

"The locals, even the Marshals," said Menendez, "are earnest but not the kind of highly trained, highly experienced operators on our team. They can't possibly react quickly unless they have someone of extraordinary talent on-site. And that is highly unlikely."

41

J ared, you have to deal with this."

"Ah. What was the name again? He called himself Ali La Pointe, that's all I know."

"You're in direct contradiction with Imam el-Tariq of Dearborn. In fact, it's his testimony that he chose you specially to act as Juba's facilitator, as he got acclimated to the United States. According to him, you spent more time with Juba than anybody. And if anybody knows Juba's secrets, it would be you."

"You know, I think I need a lawyer."

"I would agree with that, but, unfortunately, you signed that right away. You're here all by your lonesome. Your choices are somewhat limited."

"I don't know what to say."

"Silence is not an option."

"What *are* my options?"

"We can remainder you to Detroit, and the general prison population at the state penitentiary at Kinross. My goodness, I hope that doesn't happen. The results would not be pretty."

"Or?" said Jared.

"A case could be made that, in assisting Juba, you became an accessory before the fact to all his crimes. Since one took place in Israel, the Israelis, who are very interested in Juba, could demand extradition, for interrogation by their intelligence services."

"Ouch. Okay, so what's your deal?"

"Same as the one you've got. You go this afternoon to the courthouse and testify before the grand jury. That gives DEA license to pick up Raúl Menendez. You testify against him in a court of law. He goes away. You go into Witness Protection. All that stays the same. However, upon your testimony this afternoon, you are flown to a heavily guarded FBI safe house, also on military property, and you give us everything you have on Juba. I mean everything. No playing cute, as you did with DEA. We will go over it time and time again. We will medicate you, as your permission to do so will be part of the deal. We'll go deep hypnosis. You will also work at length with the finest police sketch artist in the world, and you will give us a good portrait of the sniper. And if we feel you're holding back in any other way, the interrogation will become sterner. And if we fail to stop him and he commits whatever mission he was sent here to commit, that will go very hard on you. When it's all done, we'll loan you out to the Israelis, and any other country—Malaysia, for example, or the Philippines—that has suffered at Juba's hands. Then back to Kinross. If there is a 'then.'"

Jared sighed, signaling epic self-pity at the horribleness of what was happening to him. It was so wrong. He didn't realize that it was just the world routinely, mercilessly, rotating on the fulcrum of the innocent and the idealistic.

"See," he finally said, "Menendez is shit. He doesn't matter. He tried to kill me. I was nothing to him, so turning on him, that's cool. It's kind of fun. Juba is different. He's part of the cause. I don't care about Islam, really, but I do care about the shit that my people suffer. I don't believe in Allah or Yahweh or Jesus H. Christ, any of it. But those people are so fucked by everybody, and nobody talks for them except the Jubas."

"If you become older," said Gold, "you will perhaps see the wisdom in moderation, mercy, and simple courtesy. The bold warrior archetype, so impressive to youth, will reveal himself to be psychotic, utterly corrupted by the flame of his hatred. It's fine to have heroes of force, but you will learn that it is not fine to have heroes of evil."

"No doubt you're speaking from the heart, Mr. Gold, but one man's evil is another man's heroism. I'll take what's coming."

"You poor kid," said Chandler. "You're shipping yourself to Hell."

"Do they get Netflix there?" the boy asked but was unable to laugh at his own joke.

42

Cathedral of the Immaculate Conception, Wichita, Kansas

At precisely 1410, a black SUV pulled up. The first team, six of them, were dressed as priests—if priests were weight lifters, had MORIR EL CABRÓN!! tattoos in 48-point Bodoni Light Gothic showing under their clerical collars, and wore earphones with foam-encased mics. They were highly professional, all veterans of 1st Brigade, 2nd Special Forces Battalion, Mexican army. Many fights had they seen, many operations had they prevailed in, all over South America's raw and violent regions, and many cartel members had died at their hands. Now they were on the other side, and that is why Menendez so treasured them, and so overpaid them. For their part, they got the bargain and had made friends with it: if you take El Patrón's salt, you must obey his orders, unto death if need be. Actually, they liked to fight so much that the outcomes didn't make that much difference to them. Everyone dies; their preference was to do it in battle.

Black-frocked and solemn, they found the exquisite interior of the domed cathedral largely deserted. They strode down the nave like Becket's murderers, piously genuflected before the mounted cross when they passed in front of it in the chancel, for they had no urge or need to commit blasphemy, only murder. There was no need to be disrespectful. They strode quietly, for such big guys, amid the shafts of sun and the flickering of candles and the orangish old bulbs that had been burning since 1923, and began, as discreetly as possible, the process.

It didn't take strong-arm stuff to control the building. Merely a brief opening of robes to display each fellow's AK-74 Krink, the lighter-caliber, short-barreled version of the world's most famous and prolific firearm. That made the point, and without sound or fuss the authentic clerics followed their captors' instructions, gathered in the nave of the cathedral, where they were made to kneel, were flex-cuffed and ball-gagged.

The sergeant in charge spoke quickly in Spanish, then English.

"We mean you no harm. We are true believers ourselves, and ask the Lord Jesus Christ to bless our endeavor, for its outcome favors *la raza* over the usurpers and represents the reconquest. You will remain silent for another few minutes, and, presto, we are gone, and someone from the police will arrive to free you. Do not look carefully at our faces or attempt to commit details to memory. It could haunt you at some future time."

That said, the perimeter established, a sign placed in front of the entrance reading NO ENTRANCE/NO EN-

TRADA, he spoke into the microphone held before his lips, giving the signal.

Another black SUV pulled up, and out of it climbed Unit 2, three more men in priest's robes, a fellow said to be an expert on the workings of glass, a stout and dedicated load bearer, with a gun case wrapped in a bright Navajo textile and a tripod simply wrapped in brown paper, and Juba the Sniper.

"This way," said the husky man. He was Special Forces as well, had reconned the site personally, and knew exactly where he was going. He led them into the structure.

The church held no magic for Juba. His mind was fixated on purpose. No sense of grand importance came to his mind, no urgency, no care, no anxiety. All that mattered was the shot; in the moment, faith would be a distraction. He didn't notice the vaulted grace about him, the shafts of holy sunlight, the dust floating in the air. He didn't observe the designed serenity of the place, made no comparisons between the busy beauty of Christian religious ambience and the severity and simplicity of his own faith.

He followed the man in front, who knew exactly where to lead him, which was down the leftmost aisle, around behind the altar, to a stone stairway rising into darkness, blocked by a chain and yet another sign reading NO ENTRANCE/NO ENTRADA. He stepped over the chain, following the route upward into the dome, spiraling up its circumference as he climbed. He reached a higher catwalk that circled the base of the dome, followed it as it curled around until a ladder availed itself to him. Since he was strong, he had no difficulty, though he worried about the glazier, who might not be up for such an ordeal. But the glazier was a monkey, the Special Forces trooper with the load now strapped to his back was a gorilla, and all made it without oxygen debt.

They were now in a land of spiderwebs and darkness, illuminated every sixth of the way by radiance pouring through ancient windows set into the stone a century before. It smelled of coldness, perhaps of the tomb or maybe just cellar stuff, both moist from the stone and dry from the dust. Esteban put a headlamp on to show the way and led them halfway around the dome.

"Here!" he said in English.

They had reached a particular window, and Juba peeked out, saw that it afforded, over another roof, a clear angle to target: the parking lot and steps into the rear entrance to the federal courthouse at 4th Street and Market.

"Señor?" asked the glazier—meaning, I am here, let me do my job. Juba moved down the catwalk a bit to make room while the soldier set out to open and deploy the tripod.

The glazier's work was highly professional. First, he affixed a large suction cup to the pane, then he took a Dremel tool, battery-powered, and drilled a smallish hole in the old glass to achieve purchase on the window's edge for what came next. That was a glass-cutting key, and with strong, deft strokes, he inscribed the border of the pane without difficulty. A second later, with a little scraping sound to add to the drama, he gently eased the pane out, removed it fully, and stepped back. The window was cleared of glass.

The soldier hustled into position, quickly erecting the tripod. He opened its legs as wide as possible, for maximum stability, de-telescoped the shaft to its highest position, and, with a snap, locked it solid. Skillfully, he screwed a small flanged platform to its apex, upon which could be mounted a camera or a rifle. Juba chose a rifle.

Like the surgeon he and other snipers were often compared to, he drew on close-fitting rubber gloves, while behind him the trooper tied a mask to the lower part of his face, slipped a surgical cap over his hair, and slipped a pair of Bausch & Lomb yellow shooting glasses over his eyes, hooking them over his ears. Now he was ready for the computations.

He recognized that what lay before him was a fairly simple hunting shot, but it was far enough away and precise enough that it couldn't be sloppy. He'd been told the distance and height of tower, but he was still going to check. So, since the rifle had a Leupold scope on it, he had chosen and programmed a Leupold laser range finder, the new one designated RX-1600I TBR, the TBR standing for "true ballistic range." He ran through the functions. The range finder's inclinometer verified the angle at about forty-two degrees. This meant the actual straight-line distance to the target would be about twenty percent farther—call it three hundred and fifty-seven yards versus the sea-level distance of two hundred and ninety-seven; that would seem to make a big difference with a 6.5mm Creedmoor. But the counterintuitive reality was, the shot was still two hundred and ninety-seven yards, regardless of angle and distance. Gravity is picky; it doesn't care about angle, it only cares about the sea-level distance. So, since he was zeroed at three hundred yards, his data was validated.

Now verified, he knew it was time for the instrument. He put the range finder in his pocket, bent over as the soldier opened the gun case and removed the rifle. It held four rounds of Hornady's superb 140-grain Match ammunition. Sleek and graceful, its proportions refined toward the sublime, it was, like any firearm, a weird blend of the charismatic and the mundane. It was tan through the stock, dappled with abstractions conceived to blend against someone's idea of a desert landscape. The barrel, receiver, and trigger guard were all finished in a kind of dun, somewhere between gray and tan, as neutral and invisible as any color could be to the unsophisticated human eye. The scope was black, simply because most scopes were black, and there hadn't been time or interest to find a Leupold 10 that matched the rifle.

He removed the suppressor from the case, put it to muzzle, and screwed it on. It just looked like a big black tube squashed onto the end of the smaller khaki tube of the barrel, extending its length by perhaps eight inches. It added but a few ounces weight, and although it could not by any means silence the sound of nearly 45 grains of smokeless powder igniting in a ten-thousandth of a second, it could diffuse it. If it registered at all, the noise would come from everywhere.

He hefted it, experiencing the ten pounds as just enough to be responsive yet at the same time just enough to be steady, slipped behind the tripod, and bedded the rifle forestock on a small sandbag that lay between it and the steel platform at the tip of the shaft. He fit himself to it, his eye coming to the scope and finding the right distance between scope and eye, and settled in.

The rifle was, of manufacturing necessity, generic in its dimensions and design. It was not adjusted to him, he adjusted to it. He knew exactly where to place his cheek to find dead center of the scope, he knew where exactly to place his hand on the comb to pull it stoutly to shoulder, he knew where he'd place his off hand—on top of his firing hand, just behind the thumb—for maximum control.

Meanwhile, behind him, the soldier slipped a radio to Juba's belt, ran the wire to his head, and ensnared it in the earphone-mic crown. Juba heard crackling, some Spanish chatter, followed by the clear Arabic of Alberto:

"Guardian"—using the ludicrous code name that the Mexicans had insisted upon—"are you there?"

"I am," he said into the microphone.

"Are you on target?"

"Yes, a few adjustments to make. What is the time situation?"

"Ah, they're telling me it's still six minutes until he's due. We have spotters, and—"

"I know."

"Yes, they will alert us when the vehicle is spotted, no matter from which direction."

"Yes."

"All right, now, they're telling me he's about two miles away, no traffic, ETA about four minutes."

"I receive," said Juba.

Now he was ready. He flicked the safety off, opened the bolt to reassure himself by a peek of brass that the cartridge still rested in the chamber—though, by no stretch of the imagination, could it have been removed—locked the bolt down, and began a series of microshifts and -adjustments toward perfect comfort.

"Last check through," said Alberto from wherever it was the operation was being run, presumably a nearby apartment.

"Everything is perfect," said Juba.

"Yes."

"And the distraction detonation?"

"He is on the circuit. When you say go, he will blow up a garbage can down the block. Lots of smoke and noise."

"Good."

Another voice came on.

"All units now, radio silence for the shooter. May God be with us."

The Marshals' Dodge SUV led the way, behind which was the FBI party in a nondescript Bureau Ford, and, behind them, in honor of local participation, a Wichita city police squad car, holding two sergeants, seven doughnuts, and two cups of heavily sugared-up-and-creamed coffee.

"At least it ain't a circus," said Bob.

"Their plan is discretion, not a show of force," said Nick. "Chandler, how are you doing back there? Okay?" She was alone in the backseat.

"I'm fine," she said. "No State cops are asking me out for a drink."

Around this tiny convoy, the mild and pleasant streets of the Kansas city passed, and Bob for some reason kept his scan running hard, his concentration cranked up to eleven. Of course he had no firearm, so what good would it have done if he'd spotted anything anyway?

"Okay?" asked Nick. "We'll catch him after testimony. He'll have thought about it. He'll see what being a stand-up guy will cost him and he'll come home to us."

"Hope you're right," said Bob, eyes catching on the sudden spurt of a Dodge Charger, but it signaled, then turned left, as it passed the Marshals' vehicle.

"He's a kid," said Chandler. "Behind the bravado, he's scared and fragile. Plus, he misses his mom. He'll see the light."

The courthouse was a New Deal monolith, all vertical lines and right angles, *art moderne* by way of a let's-build-shit-to-get-the-economy-going zeitgeist. It was built to withstand tornados and angry peasants with pitchforks and torches. The Marshals' SUV pulled through the gate, obediently opened by a guard, eased into the lot, and pulled up to the curb, which accessed the six broad stairs, which, in turn, accessed the double-wide brass doors. Two more Marshals stood at the doorway, like sentinels. So much drama.

Nick parked in a precleared nearby space, and the cop

car closed the gap on the SUV, nudging up to it, fender to fender.

As he exited, Bob scanned for threat. Nothing, no movement, no parked cars on the street, no suspicious traffic on 4th Street. Just America: trees, sunlight, a bit of a breeze, a few folks across the street, meandering their way through errands and visits, nobody paying any attention to anybody's business but their own. Swagger did notice one tall structure on the horizon, the dome of a church or some kind of sacred structure, off to the northwest, three hundred or so yards away. He marked it, but it was too far for his eyes to pick out details. It occurred to him that he should have had binoculars, but he also should have had a pistol, earphones, and a link to the 'Net, body armor and more comfortable shoes, and been twenty years younger.

The FBI folks reached the SUV, which had remained closed until they got there. Now the front door opened, a large man in a blazer emerged, miced and phoned up, Sig bulging over his right kidney, regulation-issue crew cut, and, like Bob, did his own threat scan. Satisfied, he nodded, and the back door opened.

Scrawny Jared got out, the puppy at the center of all this arranging. He was dressed as if for his English class at Princeton, in jeans, sneaks, and a sweater, sleeves rolled up. No cuffs, no shackles, since for this part of the operation he was a cooperating witness, not a felon. He had a pair of wire-rimmed glasses on, and he seemed like a feral beatnik cat next to the two Marshals, who quickly fell in beside him. In comparison to his boho insouciance, they were like Kansas football coaches. He did not look at, nor did he receive any acknowledgment from, the FBI party that waited for him to walk up the stairs and fell in behind him.

The stairs were gentle in incline, low in height, broad in depth, and ceremonial in execution. Everybody covered them easily, and up the party of six went.

Okay, on Fourth Street," said Alberto. "You should have them any second."

Juba gave the focus ring of the Leupold a last tweak, and it brought the scene into startling clarity, much bigger, because he was so used to tiny dot-like targets at over a mile through the Schmidt & Bender 25×. Now it seemed like a movie, blazing with color, crisp to the edges of the frame, and he saw the steps, the terrace up top, the two Marshals flanking the doors, the ornate bas-relief pictographs of Labor and the Eternal Prairie etched lovingly into the building's walls seventy-odd years ago.

"Okay, on-site," said Alberto. "Do you have them?"

"I do. Now, shut up," commanded Juba. "Wait for my command."

He didn't care to track them, preferring to let them rise as they ascended the steps into his crosshairs.

At the bottom of the perfect circle that was his field of vision, he could see motion: heads, as the party assembled itself outside the black vehicle. It seemed to take some time, as if it were a parade being set up, not a mere trudge to an appointment. But finally they arranged themselves as they preferred and they began the climb.

Three in front, three in back, the target obviously in the middle of the first rank. They moved without hurry or ceremony, totally unaware they were being observed by the predator from afar, not even in step or cadence, just an unruly batch of people heading inside.

"Now!" said Juba.

Somewhere someone pushed something—phone key, TV remote button, professional wireless detonator, whatever—and half a block down the street a KEEP WICH-ITA CLEAN garbage can, placed a foot off the sidewalk in a gilded frame, exploded. It was not a destructive blast—perhaps two ounces of Semtex or C-4 crushed into a Dixie cup, with detonator and signal receiver, as the point wasn't to destroy but to stun. The can, plastic, shattered as it rose upward, propelled by a plume of energy and oxygenation, and for however tiny amount of damage the detonation did, it indeed produced the sound of a world ending, in one one-thousandth of a second.

And it stunned totally. All six principals froze, as their human brains, being hardwired and acculturated to the noise of any blast, reacted as threat messages overcame all mental processes.

The Marshal on the left and one of the three trailers had begun to recover already, but Juba, without tremble, tremor, doubt, or reluctance, had his crosshairs square on the right-hand edge of the Marshal's haircut as his target, but, by the incomprehensible unpredictability of spontaneous movement, the Marshal had shifted slightly to the right at the noise, and his head was now obscured.

Time moved in atomic increments. Juba's finger lay into the trigger, and he felt it move, move, move, yielding a tenth of an ounce by a tenth of an ounce, but he still had no goddamned target—Allah, help me! Allah, do not forsake me!—and, in a nanosecond, the man's face began to clear, and the crosshairs exactly defined the edge of the Marshal's head and about a third of his emerging face when the trigger, obedient to its administrator's beliefs, went.

Blur and whirl, the odd no-noise of the suppressor turning the muzzle blast into generic muffled obscurity, the rifle rising off the tripod as it drove back just a bit by the recoil, and then falling again to stability, and since he had not come off the stock or out of the eye box during the recoil cycle, it restored the movie that was this chaotic event, and at that second Juba saw the face of the man in the flash of an instant before the great destruction.

43

There is no sound quite like the sound of a high-velocity bullet striking a human head. It's wet yet solid, repulsive, and full of odd aural subtexts: some cracking, some sibilance of the spray phenomenon, some twisted mach-speed splats. Of the people standing next to Jared as the bullet, sliding off the skull of the Marshal, took him dead-on flush beneath the eye, only Swagger had heard it before.

He wasted no time. The sound carried terminal information. No need to look at the results, though he involuntarily snatched a glimpse of the Marshal, also toppling, also issuing copious outflow, to determine that that man was probably not fatally hit but had a year of headaches in store for him.

In the moment of suspended animation that followed, it was Swagger who screamed, "The Dome! The Dome!" and, without a whisper of pause, bolted toward the police car behind the Marshals' SUV, yanked open the rear, piled in, and shouted again: "The Dome! The Dome!" The absurd smell of sloshed coffee filled the automobile, but indeed the sergeant at the wheel bumped into drive, squirmed out from his slot, went hard left, peeled around the lot, hit the exit gate, blew through it, sending spars and splinters of yellow-and-black-striped wood flying, cranked hard left down 4th Street and put pedal flat to floor, and the power drive of Dodge Charger Pursuit's best 370 hammered its way through the atmosphere.

"Headquarters 10-35. Shots fired, shots fired, Fourth and Main, need medical fast," said the other cop into his mic. "Officers down. We are proceeding to Immaculate Conception, shots may have originated there, all units, 10-35, Immaculate Conception, proceed under siren."

"Tell 'em, suspects heavily armed, expect to receive gunfire," Swagger said, as the two blocks of 4th Street went to a blur outside the speeding vehicle, and the g-forces tugged its occupants back.

"Be advised, all units, may encounter gunfire at site."

"Got a gun?" Swagger said.

"There's a shotgun in the trunk. I'll pop it when we bail out."

"Roger that," said Swagger, as the car reached its destination, yielding the sudden image of two SUVs halted at the curb in front of the cathedral just as a batch of priests were scurrying toward them.

"Watch it, goddammit," yelled Swagger, as one of the priests dipped and came out with an assault rifle.

All three of the occupants went down as a fleet of small, angry missiles nailed the windshield, reducing it to sparkles, veins, and glittering spray. Nobody was hit, but the car itself slid out of control, sideswiped a parked vehicle, came to a hard stop against another, throwing each occupant forward and into shock against whatever was ahead of them, dashboard or the back of the front seat. Swagger felt a bone crack, a rib twist, his heart go flat as a pancake, his lungs nearly split, and a rocket of bad pain go vertically from the center of his body. More fire splattered against the car, filling it with the sound of metal shearing, vibrations like a ripsaw, and the pungency of fried paint and gasoline. But at the same time, more sirens rose, meaning that the guys were incoming, and maybe there'd be enough of them to close this thing down.

Juba lost a second to amazement, then his combat brain took over. He turned, knocked the glazier to the ground, and said, "Stay for police."

They were halfway out of the dome, on the long catwalk trek to the last remaining flight of stairs, when the dry snap of outdoor gunfire began. How could there be gunfire? How could people have gotten here so fast? How could they tell where the shot had come from, as the suppressor had diffused its origin? Was this a betrayal or some kind of terrible stroke of bad luck? He knew he could mull these issues until capture or death, but got over them in one second. That was the soldier in him: built to confront the wretched here and now.

He and Esteban reached the stairway, two-at-a-timed-it down the steep incline from the catwalk, found themselves behind the chancel, and ran down a side aisle to the west door. They stepped into firefight city. Before them, four of the first-teamers were draped over the two

SUVs, all gone to full hammer on the Krinks. The sound of the guns eating ammo came as ripping, as if huge canvas shrouds were being pulled apart by mechanical devices. Around them an ever-growing crescent of squad and sheriff's cars had arrayed themselves clumsily, and each by this time had its own assortment of sheltering law enforcement, most with pistols, some with automatic weapons. Everybody shooting at everybody, ducking, finding a new spot, shooting some more, twisting back to hasten through a reload. A shooter went down, tried to crawl away, and, halfway through his second extension, bled dry and went still. The others kept the fire up.

It was chaos. Just men with guns shooting at men with guns, trying to maneuver under fire, and, when frustrated, unleashing bullets into the crisp air at vehicles or earth to no tactical advantage. Police flashers exploded, tires went flat, steam burst from engines, lakes of oil oozed like slime across the pavement.

"Back," yelled Juba, who, absent the abandoned sniper rifle, had no weapon.

He and his companion pulled back, even as someone noted them and sent a burst to gouge a furrow of splintered wood in the west door.

"You go," yelled the soldier. "I'll hold them."

"Jihadi hero," yelled Juba, then kissed him fiercely on the lips.

"Here," yelled the soldier, handing over the Krinkov.

As he turned back out, he pulled a Beretta and started to fire at oncomers.

Juba ran down the nave to the transept, amid slanting beams of holy light, in full view of the tortured man on the cross. He pushed his way through a crowd of frightened, bound priests, but none had the nerve to try to block him. He twisted into a hall, heard shrieks and screams from civilians in the rooms on either side, came to a corner, took a quick look back down the hall over his gunsight and saw no one. He kept moving and came to a door, pushed it open, tasted sun and air and the glories of a garden, negotiated it forcefully, and saw a street before him through an archway. He put the rifle to his side, after folding the stock, and set out. Trying to walk naturally, though breathing heavily, he hit the sidewalk, was about to turn right down the street, and then a man crashed into him, the rifle clattering away, and the two went down, tangled in each other's arms, strength on strength.

Swagger had no gun. What good was he? And each arriving officer seemed more eager to get into the fight than to pay him any attention. The FBI Ford pulled into the formation, Nick rolled out, Chandler the other way, and Neill from the rear.

He scrambled low and hard to them.

"Gun!" he yelled.

"I'm using mine!" said Nick, not really paying much attention, and leaning over the wheel well to put several Glock .40s out into the generalized target area thirty-five yards away.

Fire everywhere. The cars trembled as they were hit, the noise of the shots hit eardrums like driven spikes, the smell of burned smokeless drifted all over.

Swagger, in his quest for firepower, kept sliding car to car and reached the last of them in the barricade around the enemy position and found two Marshals blazing away with .45 automatics. They wouldn't relinquish a gun either.

That's when he saw Juba.

The man wore yellow shooting glasses, and had just emerged from the entry to the cathedral. Heavyset, intense, muscular under the priest's robes, no fear in him. Bob decided to charge. Somehow he felt that his aged body could outrun the bullets that Juba's bodyguard sent his way and overcome them both with well-executed punches, bellicose profanity, and hard-steel U.S. Marine Corps attitude. But he saw the error of his ways when the companion saw him and raised the rifle to kill him. However, in the next second, before his death was enacted, Bob saw a burst of shots riddle the huge door, drive the two back. He took this as God's belief in his mission and continued his charge after the momentary lull.

He quickly saw it was indeed a stupid thing to do, as the companion emerged again, this time with pistol, which he put toward Bob. As his trigger finger almost went into full press, someone just behind him shot the guy six times with a Glock. It was Chandler.

"Get back!" he screamed at her.

"You first," she replied.

But something knocked her flat. This burst, probably

from a gunman behind a car, spared Bob. No one would kill him! It seemed so wrong!

He ran to her.

"Where are you—"

"Vest," she wheezed. "I'm okay. Just . . . ribs . . ."

He got behind her and dragged her behind the Marshals' SUV.

"Stay here!"

"Take this!"

It was her Glock. But it was locked back, empty.

"Mag?"

"Gone."

"Shit," said Bob, and flicked the slide lock so that the gun clacked shut, even if empty. An empty gun could be better than no gun.

"Stay down now!" he yelled.

If she had a riposte—and she almost certainly did—he didn't hear it, for again he took off. But this time instead of running to the building, he ran to its side, reasoning that Juba would cut through the cathedral, find a way to reach the other side, and make his break into traffic, where he'd hijack a car or maybe just hot-wire something parked nearby. Juba would know what to do, that was for certain.

Bob came around the rear of the immense building, stepped out of its shade into sunlight, and noted that on this street traffic had stopped, pedestrians had disappeared, but all the cop cars with flashing lightbars and still screaming sirens were half a block away, clustered at the intersection. He slowed, but not much, negotiating the far side of the cathedral complex, and came to an arch, out of which, at that precise point in time, came a husky priest. As priests don't normally wear mics, yellow shooting glasses, or carry Krinkov assault rifles, he understood, in supertime, who it was. His reactions were appropriate. It was an open field tackle, low into the hips, no arms wrapping around, and, as the two crashed together, Juba's rifle flew. Each endured a moment of spangled confusion, but each came up fast.

"Freeze!" yelled Bob, the Glock locked on Juba's midsection.

"No shoot, no shoot!" yelled Juba, in English, his arms flying upward. "Please, sir, no shoot!"

But then, unaware or not caring that it was an empty gun that tethered him in place, he moved so fast, Bob could not keep up, even if he squeezed on an empty chamber. It was Systema Spetsnaz, the Russian Special Forces fighting system, which is not built of memorized elaborate moves—they break down under pressure—but the natural physics of the body relative to strength, balance, practice, and experience, the latter of which he had plenty. It began as a wave, a crest of energy, rushing through the body to accumulate at the point of contact, accelerated through the universe in warp drive, and was delivered at a speed that has no place in time, the limb going so fast, so soon, it rendered itself invisible. The hollow of Juba's foot hit Bob in the head so hard, it knocked him straight to Wonderland, and Alice and the White Rabbit played chess on his ruined skull for one or two seconds, and, when he recovered, the fight was over, and Juba, having recovered his rifle, stood over him to finish things off for good and all.

But he didn't.

Instead, he spat something in Arabic, turned, and, fleet as a deer, amazingly fast for such a big man, headed down the street.

Bob tried to rise, to look about, to yell for backup, but all the squad cars were clustered halfway down the block at the intersection, lightbars pulsing red-blue distress, men scuttling for shooting positions, though the shooting seemed to have halted.

Bob's knees went as a new wave of dizziness came over him, and he realized he had been hit so hard, he might die, as the pavement came up in a zoom shot to smash him in the nose, setting off more lights and frenzy.

44

Hospital, recovery

He came to once in the ambulance, alone, except that his brain felt as if it had nails hammered into it. It was not pleasant, and he decided to lie back and, somewhere between the lying and the backward part, he went to black again.

The next time he awoke, it was in a hospital room. Nick was there, but so were the nails.

"Welcome to the world," said Nick.

"Ahh," said Bob, "not sure I want to be here."

"No, the news is not good, but I expect you're man enough to take it."

"Chandler?"

"She made it. Broken ribs, but the vest saved her."

"Thank God," said Swagger. "Tell her to sit the next one out. You're her boss."

"You try and tell an American woman anything these days, let me know how you do."

He lay back, and didn't slide under. Meanwhile, a drip passed something medicinal into his veins, his vision was somewhat lazy in its mission to put edges on things, the smell of hospitals was its own special ordeal. A nurse leaned in to perform vital life-giving tasks, the last of which was holding a cup up for a long drink of water.

"Juba?" asked Bob after the last gulp.

Nick's expression told enough, but as a stickler for details, he then provided them.

"He got into a parking lot, hot-wired a car, and got out of town. Where, we have no idea. The report on the car didn't come in till last night—"

"It's the next day already?"

"Afraid so."

"Christ."

"Anyhow, we haven't located it yet, though now there's an APB out."

"That won't help. He'll dump it—he's already dumped it—and pick up another. He'll always be a car ahead of the APBs."

"No doubt. Smart operator."

"And fast. I never saw anybody so fast. He put that leg into me at light's speed. So give me the score."

"Not as bad as it could be. No police KIA, four wounded, not including you and Chandler. Four bad-guy KIA, including their NCO, who blew his own brains out rather than be taken. Six surrenders. Counterterrorism Division people are all over them, but since they were hired by a cutout in Mexico, and handled by cutouts all the way through, there's not going to be much. Universal soldiers, Mexican variation. Special Forces, good operators; as long as someone pays their life insurance, they'll shut up and wait for a chance to break. Also, some guy who's a glass expert, cut the window for Juba's shot. He doesn't know anything either."

Bob nodded.

Then he said, "Anyhow, when do I get out of here?"

"There's some recovery time up ahead. You've sustained a heavy concussion and skull fracture. They say not for a week."

"By then, Juba could have whacked—"

"Not your department. Your department is, tell the artist what this guy looks like. You're the only one who's seen him who's still alive and not afraid to talk."

"Jesus, Nick, it was just for a split second before he whacked me out."

"You're a trained observer. When you put your mind to it, you'll be surprised what you can recover."

"I'll try."

"There is no 'try,'" said Nick. "There is only 'do.'"

But there was no do. There was only try.

"I admit, it's not much," said Swagger.

A square-faced, rather generic Arab stared back at him from a universe of deft charcoal strokes. Whatever subtle nuance of geometry, weight distribution, underlying musculature, bone slope, and eye radiance that make a face a face was not there. Nothing was there.

He was still abed after three long days of working with a very decent guy billed as the best police artist in the world, but it came to only this.

"He looks like a cross between Saddam Hussein and Dr. Zhivago," said Swagger.

"You mean Omar Sharif, the Egyptian actor," said Nick. "Well, it does have a certain standardized, even idealized, quality to it. We'll put it out, but if it draws in over seventy-five thousand suspects, we'll know it's not really working."

"He's not a face. He's motion. He's speed, grace, battle talent, remorseless will. The face is nothing."

The door opened, and Mr. Gold appeared. He looked tired because during all the time since Juba's escape, he'd been sitting in the temporary FBI working room in the Wichita Hilton, going through reports, looking for patterns, reading the transcripts of interviews with the captured shooters and the glazier, trying to infer from the grade Z material something grade A. Again, plenty of try, no do.

He shook Swagger's hand.

"You have survived again," he said.

"Dying is above my pay grade," said Bob.

"The bravery is just this side of insanity," said Gold. "No man on earth would have launched himself at this fellow without a weapon."

"If it was about heroism," said Nick, "we'd win every fight."

"While you're here, Mr. Gold, I'd like to run my take on the shooting by you. Maybe you'll see something I missed."

"Doubtful. But please proceed."

"I have been thinking about his shot, because I never

made one so good. Nobody has, not even Craig Harrison, the long-distance champion of Afghanistan. Hitting a dime at three hundred ain't the deal, so it wasn't just marksmanship. It was, I don't know . . . They didn't teach no words for what I mean in 1964, which was my last brush with formal education."

" 'Spatial imagination'?" asked Nick.

Bob chewed it over.

"Sort of, but not quite. What I mean is, the understanding in a flash of the forces at play and understanding how they must go a certain way, anticipating that, being ahead of it, and putting the shot where the target is going to go, not where it is."

"Magic?" said Nick.

" 'Dynamic projection,' " said Gold.

"Yeah, yeah, that's the bull's-eye. He saw that the kid's head was invisible behind the Marshal's but that it was tending to emerge. By the time it emerged, other things might have happened, and if he fired on it while emerging, it might have moved too far when time in flight finally put the bullet there. But, simultaneously, he couldn't put the bullet through the Marshal's head because it might not make it all the way or it might get deflected. So he put it on the edge of the Marshal's skull, above the ear, beneath the cowboy hat, knowing that it wouldn't impact straight on and explode, deform, deflect, whatever. Basically, he shot on the deflection, like putting the cue ball off the edge to hit two walls, knocking the eight ball on the other side of the table into the sock. He deflected the bullet about fifteen degrees, and it caught Jared just as he turned and emerged, under the right eye of a target that was probably only a quarter visible. Nobody but Juba hits that shot. What does that tell us?"

"It shows that on top of everything else, he's creative in real time. A difficult man to outthink," said Mr. Gold.

"Hope I'm up to it. One other thing. You speak Arabic?"

"No outsider really speaks it, not fully and fluently. But in the shallow sense, then, yes, I speak it."

"He said something to me, even as he didn't shoot me."

"You must have impressed him. He doesn't seem the loquacious sort."

Swagger spit out clumsily the sounds that Juba had uttered as he stood over him with the recovered Krink.

"Majnun jiddo," clarified Mr. Gold. "It means 'crazy grandpa.'"

45

The ranch

The jet landed at 0345 and quickly went to black-out as it taxied toward Menendez's private hangar. Juba had sat almost inert during the trip back, seemingly gathering strength after expending so much in the ordeal of shooting and evading.

But when he climbed down the jetway, Señor Menendez himself awaited him and quickly escorted him to the Land Rover. La Culebra, in his sock, and of course the translator, Alberto, necessary to the grandee for many reasons, hovered close by. All climbed into the car and it pulled out, with Mercedeses, fore and aft, full of security.

"Ah, my friend," said Menendez, "you were superb. What talent, what skill, what a jihadi warrior you are. My God, you accomplished the miraculous, the impossible. I owe you all."

"I do not want all," Juba said. "I want safe transport to my shooting site, myself by one route, my rifle by an-other. I want a new target to shoot, because I have to resharpen reflexes and protocols ignored for too long. All now must be to my task. And if I succeeded with your problem, it was because Allah willed it."

The last was a simple declaration. By inflection, it suggested that no theological disagreement could be permitted. It also suggested that further conversation could not be permitted. But Menendez was not good at picking up cues from others. He had things to say and would say them, regardless.

"I should thank you also for exposing a traitor in my midst, and, in consequence, I have directed an intense security review. Such measures are extreme, and innocent people, alas, will die. But if we have been penetrated, the whole apparatus is at risk. The traitor must be found, and the capture and deaths of those soldiers must be answered with justice, no matter how sloppy."

"You infer from the law enforcement response that there was a traitor?"

"I do. How else could—"

"There was no traitor," said Juba.

"Then how were they upon you before you had even descended the dome? The newspapers were so proud of the police arrival before your escape and the subsequent gun battle. I presume that is cover story to mask the presence of a rat. There's no way they could have—"

"Yes, there is a way," said Juba. "I saw it. Or him, as in this case; the way is a man."

"Who would—"

"We'll find out. After I've rested, I'll contact my people, and, through them, I'll access the intelligence files of every agency in the world that keeps records on the Americans. I'm looking for the identity of a senior sniper—sixty, seventy. He was there, and it was through his experience that he understood where the shot had to come from, and it was through his reaction that the police were so quickly on scene. He led them, and he alone understood as the action unfolded where I had to be. And he was there. This has only happened once before. In Baghdad, when the Americans understood my strategy, they quietly countered it and destroyed it in one afternoon. In both cases, brilliant thought. And I'm guessing in both cases, though the men were different, the agency was the same: the United States Marine Corps. They are shooters. They still understand shooting, and can read it and comprehend its meaning, when so few others can."

He paused.

"I saw the sniper. Weathered, from a life spent outdoors. Lithe, quick, spry, even though he was so old. Without fear. What crazy grandpa assaults an armed weight lifter thirty-five years younger than him? Only one who has been in many fights and always prevailed and believes himself invulnerable."

"You showed him he wasn't."

"No, I showed him I could evade. That is not a victory. I should have killed him, as I believe it will save me a great deal of trouble in what comes next. But if I'd fired, the sound of the shot would have drawn police in seconds. If I'd paused to strangle him or to smash him with the gun, I would have extended my vulnerability. So even after knocking him to the ground, my first instinct was to evade. I made the right decision, but it feels very wrong."

46

Meetings, Wichita, Kansas

Swagger was released on the third day and got to the morning meeting on the fourth day.

It was the first get-together for Chandler, Neill, Nick, Swagger, and Mr. Gold in over a week, and, as usual, Nick had Chandler—hobbling on a walker but game—go through the APB responses and other communiqués from the police net, particularly those provoked by the circularized police artist portrait of the fugitive, under Swagger's direction.

There were summaries from the interrogations—to no effect. And, as per usual, no possibilities from monitoring bus stations, the airport, the train station, even taxi, Uber, and Lyft drivers. Of the six or seven stolen cars reported, only one had been recovered, and it was almost certainly not Juba's, as forensics found no trace of him in it.

"Sooner or later, one of the commandos will disclose where they staged the operation, and we can bust and vacuum that site," said Nick. "But everyone on the other team is operating at a very high professional level and will probably not make the kind of stupid mistake that brings down most criminal initiatives. These people are first-class. Everything is done through cutouts far from the order giver and his inner circle, always using laundered money, accounts that lead nowhere. No wire intelligence, and nobody monitored radio transmissions, so clearly they used sophisticated masking. Neill, anything in cyber? Any little thing?"

"Sorry, no intercepts. Even put NSA on it, and they went through all their satellite stuff. I have a tech full-time in D.C. going after their fall guy. If and when a phony Brian Waters email or Dark Web site or blog hits, we'll know."

"We're fucked," said Bob. "He'll do that just before he shoots. Whatever he wants the world to know about Brian Waters will hit then, you can bet on it."

"Anything else?" asked Nick.

"Did you find the other rifle? Meaning the rifle he used here in Wichita?" Bob asked.

"How did you know he didn't use the Accuracy International?"

"No point in risking the weapon dedicated to his big shot for some sideshow."

"Well, you're right—yes, a different rifle. He dumped it behind the chancel," Nick said. "I looked at it pretty carefully before we sent it off to Firearms Division. It appeared to be straight-out-of-the-box standard, which is to say, without information."

"What about all the science magic you do? DNA, hairs, atoms, that sort of thing?"

"Nothing yet. Again, it's doubtful any microtraces will be found to lead anywhere. Maybe once we get Juba, we might be able to DNA trace, but as of now, since we don't have any DNA on him, DNA is pointless. In all other respects it was just standard Remington 700, Police Model, with a standard Leupold in standard mounting hardware. No gunsmithing required, no trip to custom rifle specialists; ergo, no information. Firearms Division is running the number, and they haven't come up with anything yet, but if it follows the pattern, it'll be a straw man's purchase in some faraway state that proves to be a dead end. Meanwhile, the rifle just sits on a rack in the Hoover Building."

"It's a .308, I assume?"

"No. It was something called 6.5 Creedmoor."

Bob nodded, considering.

"Does that tell you anything?" Nick asked.

"The fact that he's onto 6.5 Creedmoor is an indication of how up-to-date he is. It's the big new thing, on all the magazine covers. Supposedly more accurate than .308. The boy don't miss no tricks."

"So it looks like no progress," said Nick. "But it confirms what we know: money is behind it, big money. Again, that tells us the target is major, and we ought to get going or something bad will happen."

"Should you go to the White House?" asked Neill. "It seems that his target—"

"No," said Nick. "When you go there, it gets all sticky politically, and other agendas beyond law enforcement come into play. That is why I would prefer if you keep speculation on the ultimate target to yourself. If you make an assumption, we're in a world of confirmation bias, and clarity is the first casualty. I want us to work in the complete context-free abstract until it's not possible. Don't you agree, Mr. Gold?"

"I do entirely," said Gold. "In Israel too, politics beclouds our efforts all too often."

"So, what's next conceptually? Tell me how to use Counterterrorism's manpower to flood a zone and flush something out. Tell me some way to aggressively proact, not just wait to pick up the pieces and hope we identify a piece of DNA or Juba's credit card."

Silence.

Gold then said, "Sergeant Swagger, his shot will be at over a mile, you think. But at a certain point, he is required to divert, and he goes on this mission, the distance being three hundred yards in a crowd. He requires a new rifle, new ammunition, a whole new program. This involves a whole new set of problems to solve. He solves them—and barely escapes. But does that mean, assuming he is back on safe territory, he'll have to reacclimate himself to the longer shot?"

"He will if he can, if he has time. It's not necessary, but he'd want to do it. Do you see anything in that?"

"Ah, there's something in there, but it has yet to clarify."

"Mr. Gold," said Nick. "Please clarify! *Clarify!* We need clarification!"

"I shall so instruct my subconscious. But it seems not to work regular hours."

"One interesting thing," Nick said. "Wichita Metro tells me that the AK Juba left behind, it didn't have a magazine. That is, he removed the magazine and took it with him. Maybe to use it as a blunt-impact weapon. He could fit it under his jacket, in his belt, and it would fit flush. Of course, that would preclude commercial flight, yet another indicator he had private means out of town. But—why? Any thoughts?"

Swagger said, "He don't do nothing on a whim. He's a careful bird. He's got a use for it, and I hope I ain't around when he comes to it."

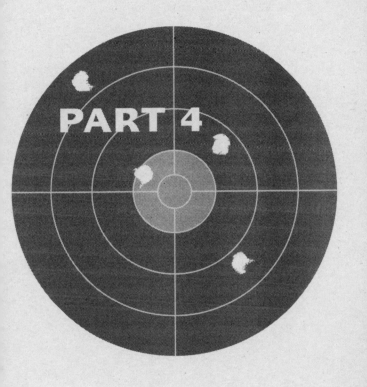

PART 4

47

The ranch

A day later, the pictures of known American snipers came through via email from Juba's control. He peered at them and, of several possibilities, recognized one: a sergeant's face like his own, something clever, alive, even wise, but without aristocratic air or expectations beyond the practical. Not interested in luxury, not softened by too much pleasure, steadfast of soul and devoted to duty, unable to relax but for the company of those who'd earned the right to stand nearby. These men—American snipers, security advisors, Green Berets, and SEALs, men of experience and talent—had all acquired the patina of an Assyrian shield, a certain cast to the eyes, surrounded by a fissure of wrinkles, a stolidity of expression, a hardness to the jawline that extended to a mouth that would never yield to gentleness or humor unless deep in the bosom of family, friends, or cobelievers. But this sergeant's face completed Juba's nightmare portrait of the American sniper who awaited him in the future. It was the face of his death.

He looked at the name, trying to make sense of it. Since its structural foundations diverged so from that of the Arabic, it seemed incoherent. It was simply an accumulation of sounds squished into a single utterance. It seemed to have no meaning.

"What does this mean?" he asked Alberto. *"Bobleeswagger?"*

"American names are simply labels. They don't carry meanings and are not adjusted to celebrate an outstanding individual or origin or heritage. His name is Swagger because his father's name was Swagger, and that is all that can be said."

"But I have seen this word 'swagger' in texts. I did not bother to look it up. But it exists independent of this man."

"It does. 'Swagger' is 'a bold walk.'"

"A sniper would not swagger. A sergeant might, an aviator certainly. A general, without doubt. A sniper? Never. The sniper is quiet, calm, without vanity and drama. This fellow would not swagger."

"They call this irony. Actually, if I understand irony, it's not irony, it's coincidence. But Americans love irony for some reason and they misuse the term promiscuously, as perhaps we do 'honor.' Irony is saying something but meaning the opposite, usually for the sake of mischief or wit. Thus, they love the fact—those who know him or of him—that his name is one thing and his character and skill another."

"I suppose I understand. I would not have until I had reached this stage and achieved so many infidel kills. In mannerism: sedate; in action: bold. It is the best way for a man to be. Now I know him a little, know what created the man he is today. *Bobleeswagger*. He has delivered much death and knows it always sets him apart—even from his children. He knows he is used, sometimes cynically, by his masters for ends of which he has no knowledge and in which he has to believe on faith alone. But he adheres to duty nevertheless and will die doing it."

"Is it him you are discussing or yourself?" asked Alberto.

"We are much the same, even if our gods are at war. I should have seen it earlier, as I now see its signs everywhere. And it explains everything. This isn't an operation. It's a game—*the* game—to be played out to the end. His death or mine."

Alberto nodded. "Or both," he said.

48

Zombieland, a clarification

Sleep. Dreams utterly incoherent, full of odd scenes, outliers, and rogues. Aches of old wounds and new—the cracked ribs, the spells of dizziness, for example—came and went at random. Sometimes his phantom hip screamed in pain, though in his wakefulness it was perfect. Old man, pins wobbly, struts bent, needs oil, lube, and some adjustments.

But worse: every so often, the face of one of the lost ones—there were so many—and things that went along with them. Regret, isolation, despair, nihilism, memories of pain, memories of the comforting blur of the bottle, memories always of folly, stupidity, cowardice, ugly words, once issued, never recalled, all the times the obvious had been missed and the impossible selected as a goal, the center not holding, all systems exposed, in their illusory nature, the cheapness of their fraud, the tawdriness of their window dressing—a night, really, without much actual rest. Then, almost a mercy, the phone.

He swam toward it.

"Swagger."

It was Nick. "I want everybody in. We've got something."

That got his attention. "Has it broken?"

"Well, I'm hoping the breaking process has started. Get in here."

"On my way."

He struggled through a shower that semi-restored him, and a cup of bad residence hotel coffee, and drove his rental down to Hoover. It was almost five in the morning, but by the time he arrived, most of his functions were functioning, his hands weren't shaking, and the surrealism of the dream world had helpfully erased itself.

The building operated at about ten percent hum in the off hours, and halls, usually so bustling, were ghost tunnels. Security was sparse, and each individual noise seemed to carry an echo and its reecho with it. Perhaps in the op center things were jumping. Everywhere else, there was too much room, not enough people. He elevatored to the sixth floor and turned in to the deserted hall that led to the task force office, entered, and saw they were all in, except for Gold. Someone had put a pot of coffee on, and Swagger took a cupful, his second of the day.

Finally, Nick looked up.

"Should we wait for Mr. Gold?" asked Neill.

"No, he's here. Going over his notes."

"This is his party?"

"The whole way."

"Is it his clarification?" groggy, gorgeous Chandler, in jeans and sweatshirt, Glock on hip, had to know.

"He'll explain. Mr. Gold!" he called.

The Israeli entered. Unusually for him, he was not in his daily wear, the jeweler's black suit and tie. His shoes weren't even black. The shirt was wide open, there was no jacket, and the slacks were radically gray. He was wearing burgundy loafers.

"Good morning," he said. "Sorry to drag you all here, but if you agree with me, I think we have to get going on this."

He sat.

"What has happened is that two unrelated pieces of information—one from Mr. Neill, one from Sergeant Swagger—have suddenly become related. Apart, they are nothing; together, perhaps something. I believe it at least demands a serious effort."

"Please proceed," said Neill. "I love it when I'm a genius."

"You had said that the kind of aerial or drone reconnaissance that led us to Juba in Syria, keyed to the attributes that would identify a long-range shooting venue, were useless in the United States without some kind of limiting or defining function. Not even knowing the region, we were looking for a rowboat in an ocean."

"True," said Neill.

"And Sergeant Swagger had said that Juba almost certainly will shoot at living targets, first to acclimate himself to the spontaneous motion of life at that distance through that magnification system, and second—and equally important—to test the killing power of his rounds at that distance, in search of one that causes potentially more damage."

"Yep," said Bob.

"Now, I assume that, as a true believer—you never said as much, but I believe the inference was there—I assume that he would use human targets at some time in his journey. He believes them to be infidels, has no scruples against using them, and it is easily within the capacity of the Menendez apparatus to arrange such a thing. Everybody with me?"

Nods and mumbles of assent.

"So a question that can be asked is this: who would he shoot? Where could he get living bodies to hit at long range? It's not the sort of thing you advertise for, nobody's going to volunteer for it, not even for a large sum to be left to the volunteers' benefactors. Those selected would almost have to be of a sort who would not be noticed in their absence, perhaps not even reported. They would have to be from a victim pool about which even the police, in reality, wouldn't care much."

He waited. Nobody had a thing to say.

"It seems to me," he said, "or, that is, it seemed to me all of a sudden two hours ago, that the one source without fail would be any city's population of homeless men. Nobody counts them, nobody really looks at them, American legalism is such that they can't be rounded up in a tank or beaten until they leave town. So they find an out-of-the-way place and fester. Under the viaduct, by the river, out with the dumpsters, in abandoned factories, zombie neighborhoods, that sort of thing. And so it seems to me that Menendez might assign men to visit these places, drug an already sleeping hobo, and drag him off.

"You can imagine the rest. He awakens a day later in unfamiliar circumstances and finds himself pinned or in some fashion imprisoned, and, from a long way off, our good friend Juba conducts his experiments. The bullets come closer and closer, and if the man screams or begs, no one is there to hear, because the site is clearly wilderness of some sort. When Juba strikes, the cadaver is examined for terminal forensics, then buried, burned, or otherwise disposed of by cartel methodology. I have heard of buzzards."

"They do use buzzards," said Nick.

"So it seems to me that as of this moment we ought to begin a national canvas for any localities that have experienced a sudden spike in homeless disappearances. I doubt they would abscond with people too far from what is their ultimate disposal site, it simply would complicate logistics. And they would be confident in their operations because the homeless have no champions, save the odd social worker or nun, and are of no interest to anyone in society, perhaps garnering some municipal social service attention, but even that is apt not to be so tightly applied. And if it were, who would care? Suppose you go to the police with fears that a number of homeless men have disappeared? What sort of response would that generate?"

Silence, of course, for the Israeli had focused on a

particular weakness in American society, one that no one seemed to have the knowledge, the will, or the funding to do much about.

"Nobody's going to win a Pulitzer Prize writing about vanished homeless, that's for sure," said Neill.

"You see the rest of it," said Gold. "If we do locate an area of usual activity, we can program a satellite to search for the attributes in that area that might show up from outer space. We winnow further by drone. We can put the tiny whirlybirds over the most promising areas and, in that way, find the location of such an installation literally right down to the bench on the ground in front of it. And, as in Israel, we raid. Six helicopters dropping off forty of Orwell's rough men—or Gadi Motter's—at oh-dark-thirty, and your problem is solved."

"So let's get on this right away," said Nick. "We want to circularize all police entities for reports of such a spike in disappearances. Maybe they have undercover sources in these communities. Maybe it's right in front of them, they just have never had any impetus to look. So they assign a clerk for an afternoon to go through the records. Maybe there's one town where, for some reason, the number had jumped."

"Boss," said Chandler, "I'd also do charity agencies, social work departments, and university sociology departments. The homeless interest researchers, and we've got to tap into that."

"Good, Chandler."

"Also, I'd be sure to get the info request read at the daily preduty briefing to beat cops. It's the sort of thing a beat cop might hear and discount or ignore, but suddenly when it's put before him and been validated by the process, he gets involved."

"You might try places where illegals congregate to find work," said Swagger. "Lots of men could go missing from Home Depots all over America, and nobody know."

"Good, good, I like what I'm hearing. Any other suggestions?"

"Anyplace stoop labor is hired," said Neill. "Harvesttime, lots of migrants come in to work the fields. Some—too many, no doubt—end up *in* those fields."

"Non-union construction," said Bob.

"Should we prioritize by area?" asked Chandler. "I mean, we have sort of assumed that wherever Juba is training, that would be the west. Lots and lots of land out there. Lots of land where he could have a mile-long shooting range and nobody would know."

"That makes sense," said Nick. "I think it's a good assumption. This is going to be a hell of a workload any way you cut it, so any help is worth it.

"Neill, you and Swagger get that software to guide the birds setup. Okay, let's get—Oh, wait. Let me say it formally: Mr. Gold, you are the best. Don't know where we'd be without Mossad."

"I only want one thing in return," said Mr. Gold. "A long chat with Juba. I want to hear his thousand and one tales."

49

The ranch, shipping out

A last man was sacrificed on the altar of accuracy, and Juba was pleased to see that the shooting instrument he had so painstakingly built and tuned over the previous months maintained its efficiency after having been laid down for the other rifle. It killed totally on the first shot at the range required. After putting the target down, he cleaned the rifle exhaustively, and, after that, all its surfaces pristine, he fired one more shot, because cold bore shots, by tradition and experience, were always better out of a fouled bore.

He prepared the rifle for its trip. He shellacked all the knobs on the Schmidt & Bender scope so that they would not vibrate in transit to a new position. To make doubly certain, he marked the settings with stripes of fingernail polish on both turret and turret housing so that the joining of the two stripes in one continuous line would signify that the turret or housing had not been turned. The bolt was removed and taped to the stock. The whole receiver-scope nexus—the heart of it, really—

was triple-swathed in Bubble Wrap so that it was suspended midair to avoid being jostled or subject to vibration. Each screw, tightened and shellacked, was also marked so that a quick glance could tell if it had been loosened.

The rifle was the sum of its tensions. It was a mesh of screws tightened to an exact position and no other. Ambiguity, drift, the random and forlorn could not be accepted. So perfectly tightened, it became a matrix of stress. In this respect, it was a musical instrument, all stops set perfectly, all reeds and spit valves dialed to the precise position. It stayed reliable to the degree it retained exact registry. Rifles—all systems—fall apart when individual components go unmonitored and unadjust themselves. Juba could have none of that.

Then he put together a case with all the necessary logistical components: the iPhone 8, with its precious ballistics program; various wrenches; LensPens; a glazier's key; a set of screwdrivers; and the ten most perfect rounds of ammunition that he had assembled. This too was wrapped and taped to the stock.

Finally, when the whole package was encased in foam and tape—it looked a bit like a mummy—it was secured in the false bottom of a high-end bookcase, invisible to the eye, which was itself skillfully packed in a shipping crate, secured tightly, made inviolate to all but the most violent accidental intrusions. It would survive a crash landing, in other words, but not a crash.

A day later, Juba watched as this object, under the rubric of a well-known custom furniture boutique, was delivered to UPS for delivery to its next destination. It would thereby enter two systems: UPS's, but also Iran's Ministry of Intelligence, whose supple and proficient professionals would be responsible for its transport from several different destinations via several different shipping agencies. At a certain point, it would become affiliated with a credit card registered, through Iranian subterfuge, to Brian Waters, of Albuquerque, New Mexico, and in that way join the train of evidence that was slowly accumulating against the dead man, on whom all blame was to be placed.

The intelligence people would discreetly monitor its progress, taking possession of it intermittently, inspecting it, then shipping it onward. It would reach its destination—only one senior executive knew the final address—at a leisurely pace but still in plenty of time. Juba wanted to be there, in the room with the rifle, facing the target, for a good while before he had to pull the trigger—one day, at least, a full week if possible. The whole enterprise disintegrated if it were rushed or improvised.

Finally, it was done.

He sat in the Land Rover, with Alberto, as they drove back to the ranch. The two Mexican Special Forces troopers, who had handled the transaction at the shipping agency, sat in front, indifferent to the Syrian-accented Arabic being spoken behind them.

"This step is finished," said Alberto. "It must be a relief. Now, only the journey."

"That part has been well planned. It will proceed routinely. No one will intercept me."

"The picture they have put out is quite amusing."

"It makes me look like a cartoon. It degrades me."

"Everybody's a critic. More important, it makes you look like me—like Gamal Abdel Nasser, Harvey Weinstein, John Garfield, Omar Sharif—like any other Semitic with strong features. The dark hair helps. It's all the same DNA, intermingled by crossfucking over the centuries. That is why there is so much hatred. We're all family."

"I do not share your theory of mongrel politics," said Juba.

"No matter. In the end, the drawing is so stereotypical, it looks like everyone and no one. It can be of no help."

"As you say. In my journey, in any event, I will remain obscure."

The Syrian laughed.

Juba showed him a finger on which he had written in Arabic, in ballpoint: "Meet me outside in swamp at 0430."

Then he rubbed it out, and said, "Who's Harvey Weinstein?"

50

It was as if her name was Detective. Her last name was Murphy, but people just called her Detective. To look at her was to know why: she had that glare of butch aggression, a face unsoftened by makeup or internal mirth, family, love. If she'd ever had any of them, it was a long time ago. You wouldn't think life in a city of twenty-six thousand would have eroded her softer components so relentlessly, but it made sense when you realized this was her second department, after fifteen very tough years in Salt Lake City Metro. She's come to Rock Springs for the landscape and the peace and quiet. She's found one—the landscape was everywhere—but not the other two.

"Detective, for some reason Rock Springs has the highest rate of homeless depletion in America," said Nick.

"I'm surprised anybody keeps tabs," she said.

"I'm not too sure that the figures are reliable, with the single exception of yours. But it's clear from the report your chief forwarded that you're the only one paying attention."

She lit a Marlboro, offered one each to Nick and Bob, who each declined, and took a deep draught. She wore jeans, packed a Smith .357 four-inch on her right hip, a plaid shirt, a five-pointed law enforcement star, boots that had been through fertilizer a time or two.

The three sat on a bench outside Rock Springs's main station, a nineteenth-century brick extravaganza, from which men with Colts and Winchesters had gone to enforce the law a century before. She would have been happy among them.

"It's mostly Indians," she said. "They get in all kinds of trouble. You tell me why. But I'll tell you how. Meth, speed, coke, Mexican Mud, now opioids. They're always doing something to fuck themselves up, and if it's off the res, it's on us to clean it up. Such beautiful folks too. But you want to hear about our hobos. Oh, wait, can't call 'em that. Our *homeless.*"

"You say that of a population you estimate at over seventy-five, at least six have gone missing in the last three months. Not moseyed away, not died in ditches, not frozen, or hit by big rigs on the interstate, but just vanished—one day here, the next day not?"

"Yep, totally. It actually stopped for a while, then, the last few days, another guy ups and vanishes. Then comes your alert."

Bob and Nick looked at each other. Without having to say it, each man thought of Mr. Gold's inquiry about whether Juba would refresh his skills with another run-through.

Detective continued. "By my calculations, Rock Springs is weird. Used to be a hard-bitten coal town, but, of late, it's shared in the tourist boom. That's why you see all the cornball Old West cowboy shit around. Anyhow, with tourists, you get homeless, as old-school settlers are too judgmental to give nickels and dimes to the scarecrows. But the tourist hands over five-spots just so they won't have to look at them. So they're drawn here in the warmer months. Progressive city council, so we can't get rough with 'em. They hang on somehow. I got to know a few, that's why I can tell what's going on. They talk to me. I try to talk for them, but nobody listens."

"We're listening."

"It started about three months ago. I picked up on it fast. 'Where's Paul?' I had to know, because one day Paul was gone."

"Paul was special?"

"Most of them are self-made wrecks. Paul was wrecked by fate. He had no character flaws. It's just that God decided it was time to squash a bug, and Paul lost the bug lottery."

"What was his deal?" asked Nick.

"Paul Finley. Beloved English teacher at Rock Springs High. By all accounts, smart, funny, generous, forgiving, concerned. One day, he backs out of his garage and kills his daughter. I guess some folks can come back from that, but he wasn't one of them. He just starts falling through pathologies. Drunk, unemployed, suicidal, drug-addicted, divorced, on the streets. We tried hard—and I mean everybody—to help out. But he couldn't make it back. Last time I saw him, he was sawing away on a Robitussin-and-Ripple high in an alley behind North's, the restaurant. Maybe if I'd pulled him in that night. But I didn't."

"And?"

"And nothing. Gone. I noticed a few days later and asked. Nope, just gone. No one knew where."

"Is that odd?"

"It is. These folks don't have homes, but they do have a kind of community. They talk. Nobody leaves without good-byes, advice on where it's better, towns that are softer, the weather easier, blue less inclined to hit. But Paul was just gone."

They waited. She took a few puffs.

"Jerry was next. Followed by Husky. Finally, Frank. Same deal, just gone. No one saw a thing. I got an old wheezer named Big Bill to talk. He said he saw three guys come into the alley—the homeless bomb out most nights in an alley that runs two blocks behind the North Street restaurants—give Frank an injection, and load the guy into an SUV. It took about thirty seconds. They'd done it before. Then it stopped."

"And you say it started up again?"

"Charlie Two-Toes. Lakota Sioux, proud when sober, a mess when drunk, which was most of the time. Gone, no trace. I keep trying to tell people. I sort of want to get a night watch set up, or something, but there's not much interest. It's a 'Good riddance' sort of thing."

They were silent. She lit another cigarette. Over the buildings, mountains filled the day with snowy grandeur and cheap irony.

"Say," she finally said, "what is this all about anyway? Nobody gave a damn, and suddenly big actors from the FBI come to town, including this one here who doesn't say a thing but has SWAT eyes."

"I do talk," said Swagger, "but not this time."

"So you can't tell me a thing?"

"We'd love to tell you the Bureau had opened a new project to examine crime against the homeless on a national scale," said Nick, "but that wouldn't be true. I can only say, this touches on a national security issue that demands immediate attention. Yours is the best break we've gotten. Thank you for paying attention and caring."

"It's just such a downer to see the waste. Most of them were something, could still be something, but they just somehow lost whatever will it takes to play the game. They floated until they went under."

"Can you give me a little insight on the area?"

"Sure. Glad to help."

Swagger said, "We're looking for a certain place. It would be big and private. Someone rich would own it. It would be way out of any town. The owners would probably keep a real low profile. You could drive by it a hundred times and never notice it."

"All the big rich are up 191 in Sublette country toward Jackson Hole. Forty miles up, maybe. Some historic spreads, like the Hanson Ranch. It's now owned by some Southern California corporation for executive retreats, but it was built on coal-and-railroad money. Huge. Goes on and on and on. You could do anything there, and nobody'd know a thing."

"Does the region have a name?"

"It's called Pine Valley. Little town at the center, some posh restaurants. There's a private airport where the haircuts jet in from their other places in the Caribbean or the South of France. They don't hang out much at the 7-Eleven, so I can't tell you too much more."

"That's very helpful, Detective. I'll send your chief a letter."

"He'd just throw it away. I'm a pain in the ass."

The drones, flying at sunset high enough to disperse their engine noise, always out of the direct rays of the sun so they didn't sparkle, came back with the goods, from five thousand feet that looked, under magnification, to be more like five hundred. Swagger went through the images at Hill Air Force Base, in Ogden, Utah, just west of Salt Lake City, which was the nearest spot with the necessary technology.

"Do you see it?" asked Neill, who'd masterminded the aerial recon with his usual nonchalant genius while making smart-guy comments the whole time.

"Yeah, yeah," said Swagger. "I've got it down to two."

He gave his two selections. Neill punched buttons at

a keyboard, the two images came up side by side on a giant screen more usually given to the display of Russian bombers on Siberian tarmacs. To the uninitiated, it was just a blur and smear in odd shades, imprimatured by a digital display at one corner that expressed latitude and longitude, altitude, time, weather. But Swagger got it, homed in on one, homed in further on a specific area and requested the blowup.

"I'm seeing what looks like, um, a post? It's not a natural structure. It's clearly man-built. Is that what everybody else sees? Can you bring it up more?"

Neill diddled—*clickety-click, clickety-clack*—and selected the piece of picture in which the post-like thing was featured, brought it to center screen, and blew it up nice and big.

They were in the darkened theater of an air force room, decorated with photos of supersonic fighters, gray-haired generals, and flags. The screen was the only thing that differentiated the chamber from a Kiwanis Club.

Nick said to Colonel Nickel, who was the USAF representative at the meet, "Colonel, wouldn't you have some guys who can read these things at a high level? Any chance you'd loan us their eyes for a few minutes?"

"Sure," said the colonel. "Always happy to pitch in."

He disappeared quickly, leaving the hard core alone.

"If we can get NSA on them hard," said Nick, "maybe we can pick up some commo linked to a foreign intelligence service. With that, we can go to FISA. If we get a FISA warrant, we can go prime time on their asses."

"That works," said Neill.

"It better, because that's going to be your job. Bob, tell me what you're seeing."

"The post is at the end of a meadow that's over a mile long. It's situated east-west, to make the sun less a problem. The trees and gentle incline work as a natural wind barrier. There are car tire tracks all over it, signifying recent activity. Somewhere in the far trees, there's got to be a shooting platform. That's key, because if we can measure the range from platform to target and weigh that against the possibles, we can find a match and identify the target. But I'm sure it's a mile-long shooting range with a post at one end to mount targets."

"So if your read is verified, we might raid."

"You'd need two elements, in coordination. A chopper insert of aggressors and a simultaneous penetration off the highway, with backup, communications, more ammo, medical, all the necessities. It's straight SEAL work. Too bad we can't get 'em."

"Sounds like Mogadishu," said Neill.

"I hope we do better than Mogadishu," said Bob.

Nick was thinking out loud. "We'll start with Counterterrorism's teams and fill in with SWAT people from a lot of field offices. Once we get FISAed up, we'll get an okay to drop the airborne raid out of Salt Lake City, where we have the assets. I'll get Ward Taylor involved, and, with Counterterrorism behind it, it'll get moving. But it can't happen tonight. Or tomorrow night. Or even—"

Staff Sergeant Abrahams arrived, in tow behind Colonel Nickel. Briefed, he laid his extremely gifted eyeballs on the two-dimensional imagery stolen from up above.

He looked hard at the first image, then directed Neill to take him through the sequence so he could see it in the context of the larger plat of land upon which it was situated.

"Abrahams is the Da Vinci of photo interp," said the colonel as Neill zoomed in on the image and then out. "He can tell you if the rubles in the bad guys' pockets are heads or tails."

"Sir," said Abrahams, a rather dapper black NCO who looked like the leading poet of the Harlem Renaissance, "not knowing what you're looking for—"

"By design," said Neill.

"I get that. Okay, I'd call that identified structure a post of some sort, apparently of wood—wood has a unique reflect pattern, which I see here. Relating its shadow to the time of day, I'd make it about six feet tall. I can even make out what I'd call some kind of cement at the base. The tire tracks are SUV weight; I've seen that same tread all over the Mideast wherever service Humvees and Agency Explorers do their work. Too deep, too wide, for regular passenger vehicle."

"Anything else?" said Swagger. "Assume we're dopes and have missed everything."

"Well, there is some reflect in the center of the meadow. Meaning wet. Meaning marsh. Meaning mud. Meaning moisture. Meaning humidity. If this is where they put it, they put it in such a position where access to it—visual, ballistic, laser, infrared, radar, whatever—dealt with differing air densities, the humid air over the marsh being heavier than the dry air over the prairie. I don't know if that was something intended or just happenstance, but my guess is, given the amount of drier land available and the many other possible access angles on the target, that it was on purpose. For whatever reason, they wanted to track the effect of the heavier air on their effort."

He's shooting over water, Bob thought.

51

It was a tangle of trees artfully positioned to give definition to an exquisitely landscaped garden that lay behind the main house, perpetually damp from water seepage, giving it the nickname The Swamp. Tactically, its great advantage was that it could be accessed on the crawl, unseen by any of the night sentries who roamed the property on predictable paths, which Juba had noted.

Thus, when he saw Alberto approaching, even on a night without a moon, he knew that the transaction went unobserved. And before the man reached the edge of the brambles, Juba attracted his attention with a small snort, diverting him yet again to the lee of a small tree.

"Nobody saw you?" he asked.

"No one. I don't think there are security cameras in my wing of the house. His fear is, people coming in from the outside, not betrayal from the inside. But he is a very paranoid man."

"Indeed," said Juba.

"What is this about?"

"Your future."

"Meaning?"

"That I suspect you want one. If that is so, you will have to perform certain tasks. Otherwise, you will be dead, cut to ribbons by the freak in the sock."

"I have done nothing to—"

"It's not what you've done, it's what you know. They will kill you within seconds after they kill me."

The Syrian-Mexican could make no sense of this.

"What? Why would—"

"He cannot let me go on my mission. It's too big a risk. Wichita changed everything. Suppose I am captured? Suppose the Americans offer me a deal to testify against him and identify him as the instigator of the Wichita thing? They offer me a new life, as opposed to sending me to some black site where Serbian mercenaries blowtorch my secrets out of me. That is now a more serious problem for him than any damage my people will do to him in suspicion of a betrayal. And, in any event, my murder will be disguised as some kind of mishap, a chance encounter with a policeman, an auto accident. He will pay an indemnity, but in that lies survival for him. He knows it. I know it. He just doesn't know I know it."

"I am only half Arab, so I lack your gift for cunning."

"I need two things from you. First, I have to know when that screwball in the sock is out of the picture or indisposed in some way."

"Easy. Two Mexican women come to him at six each

evening. He must either have sex or kill somebody every single day or it is said he becomes irritable."

"Six, then. And second: tunnels. These Mexicans, they make their living in tunnels. Illegals, drugs, whores—what have you—they move it underground. They are also escape-obsessed. They worry about the Americans, they worry about their competitors, and now that they're involved with us, they worry about us. They fear surprise attack at any moment. When Menendez took this place over, the first thing he would have done is move his engineers and construction people in and had tunnels dug. Do you know about them?"

"I know areas I have been advised to avoid."

"I need more than that."

"And I need an incentive."

"How about this? If you don't help me, I'll behead you."

"Or, how about this? You take me with you. This whole thing is beginning to feel more and more fragile. When it collapses, many will die. I have no desire to be among them. Only with that in mind can I act . . . heroically."

"I appreciate your lack of grandeur. No false idealism for the translator."

"Call me what you will, I understand that translators have a short life expectancy around here."

"Tomorrow, then?"

"No. Too soon. My explorations must be tomorrow. I will have no results till the day after, maybe the day after that."

"Work swiftly, little man."

52

The NSA intercept, a garbled satellite pickup in which someone called a number in New Jersey, which was shunted to a serving station in Manila and on to a receiver in Gstaad, Switzerland, and appeared to be confirmation for "picking up a package" three days on, at "the ranch," was pay dirt. It became an imperative, actionable at the utmost dispatch, when the ultimate address was linked via a computer deep-mining operation, with a drop site for Iranian Ministry of Intelligence operatives in Europe. It came together fast after that.

Nick got Counterterrorism's number one and number two assault teams, plus the Bureau's SWAT from L.A., San Francisco, Chicago, St. Louis, and Minneapolis to augment them. As a bonus, Ward Taylor himself was on the operation, so that the assaulters wouldn't fidget taking orders from someone they didn't know. Briefed with extremely revealing drone photos of the ranch, they put together a good plan, modeled on the SEAL raid on bin

Laden, which was the gold standard. Nobody mentioned Mogadishu.

"Expect resistance," Nick briefed them. "It will be hot. His security people are drawn from Mexican Special Forces. They are hardened professionals and, in the past, have fought to the death. Check the reports from Wichita, if you doubt. That's why the full body armor, especially helmets. That's why it's shoot to suppress from the first encounter of fire and, if necessary, full automatic. Take a lot of ammo. Waste bullets, not men. That's why night vision, for all tac advantage. But I say again, the point here is to take down one guy, not even Señor Menendez, though he would be a very nice bonus. Our guy is Arab, early forties, another extremely capable character. But he's the bonanza. Prefer him alive, but I'd rather kill him than lose any of you. The point is to stop him, not interview him. That's a good day's work."

Afterward, Nick and his team gathered at a National Guard Armory in Jackson Hole. Here, he'd assembled his ground component, mostly personnel from Salt Lake City and Denver. They would engage simultaneously with the air assault, crashing the fake gate, then the real gate, and hitting the compound as the commandos moved through the structures. Their task was perimeter containment, to stifle any escape, seal the place off and put it out of business in a hurry, under mandate from FISA, which allowed "any and all law enforcement activities deemed necessary to halt a terrorist threat." A U.S. Attorney was along with them to issue legal advice on the fly, if need be, and to help move stretchers to ambulances.

"Have I forgotten anything?" Nick asked Bob.

"Yeah, me," said Bob.

"Sorry, pal. You're sitting this one out. Explicit orders from Washington."

"Come on, Nick . . ."

"Nope. Believe it or not, they treasure your brain over your trigger finger. A first, I'm sure."

Bob didn't lose it marine NCO style, but his gray face, his narrowed eyes and slit mouth, his measured breathing, all equaled rage.

"I am going along."

"I guess you are. In a government sedan. We will need you to examine and make identification fast. I'm told he looks just like Dr. Zhivago, so that should be easy. Have you seen it recently?"

"I never saw it in the first place."

"Maybe you'll get to interview him. I hope, at least, that you get to ID the body. And following that, you'll provide assessment on any sniper activities found in place and begin to assemble data for the after action report."

Bob nodded without enthusiasm.

"Anyhow," said Nick, "you will hold well behind the perimeter and will be reached by radio and notified to come forward when the area is secured. Tomorrow, at first light, we'll be traveling to the shooting area to see what we can see. Hopefully, that'll be more like a picnic than a mission, and we can draw on that for the after action report. Hopefully, it's all over by tonight."

"Sitting out the big fight don't make me happy," said Bob.

"You will hold on the perimeter until notified. Do I need to put a three-hundred-pound babysitter on you?"

"No."

"That's a good boy."

Disgruntled, he didn't bother to listen to the radio commands tying the whole op together. He just climbed into the backseat of the last vehicle in the convoy, one of three sedans following the SUVs and armored assault trucks with FBI emblazoned on them. His driver was a rookie agent out of Denver, the guy next to him in the front seat was the U.S. Attorney, and not one of them had a thing to say to the other two, as each was in his own private stew. All wore body armor and Kevlar helmets and were linked by radio, and only Bob had his set to OFF.

The convoy left at 1715, proceeding south on Wyoming 193 from Jackson toward Rock Springs, by way of Pine Valley, where there were no pines. On the other side of the road, western scrub seemed to roll away, showing nothing, hiding nothing. To the west, farther, the crags of the Tetons could be seen, magnificent and artistic, the perfect ideal of The Mountains, as many art directors of the American western movie had discovered. Bob did not pay much attention. He was the eternal wallflower at an orgy, feeling both frumpy and invisible at once. The fun would be over by the time he got there. He didn't even have a weapon.

The convoy did not proceed under siren or at high speed. It poked along, opening and closing like an accordion, trying to stay under the speed limit, though any passersby knew that it represented government action at its apogee of force. That was the information truckloads of men in armor carried.

It took about an hour of stop and start, and when they approached, Wyoming State Police set up the roadblocks to halt civilian traffic just before and after the ranch entrance.

"Should be any second now," said the FBI driver, pulling to a stop on the road at the rear of the convoy, which had halted.

Bob flicked on the radio just in time to hear a last-minute checklist run by Nick, each vehicle okaying its position and status.

"Hammer Fifteen, green for go," said the young driver.

"You got it, son? You pull up at the inner gate, and we hold there, waiting for the all-clear."

"Mr. Swagger, my orders are to bring Mr. Heflin in by foot two minutes after the airborne drop."

"That your understanding, Heflin?"

"That's what they told me. I brought a gun in case there's a gunfight."

"Don't hurt yourself with it."

"I'm actually pretty good with it," said Heflin.

"Well, leave it in the holster. If you're shot at, that's when you draw it."

"Got you."

"Here they come!" said the driver.

And come they did. Black Hawks, Wyoming Air National Guard, six of them—low, loud, and fast—in well-crafted delta-assault formation, altitude about one hundred and fifty, low enough to rip a column of dust from the earth below so that, in the settling gloom, it looked like they led the apocalypse toward the target.

Helicopters! Bob thought. *I hope I am done with helicopters after this.*

The birds disappeared over the crest, Nick announced, "Green, green, remember your positions and your assignments, safeties off *only* after disembarking, green, green, green!"

The accordion of vehicles again opened itself up, only this time at speed, as Nick's Command truck led the way, screeched out, yanked hard right to the ranch entrance and went cascading down the road toward Hell or Glory. Three more armored trucks, riveted turtles in black with FBI in white painted on every flat surface, followed, in turn, by the SUVs and the other two sedans.

"Okay," said the young FBI driver. "I guess it's time."

"You up for this, son?" asked Bob.

"Yes, sir," said the driver.

He accelerated gently, not being part of any speed brigade, followed the column of dust ahead of him, entered the ranch, and proceeded through a mile of rolling plains before reaching the actual security gate. It was deserted. He pulled over.

Bob was first out. He waited for the sound of the guns. There was none.

"Okay," said the agent, "I'm taking Mr. Heflin into Command now."

"No guns," said Bob. "Announce yourself to the assaulters so you don't get shot up."

"Yes, sir," he snapped, and the two men set off at a half run, leaving Bob leaning on the fender under the dark sky, a bit beneath the last crest, feeling a whip of wind but no sense of human activity.

He heard the raid happening via radio.

"Hammer One, have entered house, no resistance."

"Hammer Two, entering from rear, some civilians in the kitchen, have cleared them, no weapons, they're just a mess."

"Barn clear, this is Hammer Four, barn clear, no hostiles, no fire, deserted."

"Hammer Five, in garage, all quiet, nice cars, nobody here."

"This is Hammer Six, I am in the kitchen, moving through the basement, coming up the stairs. Hold your fire, Hammer One. No tangos, no incoming fire, it's just your buddies from Minneapolis."

"Got it, Six. Yeah, see you. Hey, everybody, just waiting on upstairs report. Okay, getting signal, no tangos upstairs, upstairs clear."

"No incoming, no movement?" asked Nick, holding at his Command vehicle.

"Nothing, big dog. Oh, well, yeah: lots of bodies," said Hammer 1. "What is this, Jonestown?"

53

No signal from Alberto the next day, nor the next. Juba was just waiting. He made his call to his own control, making certain the schedule was still set, his pickup would be on time, all things were in place, and there were no imminent signs of aggressive action against the operation. It was all subterfuge, of course, as he had no intention of leaving that way. That way, he knew, was death.

But he was also certain no attempt against his life would be made here. It would raise too many questions and lead to too many difficulties. He thought, instead, when he had been picked up—he himself did not even know by whom—that the vehicle would be followed, perhaps by a drone, and when it was far away, in some state disconnected by miles of highway from Wyoming, some police incident would be arranged so that the true perpetrators could claim utter innocence.

Juba passed the time working out in Menendez's elaborate gym, went for a long run each day, and otherwise spent his time in his shop, reading reloading manuals and classic ballistics texts, if only to enjoy privacy in the world he so enjoyed. If he imagined a future—it happened occasionally—he saw himself on a large estate with a shop full of interesting rifles and, outside, a mile of free countryside into which he could shoot. It would not be shooting for purposes of politics, history, or faith. It would be shooting as shooting, an end in itself, a kind of subreligion of the larger commitment to Allah, demanding the same rigor, stamina, commitment, and vision. It would be a paradise on earth well-earned.

On the third day, a nod from Alberto told him that the tunnel entrance had been located and that things were set, to the degree that they could be. A nod in return was all that Alberto needed.

"I will see you in the big room at six-thirty," Juba said to Alberto. "Tonight, I will say my farewell to our extraordinary host."

"I will be there to perform my duties," said the old man.

At 6:30, Juba, freshly showered and dressed casually in slacks and sweater, ambled to the vast room to find Menendez by himself, reading a book in front of the fireplace. The room was a museum of images and objects from cowboy movies. Sculptures of wild animals, their muscles ripped in strain as they galloped or reared or fought. Massive paintings of the knights of the plains at full gallop across the sagebrush, dust a-rising, neckerchiefs a-fly. Buffalo and elk heads, all with massive spans of knurled, polished horn. Tapestries in tribal patterns, gaudy colors in zigzags like lightning bolts. Polished wooden tables of thick oak, wrought-iron lamps, two sofas and four massive chairs, all in burnished leather and swaddled in tribal blankets. It was a cowboy fantasyland.

"How nice of you to visit," said Menendez, rising. "I understand why you must remain solitary—it's for your concentration. You must shoot even more precisely than you did at Wichita, though that was breathtaking. But I appreciate, now that our relationship is ending, the pleasure this last time of your company. I know you do not drink, but perhaps just this once. It's a very fine Spanish wine, Sierra Cantabria Teso La Manja Toro."

He spoke so fast, Alberto had trouble keeping up.

Juba shook his head.

"No? That is fine. A man as hard as you can make no concessions to appetite, I understand. Your true test is upcoming. I feel mine has passed, with the elimination of the witness. It is time for me to relax for a bit. Soon, I will leave here—one cannot stay in any one place too long, alas—and go to houses perhaps in the Caribbean or the South of France or in Cancún. I have always said my true headquarters is, literally, my head—ha—and I can administer my responsibilities from anywhere, which is the one pleasure of the modern age and all its communications genius, though I do think, my friend, that you and I might have been better suited to an earlier age, you as a general, in silk turban and caftan, mighty scimitar in its sash, ready to go against the Crusaders at Acre or Tours or wherever, myself a king of Old Spain, as our humble peninsula achieved domination over the world, due to the guts of her conquistadors and her admirals."

He seemed flushed tonight, a bit florid, pausing now to sip while Alberto caught up. Maybe he was tipsy. Maybe he was blotto. The fire crackled, sending flickers of light and shadow into the room, which, in any event, was lit from behind ochre shades so that the illumination everywhere was gold. He smiled. He drew his arm around Juba, pulling the sniper closer.

"You know," he said conspiratorially, "this has been such a pleasure for me, so much more than mere business. I feel that we are brothers. We are both men of the dark skin, our forebears were swarthy, and only a little polish hides our true nature as men of color. I feel our alliance is determined by nature. It is time for those of us of the darkness to take over. The world has too long been dominated by *los gringos* or *les blancs*, or whatever one chooses to call them. I have lived among them, I know them. I was educated at Harvard, you know, and have studied them. It could be said I majored in White People, ha ha. You know them too. You have hunted and killed them. Such entitlement they have, such a sense of nobility and position and grace, not knowing how they are loathed among those of us who are not of them. Really, it is about race—*la raza,* as we call it—and how they have assumed for centuries our inferiority and how that time is coming to an end. And you and I, my friend, we are on the front lines—you in your way, I in mine—not just to bring down an entity known as the United States, with its capital in Washington, D.C., but an entire culture, a civilization, and the assumptions upon which it was built. They consider themselves superior because freak chance awarded them custodianship of the Industrial Revolution, but to make it work, they had to steal from us at a rate beyond calculation. Their wealth and power was built on our flesh and sweat and death. They thought they built a thing when, in fact, it was our muscle and our lives that paid the price. And, from that, they assumed possession of all material goods and all spiritual succor. It was, I tell you, the greatest crime in history, and only now are we beginning to understand the extent of the white man's thievery, not just from Africa, not just the labor of the Negro, but from the world over. From all the peoples of color, they looted and pillaged and alchemized our tears into their gold. It is my deepest pleasure to be a weapon in the war against all that.

"That is the point of the narcotics: they are weapons, not pharmaceuticals, their mission to eat at the structures and disciplines of these pretenders, so stupid in their ways that they do not see the larger picture and understand that we are rotting out their infrastructure from beneath them so that it will collapse upon itself. And, in the end, all men will have the character bred out of them or softened by the pleasures of the chemicals that we sell, crippled by their need, desperate for the effect. They have no strength left—not physical, not moral, not even metaphorical—and so they too shall pass, and the world shall become the communion of 'we,' of color and blood, well bound by the intensity of our co-struggle and our—"

"Can I see the gun?" Juba said.

"What? Why, yes, of course. Yes, what a beauty it is. A perfect symbol of our struggle. How appropriate it is at this moment."

He walked to the gun case, unlocked it, and removed the gold-plated AK-74.

"This is not a toy," he said, "or a fraud. The plating is genuine twenty-four-karat, the rubies and diamonds that encrust it are all real. It is said to have a value of close to three million dollars. It was given me by a consortium of Mexican gentlemen who understood the nature of my struggle and my commitment to my race. See how it gleams and sparkles?"

The weapon indeed gleamed and sparkled in his hands.

"It is a monstrosity to some tastes, a work of art to others, a kind of melding of fifteenth-century aesthetic drawn from the treasures the conquistadors had come to the New World in search of, as applied to the fist of the twenty-first century, that expression of guerrilla will and courage as perfected by Sergeant Kalashnikov in the workshops of the old Soviet Union at the end of the Great Patriotic War as it prepared, planned, and plotted for its next Great Patriotic War, men of the East, men of small stature, who would end the rule of—"

"May I?" asked Juba.

"Of course. I do go on, don't I?"

Juba removed the magazine from his belt, where it had been tucked under his sweater, and, with knowing hands, rocked and locked it into the mag well of the weapon, smiling mildly all along, hit the bolt latch with a strong palm, so that it flew back, admitted a cartridge to the chamber, slammed forward with the system's prototypical *klak*. Menendez watched this brief ceremony with fascination, as it was the last of all things he imagined happening, and he, normally so sure, could generate no policy toward it but instead fell into a sort of numbed enchantment.

Juba stepped toward him and rammed the muzzle of the rifle into his throat, the angle upward and just to the right of the larynx, so that the barrel pointed into the cerebral vault.

Menendez made sounds like a thirsty frog requesting water, finding it difficult to form words with the cylinder of the flash suppressor shoved an inch into the flesh of his throat.

"Gk . . . Gk . . . Gk . . ." he said, eyes opening wide in realization of what was happening.

"You should not have required me to kill my friend," said Juba.

Bang, said the AK-74.

La Culebra liked to do certain things to Rosita at one place, while Rita did certain things to her at another. Then they would change positions, and he would work there while Rita came up here. There was always a lot of delightful sound involved. It was moist, yet fricative, and seemed accompanied, if one listened hard enough, by a chorus of droplets landing everywhere. Wetness was general over the three of them, including the slide and slurp of fluids, salty, even fishy, flavors, dribble tracks zigzagging this way and that, and the skin upon which these phenomena played out was so prehensile—theirs and his—that it always found some new way to lie or arrange itself. It was so very interesting. Sometimes, comically, his mask slipped, rising or falling from the dynamics of the action, and his eyes were covered. That had become quite enjoyable because, at that moment, both women went down below and began to work on him while, at the same time, they were working on each other, all of this in warm darkness. The energy developed could be quite astonishing.

He heard the shot.

He immediately knew something terrible had happened. But he was naked with two naked women. He disengaged, reached for and pulled on his clothes.

He hated to be so unprepared. He straightened his mask, tightened his belt buckle, and slid into the harness that contained, in different locations, seven different blades. A black guayabera shirt went over it.

"What is—" began Rita.

"Shh," he hissed, hearing more shots, all single taps, suggesting careful aiming, and knew that some kind of catastrophe was occurring.

"Stay here," he commanded, and went to investigate.

* * *

The bullet killed but the gas destroyed. Roaring at supersonic speed and energy, it vaporized all before it, scalding a funnel-shaped zone of vacancy, an eviction notice from the high lords of physics to Señor Menendez's skull, emptying it of matter, which it distributed artfully on the ceiling, on supersonic zephyrs, forming whorls and pinwheels and lone dazzlers of abstraction. Droplets of crimson goo were flung everywhere, and Juba had to do a quick wipe on his eyes to clear them of the mess.

He turned to discover Alberto, standing, as if encased in amber a billion years ago.

"Stay with me, old man," he said to him, and gave him a playful smack on the shoulder.

The sounds of footsteps arose, from the main passageway, and Juba fired quickly at the shapes that suddenly filled it, not a burst, as only fools fire bursts, and placed 5.45×39s into thoracic cavities as they became available. One shot, one kill; three shots, three kills.

He turned back.

"Okay, now lead me out of here. I don't want to have to fight his whole fucking army."

Alberto came out of his shocked stupor, realized what had happened and was happening, and said, "This way, quickly, the library."

They ran, and, here and there, encountered terrified random household staff, who melted before them and did not require killing. They passed the foyer, and Juba called a halt, opened the front door, spied three armed men racing toward him from the sentry house, and, with three shots, delivered languidly but with smoothness, he dropped them.

Then an amazement: the stairway upward. Who was halfway down it, barefoot, but the man with the sock on his head.

Yet Juba did not shoot him as he could have. Instead, he smiled, nodded sportingly, and the fellow drew back.

Alberto pulled Juba along to the library. He knew where it had to be, a section of shelving with faux books, but did not understand what mechanism would spring it.

"There," he said. "Do you see? The books are fake. It has to be a door."

"And suppose it leads to a wine cellar," said Juba, but pushed hard, and indeed the shelves moved backwards on ball bearings, far lighter than its weight should have been, and revealed an alcove and a spiral staircase. The two stepped inside, pulling the door closed, and descended into darkness. Alberto saw a light panel, hit a switch, and the lights came on, revealing a well-engineered tunnel leading away from them.

"There you have it," he said. "Escape. Is this where you kill me, now that my use is over?"

"I am not a murderer," said Juba. "I am a jihadi. I have honor. Besides, you are not important enough to kill."

"Then let's get out of—"

Even inside the bowels of the house, they heard the

roar of mighty engines and shivered as the wave of vibrations poured over them.

"What is—"

"Helicopters," said Juba. "I think Bobleeswagger is here. Won't he be surprised?"

L a Culebra returned to his room, finding the two women, still naked, terrified on the bed.

Suddenly a roar arose from outside.

What on earth—

He rose and watched as six large machines settled out of the sky amid columns of dust whipped up by invisible rotors. As each landed, men poured from them, armored in the commando style, with all kinds of automatic weapons, shields, lights—the entire modern war-making trousseau. Serious customers, now running hard and low to the house, which they'd broach and penetrate in seconds. Everything was happening at once! The world was ending!

"Boots," he said. "Get my boots."

They pulled out a pair of splendid boots and set about putting them on their master's feet.

"Excellent," he said. "Now I will depart."

"What should we do?" asked Rita.

"Ah—tell no one a thing. Do you understand?"

"Yes, my lord."

"Here, this will help."

He cut her throat. The five-inch slicer, seriously curved to yield but a single, murderously sharp edge. It cut through flesh like butter, especially when guided by a sure, strong hand.

She fell, bleeding, choking, dying.

He turned to Rosa.

"Why do you do this?" she asked.

"Shh," he said, and cut her throat too.

54

The ranch

Nick got to the ranch house as soon as it became clear nobody was doing any shooting. Mostly, he found guys dressed like frogmen at a gun show poking around curiously. They had the aspect of children at a new amusement park. Maybe there was a method to it, but chiefly it was guys who thought they might have gotten into a gunfight coming down to the realization that the gunfight had been canceled.

He went to the SWAT commander—Ward Taylor, of course—and got a quick summary of the action.

"Those are the bodies?" Nick could see them in the position of the recently extinguished—that is, helter-skelter, limbs awry, grotesque and utterly still, beyond care or menace, pretty much scattered all over the place.

"We got six DOA in the big house. Three more outside. Maybe more as we check more closely. One you gotta see to believe."

Taylor led Nick into the famous Hanson Ranch's big, beautiful main room and pointed out a sack of man flaccid on floor in an elegant gray suit, silk shirt, ascot, with perfect white teeth and no upper skull. This sector of the room had been redecorated in Early American headshot.

"You sure this guy Juba isn't secretly working for DEA?" asked Taylor. "I'm pretty sure this one is, or was, Menendez, the cartel big shot. That's him. Look up and you'll see his brains. Now, looking over here, we got a batch of high-speed operators, all with snails in their ears, good tac gear and high-end assault rifles, mainly M4s, with all kinds of flashy optics. The optics didn't do 'em any good. All look single-tapped, center chest."

"That's Juba," said Nick. "He's *that* good a shot. Any sign of—"

"No, but we're running another, more thorough search. Here's the odd part. Two women, upstairs bedroom, lookers, naked, throats cut. Cowboy boot tracks in the blood. Not sure who that guy would be, but it definitely wasn't our boy Juba who took out Menendez and the security people. The tracks led to a closet, the closet led to a secret alcove, which led to a spiral staircase which led to a tunnel. I'm betting this place is honeycombed with tunnels."

"That's how Juba made it out too. Goddamn, he's a slippery eel. Let's get the dogs in here and see if we can find a track."

"They're coming in with the next relay."

"Okay, everybody," he said to the room. "Sorry, the night isn't over yet. We have to get on Juba. Maybe the dogs will bring him down."

He turned to Chandler, off the walker, still hobbling, but game enough to tag along.

"Where's Swagger? He's tracked before."

"Boss," said Chandler, "you left him on the perimeter, remember?"

"Yeah, I forgot. Okay, we need him."

He went to radio.

"This is Command. All units clear and secure?"

One by one, each Hammer element reported in, all objectives taken, no casualties. The street agents had begun to process the bewildered survivors, but that info wouldn't be collated into a coherent picture for some time.

No Swagger on the 'Net.

"Swagger? Swagger, this is Command. Swagger, report please, give me your sitrep."

"God, I hope he hasn't taken off again," said Chandler.

"I knew I should have left somebody with him. Where the hell could he have gone?"

La Culebra slipped down the low corridor, hunched, tracking his way by flashlight, smelling dirt, feeling along the timber shoring, feeling the fragility of the underground passageway. It seemed as if it could collapse at any second. There were seven tunnels out of the house; this was not the best of them. It didn't matter. What mattered was, getting out, somehow commanding a vehicle, and fleeing the area under the cover of dark. Like a vampire, he could travel only by night, for the mask made him too obvious. In rural Mexico, daylight travel was possible, but here in *el Norte* it was beyond question.

He knew he had to escape the raiders. Who were they? Again, it didn't matter. The Tijuana Cartel? Colombians? Russian gangsters out of Vegas with commando experience? Or any of a dozen other outfits who wanted to extinguish Señor Menendez from the earth and take his place as *El Supremo. La Policía*? Maybe state operators from a country that wanted the cartel business for itself. Rogue Green Berets? It didn't matter.

Only one thing mattered and that was escape.

He came at last to the end, climbed up a ladder, pushed aside a flimsy door, and climbed into night air. He blinked, checking. He was alone, over the crest from the big house, oriented toward Route 193. He had to veer toward it, somehow get out of the zone of police activity and get himself a car. If he had to, he would kill everyone who stood a chance of preventing him from doing that.

He waited a bit for his eyes to adjust to the darkness, feeling a night wind against him, though it was still warmish out. Above, low clouds, the air heavy with the threat of rain. A front was said to be coming in from the west. Good, it would cover his smell and melt his tracks. He looked back in the direction of the house, and though the crest obscured it, he could see the pulsating illumination of the red-blue staccato rhythm lighting the low clouds, confirming that the raiders were indeed police. He thanked God for the good luck that got him on the run before, rather than after, the attack. Juba may have killed Menendez, but his shot had saved La Culebra from the raiders. So it goes in the mad world. He was alive now, or at least free, with a good shot at escape because of it.

He tried to reconstruct in his mind the lay of roads and fields on this side of the house and came to the conclusion that if he trended north, which he could determine by glimpses of the highway a mile or so away, he would intercept the entry road to the property, could follow that east off the property to 193.

He knew he had to move fast. These raiders would soon be organized, and, once organized, they'd call in reinforcements. They'd organize search parties and forensics teams, interview the staff, and put together a picture of who was there and what they had done. Of course, they'd discover Rita and Rosita and understand that the Arab wasn't responsible, he was too busy killing Menendez and the bodyguards to bother with *putas*. So the staff would know another player was responsible and they would soon give up information on the man in the mask, and the search for him would begin. The raiders would be provoked by a man who liked the knife so much. And, sooner or later, they would find the other bodies and realize that his hobby was essentially killing young women, and he would shortly become a high priority for them. How could they care so much about *putas*? They lived to serve and die. That was reality. To care was more *gringo* madness.

And then—was this evidence that God had not forsaken His most wayward of children?—he saw it. A sedan, on the entry road, in the midst of the blackness. Its headlights were on. In the next second, he made out the languid shape of a man lounging against the bumper. Now, what was this strange *hombre* doing here? He didn't appear to be a sentry and was on no kind of guard duty, not from the position he had assumed. He wasn't dressed like a raider, instead basically wearing the clothes of an American at the mall, jeans and a light jacket. And he had no machine gun or helmet. He wasn't smoking, he wasn't on the radio, he just seemed sort of disgruntled, according to his posture, a bad boy exiled from the main action by a stern authority.

The Mexican reached under his shirt, selected his seven-inch, and withdrew it. Bone grip, tight, thin, and checkered by the bladesmith, a dagger meant to kill by thrusting deep into the organs, but sharpened on both edges so that a quick, strong slash would open the body, perhaps fatally, certainly enough to paralyze by shock so that he could get the point into the chest and puncture the heart. It was a good blade. He loved it. The Toledo steel whispered as it came from the leather. He began his slow approach, though he could see that the man was old, perhaps some kind of cranky derelict or local law enforcement senior citizen moved out of the action for everybody's safety and disarmed. In any event, he would die quickly under the blade, and killing him would be, as it always was, a supreme pleasure. Another one! The two women, targets of opportunity, and now this lanky, stupid *gringo*. God was bountiful tonight.

He drew close and closer, amazed at how uninterested the man was in everything around him.

It was not Swagger's best moment. He stood there, fulminating in the dark, occasionally going on the 'Net to learn that there had been no gunfight, and they were trying to get things sorted out.

What am I supposed to do? he wondered.

He went off 'Net again. Somehow, he hadn't figured on this possibility, much less figured it out. He didn't want to go in on foot alone. The boys were still nervous, not quite sure what they had uncovered. Yet at the same time, Nick had said he'd send an all-clear and he hadn't. He didn't want to interrupt the radio transmissions with his own questions, because they had too much to do and didn't need interruption. He could drive in, but some hotshot might empty a mag into a strange vehicle appearing from nowhere. His best bet, obviously, was to wait it out just a few more minutes. The secondary convoy, with forensics people and other crime scene processors, medical personnel and equipment for the anticipated casualties, as well as dogs to track escapees, was said to be on the way. He would latch on to that. It couldn't be more than five minutes or so away.

And just to fuck things up even more, a cold rain began to fall. If the skies really opened up, the rain could turn things to mud and destroy any tracks or scents left behind, assuming that, as it now appeared, the sniper had in fact again evaded them. The guy had more lives than a cat.

These things filled his mind. That meant he'd totally given up on tactical awareness. That meant he'd made the old man's most likely mistake: not paying attention. So his reflexes were shut down, and if there was a footstep, a snap of a twig, the brush of legs sprinting through bush—anything at all—he missed it, and the man hit him hard, filling his brain with chaotic flash and infinite regret, and he lost another second, wondering, *Huh? What the fuck?* and he was down and pinned.

It was too easy. The strike of the keen predator against the unaware prey. La Culebra drove his left forearm hard into the old man's head, knocking his baseball cap awry, scrambling his mind, while his full body weight, propelled at near maximum burst speed, sent the old arms akimbo and broke him fast to the earth. La Culebra knew the tricks, and, with killing speed, he laced his left arm through the old man's, pinned it, achieving maximum leverage, and put his full strength against the enemy. The old man flattened, gulping, perhaps grunting, even as he understood he hadn't the strength of his own to defy the attacker. In another second, the old man was helpless.

"You should pay attention, old one," La Culebra said in English, for he recognized him as a *gringo*, noting that he looked like an old-time cowboy, a marshal or town sheriff, all crags and wrinkles.

"Now it is time for you to go," he said, rather enjoying the moment and the intimacy between killer and victim.

He put the dagger point into the man's neck, below the ear, and the glare from the headlights showed the blue blur that signified the carotid just a quarter inch under the white skin, which even now picked up the gossamer reflection of the rain drops beginning to crash against it.

"But you should see he who slays you and know at whose dispatch your fate has arrived," he said, and, with the tip of his dagger, plucked off his mask so that his full face was bright in the beam of light.

Swagger was gone and knew it. Though thin, his assailant was extremely strong, far stronger than he was, and, more important, clearly schooled in the darkest of all the martial arts. The man had him pinned and stilled. He was the pig hanging on the hook as the slaughter boss leaned in close, with a smile on his face and no fear in his heart, and with the throat cutter in his hand.

The man seemed so happy. He seemed joyous. Swagger tried to think of something to do, but there was nothing. Of all his very bad moments, this was the worst, as death toyed with him, the knife danced quicksilver in the light. The force against him was so strong that his arms went to sleep, and his hands, even though useless, lost their grip. Now, at last, after so much. A wet field in the rain in Wyoming, some orangutan-strong screwball with a knife and a ski mask.

"But you should see he who slays you and know at whose dispatch your fate has arrived," said the man, and it struck Bob, through it all, as rather ridiculously overstated.

The mask came off and there it was, in the light: the Snake.

Inked bright green for slithering through the Garden of Eden, nose surgically reduced to a button, scales surgically etched into the leathery skin, nostrils buttonholes in the slope of facial plates, jawbone reduced to a flange.

No eyebrows, no ears, eyes vivid with the reptile's vertical yellow pupil against the green upholstery of the physiognomy, much of the cheek flesh drawn off so that the shape of the face was purified toward the primal trapezoid, the mug of he who strikes, he who preys, he who oozes, which excites in all mammals, whether bi- or quadruped, a deep shudder of revulsion and fear of dark places and things without arms or legs but which still are fast as greased death.

The Snake smiled, showing the red tattoo ink that turned his lips and gums the color of blood, all the better to show off the two gleaming reptile fangs that hooked downward from above. And, of course, the tongue. Out it came, red as the candy cane's stripe—and when he flicked it out, Swagger saw that it too had been altered by a surgeon and was split and spread, a tip going north, a tip going south.

"*El Serpiente, amigo!*" said the man, on the crest of the best laugh of his life. He leaned, and the tongue flicked out to lick Bob's forehead, almost caress it. Bob felt the dagger point sink deeper into his flesh.

The face rearranged itself around the .355-inch crater that appeared without ceremony beneath the left eye, a pucker like a chancre that brought with it vibrations of terminal penetration. Black brain blood drooled from the new orifice, spreading randomly as it cascaded downward and outward in accordance with the laws of gravity. Another bullet, less acute in angle, hit and tore out the bridge of the nose, ripping a gaping wound that destroyed any semblance of the monster and replaced it with an image that conveyed merely the banal data of what damage flesh could sustain, including eye burst, temple eruption, facial deconstruction, and a cloud of gray matter thick as July bats in the night heat. Swagger didn't even hear the second shot, much less the first.

The man toppled, hitting earth so hard, he seemed to dig his own grave.

Swagger lay flat, hungering for air. Rain pelted his face.

Then he heard his savior ask, "Is it dead?" and turned to confront someone lowering a Glock from a two-handed grip seven feet away. The rain fell like a shroud, billowing in the wind, turning reality all gray and smeared, but Swagger saw nevertheless that it was Mrs. McDowell.

55

They crested a hill but saw no relief.

A train of taillights choked the highway as it entered a valley, crossed it, and climbed the slope on the other side. There was nothing to do in the pouring rain except show patience, forbearance, and fortitude.

"Agh," said Alberto.

"Easy, easy," said Juba. At the end of their tunnel, they had found a small shed enclosing a Honda Civic, with all necessary documents, twenty-seven hundred dollars in cash, and a full tank of gas. Menendez had plotted well, knowing that if flight became necessary, a car and money were equally necessary.

Now they were on I-80, in traffic, in the rain, headed east. He was on the tail of an 18-wheeler whose trailer dwarfed him, while behind, pressing in, another 18-wheeler threatened to devour him. There was no passing, as the lane to the left was as jammed as his was. There was no exit. There was nothing to do but wait, as they crept along. Top speed: eight miles an hour.

"It must be an accident ahead," said Alberto.

Juba said nothing. The situation was self-evident. The rain crushed downward, smearing the lights into fragments, while the old windshield wipers tried gamely to scrape it away, though to not much avail. The only reality was rain distorted, turned kaleidoscopic and fractured by diffusion. *Whacka-whacka-whacka*, went the blades. The old Honda coughed alarmingly now and then.

"Suppose . . ." said Alberto, almost as if he were frightened of an answer. "Suppose it's a roadblock. Suppose they have your description. Suppose they know of me. Suppose they are looking for two Arabs heading as far away from Rock Springs as possible."

"Suppose we spend the rest of our lives in an American prison. Suppose the FBI sends us to the Jews. Suppose we are killed. Suppose we do not go to Heaven. Suppose Allah is without understanding of our failure. And without empathy."

"Everything you say could be true."

"And everything I say could be untrue. Pray, brother, even if you don't believe. That is all that remains. You are in the hands of God."

"You are said to be a practical man. Perhaps the practical thing to do would be for you to jump out and head cross-country on foot. We can pick a rendezvous site, and if I clear the roadblock, I will head there and pick you up."

"Outside is the one place I am not going. I have no idea where we are. I hardly speak the language. I am being hunted by all men and women with badges. No, it's much better to wait this ordeal out, and if indeed we get to a police blockade, to bluff our way through on the strength of our excellent credentials, all of which are professional. You have a glib tongue in Arabic and Spanish, I'm guessing that you speak English as well."

"I do."

"Then our weapon will be your charm."

"Right now, I feel as charming as a goat."

"You will astonish yourself as you rise to the occasion. I know. I have been hunted as many times as I have hunted, and under the duress of being the prey, one is capable of amazing feats."

They reached the crest of another hill. As before, what lay ahead was a long, slow transit by a barely moving convoy through the rain and the dark, across a valley, and up another hill, beyond which, no doubt, lay exactly the same.

Alberto saw it first.

"God be praised. Or cursed! Look, do you not see it?"

Juba squinted, trying to focus through the smeared light.

It was a blinking light at the top of the hill.

"Roadblock," said Alberto.

It seemed to take hours, when, in actuality, it took hours. Finally, they edged up to the crest and could see the light just over it, casting an intermittent blaze against the low clouds, illuminating the slanting rain and the engine vapors and the tire spray.

"All right," said Alberto, "should I drive? Should we switch?"

"No, this is fine. If it goes bad, and we have to make some kind of escape attempt by auto—we'll almost certainly die, of course—but if that happens, we have a slightly better chance with me driving than you. I have taken many advanced courses in tactical operations, and high-speed driving is part of them. My skill might let us escape, where yours definitely would not."

"Fair enough," said Alberto. "I can hardly see in this rain anyway."

And now it was here. They reached the crest, and, over it, just a few dozen yards, the commanding sign, even if its message was blurred in the cascade of water. Beyond, on the downslope, they could see the traffic speed up and separate.

Juba began to calculate the strategy he would take if escape became necessary. This old car, with its worn tires and problematic acceleration, trying to outrun speedy American police cruisers! The only chance would be to veer across the median, head in the other direction, look for a soft spot where he could get off this highway, and perhaps onto a smaller country road, and, if far enough ahead, abandon this car and head cross-country. But he didn't like the chances at all.

"O Jesus, please show mercy," prayed Alberto.

"You are not even of the faith!" exclaimed Juba.

"I never said I was. My father was Catholic, my mother Egyptian. I studied for the priesthood!"

"God laughs at me," Juba said. "He sends me to death with an infidel."

"I am, at this point in my spiritual life, quite flexible. If you want me to pray to Allah, I will happily do so. O Allah, I beseech Thee—"

"Shut up."

With a lurch, the 18-wheeler ahead pulled free and began to speed up, and Juba knew police would be on him with their flashlights in seconds.

But there were no policemen.

There was nothing except the sign, by the side of the road, blinking furiously as it beamed its message to the traffic it had slowed to a jam in the rain and dark.

"What does it say?" asked Juba.

"It says 'Welcome to Wyoming, Speed Limit 75.'"

56

Almost instantly, four FBI SWAT members emerged to take over the scene. They had been dispatched by Nick to follow the tracks of the bloody cowboy boots through the tunnel. Emerging, they caught his footprints to the north before they melted in the rain, followed, and there came upon Mrs. McDowell and Swagger.

At almost the same time, the long-anticipated secondary convoy, with its med technicians, forensics teams, interrogators, dogs, and locals, showed up—a long, well-lit convoy pouring in from 193, and its commander stopped to be debriefed about where the shooting had taken place. And finally the rains really let go, falling in slanting, pelting anger, turning dirt to mud, and warm to cold, and set the breeze to howling. Time to get under cover.

So it was not for a few hours before Nick and Bob—somewhat recovered from the verge of death by a carotid puncture at the hands of a man who thought he was a snake—settled in with Mrs. McDowell, herself soaked, but somewhat warmed by coffee from the kitchen that one of the cooks had started running. Why not? Nobody was working for Señor Menendez anymore. Nick ran the meet, Chandler took notes for the after action report.

The story Mrs. McDowell told: her ex-husband's sister was married to a colonel in the Maryland State Police, and one of his responsibilities was to oversee liaison with FBI, with whom he was on very good terms. When all the news about the killing and gunfight in Wichita broke, not only had she concluded Juba was the trigger-man, she'd caught a glimpse of an agent she knew from the coverage on CNN.

"Agent Chandler. She's so beautiful, the CNN cameras had to show her."

So she knew that Juba was in play, and she asked her ex-husband's sister to ask her husband for any news or info. He responded by saying that all the feds were agitated because an urgent directive had come out requesting certain SWAT teams to report to Salt Lake City for possible deployment in a big raid. Baltimore's field office was all ticked off because they hadn't made the list, though they regularly came in first or second in the FBI SWAT Olympics held every year.

Figuring that action was coming up, Mrs. McDowell had flown to Salt Lake City, where, at a Radio Shack, she had bought a police scanner, with which she quickly found the FBI Clear Channel and was able to follow the assembly of a major raid task force in Jackson Hole. She also had her Glock.

"It's completely legal," she said. "I've owned it for five years, and I have one of those crazy Utah licenses that let me carry in thirty-three states. I can't carry in Maryland, but I can carry in Florida, Texas, Wyoming, and a batch of others. I declared it and flew out with it. I drove out to Jackson Hole, monitored the FBI channel, could tell you were setting up to jump, and just followed the raid in. I parked on 193 and walked down the access road. I see this fight, I run to it, and this snake monster is on top of someone—I couldn't tell it was Bob Lee Swagger, but it didn't matter. I could see his blade gleaming in the light, and I sort of assumed if he had a snake face and was about to stick a knife in somebody's throat, he was probably a bad guy."

"So?"

"So? So I shot him in the face."

"Twice," said Swagger. "The first got his attention, but the second made sure he was listening."

"I've got guys lined up in the rain to see this guy," said Nick. "He was a piece of freak pie."

"Janet, by the way," said Swagger, "thanks for saving the bacon. Between you and Chandler, you're going to keep me alive until the next century."

Chandler said, "You want backstory on the Snake?"

"Sure," said Nick. "I haven't had a laugh all day."

"We ran the prints, and I got some preliminary info from DEA out of the Mexican State Police. Called La Culebra, Spanish for 'the Snake,' he was born in Mexico City as Antonio Jorge López and was known from the age of fourteen as a knife fighter. Very colorful teenage years. Worked freelance; his specialty was cutting out the hearts of snitches. He was so good, he signed on permanently with the late Raúl Menendez. He started this reptile bit a few years ago, since he was no longer on the road. Obviously crazy, but useful in cartel culture: when Menendez met with other cartel big guys, he liked to have the Snake standing close by, in his mask, which is a play on *lucha libre*, a form of Mexican professional wrestling where everybody's masked. Anyhow, DEA suggests that there may be some sexual dysfunction as well, since a number of prostitutes have disappeared everywhere La Culebra puts up for a bit."

"Janet, you couldn't have picked a better candidate for your first kill," said Nick.

"I had hoped to find you guys drinking beer over Juba's corpse," Mrs. McDowell said.

"And we'd hoped for the same," said Nick. "But the bastard seems to have given us the slip once again."

"Are you going to tell me what this is all about?" she asked.

"Nope. I am legally enjoined from doing so. You have no security clearance."

"That doesn't seem fair."

"It isn't. But I have to play very much by the rules, for now. I can't say a word, except to officially express the Bureau's appreciation for saving one of its delinquents. And promise a nice letter for your Glory Wall."

"I don't have a Glory Wall."

"It's your letter, do with it what you want. Now, I'm

going to have you give a deposition to the Jackson County Sheriff's Department, have them buy you a big, hearty Wyoming breakfast, and put you on a plane back to Baltimore. When it's over, maybe Swagger can brief you unofficially. He owes you that much."

"I can guess most of it already. Juba's here to take a really long shot. We all know who it's got to be."

"See, that's what I can't have," said Nick. "If we assume we know, we fall into the trap of confirmation bias, where we only see what supports our interpretation because we want to be right. I purposely haven't addressed the target issue yet, and I'm not ready to without hard evidence. Speculation is counterproductive. That's the real reason I'm chasing you out, Janet. I don't want you tearing down the weeks of professional discipline these guys have shown. That may be their best attribute: the ability to keep an open mind."

"Janet," said Chandler, "Nick's right. We can't go in all oriented to something. This is too important. That's also why nobody on this team is political. We're professional, we're trying to solve a problem, that's all it is."

Like a guest star brought in for a flashy scene or two, she was indeed gone the next day, driven off by two junior agents to Salt Lake City and put on a late flight back to Baltimore. It really was the right decision, cruel as it may have seemed, because much had to be done and there wasn't time to bring anybody new up to speed.

The various teams went to work. Nick spent a long, awkward time on the phone with the Director and an assistant attorney general, but somehow managed to survive. And, gradually, some sort of intelligence picture emerged.

Meanwhile, Swagger accompanied a crew of agents to the meadow where the drone pix showed that the shooting range was located. Fresh from the rain, it looked like Paradise Found—a sunny roll of lush land sparkling with droplets that had collected on the grass—a pure mile of open space. Above, of course, azure sky, clouds like melting vanilla, piercing late-summer sun, and, rimming all this glory, the Grand Tetons.

"He chained 'em here," Swagger said, pointing to the four-by-four-inch post sunk in a wad of concrete and impervious to human influence, immobile even when subjected to the desperate energy of approaching death. The post bore grisly signs of struggle. It was smeared with the dark ochre of dried blood, and a few frags had blasted through the bound bodies and ripped shreds from its surface. One high miss left a perfect pucker drilled into the wood, at the bottom of which lay the expended and battered .338 bullet. Forensics would recover and analyze it.

"Mr. Swagger, we'll also look for latent prints on this post. We'll run chemical tests on the ground for blood, and if we find it, we can extract DNA."

"That's great," he said. "You got corpse-sniffing dogs?"

"No, sir, but we have methane probes that are very

efficient at locating buried cadavers, if we can just find some recently disturbed earth."

"One more thing," he said. He took out his iPhone and quickly prompted an app called My Altitude. Preset to southeast Wyoming's general elevation as a baseline, it quickly placed this spot at 1,505 feet above sea level. He wanted to save that for future use.

"Now, the shooting platform?" he said. "This bird is so careful, and so committed to preparation, that he'll have the distance down perfect."

"Yes, sir."

It took an hour.

"Got it!" someone cried, as all had moved a mile to the east and began to pick their way carefully through a scattering of elms and oaks, before it gave way to denser pines.

The men congregated at the site of the announcement, and indeed there it was, maybe seven feet up, a stout platform, well-braced and well-built, hammered into the vee of a giant tree. Branches had been clipped to allow for clear lines of fire to the faraway target, and a few wooden slats had been nailed into the trunk as steps to get up and down.

"Do I mess things up if I go up there?" Swagger asked.

"I don't see how. There's probably no prints on the bark, as it doesn't take to prints. DNA? Maybe, but I'm guessing it's more important to get the distance data than prove that a guy we know was here *was* here."

Swagger was gloved and masked, and with a little

help, managed to haul his old frame up to the platform. There, he saw what he couldn't from below: a shooting bench, solid, built at the edge of the platform to provide stability for the rifle as the shooter oriented toward the target. That told Swagger that wherever Juba would be shooting from, he'd be sure he was solidly anchored.

From this position, Swagger looked out across the meadow. He had never made a shot at anywhere near that distance, only an eight hundred and fifty in Vietnam with his .308—so long ago, it was impossible to recall details.

But a mile was different country. It was way the fuck out there, practically on a different planet, with winds that played on the bullet's flight, humidity that thickened or thinned the air, a trajectory like a rainbow's arc but without the colors, and time in flight of more than five seconds. Its execution demanded the rifle be placed as if embedded in rock, while, at the same time, administered with so delicate a touch that a heartbeat, a tremor, a microscopic twitch in the trigger push, or a moment of doubt or broken concentration, and the whole thing was off. Even with a 25× Schmidt & Bender, the finest optical system in the world, the human figure was but a dot. For its part, the post was impossible for him to pick out, even if the image was clear. It was just too small, too blended into the jagged background of trees. Through his binoculars, he saw nothing.

First move: the iPhone with the Altitude app. That drill revealed an altitude of 1,572, a difference of sixty-seven feet. He noted that figure as well.

"Okay, hand the thing up."

The thing was a Tecna LH40 military-grade range finder, borrowed from the FBI sniper school and good out to twenty thousand yards. Oddly enough, it didn't have the Star Wars look, with dials and buttons and all kinds of sci-fi stylistics. Instead, it resembled a slide projector from the '60s, with which the family's trip to Disneyland was documented for the neighbors. It took Swagger a bit of fiddling to get it set up on its tripod on the bench, then some more fiddling to get it on the target and focused, but finally he was ready.

Nothing.

"Can you get a guy to stand by the post? I can't see it to take the reading," he called.

He heard the team commander on the radio, and in a few seconds somebody—presumably, one of the men of the cadaver team that was looking in the area near the post for buried bodies—walked out and stood by the post. Swagger put his eye to the device, put the red dot on the tiny figure, and pushed the button to shoot a laser beam that far. The device would measure how quickly it bounced back and, in that way, solve the distance algorithm. He did it five times. The distance consistently turned out to be 1,847.5 yards.

He wrote the figure on the back of his hand in ballpoint under the altitude recordings, as insurance against a seventy-two-year-old memory.

"You get it?"

"Yeah, a little over a mile. Hell of a long way."

It also might do, he figured, to find out from the

household help what times of day the shooting took place, as those could be run against average wind speed, so he would also shoot when the speed of the wind was closest to the speed of the shot he'd come all this way to make. The position of the sun was another issue; he'd shoot when it most precisely matched the position it would be on the day of the shot.

So: he had direction, distance, the difference between the shooting site's elevation and that of the target, the presence of water between himself and target, the wind speed, the position of the sun. All of these factors Neill could magically enter into a computer program and test for real-world matches, particularly at places, as yet to be determined, where likely targets would likely be. In that way, perhaps they'd unlock the secret and could deploy in time to prevent.

Anything else?

He racked his brain, came up with nothing. But of course Mr. Gold had yet to run his fine mind over the data. The Israeli was back in Washington, not being a necessary raid component.

"Mr. Swagger?"

"Yes."

"Just heard from the cadaver team. The methane probe has turned up a batch of bodies. We have forensics on the way."

"Got it. Can you have the guys do a fine-tooth-comb search of this area? Maybe there's something here worth looking at."

"They're already on it."

"And I guess they ought to do the same to this shooting platform."

"Just waiting for you to come down. Be careful, now."

"I'm fine," he said, then slipped and fell down the seven feet and landed on his rear.

Men rushed to him, hands helping pull him to his feet, urgent faces projecting worry that he'd hurt himself seriously.

"I'm fine," he said, flexing, stretching, bending. "I only hurt my dignity. And my ass."

57

There it is," he said.

It was a building new to this ancient neighborhood, glassy and still clean, and full of optimism, when around it were so much blight, sadness, desolation, and dismay.

It was night in the city. In this far zone, separated by a river from the storied downtown, there wasn't much in the way of nightlife, street activity, vibrancy. In fact, the glory of the building had exactly the opposite effect that its designers had hoped for. Instead of livening up the street, by contrast it pointed out the tragedy of urban decay that surrounded it. Maybe it was a new start, maybe it too would lose its glamour and go the way of the sad brick and peeling paint that had claimed all the other structures. Who could know?

"Is our trip over?" asked Alberto.

"No. We will make a circuit of the block, then head out, find someplace to put up and stay the night."

It had been a long, dull trip across the United States.

There wasn't much to see from interstates at night, and they never entered cities, only the fringes, staying in cut-rate motels, eating fast food picked up from drive-thru windows. So to Juba, America was a blur of lights smeared by night, neon-basted plastic eat joints, and the ever-present cop fear. The last was misplaced, as, over the week of travel, no cop had paid them the slightest attention. Now, finally, chunk by chunk, five miles under the speed limit the whole way, they were here.

"Tomorrow," continued Juba, "you will take public transportation here and spend three hours in the neighborhood. Your job is to look for signs of police or FBI observation. Maybe, somehow, they already know, maybe they are just waiting. Maybe Bobleeswagger has figured it out and he's up there, waiting for me to walk into his trap."

"I doubt it. It seems to me you have accomplished the impossible. You have been trapped three, four times, have escaped each time, and have left behind exactly nothing. They could know nothing. Menendez knew nothing, not that he could have told anyone anyhow, not with his brains on the ceiling."

Juba nodded. "We know that they have studied the ranch, studied the remaining evidence. They have found the shooting site, measured the distance to my targets, examined my shop, seen my dies, my powders, the bullets I acquired. They know what rifle I am shooting."

"What can they know from all that? Nothing, it seems to me."

"They know the range, they know that I will shoot soon, because my data is only good as long as the weather here is similar to the weather on the ranch. They will try to infer from that my target, my shooting site, and my schedule. Their computers will help them in all this, which is my biggest fear. A computer could put something together in a second that no human could in a century. That is why Bobleeswagger could conceivably be up there, waiting."

"He is just a man. And not as good a one as you."

"Maybe. But to underestimate him is to court catastrophe."

Juba drove around the building, which occupied a whole block. He could see nothing that indicated observation. Other than a random police car manned by two listless officers, he saw no signs of authority.

"Maybe drive around again?" asked Alberto. "Just in case?"

"No," said Juba. "You are not thinking like a pursued man. What if, unknown to us, there have been burglaries in the area. So those two sleepy policemen aren't as sleepy as they seem. Instead, they are carefully watching for cars that are performing reconnaissance for an upcoming robbery: orbiting blocks, parking and watching, hanging out in nearby stores. If they see a vehicle, sirens sound, and other cars arrive out of nowhere in seconds. No rifle, but they find your little bag of diamonds and rubies from the rifle, they check the wires and see that the authorities are desperately searching for two 'Arabic-looking' men our age, and, by morning, I am on a plane to a country I've never heard of where certain men with blowtorches await. You see, you must account for the unaccountable as well."

"You must be the most careful man who ever lived," said Alberto.

The next day, Alberto took the subway to the area, spent time in a coffee shop, had lunch at a sandwich shop, bought a T-shirt and a ball cap at a souvenir shop, and, through it all, kept his eyes open for unmarked sedans sitting idly by, dull, thick men on the lookout, chats into radio microphones, odd rendezvous where one unmarked car pulled out to be replaced by another. Of those phenomena, as charted out for him by Juba, he saw nothing.

Back in the low-rent suburban motel, he said, "I saw no movement, no action, no sign. The building is completely unguarded and unobserved. I went into the lobby and found it without attention. I watched the people come and go. They were black, most of them. It is safe, I tell you."

"Tomorrow, you will go to one of those big stores and buy a disposable phone. I will make one call on it and it will be destroyed. The chances of an intercept are minimal, but we will take all precautions. If I am satisfied that all is well, I will arrange to take delivery of the key that admits me to a certain apartment in the building, and then I am where I must be. You and your little bag of diamonds and your junky little car—you will be free to go."

"I could stay," said Alberto. "I feel now as though this mission, whatever it is, is my mission."

"No, go far away. Return to your life. Or buy a new one, if you want. Do not get involved in cartel affairs—"

"I wasn't, to begin with. They dragooned me. I am lucky to be alive."

"Yes, you are. So am I. You go, you disappear. If I am successful, you will read about it in the newspapers. If I am not, you will not hear a thing. If you hear nothing, tragedy has occurred."

"Is there a date for all of this?"

"Yes, but I cannot tell you. You see why. Still playing against the tiny chance that somehow you'll end up in deep conversation with the FBI. They'll have the rubber hose, and you'll want to cooperate."

"I would die first."

"Everybody says that. But the hose always wins. The only issue is, how quickly."

58

The Theater of Insane Security continued into a second act. Mr. Gold remained in the lounge below Cyber Division, talking by phone with Memphis, while Swagger and Neill were nine feet away through the floor. It was feared by someone important with not enough to do that Mr. Gold would identify the brand of computers the FBI used and share it with Mossad. It never occurred to anybody that Mossad already had its own computers and wasn't looking for new ones.

"Okay," said Neill, "this is what I've got." He ran through the attributes listed by Swagger. "Everybody's in accordance? That's it, from 1,847.5 yards at a westward trajectory, in a south wind of four to six miles per hour, with sixty-five percent humidity, over a significant body of water . . ." And on and on, through all iterations of the attributes Swagger had determined were in play with Juba's upcoming shot.

"Can you think of another one, Mr. Gold? Any breakthroughs?"

"Not a thing," said Gold, from nine feet straight down.

"Anyone else? Chandler, you have anything?"

"I think we've got it covered," she said.

"Okay," said Nick. "So now we are going to run these attributes against the locations of appearances of high-level officials over the next three weeks, as recorded on the highly classified Secret Service master schedule. We begin with the Cabinet and the Executive. We assume any Cabinet or Executive officer to be the high-value target that would incite a plot. But we will move on to talk-show hosts, movie directors, star athletes, best-selling authors—whatever—anyone whose prominence might incite elimination with grievous consequences, not merely to morale but, really, to everything. We'll come up with—"

"It occurs to me," said Mr. Gold suddenly, "shouldn't time be a consideration?"

"What do you mean?"

"Well, we first became aware of this possibility upon acquisition of Juba's south Syrian location, courtesy of Mrs. McDowell, where, after our raid, the intelligence indicated he was preparing a shot in America with an ultra-long-range rifle. That was fifty-four days ago. Since he was in preparation for the shot for some time before then, it means that their plans were suppositioned on something that had to be on the schedule and immovable for at least fifty-four days, and almost certainly longer. So does it not make sense to limit the inquiries by focusing on those few dates that were in place early enough for them to be planned against?"

"Excellent," said Nick.

"Got it," said Neill. He sent an email to his staff of programmers and analysts in the bay who were the actual mechanics of the cyberoperation.

"I hope that cuts down on the possibilities," said Mr. Gold.

"Absolutely," said Neill. "The name of the game is winnowing. Winnow, winnow, winnow. When we are down to what cannot be winnowed, we ought to have something."

The time passed—*tick-tock, tick-tock, tick-tock*. In the big computer bay, people did what they had to do, lights blinked, strange whirring noises were raised by hard-drive fairies beating their wings furiously, a giant cleared his throat, printers yawned and printed in vacuum-cleaner-like hum, and the inquiry proceeded.

"Our program will examine all the potential sites for the shot attributes, as observed from the national satellite recon database. They'll bring the matches to us—that is, satellite recon images of potential shooting sites where the target will be accessible that fit the attributes. That's when sniper genius Swagger puts his brain to work, and let's hope he's still not cuckoo from the kick in the head Brother Juba laid on him, or the fall out of the tree."

"No problem, Bill," said Swagger to Jeff.

Nick laughed.

"The program can only do so much," Neill continued. "That's where human intelligence comes into play. The computers are as literal as a German schoolmaster. They don't do ambivalence. But when we look at the results, maybe we'll see ways in which something the computer is not impressed with might nevertheless be in play."

A young woman came over from Machine City.

"You'd be surprised at how much stuff we're getting," she said, "but here is the initial output."

She put a stack of heavy printout paper in front of them. Nick looked. "Wow," he said. "Well over a hundred."

"The field is too large," said Neill. "We've got to find a way to trim it down. The more attributes, the fewer the possibilities."

"We'll start with these, though," Nick said. "Meanwhile, somebody smart thinks up some new attributes. I see long-set appearances by the big guy nine times, the secretary of state five, the secretary of transportation—why would anyone target the secretary of transportation? Swagger, who is he?"

"No idea," said Swagger.

"A *she*," said Chandler. "And extremely unlikely."

Nick resumed: "The secretary of the treasury four times, and on and on—"

"It's pretty obvious we should go straight to President Tr—" started Bob.

"Stop right there," said Nick. "We've moved on to target possibilities, but I don't want to hear any names. Names carry connotations—history, backstory, political biases—all of which we must put out of our process. Thus, the gentleman you were about to call by name shall henceforth be known by his Secret Service code name, which is Mogul. To us, he is not a man, he is a cipher standing for an office only incidentally occupied by a human being. We are protecting the office, that is all. Is that understood?"

"Since you brought it up," said Bob, "it seems like I ought to ask something everybody's been thinking."

"Been waiting for this," said Nick.

"If you read the papers, or breathe, you know in some quarters Mogul is not popular. What if in all our digging and probing and chasing, we come upon some evidence of Americ—"

"Again, stop," said Nick. "I don't want to hear that. It is groundless speculation, and in this part of the forest, groundless speculation is poison gas. That is why we are proceeding on this one totally as a criminal investigation, not as some kind of coup. That is why I have tried to keep the Agency out of it and stay as low-key as possible with the Secret Service. That is why I have not made overtures to the White House. We need clarity, not a drunken-monkey orgy. If—and I say 'if'—you come across any such thing, it is only to be discussed with me, not among yourselves. I will make a determination whether to take it to the Director. But if it gets out—if even the possibility gets out—that, using foreign assets, someone, somewhere, with influence and connex here in D.C. has set up the elimination of Mogul, you know as well as I do that a drunken-monkey orgy is definitely in the cards. Not good for anybody except the drunken monkeys. So, barring hard evidence of that scenario, noses down, eyes locked in, small picture, not big. Understood?"

The lack of comment and response meant yes.

"Okay, handing these out, look hard and see what you're getting. Sorry, Mr. Gold, can't show 'em to you."

This was the real work of the day. Swagger ran his eyes over the photos, which were hazy, blurry sky-down views of unknowable zones, each with a circle centered on the executive's appearance location, the circle being 3,694 yards in diameter, putting anyone on the circle the required 1,847 yards from the center—that is, the target. That meant the shooter could be hiding anywhere on the circle.

He tracked directions and angles without regard to identified targets. The best shot clearly would have been on the secretary of transportation, where Juba could have perched atop what looked like an oil storage tank in Illinois and gotten a bullet across the Mississippi into Busch Stadium, where she was slated to throw the first pitch at a Cardinals game. But it just made no sense.

The Mogul sites were less promising, but not without a whisper of possibility. Of course, Mogul was so improvisational in his day-to-day, the long-term aspects seemed problematic. He might take off for golf in Florida that morning. He could do anything he wanted. He was the president!

The best shot would have been at an appearance in Baltimore, where he was more or less slated to appear at a luncheon at The Center Club—prominent, big-money businessmen—in the USF&G Building. He might be accessible from a mile-plus out from the Exelon Building across Baltimore Harbor, but that would involve shooting through glass, which hadn't been in the specs. Could there be another shooter who could fire at a raking angle from closer and shatter the glass, and in that frozen moment, Juba could take his long shot on the target? Well, theoretically, but . . . so many moving parts.

At a certain point, it was time to break for dinner. But they didn't break for dinner. Then it was time to break for coffee. They didn't break for coffee either. They didn't break for anything.

Finally, it was Chandler who said, "Everything we're coming up with is vaguely possible but, for this reason or that, unlikely."

"And your point is?" asked Nick.

"Maybe there's a fundamental error at a crucial spot."

"Did you hear that, Mr. Gold?"

"I did, and I think she has a point. But the question would have to be, at what crucial spot?"

"Well," Chandler said, "the servo mechanism that puts possibilities before us is the Secret Service master schedule, right?"

"Yes."

"Of all the attributes, that seems the most fragile. I mean, Swagger measured the yardage. That's a hard figure, empirical, unarguable. All the other things—the weather, the wind, the angles, all that stuff—is hard data. But the master schedule is assembled by people acting on information from other people. People talking to other people often have motives in the mix, even unconsciously, and there's miscommunication, it's imperfect, any of a dozen things can go wrong."

"All this is true. Do you want to call Secret Service and lean on them to recheck the schedule?"

"Here's my thought," she said. "Maybe what's upcoming isn't considered a Secret Service enterprise. You know, requiring special planning, the movement of assets, additional personnel, ground recon, prior coordination with local authorities. It's not special. It's normal, run-of-the-mill activity. So it's not on any schedule."

"How do we find out about it?"

"Do what Mr. Gold said: assume that it has to be something locked in early. It's been on the sched early enough for the bad actors to plot to it. So, chronologize the data by the length of time on the schedule. Not the master schedule of appearances, just daily operations."

"What have we got to lose?" said Nick.

He made the call, getting his Secret Service liaison out of bed. However, that guy was good at the job, got on the horn to SS operations—a 24/7 shop—and the larger schedule was emailed over to the FBI in a matter of minutes.

The data it contained hardly needed a program to be analyzed. It was just a matter of finding the earliest date of entry. That happened quickly enough.

"New York" was all it said, and ID'd a date a week further on, the next Thursday, the eighth of the month.

"So Mogul is going to New York on the eighth," said Nick. "Why? And why would he know so far in advance? And why would it be ho-hum to Secret Service?"

Obviously, nobody had any knowledge.

The next call was to the FBI–White House liaison. It

took a little longer because the guy was at the movies, he had to get home, go to his monitor, bring all this stuff up, check his numbers, call a good source in the White House, before he got back to them.

Nick took the call, listened, nodded, and looked up.

"Okay," he said, "we have a date. We also have politics, ego, vanity, media manipulation, and personal enmity in the mix. In other words, any day in D.C. since 1784. On that date, Renegade is scheduled to give a speech here in D.C. At some Arab–American Co-Prosperity function, funded by the Saudis."

"Who's Renegade?" asked Bob.

"Think hard," said Nick.

"Oh, I get it. The predecessor. Number forty-four. The—"

"You got it," said Nick. "So Mogul knows Renegade's talk will get a lot of attention and press. He doesn't like it. So he counterprograms. He learns that on that day a certain newly constructed building is being officially opened. No, Mogul doesn't own it, his company didn't build it, but he's pals with the guy that does and did. It's in the East Village, overlooking Roosevelt Drive. The guy's a big contributor, but, more, he's a deep and abiding enemy of the mayor of New York City, who definitely won't be at the ceremony. He hates the mayor, Mogul does, so it's a New-York-in-your-face-schmuck kind of thing as well as a Renegade-in-your-face-schmuck kind of thing. So it's been widely known for some time in New York political circles that Mogul would make a day trip up there, unannounced, and say a word at the ceremony. Maybe make a major announcement and pull the spotlight off Renegade."

Everybody looked at everybody else.

"The building overlooks the East River," said Nick. "Can someone go online and find an address?"

It took Chandler about seven seconds.

Neill called to one of his long-laboring computer techs, who came by and got the info and went off to run it against the shot-attribute program.

"Okay," said Bob, "is this just a party for geniuses like Mr. Gold and Chandler or can a country boy get a word in?"

"Go ahead," said Nick.

"I just thought of another attribute. Sorry I didn't think of it earlier, but it's crucial."

"Does it help us winnow?"

"I think it does. It just come to me like a kick in the head. See, there's been a key component missing. My fault, nobody else's."

"Go on."

"Most folks think you point a gun at someone, pull the trigger, and down he goes. Instant, like in a millionth of a second. But it ain't that way."

"Go on."

"The bullet takes some time to get there. The farther it travels, the longer it takes. If you're shooting at over a mile, it would be somewhere in the five-second range. It's officially called time in flight. Could figure it out more precisely, but trust me on this."

He waited for the import to strike them—but it didn't.

"That means the target has to be still. The shooter has to be assured he ain't going to leave to get a Coke between the pull of the trigger and the arrival of the bullet."

"So he's stationary?"

"Totally. He's giving a speech, he's sitting on a chair, he's at his desk. He's sitting down or standing still."

"We could cut out three-quarters of the possibilities by that test," said Neill.

"On the dais at that New York opening, he'd be still," said Chandler.

The young woman came back with a new sheet of paper.

"I think you'll like this," she said. "It's fourteen for fourteen on the attributes."

They all clustered around and saw about half a mile's worth of circle arcing through the dockside real estate across the East River in Brooklyn, and, 1,847 yards away, across a broad expanse of river, the docks, Roosevelt Drive, the building at which Mogul would be in place, still as a posed portrait.

"So that's got to be it, then," said Nick. "Next Thursday, the eighth, at three o'clock in the afternoon, shooting from an unknown site in Queens a mile out, Juba's going to kill Mogul."

59

The key pickup was without incident, and Juba said farewell to Alberto. He understood that the man now had a chance to turn him in to the FBI and become a hero. But he simply had to bet he wouldn't. Alberto was Arab where it mattered: in blood, in heart, in mind. He could be trusted.

The apartment to which the key admitted him had been rented, again by elaborate ruse and considerable bribery, to get him where he had to be, in a building subsidized for lower-income families by no less than the Department of Health, Education, and Welfare. Everything was seemingly legal and had been handled by a completely innocent contract employee of Iranian intelligence on money supplied by—well, that was unknown, even to the most intimate of conspirators, but by somebody with an interest in havoc, mayhem, anarchy, and collapse, especially in the United States of America.

The apartment was sparsely furnished with furniture,

also rented. The dining room table could be shored up for stability and used as a shooting bench upon which he would execute his mission. Nothing else was memorable, except for a crate that had been delivered a few days before he arrived: it was from a boutique furniture craftsman in Rock Springs, Wyoming. Examined carefully, it revealed no signs of tampering. He disassembled it, first the crate, then the bookshelves themselves, reducing both to wooden slats neatly stacked against the wall. The process revealed the rifle.

Accuracy International Arctic Warfare model, .338 Lapua Magnum, Schmidt & Bender 5.5×25×56 scope calibrated in MOA. He pored over it, checking the fingernail polish marking on each screw to make sure that they remained tightened exactly to the torque he had applied in Wyoming for maximum accuracy. In the kit of tools, he'd packed, along with the ten rounds of ammunition, dedicated wrenches, a lens-cleaning pen, his iPhone 8 with the FirstShot app already calculated to zero on the rifle at eighteen hundred yards, a Kestrel Pocket Weather Meter, and, among other shooter knickknacks, a bore sighter. This instrument allowed him to test for the scope setting for inadvertent alterations against the valuations he'd made in Wyoming. Again, it was unchanged, perfect.

Juba slept on the floor without a problem, took all his meals out, bought a few clothes with cash left over from the trip and washed them out every night, to dry overnight, so that he didn't attract attention due to shabbiness. Occasionally, he met other tenants in the lobby or in the elevator, but nobody here cared about anybody else's woes, much less existence. The tenants were in their own world.

In the apartment, he wore a mask, a hairnet, hospital slippers, and tight rubber gloves to safeguard against inadvertent DNA deposits in order to sustain the fiction that the occupant of the room, when it was discovered after the event, was one Brian Waters of Albuquerque, New Mexico, NRA life member, thousand-yard rifle champion, well-known hunter and gun crank, and author of some hideous screeds as yet to be deposited on the Dark Web. He would do that in the aftermath of the shooting with a single keystroke. In the next minutes, Juba would scrub down the rifle with acetone and apply certain biological traces of Brian Waters. Then he would disappear, and what would happen would happen.

He confronted the view. He initially was almost afraid to look, but it was all right. He was on the sixth floor, sixty-seven feet off the ground. He overlooked the building across the street and, beyond that, the roofs of smaller buildings, descending to the broad band of river three blocks away, and, across the river, his target zone.

Everything was as it should be, yet everything was different. It was as if he were confronting the reality of a dreamscape. He had seen this view in his mind, consciously and unconsciously, for over four months. Everything familiar, yet nothing familiar: that was the dynamic. He had to learn it, adapt to it, not let it throw his concentration off.

He understood that to make his shot, he had to be on-site days before. Unlike combat sniping, it wasn't a case of putting the crosshairs on the target, letting your reflexes squeeze the trigger, scrambling away before they could locate you and send incoming fire after you. It had to be his reality, as familiar as his mother's face, known in all its nuances, comforting in its exactitude. So he spent hours each day on the rifle, on the scope, on the table, his fingers learning anew—as if they'd forgotten—the shape and feel of the design via the exercise of the dry fire, his muscles learning the weight, his arms reacquiring the sensation of holding the rifle in that perfect merger of strength and gentleness. He had to become one with the rifle, a kind of exalted state of biomechanical intimacy, not easily achieved, not achieved, in fact, except through great effort and with practice, especially on demand. And he had to be able to do it on demand.

He prayed the required five times a day. It was pleasing to be back to such discipline. That was of great benefit. In speaking to Allah, in beseeching His holiness, in putting his petition for assistance before His greatness, he calmed himself. Was he speaking to God? That wasn't the point. The point was, his brain thought he was speaking to God, and Juba's respiratory system, his musculature, his digestive track, even his subconscious, felt subdued by the rigor. A great calm spread through him, and his limbs and veins thrummed with energy and confidence. No man in the world could do this thing, save him—not even Bobleeswagger—and his prayers enabled his effort.

Of course, he made sure to be on the rifle, eye locked on the scope, at the same time each day as the shot so that he could learn the play of the light in different weather conditions. *Snap!* went the dry trigger, over and over again. Maybe the day would be cloudy, maybe bold with sun. *Snap!* Shadows would cut the image, maybe not. Trees and the rills on the river would describe the wind, and he would have to understand how to read them. *Snap!*

Each day, afresh, he ran the program on the FirstShot ballistic calculator, and, each time, the solution came up the same for the preset eighteen-hundred-yard zero, arriving at the setting to which the scope was now set, 48 MOA elevation and 24 MOA right windage, which took it all into consideration—the wind, the temp, the humidity, the air density.

In the afternoons, after a brief lunch at a fast-food place and a cup of god-awful American coffee, he walked down as close to the river as he could get. Various barriers prevented actual riverside visits, and he couldn't risk violating them, for if nabbed by security or police, how could he explain the Kestrel?

He ran the Kestrel to record the exact weather conditions. He marked the waves in the water to match them to wind speed and learn it. There wasn't much variation, only in the cloud cover. No rain expected, humidity not ominous, wind tepid. It was as if Allah were sending him the ideal conditions. He looked across the river at the cityscape, the skyline. It was, as he expected, majestic, with proud towers and soaring structures, alive with the reflection of the sun off a million windows, humming with power, the dynamo of the West in one image.

He loved it. He hated it. It beckoned him. It sickened

him. It mattered so much to him. He mattered so little to it.

Your buildings tell us our place, which is in their shadow, bent and craven. We reject that, and you declare us monsters. We fight that, and you call us murderers. Your airplanes drop bombs guided by technical magic we could not understand and smash our children to jelly, and yet we are the beasts.

Tomorrow, I will destroy you.

Snap!

60

Zombieland, the sixth floor

Nick was back from the big meeting, and all waited for his account and direction. He'd worn his best suit, blue with banker's pinstripes, peaked lapel, white shirt, red ancient madder tie, black Alden Long Wings. He looked like a Washington power player.

"Good news, bad news," he said. "Anybody want to pick the order?"

Nobody did. Maybe the game wasn't appropriate for them, as they were tired from the hours spent on The Problem, and eager to move on, and had no need for Nick's charm, though on many other occasions they'd appreciated it.

"Boss," said Chandler finally, "whatever."

"Okay, nobody cares," said Nick. "So I'll start with the good. And it's really good."

He paused, smiled.

"Congratulations to you all, and I suppose to me too. At the top levels, they are extremely pleased and extremely eager. They believe your work represents a major victory over the threat of jihad in the West and the opportunity for a major victory. Not only have we saved a life and prevented the political and cultural chaos that would ensue from a terrorist event against a high-value target, they see a chance to be proactive and turn it into a major advantage. Even as I speak, that response is being organized. There's just enough time to set the trap, and the people involved are talented and skilled enough to bring it off."

"We ought to be on the Acela for New York right now," said Neill. "I'm packed, and I've told my wife—hmm, what was her name? Wendy? Susie? Something like that—anyway, I've told her we're going."

"Neill, we've all worked long hours and gone without spousal visitations," said Nick, "but the point is taken: you want it done fast so you can get back to normalcy. Me too. But that brings me to the bad news."

He paused. "We've been fired."

He let it sink in.

"I don't see this as an insult, a gesture of contempt, a reaffirmation of the principle that no good deed goes unpunished. It's not 'Thank you very much, but what have you done for me lately?' It's simply the way the system works, and I should have prepared you better for it."

"Is it politics?" Swagger asked.

"Well, I'd rather not speculate on meaning," said Nick.

"Does this kind of shit happen in Israel?" Swagger asked Mr. Gold.

"Never. Except every day. And twice on most."

"From a management point of view, I see the issue," said Nick. "If we're up there, we're another layer that has to be briefed, kept in the loop—and, worst of all, listened to. We just get in the way of the Incident Command staff and turn it all murky. We think it's our turf, and we're hardwired to protect turf. Maybe we make different calls than they do, maybe we know too much, which can be as destructive as knowing too little. Maybe—and they're right on this—Nick Memphis doesn't have the experience to run something this big and complicated, and maybe the loyalty his people feel toward him clouds their judgment. Not saying it's so, just saying that's how it could be seen. And, once seen, it has to be avoided."

"And maybe some Bigfoot wants the credit," said Bob. "And maybe someone has a debt to be paid or wants to advance a protégé up the ladder. Or maybe someone thinks Nick's shoes ain't shiny enough or he should have worn cotton socks instead of wool ones, which he would have learned if he'd gone to a university that didn't have 'State' in its name."

"These are silk," said Nick. "My only pair. So it's not that."

"So what happens to us?" asked Chandler.

"We stay here. We are copied on everything but asked to comment on nothing. If questioned, we answer to the best of our knowledge. On operation day, we will set up in the Command Center and will be able to follow the action by uplink to the New York Field Office in real time. We get a front-row seat, watching it all go down. That's what everybody wants—and I do mean everybody."

Again silence, as each tried to work his or her way around what was deemed necessary by upper management.

"I smell the White House," said Neill. "I smell Mogul."

"Okay," said Nick, "maybe you do. Off the record, this was always in the cards, we just didn't see it. But upper floor reads the Juba operation as a win-win. You all know there's a cloud over the Bureau, and maybe a big triumph helps it go away. That's the first win, and you better believe the Director is hot for that one. Then there's the White House. You all know that elections are coming up, and if Mogul can get a victory over Islamic fundamentalism, that's another big win. If he looks like a hero, it's big enough to get him that second term. So everybody's salivating, and intelligence concerns, strategic implications, and plain old justice just go out the window. Too much to be gained, in that superficial Washington way, with no downside. The best I can offer is, you've really pissed off the CIA, and they want in. But since it's our baby, Mogul won't let them in. So in the eternal war in Heaven between the angels, our side has won a big one, and you are the angels that did it. Recompense will come in many forms—promotions, Glory Wall photos and letters, commendations, everything that should make good little boys and girls happy. Swagger gets a new BarcaLounger at Bureau expense. And when it's all over, Mr. Gold, maybe there'll be enough Juba pie left over to send to Israel. Wouldn't that make you and the boys in the black cube happy?"

"Indeed," said Mr. Gold.

"It should even make Mrs. McDowell happy," said Nick.

"What have these geniuses come up with?" asked Swagger.

"It'll be run out of the New York Field Office, with a lot of New York SWAT and aviation thrown in. Real big, but I think it'll work out."

"Are you afraid to tell us?" asked Neill. "Is that why you're buttering it up?"

"Neill," said Chandler, "show some respect. Nick has been with us and behind us every fucking step."

"You're right," said Neill. "Sorry, Nick, I misspoke."

"Emotions running high. Everybody, please drop down into second gear, okay?"

He waited a few seconds.

"Okay, there's a countersniper technology that turns on luring the bad guy to shoot through a microphone pickup field. It's called Boomerang II, much improved from Boomerang I, from the folks at Raytheon. Maybe Swagger can explain it better."

"I can't," said Bob.

"Anyway, the microphones yield data that the program can solve, and, in one millisecond, get you velocity, caliber, weight. But, most important, it can source the bullet. I mean, fast. They've used it hooked to artillery in the sandbox, and they can send a flight of 105 howitzer shells to point of origin inside a second. Takes care of the sniper and the city block or village in which he was hiding."

"How do they get Juba to shoot in the right spot?" asked the annoying Neill.

"They're arrayed, under camouflage, around the podium. They look sort of like a ball with spikes sticking out of it. The hardware isn't gigantic or obtrusive, and it flashes the data back to the receiving station, in the Incident Command van."

"So they're going to get Juba to shoot over the microphones, then track him and blow him up?" asked Neill. "Bye-bye, Queens."

"No. They get the read back to origin, and instead of sending 105s after him, they send assets that were put in place the night before—that is, NY SWAT teams airborne in choppers. They feel they can get them on-site inside a minute or two from various hidden locales, rappel the boys onto the rooftop while squad cars beeline in from just outside the zone, and, in that way, take him alive."

"Meanwhile," asked Swagger, "is Mogul dead?"

"No. The heavyset blond guy isn't Mogul. He's career Secret Service, in a blond wig, said to bear a pretty good resemblance to the real thing. Under his blue suit, white shirt, red tie below his zipper, and Elvis rug, he's packed in enough Level IV Kevlar to stop a truck, no problem with a bullet that's traveled eighteen hundred yards and whose velocity is way down, under a thousand pounds, like a handgun. From a hundred yards out, he'll convince—let alone a mile out. First shot, he goes down, behind the armored podium. He's risking a headshot, but that's the name of the game. He's a stud."

"I'll say," said Swagger. "I wouldn't do that job for all the money in the world. Or all the glory."

"Anyhow, maybe Juba goes down hard, and it's just a kill and a great success. But, Jesus, if they get him alive, what a bonanza. A live terrorist with a long and interesting past tasked with and almost succeeding at taking down Mogul. Everybody looks great, the Bureau looks fabulous, our real enemy, the CIA, looks pitiful, Mogul gets to strut and brag and do photo ops with the head of NYPD SWAT and the blond guy in Kevlar. Meanwhile, the interrogation and trial go on all through election season."

"Too many moving parts," said Swagger. "Wrong goal. Goal should be to stop him—first, last, and only. 'Capture' is overambitious bullshit. If you don't fixate on 'stop,' it can go south hard and fast."

"Our masters have spoken," said Nick. "It will be as it will be."

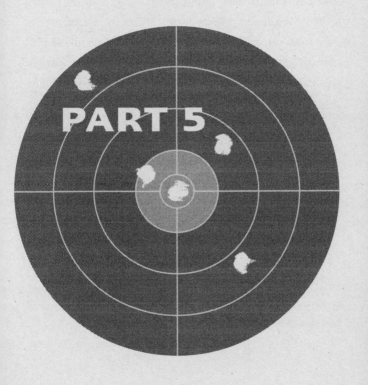

PART 5

61

Allah sent him a wonderful day, on the cusp of a wonderful night of deep and restful sleep, untroubled by a visit from his darkest nightmare visitor, the American sniper sent to destroy him and his mission. He awoke to a blue sky, lightly feathered with high cirrus clouds, not much breeze. The air was fresh, even perfumed. The leaves vibrated in the gentle breeze, turning first their dark faces, then their light faces, to him—in effect, shimmering.

At the river that morning, he took his Kestrel readings, came up with a two- to four-mile-per-hour north-northwest breeze, a temperature of sixty-seven degrees, probably to rise a few degrees by midafternoon, and only forty-four percent humidity. The sun was bold, casting sharp shadows, but it would be high in the sky by shooting time and thus would render the image shadeless. The buildings, the grounds, the vegetation, the colors, the lack of activity, the lack of security vehicles or men: all as it should be. On the water, the rills were low.

Praise be to Allah, He who provides.

There was no hurry. He ambled back to the building, halting again for a long, keen observation. Again, nothing, nobody, no cruising police vehicles or plainclothes men in nondescript sedans. No helicopters above, and, with his gifted eyesight, he was sure there were no drones high in the sky.

He entered the lobby boldly, knowing that the TV monitor was down, had always been down. He took the elevator up with a young woman and her two children. Nothing was said, but the mood was calm. The children were well behaved, the mother attentive. They got off on 3, he continued to 6. Hallway empty. He unlocked, entered, and locked again, checked his watch. Time for prayer.

He slipped on his mask, hairnet, and rubber gloves, as always. He went to his prayer rug—a towel—and prostrated himself for seven minutes.

Allah, I beseech Thee, look with favor upon my enterprise today, for it is enacted to Your glory, on Your behalf, for Your war. I give up my life to You, O Allah, and will gladly leave it if that is Your decision. I pray that You make my eye sharp, my hand strong, my heart calm, my finger delicate. In Your interest and according to Your laws I dedicate that which is to come, O Beloved One, and ask as well Your favor on my ancestors and my descendants, for all are a part of this holy moment.

On and on it went, a litany of loyalty, love, and dedication. It poured the lubricant of faith throughout his body so that all processes became easier, slick with grace, beauty, and precision. His mind was narrowing, his breath was smoothing, his fingers were strengthening. Only one thing occupied his mind.

He went to the closet where he had stored a purchase he had made: it was a can of acetone. It would chemically obliterate any traces of himself on the weapon. Using a cotton ball to blot, he assiduously wiped the steel and plastic down, even if the plastic was favored not to preserve fingerprints. He worked at a slow, sure pace, watching the liquid as it spread to a sheen and evaporated, not missing any plausible surface, taking all traces of Juba with it into the ether. The scope, particularly the turrets, demanded special attention, as it could easily retain evidence if not carefully purified, though he had never touched any part of the weapon with his naked fingers.

Next, he drew out several plastic bags. Each contained DNA-carrying microdebris from the actual corpse of Brian Waters—dandruff, flakes of skin, filaments of nostril and head hair—and applied them gradually to the rifle. A piece of tape yielded a thumbprint, and by applying it to the Thunder Beast suppressor—a long tube with chambers and aperture that would dissipate the sound of the shot—then peeling it off, he transferred the image. He applied and then removed another tape—this one for the sake of the trigger finger—around the trigger guard and the trigger itself. In the end, he had rendered the rifle appropriate to the biological reality of his avatar's presence and his own invisibility.

He did the same to the iPhone, smearing it with the detritus of poor Mr. Waters. A close investigation would reveal nothing except the FirstShot app and the occasional posts of Mr. Waters on his all-but-deserted Facebook page. He checked and saw that certain pages had come to his queue, and he knew exactly the stroke to send them instantly to post on the Dark Web, where they would be found and tracked to this iPhone and to Brian A. Waters. The pages contained superb screeds of hate and blasphemy, which would make the man's sickness manifest to all and provide the motive for his crime. Brian A. Waters was about to become the most famous man on earth, as well as the most wanted. Too bad he'd been dead for over three months and wouldn't be around to enjoy all the attention.

Next, he checked his getaway bag. Yes, passport, ID, cash. He knew exactly his escape route, where he would be picked up by Iranian operatives and how he would be smuggled back to Syria.

It was almost over.

He checked his watch.

So little time.

He went to the window in front of the rifle. He had been prepared to cut the glass, use a suction cup to remove the appropriate fragment, shoot through it, then wedge the glass back in place so that no one observing from the outside would know that this room, automatically, was the source of the assassin's bullet. But a happy surprise had been that the larger pane of glass was flanked on each side by two narrower ones, either of which could be cranked open, revealing a screen, through which fresh air could circulate if the building's air-conditioning went down. Cranking it open also revealed ample room for shooting, with a perfect vantage on the target. At the last second, he would cut the screen, peel it back, and open a square through which he could shoot. His plan was to fire once as carefully as possible, crank the bolt as quickly as possible, fire nine more rounds, forming a kind of beaten zone, so that the man would take bullet after bullet. He would quickly close the window to obscure the location. The authorities would find the sniper's nest eventually, but he would be long gone.

Now there was nothing left to do but wait.

1000

It turned out there wasn't really space in the operations room for Nick and his crew, not with all the bigs who'd crowded in to watch the triumph. Probably that was best for all, as it prevented the bigs from noting the annoyance of the passed-over Nick team, and it prevented the passed-over Nick team from expressing snarky resentment.

At one point, the Director and some otherwise anonymous factotums came up to express gratitude for contributions, creativity, and the success about to arrive, although the leader himself spent more time with Chandler—as what sane man would not—than the others combined. He lurked, breathed, smiled unctuously, closed in too tight, and was too fulsome in attention.

Such is the expression of power in D.C., and, for her part, she stayed cool and professional and paid no acknowledgment to his interest. When the ceremony was over, the bigs left, and Nick's people were left alone in their upstairs warren, watching the drama on a closed-circuit TV, where they were free to go as smart-ass as they wanted, though, as it turned out, no one was in any sort of smart-ass mood.

Still, they followed as the parts were carefully layered in. The choppers weren't airborne yet, but when they were, they would hang in the air about a half mile behind the zone, which was that part of the arc 1,847 yards out in Queens that fronted on the new building over Roosevelt Drive and the East River. The Mogul sub was suiting up in Level IV Kevlar for his shot at glory; Mogul himself would arrive shortly. Teams were locked, loaded, and in place all over, the various Raytheon marvels needed for the intercept in place and tested.

Meanwhile, in Queens, SWAT units had parked during the night on blocks not far from the potential shooting sites—one of twenty-three buildings on the arc—and could get there almost as fast as the choppers. The plan was to hurl them to the newly identified shooter's building simultaneously with the arrival of the choppers—a classic pincer move.

Swagger had little to say. As much as he hoped it would work, he didn't believe it would. Juba was too good. Juba was better than he'd ever been. You couldn't match ordinary brains against his and expect anything good to come of it.

"Cheer up, Bob," said Nick. "We do this thing, have a couple of days of Mogul love and an open bar, and it's back to Idaho and the front porch. I'm sure the deer and the antelope have missed you."

"May I say something?" said Mr. Gold.

"A breakthrough?" asked Nick.

"Not exactly," he said.

"Well, go ahead anyway."

"I believe we have made an astute analysis of the evidence, and the plan itself is sound and well staffed, no half measures—and I know, from experience, that half measures are frequently catastrophic."

"Okay," said Nick.

"However—"

"Here it comes," said Neill.

"It does occur to me that in one respect, hard as we have worked, we are all Juba amateurs. We've been in the game only a few months."

"Yes?"

"There is only one Juba professional in the world. We are here only because of her efforts over long years. She has been tracking, imagining, stalking this fellow for over a decade."

He paused as they all took it in.

Finally, Nick said, "Go on."

"My thought is, at this late hour perhaps security mandates could be waived and we could reach out to Mrs. McDowell. We could put all we have—our conclusions, the time frame, the immediate anticipation of action in the countersniper plan—before her and ask her for an opinion. Well, not so much about what we plan to do but on our reading of what Juba wants to do. Maybe she'd see something we missed, maybe she'd bring an outside-the-box freshness to it, maybe there are vibrations, memes, motifs, indications, resonances, some sort of clues that we've missed to which she'd be sensitive. After all, we have several hours, by my watch, until the event itself is thought to transpire, so there does seem to be just enough time."

Nick thought it over. It involved logistics, not his strong suit. He turned to Chandler.

"Is this possible?"

"Well," she said, "I don't think Mr. Gold means by phone, does he?"

"Face-on-face would be preferred," said Gold. "That way, we could read her expression as she considers the analysis, which may be more elucidating than anything she might say."

"She's where? In the suburbs of Baltimore?"

"In the city itself, northwest Baltimore," said Swagger. "It's called Dorsey's Forge."

"What aviation assets do we have?" Nick asked Chandler.

"None. They're all at Quantico, out of play."

"Maryland State Police has aviation," said Neill. "At Martin airfield, just north of Baltimore."

"Chandler, could it work?"

"Maybe get Maryland to pick her up at some park near her home. They get her to our roof inside an hour.

That would give us two hours with her to go over the stuff. I think it could be valuable."

"Swagger?"

"She ain't no dummy."

"Neill?"

"Well, if nothing else, it would dispel all those little 'if only' doubts we have. It would represent us making every last effort, all the way to game time. No stone left unturned, that sort of thing."

"Bob, can you call her and see if it's even possible?"

Swagger took out his phone, punched in the number. Two rings, three, halfway through a fourth: "Yes?"

"Janet, it's Swagger."

"Oh, hello," she said.

"What's your situation?"

"I have no situation. I'm about to clean the upstairs bathroom, in an attempt to forestall my daily martini spree another hour."

"Is there a field, an open space, anywhere near you?"

"There's a schoolyard two blocks away. Scott Key Elementary School."

"Hold a second. Oh, better yet, don't start on the bathroom. Let us do some checking at this end. Put on some comfortable shoes."

He hung up.

"Okay," said Nick, picking up a phone.

On-screen, they saw as in the Command Center, somebody came to the Director, and he rose and was led to a phone off camera.

Nick made the pitch.

Some chitchat, maybe the Director consulted with the White House and his staff, but, in the end, the assent was given.

"Okay," said Nick. "Bob, call her back, read her in, and get her to that schoolyard. Chandler, get me our State Police liaison."

"Yes, sir."

"We'll see what she has to say."

1145

Finally: the ammunition.

Maybe this is how it begins. You cannot love the rifle if you do not love the ammunition. Something dense, deadly, charismatic in the heft and glint of it. Nothing on earth quite like it.

He had, after all the experimenting and all the lives of chained men perishing at a mile-plus in the wild beauty of Wyoming, settled upon this.

With the tip of his knife, he peeled open the package he had prepared in Wyoming. The ten Kings of Hell spilled out, each 3.681 inches long, slightly front-heavy, somehow oddly dense for volume, a function of the 250 grains of Sierra .338 diameter MatchKing hollow-point boattail bullet inserted and crushed into place by the pressure of Wilson's .367 seating die.

He loved the cartridges. He loved to build them, to think them, to imagine them, to feel the weight and roll of them in his hand. He'd scrubbed them with acetone in Wyoming and now touched them with rubber-gloved fingers only. Thus, no Juba would be evident to investigators on their ultimate discovery, even if the brass was notoriously averse to recording the prints of its handlers.

He held each one. Slightly overpressured with 91.2 grains of Hodgdon H1000 smokeless powder that filled each once-fired Hornady tube, to be ignited by a Federal 215M Magnum primer. The shell had been chamfered for smoothness, its burrs and eccentricities milled away. It had been neck-turned so that the grip of brass that secured the bullet was exactly .004 thick all the way around. It had been tested for runout—that is, deviation from the axis—and found to be within the metric of .001, which meant as close to perfect as humanly possible. It had been annealed, a brief heat treatment that made its consistency profound. The bullets themselves had been sharpened in the Whidden die, improving their long-range accuracy. All these boutique touches, which the same investigators would eventually discover, were consistent with the high craftsmanship of a champion shooter like Brian A. Waters. They matched perfectly, both as an object and as a product of a culture, with what would be observed when, weeks from this day, his house was unlocked and subjected to the most intense of forensic examinations. No one looking at the recovered shell could doubt that it had been produced by the man from Albuquerque, about to be revealed to the world as yet another lone gunman on a grassy knoll—well, an apartment—administering hatred via a death that would change the world.

He took the shells and, one by one, loaded them into the Accuracy International ten-shot magazine. As the box filled, the spring tightened and fought him more urgently. He squeezed the last one in only by applying the full pressure of his thumb against the shaft of the brass, after sliding it between the flanges of the mag and urging it back flat against its rear plate.

There! Again, something about a magazine fully loaded. You held it, feeling its density, feeling the pressure of its compressed spring, feeling its urgency to offer its cargo up to the slide of the bolt, which would pluck them, one by one, into the chamber, like a burnt offering of some kind.

He rocked the magazine into place, felt it catch, rotated it upward, felt it lock in place with a satisfying reverberant click. He had only to ram the bolt home, to insert the first of the ten into the chamber, and wait until at last his target came into view, a small human speck in the lens from so far away, who, as he would have to, would go to stillness, not knowing he was setting himself for the shot that would kill him.

Juba checked his watch.

More than an hour to go.

Now to relax, perhaps pray again, perhaps let serenity and will roll through his body, until he became one with the rifle, one with the ammunition, one with the mission.

Something moved in front of him. But it was only a

helicopter, a speck in the sky miles away, vectoring in for some kind of rooftop landing in the far, magnificent city across the river.

1350

She tried. You could see her trying. She gave it her all, her belief, her imagination, the intelligence leveraged into her brain by the weight of a mother's endless grief, all the pain of back alley beatings and rapes, all the subsequent pain in the recovery, all the willed forgetting. She tried.

Still, the message was clear: no sale.

"You don't have to say a thing," said Mr. Gold. "I can read your face."

"It's magnificent," she said. "You're so brilliant, each of you. I sense your intellect in every stroke, in every inference, in every leap. And it makes sense. It follows so logically, one point to another, one clue to the next, all of it coheres, makes policy sense, makes world-historical sense, makes religious sense, even by their standards. As a Moslem, it makes sense to me. As a tourist in Baghdad, it makes sense. As an amateur spy, it makes sense. As a rape victim, as a pauper who's spent a fortune on the same goal—on all of that—it makes sense. I applaud you."

"But," said Mr. Gold, "you do not buy it?"

She smiled, though deep in that smile was the weight of loss, and the whole room read it: Mrs. McDowell regrets to inform you that you are full of shit.

Silence in the room. One of the fluorescents had gone out, so shadows haunted the place. The batch of them faced the woman, who wore no makeup, as she hadn't had time to put it on, who sat before them in dumpy jeans and a Boys' Latin T-shirt, her cheap reading glasses slightly askew. Her hair had looked better, as had she. But none of that mattered. Only her reaction mattered.

"Is it a feeling you have?" asked Nick. "Or is it something specific?"

"It's that I love everything about it except *it*." Then she said, "Do all of you love it? Do you have any doubts?"

"I will not let them answer," said Nick, "because that would give you a frame in which to couch your own objections, and that is of no use to us. What is only of use to us is what you bring to it."

"I will try to put into words what I feel," she said. "If you find value in it, that's well and good. How much time do we have?"

"Don't worry about that. Time is our concern, not yours. No one here will look at a watch, no one will sigh."

Swagger realized how professional Nick could be. It must have killed him to say such a thing, for indeed time was clicking away, remorselessly, as it was now 1440, and the thing would happen—or so they reckoned—at 1500. Each second made any kind of response to anything she said more unlikely.

"Do you want a Coke? A cup of coffee?" asked Nick.

"Get the Coke," said Swagger. "The coffee here sucks."

Everybody laughed. Maybe that helped a little.

"I'm fine," she said. Then she said, "His mind doesn't work like that."

They waited for an amplification, but nobody said a word to rush her. They found the discipline to let her form her own words in her own time.

"I have been on this guy since he killed my son. That's over fifteen years. I have learned a little. Not much."

What had she learned?

"It's too straightforward. You've concluded *he wants to kill Mogul.* Even if you didn't want to say it, or were prevented from saying it, your country's history forced you to think that he wanted to kill Mogul."

She was right. Maybe Nick had been wrong. Maybe in suppressing that interpretation he had made it all the more inevitable.

"But if he really wanted to kill Mogul," she said, "you would be all set up to prevent him from killing somebody else. You wouldn't know it was Mogul. You'd think it was, say—oh, I don't know—Hillary. There would be indicators all along—hints, subtle suggestions, the whole shadow show—all of it to convince you that it was Hillary. And the shot on Mogul would come as a complete surprise. It would utterly stun you. You'd have invested everything in saving Hillary from a threat that didn't exist."

Again, silence. Not a single Hillary joke.

"Think how he did it in Baghdad. The IED detonations drove the marines back to what they thought was safety. But what they thought was safety was the kill box.

Lure and distraction: that's his specialty. He lures you into one situation, twists it against you."

"We thought we were hunting him," Bob said. "He was hunting us."

"Exactly," she said.

The room went still.

"He's very tricky. It's not what you think it is. He's come up with something else."

Finally, Nick spoke—but not to her.

"What have we missed? Anybody?"

Swagger said, "All the gun stuff is hard. He will shoot at 1,847 over water in close to fifty-degree humidity with very little wind. He will use a .338 Lapua Magnum of a certain powder load, case preparation, and bullet choice and weight. You can't argue that away."

"So what isn't hard? What is interp, as opposed to fact?"

"Behavior," said Gold, from his well of ancient experience. "The hardest thing. You count on one thing, another happens. *Always.*"

"Let's ID the behavior, then," said Nick.

"Mogul will show up today at 1500. Juba's known it. It seems solid. They believed it to be solid enough to plan on," said Chandler.

"Mogul will address the crowd," said Neill. "It isn't planned, it isn't announced, it's on paper nowhere, but it's his behavior: give him a friendly crowd and there he is, screwing Renegade out of attention and getting big pleasure from that, big as life, ready for a bullet."

"Ready for a bullet," said Chandler. "Meaning 'still.'

He has to be still because of Swagger's time in flight data. Time in flight is not negotiable. It's the iron law of physics."

"Stillness," said Gold. "The young woman is onto something."

"Go on," said Nick.

"The time in flight," continued Mr. Gold, "demands that he must be still. We *assume* that stillness is a speech near a body of water, and it turns out that Mogul indeed had a long-settled speech planned for that day right at the banks of the East River. Knowing that, anyone could plan backwards from it, could see what a brilliant body-guard of lies it would make, how perfectly it might cover the real operation at about the same time, but which would turn on another form of stillness."

"Stillness," said Nick. "Anybody?"

"Eating?" said Neill.

"Inside a restaurant. Not likely."

"No joke: going to bathroom?" Bob said.

"Again inside, not available to a long shot from far away across a river."

"Reviewing stand?" said Neill. "Parade ground. The theater? A movie? I can't—"

Then Mrs. McDowell said, "My father was one of those go-getters. Never still—*anywhere, anytime, any way*. Except one place in his life where his stillness used to drive people crazy. I know. I caddied for him. He was putting."

1445

Allah, Thy servant beseeches Thee again. O Lord of all, it is in Your favor I commit myself and give myself, for life, for death, for fate, for destiny. I smite Thy enemies. I drive them to destruction. I ensure our triumph. I ensure Your mastery over all. I enable their submission and the power of Your will as it becomes not regional but global, as it destroys the Satan that is America, as it ruins this land of decadence and corruption and evil. I evoke in Your name all of those who have died to put me at this spot and make me Your instrument, and, consecrated in their blood, I perform my act. I am humble and contrite before You, knowing that now You shall reach down and infuse Your servant with power, serenity, vision, and brilliance.

It was almost time. He gently shoved the bolt forward, feeling it take one of the cartridges off the stack in the magazine, engaged it, and slid it gently, smoothly, forward into the chamber. He locked the bolt down and, with his finger, touched the safety switch on the right side of the receiver, checking that it was off.

1455

On one of the screens they could see the crowd gathering in New York, the dais beginning to fill. The other showed men in calm control in the Command Center downstairs, as they orchestrated the pieces for the checkmate that nobody watching now believed would never happen.

Nick was on the phone.

"Get me Secret Service, their Command Center. Yes, ASAP, this could be Code Red."

He waited.

"Jackson, Command" came on the voice at the other end.

"Bill, Nick Memphis over at Hoover, I'm going to put you on speaker for my people, okay?"

"Yeah. But, Nick, shouldn't you be engaged in the New York op? Aren't you up there, and—"

"Long story. Politics."

"In this town? What a surprise!"

"Something just come up. Assuming our bad guy is going to go today, I have to ask, do you have any protectees on a golf course?"

"On a golf course?"

"Yeah, I—"

"That's *mucho* classified, bud."

"Secure line, emergency procedure, maybe go to Code Red on this one. Come on, Bill, give it to me, this is real important."

"I don't know how you found out. *Nobody's* supposed to know this shit."

1458

He could see them now. Still too far out, but sharply outlined in the Schmidt & Bender, two figures, next to the golf cart. A good one hundred and fifty from the green. The tall one—too far to make out details, he was an amoeba to the eye, even blown up twenty-five times due to the genius of Germanic glass grinding—addressed the ball, concentrated, and rotated back smoothly to equipoise, paused a second, unleashed a swing.

Through the scope, Juba could not follow the ball, but he could tell from the instant dejection in the tall man's posture that the shot had not gone well. But instead of relinquishing his club and jumping into the cart for taxi service onward, the man reached into his pocket, took out a second ball, and dropped it on the grass. The same ceremony of addressing, shifting, fidgeting, adjusting and counteradjusting, gathering, squeezing his concentration to an even higher degree, and the silver shaft flashed in the sun, and another slashing stroke was delivered.

This time, success, as the tall man pivoted in follow-through, turned back, putting hand to eyes to shield them from sun, following the ball as it went where it had been directed. He could not contain a bit of leap as the ball must have smacked on the green and rolled toward the hole. Elated, he accepted a handshake from his assistant and got into the cart, which now began its short journey to the green, some 1,847 yards from Juba.

1459

"Whenever he's in town on a Thursday, he goes to a certain course and has a private round. It's secure, because it's on a military post closed to the public, and of

GAME OF SNIPERS   481

course the MPs do a security sweep and close the place down for the afternoon. They close the whole post down, in fact. It's just our guy and his caddy, for therapy, for escape, for fun. Every Thursday. He carries a bucket of balls, and he'll hit—"

"Who?" yelled Nick.

"Renegade."

It made sudden, savage sense. Renegade was beloved by millions, a beacon of racial pride, honor, and integrity, a hero to the left. Dump him with a .338 to the thoracic, and those millions would go insane with rage, especially as it came out the shooter was a white racist who'd just unleashed a ton of vile racist hate speak under his own name—Brian A. Waters—on the Dark Web and had escaped, cleanly and mysteriously, as if abetted by some Deep State conspiracy. Would we ever come back from that one?

"Where?" said Nick.

"The golf course at Fort Lesley J. McNair in the southeast, off the Anacostia. About a mile from you."

"Is there any spot on the course where he's vulnerable—"

"The eighth green is at the edge of the river, nearly a mile wide at that point. Next to the National War College. I suppose if you knew he was there and you were on the other side of the river and had a high vantage point—"

"He's there now?"

"He would be. Arrived at one. Usually on the course about three hours on a Thursday afternoon. He'd be just getting to the eighth green about now."

"Call your detail and get him off the course, and I mean this fucking second."

"No detail. No iPhone. That's the point, he enjoys being cut off, so it's just him and the golf ball. I can get the guys in the clubhouse out there, but I don't know if they can make it in time."

"Do it, do it, do it!" said Nick.

He looked up.

"They knew some Saudi billionaire had hired him for a speech. Big dollars. They knew that would keep him in town this day, and since it was Thursday, he'd go to the course. Later, they found out about Mogul's reaction, and Juba saw how he could run that as cover story."

"Mrs. McDowell's helicopter on the roof," said Swagger. "I need a rifle."

1502

It turned out the ball hadn't quite made it to the green. It landed a few feet short, fairway all the way, far from any sand, but a few feet shy of the manicured grass. Good chance to work on the short game.

Hmm . . . Long putt or short chip? Decisions, decisions.

Why not both?

Do it, thought Juba. The tiny figure stood exactly against the red dot at the center of the scope, the adjustments perfect, everything as it should be, as Allah had willed it.

But he wouldn't be 1,847, not just yet.

He'd be at about 1,865, a few yards off the edge of the lush green circle that sported its silly little flag, which, incidentally, was limp, testifying to lack of wind.

Do it! he told himself again.

But the target was not at 1,847. Everything was set for 1,847. Another few seconds, a minute perhaps.

The golfer elected to go with a chip. The drill—address, adjust, square up, bear down—all over again. Then a short, clipped backswing—more chop than swing—and he uncoiled, very much under control.

Whatever happened, it was not good.

He laughed—the man was enjoying himself—and waited until his assistant brought another club and another ball.

He dropped the ball to earth.

Address, adjust, square up, bear down, head still and down. No backswing, just a kind of controlled shove, and this time the result was better.

His assistant came to him, and the two men slapped hands.

Renegade walked onto the green.

1502.37

On the roof, under the thunder of beating rotors, Nick was leaning into the cockpit of the State Police helicopter, screaming at the pilot.

"Stay low, due east, Lieutenant, you're zeroing in on

the National War College at river's edge, can't miss it, huge building, like a temple, or a capitol, or something."

"Yes, sir," the pilot was saying.

"You have to go beyond to the middle of the river. We'll be looking at the tallest building in Anacostia with river frontage—say, a mile off the War College. Your co-pilot is on binocs, I'm on binocs, we're looking for an upper-story window that's open. He won't be hanging out, he'll be well back. You want to insert yourself between him and his target. We'll take the shot if we have to, Swagger will counterfire if he gets—"

"Sixth floor," shouted Bob. "He was sixty-seven feet higher than the target in Wyoming. Each story ten feet. He'll be on the sixth floor!"

And at that point, Neill spilled onto the roof, rifle in one hand, box of red Hornady ammo in the other. Chandler was just behind.

"It's Juba's," he said. "It was one floor down, so much closer."

Swagger and Nick ran to the chopper and climbed in, and Neill reached them a second later. He handed the weapon to the sniper.

It was familiar to Swagger, knowing its curves, its feel, its distribution of weight, its easy pointability. He'd used it in Vietnam, Remington's classic 700, as solid and tight as any assembly line could turn out.

"They haven't touched it?"

"Not yet," said Neill.

Swagger rotated into the hatch of the helicopter, going naturally to prone, rolling slightly to the right to pry open the red box of Hornady 6.5 Creedmoor—one was missing, and he knew what had happened to it—and began threading them into the well in the receiver revealed by the pulled-open bolt.

"Time to hunt," he said, but nobody heard him.

1503

The man walked to the ball on the green, bent to examine it, walked to the pin, bent to examine it—had he never seen one before?—but would not be still. He was mapping his stroke to the most precise degree, he stopped for a brief chat with his assistant, who offered him some sort of counsel, he stepped off the green to squat and peer at the ball in relation to the hole and the course its trajectory had to follow to arrive squarely, then stood up.

It was evidently an important shot, even if he had balls in his pocket and in the golf cart.

But he would not stay still, he would not begin his fatal address of the ball, which would put him in the kill box.

Juba monitored his own breathing, enjoying the fact that he was so calm, that things were progressing so well.

He had a brief flash of what happened after the shots.

Close the window.

Launch the hate pages to the Dark Web.

Make a last quick check that no traces of Juba remained.

Dump the gloves, mask, and cap in the getaway bag.

Slip out the door, which would lock behind him.

Go to the street without hurry or urgency.

Walk due south on Martin Luther King Jr. Drive and look for a black BMW SUV to pick him up.

He came out of his projection and back to the scope.

The golfer finally had come to the ball and was preparing for the putt.

1503.23

City and river slid by in a blur as the craft ate the distance between the FBI roof and the Anacostia River. Vibration, like a charge of electricity, roared through everything. The wind was a primal reality, bashing at him.

Bob lay prone on the deck of the bird, legs splayed for stability. He hadn't gone to a shooting position yet because he didn't want to hold it before he had acquired a target. But the rifle against his shoulder, its barrel projecting outward to the broad bright expanse of reality that was before him, was reassuring.

He wore a headset and throat mic, and now used it to address the pilot, "Lieutenant, if I have to shoot, can you hold her steady?"

"Yes, sir," came the pilot's reply. "Give me a second's notice, and I'll go to autorotate, which means I cut the engine, tune the blades, and we just sustain ourselves on the rotation without the buzz. I've only got about ten seconds, though, before I have to power up."

"Got it, and great. I'll sing out."

The copilot said, "It's got to be that newer building. The upper floor would get you the vantage."

"Yeah," said Nick. "If he's anywhere, he's there."

"Okay, boys," said the pilot, "I'm laying myself right in his angle on the target. I'm coming around and holding. Find him for the sniper. Find him."

1504

Now at last.

The man was still. He bent over the ball, addressing it squarely, all his attention focused on it. He did not know that the red dot of Juba's 5.5×25×56 Schmidt & Bender lay without tremor or remorse upon the center of his body and that Juba's finger caressed the curve of the trigger, that all systems were perfect, that it was only a matter not of technique but will.

Juba's focus went to the dot, not the target, and his trigger finger began its microprogress—

And then the image disappeared.

Something blurred and heavy settled between himself and it, and he recognized the shape as a helicopter. His fingers flew to the focus ring, and he dialed the blur to sharpness. And now he recognized the open hatch and, in one corner of it as if from his nightmares, bent and concentrated and unmoving, the American sniper.

1505.5

"Open window, middle, top floor!" screamed Nick.

"On it," Bob replied. "Lieutenant, go to auto."

The bird's roar ceased, and there was a moment of stillness as the rotors sustained the machine of their own without the assistance of power but purely on the laws of aerodynamics, sucking the strength of the atmosphere through their canted blades. And in that pause Bob went hard to shooting position lock-in, rifle tight, eye centered on scope, finger on trigger, saw the open window and, though darkened, what could only be the silhouette of a man hunched over a rifle.

Without willing it, he fired, even as he read the flash from the other's muzzle.

1504.066

He fired. The American sniper fired.

It was too late, of course.

He was where fate and destiny had decreed, in another's crosshairs, even as that other was in his own. The flashes were simultaneous, even at that range, and the time in flight was as well.

It had to happen. It did. Now, here, today, this minute, this second, this fraction of a second.

He entered the light.

1504.079

"Bingo!" screamed Nick. "Brains on the ceiling, baby, you nailed his ass. Oh god, what a shot, what a shot, Swagger is the best. Did he shoot? I thought I saw flash. Did he—"

He looked down to see Swagger, face flat on the deck, as if dumped loosely on his rifle, now flattened under him.

"Swagger!" he yelled.

He bent, touched the man's neck for pulse and found the feeblest excuse for one, a weak pumping. A pool of blood began to roll across the deck, vibrating as the pilot powered on and revved the torque.

"Swagger?"

He pulled him half up, saw the chalk-white face, the unfocused eyes, just the faintest tremor of breath.

"Lieutenant, go to nearest shock trauma, fastest, someplace set up with helicopter pad, fastest. I say again, fastest! Copilot, radio ahead, tell them we have medical emergency incoming, severe gunshot trauma, lung or chest. Get people on roof to get him into surgery. I say again: Emergency! Emergency! Emergency!"

"Roger, FBI, wilco," came the reply.

1504.082

Where had it gone? It had vanished—rifle, helicopter, target. Someone was yelling. It was Nick.

"SWAGGER!"

Nick yelled again, from farther out.

"SWAGGER!"

Where had he gone?

"SWAGGER?"

"SWAGGER!"

It was so far away.

"SWAGGER!"

62

F all came hard, winter harder. Bleak, even savage, months, with harsh winds and blankets of snow that lay across the prairie like the base coat for the end of the world in ice. He saw none of it.

The collarbone wasn't the problem. It was replaced by titanium, coated in nitride to prevent tissue stain. The bone chips weren't the problem. They were picked out, one at a time, all two hundred and thirty-one of them, ranging in size from .25 inch to .004 inch, scattered throughout the thoracic cavity. The clavicle, hit by the .338 Lapua traveling sideways after having been slowed and deflected by the helicopter's fuselage, had exploded like a grenade, deflating his left lung, pricking his heart. But that was not the problem. The lung was patched and reinflated, the heart de-pricked.

The problem was the chip of bone shrapnel that had cut into and almost—it was a matter of a few thousandths of an inch—destroyed his aorta. That would have been fatal in a few seconds.

But in minutes they cracked his chest, pried him open like an oyster, and went to work. They delicately removed the intruder and sutured the artery up. It was fourteen hours on the table, with relays of surgeons and nurses, the whole thing a close-run battle of its own, leaving exhausted participants soaked in sweat and limp from fatigue all over the surgery floor. But they were brave and tough and the best, and they saved him in time. Somehow the major vessel eventually healed. Seventy-three-year-old blood highways are not noted for such cooperation, but his nevertheless came through for him.

He sat, he rocked. No horseback riding, but each morning two hours of physical therapy, administered by a no-nonsense young woman from the hospital who saw him merely as a data unit to be manipulated toward certain goals, and who was always behind schedule and always cranky. Not much love flowed between them.

Audrey the Evil gone, he sat, he rocked. Late March. Scabby patches of snow on yellowed prairie grass. No buds yet, just nodules. The smell of wet everywhere. The clouds fat with rain, low and surly, moving remorselessly, a breeze that cut. One color and few variations, all off the murkiest part of the spectrum. It was a landscape designed by Nietzsche to melody composed by Wagner, both men in their deepest depressive phase of their bipolarity. He sat, wrapped in an old Indian blanket, his walker on the porch beside him. He had a thermos of coffee, black as usual, and a nice pair of binoculars in case any animal life decided to acknowledge his existence.

Phone made that god-awful sound and showed the front gate, where a new, expensive, and, hopefully, temporary guard spent the day, chasing off the too-many assholes who had propositions.

"Mr. Swagger, woman here, says she knows you. What is it, ma'am? Yeah, McDowell—a Mrs. McDowell."

"Yeah, she's okay."

He knew she'd come this way as before, unannounced, so that nobody would feel the need to make preparations, and in a cheap rental car, this one in an even more insane shade than the last, some kind of econo Chevy that pushed its underpowered way over the crest and into the yard.

The same old Janet got out, no more chic or polished up than the last time, in jeans and a sweater under some kind of waxed outdoorsy jacket. As usual, running shoes, as if she still had a marathon to run when she'd just finished one.

"Well, hey," he called.

"Was in the neighborhood," she said, "thought I'd drop by."

"Yeah, I'm halfway between the 7-Eleven and the dry cleaners."

She laughed. "Well, it's a big neighborhood."

He didn't rise; he couldn't. She bent and hugged him, he nodded toward a chair nearby, and she pulled it over.

"So, how's the hero?" she asked.

"I don't know. Ask him, if you can find one. I just pulled a trigger."

"Knowing he'd be pulling a trigger too."

"Didn't think that far ahead."

They caught up. The news was good, as everyone had prospered. Nick got to retire again, this time as an Assistant Director, a goal finally achieved. Neill and Chandler got promotions, commendations, and Glory Wall photos with Mogul. Mr. Gold was back in the black cube, and even Cohen was respectful—at least for a little while.

"All you got was a bullet," Janet said.

"I'm a big boy. It's okay."

Health notes: his progress, his mood, his day-to-day, his expected recovery rate.

"I'll be back on the horse in three months. Not sure about the motorcycles. Doctors *do not* like motorcycles. I've recently started working in the shop again—you know, the crazy gun tinkering that I enjoy. Still be a few weeks before I can get behind a rifle. Lucky he nicked me in my left shoulder, not the right."

"Some nick," she said.

And finally: the thing itself. Who was behind it, who put up the money? The Iranians facilitated it and supported it, but nobody at the CIA thought it was their sort of operation. They sensed a bigger, smarter state actor, maybe a Putin, drawing on five centuries of Russian intelligence tradecraft. The Chinese? They were that good, so that was a possibility. Or maybe some "friend" who saw the ingredients on the table to take an ally down hard and move to the front of the line. Anyway, a joint Bureau–Agency task force was on it.

"Tell me your thoughts," she said, "who saw it as a possibility, where it could have come from. Is there anything like it?"

"More than anything, it reminds me of our job on a Japanese admiral in World War Two. We were reading their code. Their guy Yamamoto was on an inspection tour. Our intel guys worked out the route and saw that on one tiny stretch of his flight he would be in range of our fighters. When he got there, the P38s were waiting and jumped him. Remember Pearl Harbor, and all that. Same thing here. Renegade's in range for the few minutes he's on the eighth green. Juba knew. Like the P38s, Juba was waiting."

"And the cover story: New York? Did they just get lucky it was the same time?"

"Not really. They knew Mogul's personality would compel him to show up Renegade. So they knew something would happen and that they could use it. That's the kind of thinking the Agency people consider beyond the Iranians."

She nodded, as if she understood or even cared. But it was clear she didn't. She'd come for one thing, and, finally, it was all that was left.

"So I really came to ask a question," she said.

"Figured as much."

"How should I feel?"

"Pretty good, I'd say. You got him. Seemed impossible, but you got him."

"I don't really feel it was me. I had help from the best

folks in the world. They believed, and, on that, I could keep going."

"No, it was you. It all happened because you made it happen. The rest of us did our parts and got the screws tightened up real good, but no Janet, Juba gets away with it. No justice, nothing for Tommy, nothing for Baghdad, nothing for the bus, nothing for the New Mexico gun guy, nothing for the homeless fellows popped at a mile, nothing for a former president and the chaos his death would bring to us. We're so fragile these days, maybe some kind of civil war. Nothing for the others on down the line that Juba would have put down. All that's because Janet made it so."

"Maybe," said Janet.

"But you don't feel any better, is that it?"

"Not really. Not where it counts. I'm a mom, that's all. I'd rather have my son back than all that other stuff, and no matter how much of what someone calls good came from it, the price was too high. That's how I feel."

He didn't say a thing. What was there to say?

"How long will that last?" she said. "That's my question. You would know. You lost so many over the years."

"Oh, you can do things. Help veterans, write an inspirational book, and if you make some money—and you should—endow a scholarship, fund a school, contribute, keep Tommy alive that way."

"Sure," she said. "Good advice, all of it. But you know it only takes you so far. Bob, tell me the truth. How long does it really last?"

"It lasts forever," he said.

Acknowledgments

This book began with and is respectfully dedicated to Tracy Miller, whose son Nick Ziolkowski—"The Sniper from Boys' Latin," dedicatee in *Dead Zero*—was killed in Fallujah in 2004. Instead of letting her grief cripple and destroy her, she turned it to energy, the energy to engagement, and the engagement to help others. She has spent her last fourteen years as an advisor to veterans and other recent arrivals at Towson University, where she is an adjunct professor of education and serves on the Veterans Committee, among about a thousand other things. That's heroism. I have taken the kernel of her story and done what I do, which is dramatize, romanticize, exaggerate, and open fire. Hence, *Game of Snipers*.

Now, on to apologies, excuses, and evasions. Let me offer the first to Tel Aviv; Dearborn, Michigan; Greenville, Ohio; Wichita, Kansas; Rock Springs, Wyoming; and Anacostia, D.C. I generally go to places I write about to check the lay of streets, the fall of shadows, the color of police cars, and the taste of local beer. At seventy-three, such ordeals-by-airport are no longer fun, not even the beer part; I only go where there's beaches. For this book, I worked from maps and Google, and any geographical mistakes emerge out of that practice. Is the cathedral three hundred yards from the courthouse in Wichita? Hmm, seems about right, and that's good enough for me on this.

On the other hand, I finally got Bob's wife's name correct. It's Julie, right? I've called her Jen more than once, but I'm pretty sure Jen was Bud Pewtie's wife in *Dirty White Boys*. For some reason, this mistake seemed to trigger certain Amazon reviewers into psychotic episodes. Folks, calm down, have a drink, hug someone soft. It'll be all right.

As for the shooting, my account of the difficulties of hitting at over a mile is more or less accurate (snipers have done it at least eight times). I have simplified, because it is so arcane it would put all but the most dedicated in a coma. I have also been quite accurate about the ballistics app FirstShot, because I made it up and can make it do anything I want. The other shot, the three hundred, benefits from the wisdom of Craig Boddington, the great hunter and writer, who looked it over and sent me a detailed email, from which I have borrowed much. Naturally, any errors are mine, not Craig's.

I met Craig when shooting something (on film!) for another boon companion, Michael Bane, and his Outdoor Channel *Gun Stories* crew. For some reason, he finds it amusing when I start jabbering away and likes to turn the camera on. Don't ask me why. On the same trip, I also met the great firearms historian and all-around movie guy (he knows more than I do) Garry James, who has become a pal. Gentlemen three, God bless them all.

In Baltimore, the usual suspects came to my aid. First, my friends John Bainbridge, Lenne Miller, and Gary Goldberg were diligent and thorough on my behalf. Why, I cannot say. Meanwhile, Mike Hill and Jim "Six Days of the Condor" Grady had useful insights and enthusiasm, as did Bill Smart and Barrett Tillman. And in Elizabethtown, Pennsylvania, my good friend Dave Dunn, owner of Trop Gun Shop, offered me cigars, bourbon, and deals—all important to morale. In Baltimore, Ed De Carlo, maître d', majordomo, and NCOIC of On Target, kept my shooting life running smoothly. In L.A., old pal Jeff Weber pitched in as usual. Thanks to all, and particularly to Lenne, who also had a major health crisis to deal with but stayed on course.

Professionally, the great Esther Newberg supervised the shift from the late house of Blue Rider to the very much alive house of Putnam, and editor Mark Tavani added his guidance. My wife, the great Jean Marbella, made the coffee that pulled me from the sticky miasma of old man's psychedelic dreamworld every morning and got me upstairs to the writing machine. Without that coffee, I'm the bitter crank whining to strangers in grocery store lines about what might have been.

And finally: did I steal the excellent title *Game of Snipers* from the immensely successful Game of Thrones series by George Martin? Sure. Why would I not?

STEPHEN HUNTER

"Stephen Hunter is a master of the tough thriller."
—*Los Angeles Times*

For a complete list of titles and to sign up for
our newsletter, please visit prh.com/stephenhunter